THE
HALF
DROWNED
KING

THE
HALF
DROWNED
KING

LINNEA HARTSUYKER

Little, Brown

LITTLE, BROWN

First published in the United States in 2017 by HarperCollins Publishers
First published in Great Britain in 2017 by Little, Brown

1 3 5 7 9 10 8 6 4 2

A CIP catalogue record for this book
is available from the British Library.

Hardback ISBN 978-1-4087-0879-8
Trade paperback ISBN 978-1-4087-0880-4

Printed and bound in Great Britain by
Clays Ltd, St Ives plc

Papers used by Little, Brown are from well-managed forests
and other responsible sources.

MIX
Paper from
responsible sources
FSC
www.fsc.org   FSC® C104740

Little, Brown
An imprint of
Little, Brown Book Group
Carmelite House
50 Victoria Embankment
London EC4Y 0DZ

An Hachette UK Company
www.hachette.co.uk

www.littlebrown.co.uk

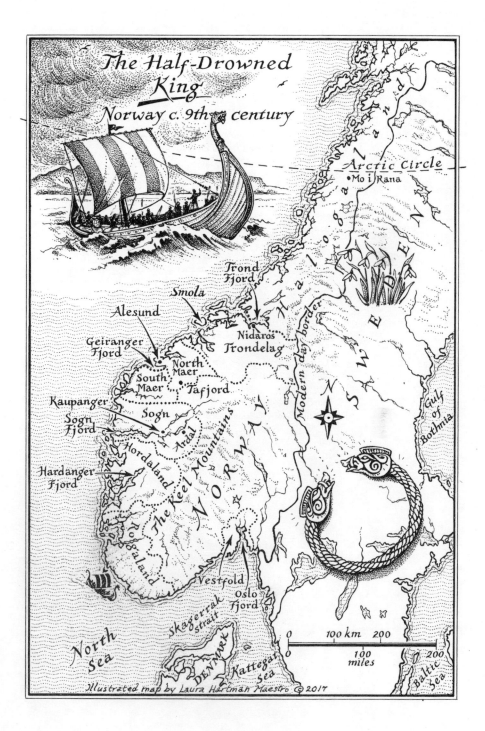

The Half-Drowned
King
Norway c. 9th century

Arctic Circle
• Mo i Rana

Trond
Fjord

Smola

Alesund

Nidaros
Trondelag

Geiranger
Fjord

North
Maer
South
Maer
Tafjord

Kaupanger

Sogn

Sogn
Fjord

Ardal

Hordaland

Hardanger
Fjord

The Keel Mountains

N O R W A Y

Rogaland

Vestfold

Oslo
Fjord

Skagerrak
Strait

North
Sea

DENMARK

Kattegat
Sea

Baltic
Sea

Halogaland

S W E D E N

Modern day border

Gulf
of
Bothnia

0   100 km   200

100
miles

200

Illustrated map by Laura Hartman Maestro © 2017

THE
HALF
DROWNED
KING

I

RAGNVALD DANCED ON THE OARS, LEAPING FROM ONE TO THE next as the crew rowed. Some kept their oars steady to make it easier for him; some tried to jostle Ragnvald off when he landed on them. The wind from the mountains, a breath of lingering winter, swept down the fjord, whistling through the trees that lined the cliffs. But under the bright sun, Ragnvald was warm in his wool shirt and heavy hose. He had worn them during the whole journey back across the North Sea, through the storms and mists that separated Ireland from home.

He touched the bow post and hung on for a moment to catch his breath.

"Come back," called Solvi. "You cling like a woman to that dragon." Ragnvald took a deep breath and stepped out onto the first oar again. His friend Egil held this one, his bleached hair shining in the sun. Egil smiled up at Ragnvald; he would not let him fall. Ragnvald's steps faltered as he leapt back the other way, against the direction of the oars' motion, the sun shining in his eyes. He moved more quickly now, falling, slipping, each upstroke catching him and propelling him onto the next sweep, until he reached the stern again and swung over the gunwale onto the more stable deck.

Solvi had offered a golden arm ring to whoever could make it the length of the ship and back, stepping from oar to oar as the men rowed. Ragnvald was first to try, for Solvi valued daring. He thought after he stood on the deck again that his run might have been one of the best, hard to beat, and he grinned. A lucky star had lit his path on this journey, finally guiding him away from his dour stepfather. He had not succumbed to disease in Ireland, when so many others had died, and now he had earned a place on Solvi's ship for another summer's raiding. He had grown into his long limbs over the winter, no longer tripping over his feet with every step. Let any of the others match his run.

"Well done," said Solvi, clapping him on the back. "Who will challenge Ragnvald Eysteinsson?"

Solvi's forecastle man leapt out next. Ulfarr was a grown man, half again as wide as Ragnvald in the shoulder, with a long mane of hair, yellow from the lye he used to lighten it.

"This is a game for young men, Ulfarr," Solvi called out. "You wear too much jewelry. The goddess Ran will want you for her own."

Ulfarr only took a few steps on the oars before his shoes slipped and he fell into the water with a splash. He emerged breathing heavily from the cold, clinging onto one of the oars. Solvi threw his head back and laughed.

"Pull me up, damn it," Ulfarr said.

Ragnvald reached over and hauled Ulfarr in. Ulfarr shook his head like a wet dog, covering Ragnvald with seawater.

Egil tried his luck next. He looked like a crane as he clambered over the gunwale, gangly and awkward where agility was needed. Ragnvald winced, watching him. Still, Egil almost reached the bow before losing his footing. He clung on and only wet his boots before Ragnvald helped him back in. Ragnvald settled on a pile of furs to watch his other competitors as they tripped and splashed.

The high walls of the fjord slipped by beside them. Snow from Norway's great spine of mountains turned into the water that cascaded down the cliff faces in waterfalls where the spray caught the sunlight in a scattering of rainbows. Seals, plump and glossy, sunned themselves on rocks at a cliff's base. They watched the ships go by curiously, without fear. Longships hunted men, not fur.

Solvi stood at the stern of the ship. He applauded good attempts and laughed at the poor ones. He only seemed to be giving the race half his attention, though; his eyes moved constantly, flicking over cliff and waterfall. He had shown the same careful watchfulness when they were on a raid, which had saved his men from the Irish warriors more than once. The Irish fought almost as well as Norsemen did.

Ragnvald had studied Solvi on this voyage, for he merited it: both clever and good at winning his men's affections. Ragnvald had not thought to find those characteristics in one man—so often a boaster and a drinker won many friends but was too careless to live long as a warrior. Ragnvald's father, Eystein, had been like that. On this journey all of Solvi's men had tales of Eystein, and seemed disappointed that Ragnvald was not more like him, a man whose stories were still remembered a decade later, a man who abandoned his duty when it suited him.

Solvi laughed at another attempt, another fall, another one of his men who climbed, dripping, over the gunwale and flopped on the deck, chest heaving from the cold water. Solvi had a narrow, handsome face, with high cheekbones, red like ripe apples. In infancy his legs had been badly burned by a falling cauldron left to spill, rumor said, by one of King Hunthiof's lesser wives, jealous of the regard he showed Solvi's mother. Solvi's legs had healed well—he was as deadly a fighter as any Ragnvald had ever seen—but they remained bowed and crooked, and shorter than they should be. Men called him Solvi Klofe, Solvi the Short-Legged, a name that made him grin with pride, at least when his friends said it.

On the other side of the ship another warrior leapt, and nearly fell. Solvi laughed and shook an oar to try to dislodge him. Few men remained to challenge Ragnvald's feat. The pilot's son, slim and sure-footed as a mountain goat, was the only other who had completed the challenge, dancing stern to bow and back to stern again.

Behind them sailed the five other ships that still remained in Solvi's convoy. Here and there others had turned off, to return sons back to their farms and fishermen back to their boats. Before that, other ships had taken other paths to islands on the inner passage, where their captains called themselves sea kings, their kingdoms made of no more than rocks, narrow channels, and the men who would flock to their raiding cries. Solvi's father called himself a sea king too, for though he demanded taxes from the farmers of Maer, he refused the other duties of kingship, and maintained no farm at Tafjord.

It was early in the year yet, time enough for another raid across the North Atlantic to winter over again, or a short summer trip to the unprotected shores of Frisia. Ragnvald was glad to be going home, though. His sister, Svanhild, and the rest of his family waited beyond the foothills of the Keel, as did his intended, Hilda Hrolfsdatter. He had won a pair of copper brooches for Hilda, worked by the Norse smiths of Dublin. The Norse king there had given them to Ragnvald as a reward for leading a daring raid against an Irish village. They would look well on Hilda, with her height and reddish hair. In time, she would oversee the hall he planned to build on the site where his father's hall had burned. Ragnvald would be an experienced warrior by then, as thick with muscle as Ulfarr, and wear his wealth on his belt and armbands. Hilda would give him tall children, boys he would teach to fight.

Ragnvald planned to claim her at the *ting* this summer, when the families of the Sogn district gathered. His family had an understanding with hers, though they had not yet gone through the betrothal ceremony. He had proved himself raiding, won wealth to buy more thralls to work on the farm at Ardal. Now that he was twenty, and counted a man, he could marry Hilda and his stepfather would have no more reason to withhold his birthright, his father's land, from him.

Over the winter he had also found a silver necklace that would suit Svanhild perfectly. She would laugh and pretend not to like it—what use had she for silver when she spent her days tending cows?—but her eyes would sparkle and she would wear it every day.

Solvi called Ragnvald and the pilot's son to him. He touched the thick gold band circling his arm, forged by Dublin goldsmiths, set with carnelian and lapis. A king's adornment. If he meant that for a gift, he was a generous lord indeed.

"I have rings enough for both of you, but I'd rather see one of you fall," said Solvi. He grinned at the pilot's son, seeming not to see Ragnvald. Well, Solvi would notice Ragnvald after this race, Ragnvald would make sure of that. "Whichever of you returns to the stern fastest gets the ring. Ragnvald, you take starboard." Now his eyes met Ragnvald's. A breeze shivered Ragnvald's skin. He preferred larboard, and Solvi knew it. He had sensed this odd shift between them many times on this voyage; one moment Solvi seemed to value him, giving him advice and praise, and the next forgot he existed. In that way, he was like Ragnvald's stepfather, Olaf. With Olaf it meant that Ragnvald must simply try harder to gain his notice, be perfect at every deed. He was not sure what it meant with Solvi.

Ragnvald rolled his shoulders and shook out his legs, which had grown stiff from sitting. He climbed over the side and glared a challenge at the pilot's son across the ship. Oar-dancing required shifting his balance, always on the verge of falling before catching himself again, another oar ready to slide away beneath his feet. He must trust his body and the rhythm of the sweeps, pay attention to the variations between one man's pull and the next, as one oar cut deeply into the water and another slipped shallowly in the trough of a wave. Agni, the pilot's son, was smaller and fleeter than Ragnvald. He had grown up on ships, and would be tough to beat.

Solvi roared their start, and Ragnvald began. He would not have to touch every oar this time, now that he had the feel for it. He leapt in time with the strokes, letting the movement pitch him forward. The wind picked up, making the ship move stiffly over growing swells.

Ragnvald reached the bow again, ahead of the pilot's son. He turned back and had almost reached the steering oar when Solvi called out, "That's enough."

Ragnvald put a hand out toward the ship's gunwale, preparing to swing himself back onto the deck, so he could help with the heavy wool sail. Solvi would need every pair of hands to lash it into place and turn it against the wind.

"Not you," said Solvi. He stood quite close to Ragnvald now. The words were meant for him alone. The oars that rowers had been holding disappeared from beneath Ragnvald's feet. The water he had danced over so surely a moment earlier sucked at his legs and drew him in. Cold water seeped up his britches. He clung to the planking of the gunwale and looked at the men wielding these oars. Those who met his eyes quickly turned their faces away.

"Help me up," said Ragnvald. He could not quite believe that Solvi meant to put him overboard. "Help me," he called again, to the only friend he could still rely upon. "Egil, help me." Egil looked confused for a moment and started forward. Solvi's men put their shoulders together, blocking him at the narrow end of the boat.

The wooden edge of the gunwale dug into Ragnvald's arms where he clung. He was still scrambling to find footing when he saw Solvi reach toward the dagger at his belt.

"I had rather not," said Solvi, "but—"

"What?" Ragnvald cried. "Wait, don't do this—pull me up." Solvi's face was set and hard, all good nature fled. Ragnvald froze as Solvi drew his dagger from its sheath and thrust it toward Ragnvald's throat. Ragnvald angled his chin down to avoid Solvi's stroke, and the blade bit into his cheek.

The pain broke his paralysis. Blood pounded in his temples. Egil was not going to break through the wall of Solvi's warriors and help him. At least Ragnvald still had his sword—he was so used to wearing it now that he had kept it belted on for balance during the race. He let go of the ship with one hand and grabbed for it, but could not get the blade free, not at this angle. He took hold of the gunwale again and swung himself behind the stern post, trapping his sword between his body and the ship.

Solvi grabbed Ragnvald's wrist and tried to haul him up for another blow, while Ragnvald's feet churned, still looking for a place to stand. Solvi grunted and brought his dagger down again as Ragnvald went limp, hoping he was heavy enough that Solvi could not hold him and get in a killing stroke. He kicked against the side of the ship, now desperate to drive himself out of Solvi's reach. Solvi leaned forward, clinging to Ragnvald, half his body out over the gunwale. Solvi managed another shallow cut on Ragnvald's throat and then let go rather than be pulled overboard as well.

Ragnvald gasped when the icy water hit his face. He inhaled and choked. The saltwater stung his wounds, but distantly, the pain from them weaker than the searing knives of cold in his limbs and the shock of Solvi's betrayal. The fjord's current ran swiftly here, and would carry him away from Solvi's ship if he let it. He stayed unmoving, head hardly breaking the surface, and counted through a hundred heartbeats before lifting his head and opening his eyes.

The current bore him almost under the oars of the next ship in the convoy. Laughter sounded from it, as it had from Solvi's ship. Ragnvald raised his head and pulled a sodden arm out of the water. He had marched into battle with these men, held a shoreline fort over a long, cruel winter with them, and shared women with them after the hot flush of battle. They should help him.

Then he remembered the men who had blocked Egil's way. More than Solvi were involved in this. Yesterday he would have vouched that these warriors would risk their lives to save his, as he would for theirs, but if Solvi could not be trusted, how could he know about the others? He let the current carry him past the ship, and did not cry out.

The cold shuddered his limbs. His teeth chattered together. Any anger at Solvi seemed far away, lost in the water along with Ragnvald's warmth. The cold took him away from himself. He tongued his cheek, the one that Solvi had cut, and tasted the iron saltiness of blood, mixed with the brackish water in the fjord. Solvi had cut clean through the flesh in places, although Ragnvald's mouth was still whole. He thanked the gods for that small mercy.

He had seen a wound like that, cheek and mouth opened by a monk's ax, fester and rot until the warrior's face was half gone and he was screaming from the pain and fever dreams. Ragnvald would seek Solvi out and let Solvi kill him outright before succumbing to that fate. At least then he would find Valhalla in death, rather than one of the cold, stinking hells of fallen cowards.

The sun fell fast below the line of cliffs, and the air on his face, which had seemed warm against the cold of the water, grew chilly. His limbs were heavy and numb now, his body passing quickly through cold to the empty doorway that waited beyond. He could slip easily here into death, and none would know where his body lay. It would be almost as shameful a death as that from fever. He could have fought back on the ship, but instead he had taken the craven way, and played dead rather than face that uneven contest. His stepfather, Olaf, had been right; Ragnvald was not ready to stand among warriors, and now he never would be.

His wool tunic weighed him down, dragging him deeper under the water. He tried to swim toward the shore, but the current in the middle of the fjord flowed swift and strong and resisted the movements of his arms. Something tugged on his ankle, the cold and grasping fingers of Ran, goddess of sea and shipwreck, pulling him down to her chilly feasting hall.

It would not be a terrible death, it seemed, perhaps better than lying forever alone, a cold body in a barrow, for Ran's hall was filled with sailors and fishermen. He saw them, raising horns of seawater slowly in a silent toast. Every sunken ship sacrificed its treasure to the sea goddess, and her warriors ranged far and wide to retrieve it. Beams of light reflected from the gold that adorned her hall, filtering up to where Ragnvald floated.

He looked in wonder at the shifting shapes below, forms of dark and light. Nets of gold decorated the high ceiling of the hall. A sea maiden took Ragnvald's arm and guided him into that cold feast. Is this my place? he asked. Will I eat fish every day? Will I drown sailors in my turn?

The gills on her neck fluttered. She bade Ragnvald sit at a bench in front of a long fire that gave no heat, and burned with a blue and green flame. He did not know how long he stayed there, among that silent host. The sea maidens brought food and drink, but all tasted of salt, all smelled of fish. And he was cold, so cold.

Then the great doors flew open, and in strode a great wolf, golden-furred and blue-eyed. Sparks flew from the ends of its fur. It stalked slowly down the length of the hall. Where it touched its muzzle, some men burned, but others grew burnished, losing the green cast of seawater. Ragnvald watched as it weaved between the men, wondering if it brought him ashy death or shining glory. When it came near Ragnvald, he saw that its fur was matted and dull in places. He reached out for its pelt, and where he touched became bright, shining like fresh forged metal. Its eyes were the blue of a summer sky, and its fur was so warm on Ragnvald's hands that he hardly noticed the flames crawling up his fingers, his forearms, only warming him where, elsewhere in the hall, they had consumed flesh and wood. He reached forward, embracing the wolf. Its tongue of fire licked at his throat, filling his vision with blue flames. He could be destroyed here, he knew, in this wolf's embrace, and yet he could not do other than meet this death.

This could not be a shameful death, here with this wolf sent by the gods. He wanted to give himself up to it, but something pulled at his ankle. Not the chilly fingers of Ran's handmaidens now, for he was already in her domain. He thrashed against the pull, crying out in protest, as strong hands grasped him and drew him from the water.

2

A LOUD CRACK WOKE SVANHILD FROM A SOUND SLEEP, AND SHE sat bolt upright on her pallet. The same sound had roused her a month ago, when the raiders came. They arrived in the middle of the night, surrounding the hall, keeping silent until their attack, which began when one of their axes struck the barn door.

Under the eaves, a few pricks of light entered through chinks in the turf. Her stepmother, Vigdis—her stepfather's favorite wife—still slept on the pallet next to her. Vigdis smiled in her sleep. She had much to smile about. She was still beautiful, and she was not subject to the many humiliations that Olaf visited on Svanhild's mother, who he had married out of obligation to a dead friend.

Svanhild listened for the other sounds she had heard that night: the low voices of men, the cows fretting. She heard none of those now. She smelled smoke, not the sweet and terrifying scent of burning hay, but the tang of half-dried firewood that fed the kitchen fire. The sound had only been the servant, Luta, breaking kindling to build the fire from embers back to a blaze. Svanhild breathed deeply. Today would not bring death.

Beneath the smoke, the air smelled fresh, like sunshine and new growing things. Svanhild pulled her furs up around her face for one last moment of peace, before climbing off her sleeping bench and pulling on her shoes. She had a good spot, near the fire, with a mattress of feathers rather than rushes. A hanging curtain divided her and the other women from the gazes of men. Her stepfather, Olaf, had a chamber to himself, and whichever wife he chose to share it—usually Vigdis, although not tonight. The nearly thirty other residents of the farm, the enslaved thralls and free servants, and Olaf's armsmen, slept on the long, deep benches that lined the hall, the same that were packed with the poorer farmers at the year-turning feasts. The morning would not be quiet for long.

In the kitchen, Svanhild's mother Ascrida was already overseeing breakfast, nothing more today than oats boiled in milk and some dried cloudberries. Ascrida poked with a stick at the fire that a thrall had built, never satisfied with the work of any but herself.

She stood up and smiled when Svanhild walked by. Svanhild ducked her head and smoothed down her hair. It fell past her waist unbound, fine as mohair, and, having slipped out of its braid overnight, now stuck up in a lump above her forehead.

"Here, let me, child." Ascrida wiped her hands on her apron and tucked the errant strands behind Svanhild's ears. Svanhild smiled back tentatively, glad her mother seemed happy this morning. Days came, more often than ever since Ragnvald left, when she retreated into herself, hardly speaking, her own hair poorly dressed and hanging, stringy and unwashed, out of her wimple. Svanhild never knew what brought on those spells, and even now she walked carefully. Even when her father lived, her mother had been watchful, always worried. As Svanhild grew older, and heard more stories of him, she understood that a careless man must have a careful wife. He had died when she was only five, and his friend Olaf had taken over his wife and his farm. But now that Ragnvald had reached the legal age of manhood, Svanhild's fate was his to decide, not Olaf's, and he said he would bring her home news of a husband to take her away from here.

At least the days were long enough now that Svanhild would not have to pass them inside, spinning unwashed wool for ships' sails. Her fingers might grow less rough from finer work, but neither Vigdis nor Ascrida trusted her with the small stitches that garments required. Her tunics looked as if a peasant child had sewn them, Ascrida said; even Olaf's servants could not go about dressed like that. Best to stick to the unending skeins of coarse sail wool. It must only be strong, not beautiful, and Svanhild had mastered that much.

"I have to see to the cows," said Svanhild, scooping up a handful of berries from the soapstone pot where Ascrida had put them. The seeds cracked against her teeth, reminding her of the noise that woke her. The sea ice would be breaking up now, and Ragnvald would be coming home. They would need his sword if raiders came again.

More than that, Svanhild missed her brother. Five years separated them, but they had always been closer than Svanhild was to her step-brother, Sigurd, only a year older than she. In those terrible days that formed her first memories, after Olaf brought the news that their father had been killed, after raiders had burned their first hall, her mother sat too numb and shaken to do anything. It was Ragnvald, only ten, who had comforted her. He took her out into the forest and showed her where the squirrels nested, in a burrow in the roots of a great oak. They sat and watched as the mother squirrel emerged with her tiny little ones.

"It is like the world tree that holds up all of creation," Ragnvald told her. "The squirrels carry news from the serpent at the roots to the eagle in the treetops, where Odin sits. Squirrels are the message carriers of the forest. Watch for them. If you cannot see them, the message they carry is death, and you must hide."

"If I can't see them," Svanhild replied, trying to jolly Ragnvald out of his seriousness, "how can they carry a message?" But that day's advice and many others' had served her well when she visited the forest to gather mushrooms, to trap small animals for their furs, keeping her safe from predators that walked on four legs and on two.

Svanhild walked through the hall to the cow byre at the north end. Now that Ragnvald was gone, and Svanhild was nearly grown, she spent more time with the cows than in the forest. She liked them, too, for they did not speak, did not argue or order her about. They made impatient noises when she opened the door. This time of year they were still recovering from the near starvation of winter and were always hungry.

As she led the cows out of the byre, Olaf's foster son, Einar, left from the kitchen door. He walked impatiently, as fast as he could with his limp. She waved to him.

"Doesn't your mother wish you inside?" asked Einar with a smile.

He was not a comely man, not with that limp, but young, and hugely muscled from his work. He had a pleasant smile, slow and shy, all the more winning for how rarely he showed it. Every free man should know how to forge a sword, carve a shield, build a boat, set a trap, and defend himself with sword, dagger, and ax, but some men had more talent for the arts of heat and hammer than others. Einar was one of these. When the old smith died of the cough three winters ago, Einar, young though he was, took over iron-smithing for the farm.

Svanhild tossed her hair. "She may wish it."

"What if raiders come?" Einar asked.

Svanhild shivered. "If raiders come, I shall send them to Thorkell's," she told Einar. Thorkell was Olaf's cousin, a huge man who had been known to bodily throw cow thieves off his land. He had been hinting lately that he wanted Svanhild as a new wife for him, or his eldest son, when she grew old enough. "Perhaps they can destroy each other."

He stepped in closer. "What if they came for you, fair maiden?"

Svanhild hesitated. Einar's flirtation made her uncomfortable. Ragnvald had promised to find a strong, young warrior, a jarl's son, she hoped, among Solvi's men for her to marry. Their father had been jarl of Ardal and its surrounding farms. Her grandfather had been king of Sogn. She could aim higher than a lame smith, no matter how blue his eyes or broad his shoulders. Still, she liked Einar. He and Ragnvald had been as brothers growing up, for Einar was a good and friendly companion, even with his lameness.

If Ragnvald did not return at all, she would far rather be Einar's bride than Thorkell's. Thorkell had put three wives in the ground already, all having died while giving birth to his children. She did not know how much choice Olaf would give her. The law said her guardian might choose a husband for her, and the only power she had was to divorce him later. After a divorce, she would have no home, no more wealth than the dower Olaf gave her, and might find herself the cause of a feud between his and Thorkell's families. If Olaf was cruel enough to try to marry her to someone she disliked, she hoped he would not want to risk that.

"They can have me," said Svanhild, "for they would surely fight less than Vigdis and my mother."

Einar would have nothing to say about that—Vigdis was his aunt, and Olaf his foster father these last seven years—but his lips quirked.

"Do you think Ragnvald is coming home soon?" Svanhild asked.

Einar's eyes lost their teasing sparkle. He glanced over Svanhild's shoulder at his smithy. "I think it would be better if he did not. Many men have found land and wives in Iceland and the south isles," he said, meaning Norse Orkney. "Ragnvald would be better off if he did the same. Will you try to make him see that, if he returns?"

"Why would you say that?" Svanhild asked. "This is our father's land. Ragnvald's land. Olaf promised—" She could not quite recall what Olaf had promised; Ragnvald had been telling her, as long as she could remember, that Olaf only held the land in trust for their father. She was unsure of the legality, but Ragnvald had said that if Olaf wanted to take the land from him, he would have to do so in front of the Sogn district *ting*, make his shameful case before men who knew their family of old, and knew the land belonged to them.

Einar looked pained, as well he might, for any conflict would put him between Olaf and his foster siblings. Svanhild could not care about that, though—Ragnvald was in the right.

"Be reasonable, Svanhild. Your brother is still a boy—"

"He helped Olaf fight off raiders for the last three summers, while you—" She stopped before she could insult his manhood, but his face told her she had already wounded him. "Einar, I didn't mean—It was Olaf who was too miserly to keep enough men here . . . and if what you're saying is true"—she had to swallow to get the next words out calmly—"he probably wanted Ragnvald to risk his life against the summer raiders so he would die rather than get the land."

"Ragnvald is my friend," said Einar stiffly. "But he has surely realized that Olaf means to keep what is his now, and he has powerful friends. Ragnvald would be better off starting anew, elsewhere."

"I will not tell Ragnvald you said this," said Svanhild, in shock. She was sure Ragnvald had not realized anything like that and would think it a grave injustice. And Einar was his friend. "I must get to work. And the cows look hungry." They had started to nibble on the short, already chewed grass at her feet.

"Svanhild . . . ," he said, pleading.

"My brother values loyalty," she said, "and so do I. Good day."

Einar bid her good day with a painful-looking bow and walked slowly toward his smithy.

Svanhild applied her switch to the cows at the rear of the herd to drive them along the path that led around the southern edge of the lake. Olaf ruled the stretch of land and tenant farms along the south coast of Lake Ardal and several leagues farther south, more than the work of a day to walk around. Near the western end of the lake stood the remains of the hall her grandfather Ivar had built. He had been the king of Sogn while he lived, and passed the lands on to his son Eystein, who had lost pieces of that land every year, and lost his life raiding with Olaf. When Olaf returned with the news of Eystein's death, he had married his friend's wife and built a new hall, farther back from Sogn Fjord and the Danish raiders. Farther from ships that bore news and trade goods, as well.

One of Svanhild's earliest memories was picking over the charred remains of the hall, prying melted pewter off rocks. Now grass covered the post ends, though she could still find pieces of charcoal between them if she looked. The cows liked to graze here, for the grass grew lush over the burned ground. She had little more than tales to remember her father by, while Ragnvald had some boyhood memories. When they were younger, Ragnvald's tales were all of their father's adventuring, for he had visited every district in Norway, and every land around the North Sea. As they grew older, Olaf's doubts made Ragnvald remember their father's lies, the winter he had been gone without word and their mother thought him dead. "He earned every man's love and no man's trust" was what Olaf said of him, on a rare Yule when he had been moved to speak of his fallen friend. While Olaf had no man's love or trust.

Svanhild pulled her spindle and a piece of wool roving out of her pocket and perched on the stone wall that separated this field from the next. She gave the spindle a flick of her fingers to set it whirling, and began drafting out the greasy wool. Twice she pulled it too thin and the spindle clattered to the ground, the unspun fleece picking up bits of moss and earth that Vigdis would scold her over. She wrapped the wool around the spindle and tucked it into her pocket. Her fin-

gers would not bend to the task today, not after Einar's words. Ragnvald would not have chosen to settle abroad without her, not after his
promises to her, but he could have died while raiding, just like their father had. If Ragnvald was dead, they would never again walk through
the woods to the witches' cave, never hike out to the cliffs overlooking
Sogn Fjord and watch the seals play. If Ragnvald was dead, she did not
like her prospects here: Olaf would marry her to Thorkell or one of
his sons to keep the peace. Thorkell was a brute old enough to be her
father, and his sons were either weak or brutish themselves. Ragnvald
could not be dead.

Slanting sheets of rain chased from one side of the fjord to the other.
The sun shone where Svanhild sat, though clouds approached from all
directions. When the rain reached her, Svanhild pulled her cloak over
her head and sat in the lee of a rock outcropping. She grew hungry in
the afternoon, and rounded up the cows to drive them home.

As she left the cows to graze in the field closer to the hall, she heard
the clatter of wood blades against one another from the practice yard.
She walked around a fence corner, and saw her stepbrother Sigurd
make a few hacks with his wooden sword against the practice post,
then rest it against the wall. He slumped down next to it. Perhaps he
had the same worries about Olaf's intentions that Einar did—surely
he did not want the land any more than Svanhild wanted him to have
it. Sigurd needed someone to tell him what to do at every hour of the
day. He could not hold Ardal against raiders.

She walked over to him and picked up his practice sword. The iron
core inside the wood made it heavy. She had wanted one for herself
once, and Olaf had beat her for it, saying she would make herself too
ugly and scarred for marriage if she fought among the reckless boys.
Ragnvald had taught her as much as he could, but she had been too
small and impatient, and then her housework left her little time.

Sigurd was tall for his age, spindly as a beanstalk, and neither as
strong nor canny as Ragnvald had been at his age. He was the son of
Olaf's first wife, a woman long dead, replaced by Vigdis and Svanhild's
mother. Sigurd had been young when he came with Olaf to live here
in Ardal. Where both Svanhild and Ragnvald were dark as their father

had been, Sigurd had Olaf's washed-out coloring and a flaxen shock of hair above a face reddened by exertion and pocked with acne.

He sneered at Svanhild when he saw her. "You should be inside, caring for my little brother." Vigdis's new son was still young enough to be crying for milk at all hours of the night. He needed a wet nurse, not Svanhild.

She put the sword up under his chin. "It doesn't feel that heavy." She shifted her weight to hold it steady so he could not see how her arm began to shake.

He batted the blade away. She moved it back to his throat. "Try waving it around for a few hours," said Sigurd. "It's heavy enough."

"Do you think Ragnvald did well on his raiding?" she asked. Einar's words had stayed with her. The dull edge of the wood pressed into the soft flesh under Sigurd's throat, where the first threads of beard had started to grow. "Why isn't he home yet?"

Sigurd grabbed the blade and pushed it away more forcefully. Svanhild let it clatter to the ground rather than allowing Sigurd to make her fall.

"I don't know," said Sigurd sullenly. "Are you scared? If he doesn't come home, I will take care of you."

Svanhild put her hands on her hips and regarded him skeptically. "Is that why you're practicing?"

Sigurd puffed out his chest. "Olaf wants me to go raiding this summer."

"Just like he wanted Ragnvald to do?" Svanhild asked, her voice growing high. "Einar says he doesn't think Olaf will let Ragnvald have his birthright."

"And why should he?" Sigurd asked. "My father held these lands when your father couldn't."

"These lands belong to Ragnvald," said Svanhild angrily. "Olaf should only be holding them, as he agreed."

"The land belongs to the man who can keep it," said Sigurd. He sounded both pleased and ashamed, as when he had burned all of Svanhild's dolls when she was little. "Anyway, my father said Ragnvald might not be coming home. Raiding is dangerous work."

Svanhild stared at him. "Especially . . . especially if you can't trust the men you sail with? Especially if someone doesn't want you to come home." Her guess had been half formed when she voiced it, but suddenly it made terrible sense. Olaf had refused to let Ragnvald go raiding until this year, until his son by Vigdis had survived the dangerous years of early childhood.

Sigurd gave her a guilty look, confirming her guess. Her face went hot. "You—you—*nithing*."

Sigurd bent down to pick up his blade. Svanhild clenched her fist and swung wildly at him, catching his jaw with a lucky blow as he started to stand. He let out an aggrieved cry and fell, sprawling back on the grass. Svanhild stepped on his hand where it reached toward his blade.

"That's my sword hand," he said.

"If you don't use it to defend your family, what good is it?" She ground her heel into his palm.

"Olaf is my family. You're just—"

"Olaf and my father were sworn brothers," Svanhild cried, pressing down harder.

"That hurts, you little troll," he said.

"Good! It's supposed to." Svanhild's hand hurt too from hitting him, a dull ache that was getting worse by the moment. Nothing was broken—she knew how that felt—but if she did not plunge her hand into a snowbank soon, it would be swollen and useless for a week. "Tell me why he's not coming back," she demanded.

"I only heard rumors." He swung a kick that knocked her off her feet. She landed on her seat and sat up in the grass, cradling her hand.

"I'll hit you again," said Svanhild, but Sigurd had seen how she held her hand, and now that she had lost the element of surprise, she had little chance of hurting him. He sprang to his feet and grabbed her by her bruised fingers, drawing her half off the ground and grinding the knuckles together painfully.

"No, you won't," he said shrilly. "You'll never hit me again, or I'll beat this hand into a pulp, and the forest witch will have to cut it off." Sigurd held her there for a moment, as tears stung her eyes. She could stamp on his foot and maybe he would let her go, or maybe he would make good on his threat. The anger that had given her the strength to hit him was replaced by a sick fear that left her shaking.

Ascrida stormed toward them then, her skirt flapping behind her. "Sigurd. Let go of your sister." She looked from Svanhild to Sigurd and nodded. "Svanhild, come with me."

"But Sigurd said—"

Ascrida glared. Svanhild closed her mouth.

✛ ✛ ✛

"USELESS GIRL," SAID Ascrida as soon as she had pulled Svanhild into the women's chambers.

"He said that Ragnvald wasn't coming back."

Ascrida set her jaw. "No one has returned from Solvi's raids yet."

"Don't you care?" Svanhild cried. "He's your son! But I suppose you didn't care about my father either. Why didn't you make Olaf avenge him? They were friends." Ascrida squeezed Svanhild's bruised knuckles together as Sigurd had. "Ow, you're hurting me."

"You speak of things you do not understand," said Ascrida wearily.

Svanhild wrenched her hand out of Ascrida's grip. "I need to cool it, or I won't be able to spin." If her mother did not care about Svanhild's pain, perhaps she would at least care about the household's chores, the endless spinning that must be done to keep them all in clothes and sails, sheets and shrouds.

"You shouldn't hit Sigurd." Ascrida sounded dull and tired.

Usually Svanhild let her be when she sounded like that, but she was too angry now. "Why?" she said. "Because he can't take it?"

Ascrida gripped Svanhild's shoulder now, her fingers digging in, causing welcome pain that distracted Svanhild from her throbbing hand. "No," said Ascrida. "Because if Ragnvald does not come back, one of Olaf's sons will be master here when Olaf is gone."

"You don't think Ragnvald is coming home either?" asked Svanhild angrily. "Did everyone spend the winter plotting murder while I learned my weaving?"

"Murder? No. I think your stepfather hopes that your brother will settle abroad."

"You are blind, Mother," said Svanhild, tears blurring her vision. "Olaf doesn't mean for Ragnvald to come home."

Ascrida sucked in a breath. "And you have too much imagination. He has been your father these last ten years. I do not think he would do such a thing."

"You don't think? Do you never wonder how he and our father went raiding, and only one came back?" Her mother had told Svanhild to forget those rumors long ago, that evil-minded people always wondered, that Olaf might be a stern man, but he was no murderer.

"I think of many things," said Ascrida. "More than an empty-headed girl like you. And when Olaf's sons are masters here, they may do what they like with you. They may marry you to an abusive drunkard, and you would have no say in the matter. Olaf will never love you—you are too independent—but your stepbrothers still might."

"No one will marry me off to an abusive drunkard. I would give myself to the roughest raider before I let Sigurd punish me like that."

Ascrida raised a hand to slap her. Svanhild caught her mother's blow on her forearm instead and turned on her heel before Ascrida could say anything more.

She met Vigdis in the corridor. "You must be gentle with your mother," Vigdis said.

"Must I?" said Svanhild. The tears that had threatened were beginning to overspill her cheeks.

"The roughest raider is likely to be a drunkard as well, my dear. Other threats will have more weight."

At least Vigdis's sarcasm made it easier for Svanhild to quell her tears. "I don't want to marry. I want my own land, and men to farm it and to go abroad sometimes and—"

"Women must marry," said Vigdis. "Marry a rich old man, so when he dies he will make you rich enough to choose whatever husband you like. I think Olaf wants to marry you to Thorkell."

"So I can die bearing his son?" The idea made Svanhild's stomach twist, as though her very organs already feared it.

"Perhaps he will die and leave you a widow who can do what she likes."

"Is that what you were trying to do with Olaf?"

"Svanhild," said Vigdis sternly.

"You can't tell me what to do." Svanhild shook her head, scattering the tears she was trying to hide, and pushed past Vigdis and out into the pasture.

She rushed across the fields and into the woods, where some shadowed grove would still shelter winter's snow. She found a cache of not yet melted snow in the roots of an oak, and there she sat, numbing her hand, while the sun set.

3

SOLVI SAT IN THE STERN OF HIS SHIP, WITH HIS HAND ON THE steering oar, and guided it through a long curve into the harbor. The wind blew ever away from Tafjord, shielding it from all raiders except those who lived there. It was a difficult spot to attack by land as well, flanked by mountains and ravines. Solvi's father Hunthiof and his father before him had been sea kings since the founding of their line, descended from the sea god Njord, who briefly loved a woman of the land but left her lamenting, to raise up sons who would leave her as well. The descendants of that sorrow grew into a line of hard men who raided up and down the Norse coast when lands across the North Sea were no more than legend, before these crowded times when every farmer's son dreamed of sailing and raiding across the ocean. They had never been farmers. Their bones kept guard over no land.

Usually Snorri served as pilot, but Solvi liked to guide his ship in these last leagues to Tafjord and his father's hall, so he could control his approach. His father would find something to criticize in Solvi's decisions on this journey, though his memories of his own raids must have grown hazy by now. Solvi fingered the pommel of his dagger with his free hand. Some blood speckled the gold inlay. The deed was done; Ragnvald had been sacrificed to Njord and Ran. If he did not die of his wounds, he would drown, pulled down by leather armor and choked by cold.

The memory troubled Solvi. He could have found a dozen other times to end Ragnvald's life earlier, out of the view of the men who now glanced at him with suspicion and fear. It was good for men to fear those who would rule them, but fear could also be tricky; a man might think it better to put a dagger in Solvi's back than risk his own unprovoked murder when Solvi's mood turned.

He wondered if his father had not backed the wrong ship in this race. Ragnvald's stepfather, Olaf, was a cunning enough warrior—it was he who had brought Ragnvald's father, Eystein, low and taken his wife. But Ragnvald had the gift of leading men, something the taciturn and tight-fisted Olaf did not. Olaf squeezed cruelly the lands he took from Eystein and lost them, farm by farm, to other leaders who required less of them.

"We need strong men like Olaf," his father had told him, "and he wants this done." If Ragnvald lived, he would surely go after his birth-right, and with determination such as his, Solvi had no doubt he would win, and guard his land better than Olaf ever had.

When the wind brought him close to shore, Solvi saw that ships other than his fathers' had made landing here, fine ships, though new; their beams shone with a varnish of fat that weather had not yet stripped from them. High company.

The shallow pebble beach crunched under the keel of his ship. Solvi jumped out, wetting his feet in the waters of home. The halls of Tafjord sat at the bottom of the valley at the end of Geiranger Fjord. A patchwork of fields and wooden fences stretched up the bowl of the valley to the crests of the rocky cliffs. Beyond the cliff wall rose the mountains of the Keel, hard and white and impenetrable.

Solvi reached down and splashed water on his face, washing off days of sweat and grime. His father's servants waited on the beach, ready to unload the ships. The watchmen must have seen them approaching.

Solvi leapt up on the pylon where his ship was tied. Long practice let him land lightly, not betraying with even a twitch of his face how his scarred feet pained him, how he struggled to make his legs obey him after so long at sea. He spoke loudly enough that the warriors on all five of the ships that had followed him the long way to Tafjord, now beached alongside one another, could hear him.

"You all have homes to go to, and maidens to impress with your riches and your stories. But if you feast with my father tonight, you can tell your tales to our skalds so they can write songs of your adventures, and then they will be sung not only in your houses, but in the halls of kings."

The men let up a cheer, all except Ragnvald's friend Egil, who looked up at Solvi from where he sat, eyes wary. As Solvi finished speaking, Egil turned his attention to packing up his gear. Solvi's other men bounded out of the ship, hurtling over the gunwales and splashing down in the shallow water. On their backs they carried the treasure each had won personally in Ireland. They would come tonight, though, to see what else Solvi might give them. He made sure to be known as a generous lord; his ships had taken rich plunder, and there was more to share.

Solvi drew his father's steward to him as the men trooped toward Hunthiof's hall. "Who is here?" he asked. "I don't know those ships."

"Warriors from Vestfold," he said. "King Guthorm and his nephew Harald." The man spoke blandly enough, but Solvi knew those names from skald's songs that mentioned them in the same breath as gods and giants. Harald could not be more than sixteen years old, yet tales had spread from Vestfold of his strength at arms. They said that he could best any man with any weapon, and with a sword he had fought off ten blooded warriors. Harald's mother was a sorceress who had prophesied that he would be king of all the Norse lands. And he was here. Solvi's father could not like that.

Three of Solvi's elkhounds bounded down to greet him. The largest and darkest of the trio jumped up to lick Solvi's cheek and breathe meaty air into his face. Solvi chucked him under the chin, keeping one eye on the ship. Egil still sat on one of the oar benches, cleaning under his fingernails with his dagger.

"I'll be starting off home, my lord," said Egil when Solvi looked his way. He heaved his pack onto his shoulder. Solvi did not wonder why he and Ragnvald had become friends. They both had an eye on the horizon, which boys their age often lacked, and Ragnvald was promised to Egil's sister Hilda. At the coming Sogn *ting*, the union was supposed to be formalized, making Egil and Ragnvald brothers in truth.

"You are welcome to the feast as well." Solvi walked closer. Egil scooted back, losing his perch and falling back onto the deck.

Egil's eyes locked on Solvi's sword hand. He made no movement to defend himself. He was a skilled enough fighter in a shield wall or a nighttime ambush, but against Solvi he would lose. Solvi had layers of muscle and five years' fighting experience, years that made the difference between boy and man. And he was not afraid to cheat—fate had dealt him too many blows for him not to take every advantage. Egil would know that now.

Egil struggled to find his feet, hand on the gunwale. Solvi put his steel wrist guard on Egil's fingers, pressing until Egil flinched and sat again. He pulled his hand free and rubbed at it like a child.

"You have nothing to fear from me, my lord. But I must bring the news to my sister."

Solvi smiled. "Take a ring for her," he said.

Egil's glance darted to the pile of treasure that spilled loose from a broken sack. He pulled out a thick gold arm ring from the nearest sack of Solvi's treasure. It was worth more than Egil's father's farm, and he knew it. His eyes met Solvi's.

"Like this one?" he asked. What price silence?

That ring was destined to buy the favor of kings, not a boy still growing in his first beard. If Solvi chose, he could lead men to raze Hrolf's farm, burn him in his meager hall, and take Egil's sister as a lesser wife. But Solvi had seen enough blood today. His father had ordered him to kill Ragnvald, not Ragnvald's friend. He nodded. Egil looked surprised at his fortune. It was a beautiful piece, pure and soft.

"You will not stand witness for him, no matter what happens," said Solvi.

Egil nodded and tucked the ring into his pack. Solvi steadied him with a hand under his arm as Egil climbed over the gunwale, and then watched as he trudged up the steep path that would take him over the moon-bathed cliffs, back to his peaceful farm, and a sister who would have gold to ease her mourning.

✝ ✝ ✝

ON THE SLOPE above the shore, Solvi's father's hall blazed with light. The smell of roasting meat carried down over the beach on the evening breeze. Solvi walked toward it. Row upon row of stone oil lamps

hung from ropes attached to the ceiling, burning brightly, displaying Hunthiof's wealth as surely as the silver on his belt buckle. The
sounds of his warriors fighting, talking, and already growing drunk
greeted him.

On the dais, Hunthiof sat with a man who must be Guthorm of
Vestfold, and next to him an eager blond boy—Harald Halfdansson.

"Solvi, my son," said Hunthiof, his voice booming out so all could
hear. He stood and spread his arms to welcome Solvi to the high table. Hunthiof wore his beard full now that he no longer made yearly
raiding trips. His father had seemed hale and tough when Solvi sailed
out the previous summer. Now his eyes were starting to lose their
brilliance.

Solvi walked the length of the hall as steadily as he could, his balance still shaky from the weeks spent at sea. All eyes were upon him
here in a way that never bothered him when he was in command of
a ship or a raiding party. At sea none doubted his dominance, so he
never thought of his deformity.

"Is it done?" Hunthiof whispered in Solvi's ear. He smelled like
mead, sweet and alcoholic, rather than the brine Solvi had always as-
sociated with him.

"Yes," said Solvi.

His father peered into his face, eyes narrowed. "Later you must tell
me how, so I can make Olaf sure."

He turned and presented Solvi to his guests. Guthorm of Vestfold
was a monster of a man, with the kind of broadness that would turn
to fat if he ever stopped fighting. Solvi did not even reach his shoulder.
His mouth was a thin, downward slash through his beard, his cheeks
pouching into the beginning of jowls.

When Harald stood, Solvi saw that he was almost as tall as his uncle. Wisps of a golden beard blurred the line of his jaw. A young giant
then, grown into manhood early. Seeing him made the stories more
believable.

Solvi's men had taken up places by the fire, arrayed around the dais,
telling of their travels, their exploits. The boy Harald listened with
excitement, a child thrilling to tales of battle. Solvi glanced up to the
foot of the hall, searching among the servants bearing skins of ale,

platters piled with meat. His wife Geirny was not behind them, direct-
ing them, as she should have been.

He frowned. He should not have expected her. In the years they
had been together, she had given him only daughters and one son who
was too ill formed to take a breath. He would not put her away, for
he feared the taint was in his own seed, but neither would he seek her
out. He had a Scottish thrall who had warmed his hide sleeping bag on
the journey back from the Hebrides. She would do for tonight as well,
especially after she had a chance to bathe.

Hunthiof rose to his feet and stood on his seat. Raising his horn,
he spoke out, his voice echoing to every corner of the hall. "My war
serpents, my treasure hands, welcome home. You have roved and
plundered and come back rich and proud. My skalds will sing of your
glories. But even their boasting will not drown out the cries of your
slain." The warriors roared their approval and banged their fists on the
long plank tables. "Let my son tell me what you have done, and I will
reward you accordingly."

Solvi gave a practiced grin. His father might want to remind Solvi's
men that he, not Solvi, was king, but it was Solvi these men would
remember as their lord, the one who led them into battle and brought
them back richer than they had left.

His men drank deeply. Hunthiof took up the bag of arm rings
and called forth the men who had raided along with him, Solvi naming their deeds, and Hunthiof giving them each a ring, of pewter, of
bronze, or of silver. Some were not happy with their rewards. Well,
they could blame his father for that, at least, and fight when they were
drunk enough. It was a poor feast that did not end with at least one
bloody nose.

Ceremonies done, Solvi sat down on the bench next to his father
and dug into the hot pile of roast beef the thrall had set before him.
The rich red juices had already soaked through the trencher. Solvi's
stomach growled. He had eaten nothing so bountiful since leaving the
autumn before—his warriors were terrible cooks. This would likely
make him vomit during the night, and he would enjoy that too, the
spoils of home.

"Why have you come so far?" Solvi asked Guthorm. Harald and

his uncle had already finished their meat while Solvi spoke his warriors' deeds, and now Guthorm gestured for a serving girl to refill his
cup, then frowned and waved her away when Harald did the same. At
his father's warning look, Solvi added, "Vestfold is far richer than our
poor land."

"The fjords here are so steep," said Harald. "How do the men farm
it?" He pitched his voice deep, as though he were trying to keep it from
breaking.

"We do not farm," said Hunthiof. "Farmers are slaves to their land."

"Yet I see cows on the high meadows," said Guthorm. "Surely they
do not all belong to the elf maidens and trolls."

"I don't believe in trolls," said Harald.

"But you should, for they come from our mountains," said Solvi,
and was rewarded with a flicker of uncertainty from Harald. He took
a piece of meat and worried a piece of gristle off it before throwing it
to the dogs. "And you did not answer my question."

"Harald should see the land he would rule," said Guthorm.

"Farmers tie their cows to trees so they cannot fall off the steep
meadows, for if they did not, the cows would drown in the fjord," said
Solvi. "Many fall and drown, and not only cows. This land is hard on
those who would rule it."

Guthorm's mouth tightened. "We are your guests."

"Yes, you are," said Hunthiof, giving Solvi a pointed look. "What
do you want of us?"

"Your support, of course," said Guthorm. "King Hakon has already
promised his daughter to Harald."

"King Hakon has many daughters," said Solvi with a leer. "I've
known a few of them myself. Which one did he give you?"

The boy's sunny eyes darkened, and he put his hand to the knife at
his belt.

Guthorm stayed him with a look. "Your son comes dangerously
close to insult," he said. "Do you want a duel over it?"

"My son is drunk and just returned home," said Hunthiof. "Do not
mind him."

"You know what the tide brings, Hunthiof," said Guthorm. "Thirty
years ago we fought a Danish army together. They found better pick-

ings in England, but in going there, they unified that country under one king. Sweden now has a king, and Denmark. The Holy Roman Empire sends its bishops north backed by armies. The time when every man who owned a valley could call himself a king is passing." Guthorm paused and looked up at the walls of the hall, where the torchlight cast flickering shadows. Solvi thought he looked further, to the cliffs that bounded Geiranger Fjord.

"If you do not bend the knee to Harald now, he will bend it for you later, and you will not rise again," said Guthorm. "The kings who join us now will be made rich beyond their dreams. Those who do not will lose all they hold."

"A bold threat, when you travel in only three dragon ships, and claim a beardless boy as your champion," said Hunthiof. Solvi looked at his father approvingly. The ships were finely built narrow warships, with carved dragon figureheads, but those dragons were only wood. This Harald, this champion who had never seen defeat or hardship, could not amount to much. He would not be the first king to sit in his flat, easy lands to the south, while claiming to rule territory he had only seen once. No man could be king of all of the Norse peninsula; the mountains and fjords were too isolated from one another. The advantage would always go to a king who ruled no more than the land he could guard by ship, and raid the neighboring lands to keep the borders safe.

"Will you murder us here, Hunthiof?" asked Guthorm quietly. "I would think that since the gods had already cursed you with a crippled son, you would not want to risk their wrath again by guest-slaying."

Solvi leapt to his feet. "I will not be insulted in my own hall."

"Sit," said Guthorm. "I insulted your father, not you. I only insult whole men."

Hunthiof stood as well. "Is this the kingcraft you would teach the boy? To offend his would-be allies? You will leave, or we will throw you out."

Guthorm stood, so huge that Solvi, long accustomed to being the shortest man in a group, still felt cowed. "In truth, we never meant to make you our allies," Guthorm said calmly. "King Hakon would never have agreed."

"Then why are you here?" Hunthiof roared.

"To give you warning. Depart these lands. Leave them to us and your neighboring kings, and you will survive. The wolf is at your door." With that, Guthorm swept out of the hall, Harald trailing behind him. Before he left, Harald cast a worried glance over his shoulder.

Solvi marched over to his man Ulfarr, who had his hand up the skirt of a pretty thrall, and shook his shoulder. "Get the men up and out." He sniffed the air, trying to detect the scent of the pitch that Guthorm would need if he intended a hall burning.

Outside some of Guthorm's men stood guard as others made the ship ready, putting out the oars. In this calm night, they must row away from Tafjord and wait for a morning wind.

"It is bold," said Hunthiof, coming to stand at Solvi's side, his own sword drawn. "They wish to make a song of it, how they came and gave us warning."

Solvi's blood was still up; he hated watching them row away unharmed. He should take his men after them, board them and sink them, drown their prophecies and their insults. His father should not have let such words stand against his son, except if he agreed. Hunthiof put his hand on Solvi's shoulder. "Let them go. It is foolishness."

"King Hakon is powerful," said Solvi. "If he agreed . . ."

"As you said, he has many daughters. If he hedges his bets with one of them, what harm in it? He can always make her a widow."

Solvi swallowed. He thought of killing Ragnvald, how the blow had gone awry. He could redeem himself here, erase Guthorm's insults. In sailing away, Guthorm and Harald had passed beyond the bounds of hospitality.

"Solvi," said Hunthiof, a warning that would allow no dissent.

"Yes, Father," said Solvi. The oars of Guthorm's ship dipped cleanly into the water, and before Solvi could draw breath again, it had disappeared in the shadow under the cliff.

"Now, tell me of Ragnvald Eysteinsson," said Hunthiof as they walked back to the hall. Solvi swallowed hard.

"Under the eyes of the helm in the cliff's face," said Solvi, "I cut his throat and gave him to Ran."

"You saw his life's blood? He breathes no more?"

Only Solvi's father could question him like this and make Solvi doubt his actions. His father was an old man now, past the age of fighting. He had given Solvi men and ships, but never trusted him entirely. And why should he? Solvi was a trickster dwarf, not a real son, his father sometimes reminded him. Solvi's memories of his childhood, fragmented by the pain of his burns, were of long days in the dark hall, no more cared for than the dogs that fought under the tables.

Solvi turned his mind to the recent past, away from those shadowed memories. Ragnvald's killing had not gone easily. Ragnvald eyes had been horrified, accusing. There had not been much blood. Solvi's fingers clenched. Ragnvald had dropped out of them like a dead man, impossible to hold against the current with his wet clothes dragging him down. His skin had been cold.

"If he breathes, he breathes water," said Solvi.

Hunthiof frowned. "Some men can. Do not lie to me. Is he dead?"

"He may yet live," Solvi admitted, and told his father what had happened in as few words as possible. "It is in the fates' hands."

"I thought it was in your hands." Hunthiof's grip on the back of Solvi's neck tightened.

"The waves stole him from me," said Solvi. He might have done the deed earlier, but he had needed Ragnvald over that long winter, besieged by Irish tribesmen in their stockade. Ragnvald had always been the first to attack, the last to retreat, and more importantly, the first to sniff out treachery. Except the treachery Solvi had practiced against him.

"If he lives, he is your enemy," said Hunthiof. "You will make good the promise to Olaf."

"Olaf is an old—"

"You will make good," Hunthiof said between gritted teeth, his fingers still digging painfully into Solvi's flesh. Eyes in the hall had started to turn to them. Solvi shrugged off his father's hand and pulled himself up to his full height, such as it was.

"I will do what is best for our family," said Solvi, "and our kingdom."

4

EGIL APPEARED AT SUPPER TIME, BLOWN TO ARDAL LIKE A bird by the spring storms that had kept Svanhild penned inside for the past three days. He looked like a bird too, a bedraggled stork with all his feathers hanging down and water pouring over his hat brim. When he arrived, Svanhild's heart skipped; she imagined for a moment that the news he brought would be good, that Ragnvald would appear out of the mists behind him.

Vigdis pushed past Svanhild to let Egil into the hall. She bid him strip out of his clothes in front of the fire, and brought him a dry tunic and trousers—Ragnvald's, Svanhild noted. He would not begrudge his friend dry clothes.

"I have news for you," said Egil while he was dressing.

"Now that you are dry, you must greet us properly," said Svanhild, stalling him. She moved to tidy up the hearth, avoiding his eyes where he tried to meet hers. "You are almost my brother."

"I must tell you." He reached out toward her. "It is Ragnvald."

No, she did not want to know this, confirmation of all the hints, of the death of her hopes, hopes that Ragnvald had fed all these years of the happier life they would have when he reclaimed his birthright. Raiding with Solvi was to be the first step.

"Tell me," said Svanhild. She wrapped her arms around her ribs, against the ache there. Vigdis offered a towel for Egil's hair, but Svanhild took it from her and held it. "Tell us," she said.

"I am sorry, I tried to save him. It was Solvi." He told them, then, how it had happened, how he had tried to defend Ragnvald, but other men held him back. "He killed your brother, and dropped him in the water," he said finally.

Svanhild felt Olaf come up behind her, towering over her. His nearness made her uncomfortable. "You saw him die?" Olaf asked. "You are sure he is dead?"

It was the same question Svanhild wanted to ask, yet when Olaf spoke, Svanhild was suddenly sure that her suspicions were right, that Olaf had not meant Ragnvald to return from this trip.

"I am sure," said Egil. "He fell like a stone. He is in Ran's hall now." He met Svanhild's eyes, briefly, then looked away. Hiding his shame, Svanhild guessed, that he had not tried harder to save her brother, his friend.

"You will be tired," said Vigdis. "You must rest a few days with us, wait until the weather clears before you return to your father."

Egil sought Svanhild's eyes again. "He died well," he said. "He had his dagger in his hand. He fought bravely in Ireland and Scotland. He will find a place with Odin. He will not lie with the drowned." Svanhild hugged herself tighter. She could not spare any kind word for Egil now. Ragnvald was dead, lost, so his body would never rest in the barrow next to his forefathers. He would never become part of the land that his family had fought and died for. She clapped her hands over her mouth and ran from the room.

Alone in the byre, she could not make herself cry, although her breath came in little sobbing gasps. She had thought of Ragnvald every day since he had gone, imagining what he did, where he fought, as best she could from skalds' viking tales. She spent so much time with him in her mind that she felt as though she had followed him home, through the sleepless nights on the open ocean, back to the shores of Sogn. He could not be gone.

The cows pawed nervously, sensing her upset. She wondered what they would do if she started screaming. Would someone then come to find her, to comfort her? She half expected Vigdis, her mother, perhaps Egil himself, to come and fetch her. Instead she heard the sounds of platters placed on the long table, small pewter cups next, then low

talking and chewing. Out in the main room, the household was gathered and eating dinner. The smell of roast goat made Svanhild's stomach turn over unpleasantly. She swallowed and brushed the straw off
her dress as she pushed open the door.

"I would like to stay longer," Egil was saying, "but I have to bring
these ill tidings to my sister."

"Did no one think I might want to eat?" Svanhild asked angrily.

Vigdis stood over Olaf's shoulder, pressing the side of her body
against his while she poured more ale into his cup. "I thought we were
letting you mourn alone," she said smoothly. "Of course, you must
join us if you are hungry."

Svanhild looked around the table. Her mother was not there either.
She must be grieving on her own now. Svanhild had not looked for
her, nor she for Svanhild. That thought brought the tears stinging to
her eyes, though news of Ragnvald's death had left them dry.

"My brother must have won gold and silver raiding," said Svanhild
in a high voice. "That must go to his family. Did you bring any of it for
us, Egil Hrolfsson?"

Egil looked up at her, surprised. "No," he said. He opened his
mouth as if to give an explanation, frowned, and closed it again.

"Then we must ask for it at the *ting*," said Svanhild. "My stepfather
has not much silver to spare for my dowry. Ragnvald was meant to
win it for me." For both of them.

Olaf looked ill pleased. He glanced at Sigurd. "Yes, Solvi owes our
family an explanation, and the treasure Ragnvald won."

"He owes . . . Ragnvald's murder-price," said Svanhild. "Unless he
has already been paid for Ragnvald's murder."

Vigdis put the pitcher of ale down on the table with a clatter. "Come
with me, Svanhild. Your mother will need your comfort now. You are
her only living child."

Svanhild let Vigdis guide her into the kitchen. There sat her
mother at the table, slowly grinding grains. She looked up at Svanhild blankly. Svanhild wished she saw some sorrow she could share.
That look on Ascrida's face, that emptiness, was the expression she
had worn for so long, whenever Svanhild went to her with hurts large

and small. Even Vigdis, with her selfish cat's ways, had more comfort to give.

"I am grinding grain for the morning porridge," said Ascrida. "People will need to eat."

Svanhild sat down across from her and pulled the stones gently from her grasp. They had little to offer one another, but she would not leave her alone. "Let me, Mother," she said. "You are tired."

✟ ✟ ✟

SVANHILD GROUND GRAIN in the stone quern until she could hardly keep her grip. All the muscles in her hands and arms ached. She emptied out the bottom stone and put another handful of grain in it. Why care if her hands hurt too much for her to spin tomorrow? If she did not hurt herself this way, she would scratch her flesh instead with the grinding stone, anything to distract from the pain in her throat.

The rest of the household had gone to sleep. Still Svanhild worked on, while her mother tied up bundles of herbs to dry, hands deft, eyes unseeing. Finally Svanhild grew too angry even to keep grinding the grain. She flung the stone down on the table, sending a fine mist of flour into the air.

"Svanhild, you'll waste it," said Ascrida.

"Mother, what will happen to us now?" Svanhild asked. "Ragnvald was supposed to—" She stopped. The list of things that Ragnvald had left undone was too long. Add it to the list of things that their father had not done, like live to protect their land from raiders, from Olaf.

"Did Olaf kill our father?" she burst out.

Ascrida sighed. "Ragnvald asked me that too. Come here." She opened her arms, weariness written on her face. Svanhild wanted to fall into them as she had done as a child, but she recalled her mother's treatment of her after she had confronted Sigurd. Her mother shared Olaf's bed.

"No, Mother," she said, crossing her arms. "Tell me the truth."

Ascrida pressed her lips together. Had she judged Ragnvald a necessary sacrifice? The Norns, the three fates, sat at the foot of the world tree, spinning, measuring, and cutting the threads of men's lives. Had Ascrida measured Ragnvald's as well, and decided its end?

"The only person who knows that is Olaf," she said, "and he has not seen fit to share that with me. If he truly tried to plan Ragnvald's death—"

"If? Mother, he is friends with King Hunthiof. He held Ragnvald at home, refusing to outfit him for a raiding trip with any other king. And now—"

"I will tell you what I told your brother," said Ascrida. "I did what I must so our family would survive." Her voice sounded hollow. "You love the old songs so much: Brunhilda's revenge for being married to the wrong man, Gudrun who survived as wife to her husband's killer and murdered her sons as they issued from her womb to avenge his death and her captivity. Life is not like that. You must learn how to survive, and how to make the hard choices. Men can be uncompromising. They can kill or die. It isn't so simple for women."

"You could kill him," said Svanhild. "He still takes you to his bed. He killed your husband and your son."

"I am no warrior. And no Gudrun either." She touched Svanhild's chin and pushed it up so Svanhild must look at her. "Neither are you. You still turn your face away at the summer sacrifices when the animals die—could you drive a blade into a man's throat?"

Svanhild thought of hitting Sigurd, of the anger and impotence that had gripped her, how she had only managed to hurt him by surprise. She could kill an animal caught in a snare, because they had no weapons to hurt her back.

"You could still try," she said. "Your family deserves that much."

"What happens next in this story of yours, daughter?" Ascrida asked. "When you kill your husband who has kept you safe these ten years? Do you then take up a sword to defend those lands from raiders and predatory neighbors? A woman waits and watches. She swallows a bitter draught when she must. As I did when I took Olaf to my bed. Wait now. Choose a strong man who will keep you safe." She picked up the corner of her wimple and brushed a smudge of dirt off Svanhild's face. "And go to sleep. It is too late. You will be tired tomorrow."

"I don't care," said Svanhild.

"Thorkell comes to feast before the Sogn *ting*," said Ascrida. "You should rest so you can look beautiful for him."

"I don't want him to think me beautiful," Svanhild cried.

"You should," said Ascrida sadly. "It is the only power you have now."

+ + +

EGIL DEPARTED THE next morning, to bring his terrible tidings to his sister Hilda. It comforted Svanhild to imagine Hilda crying for Ragnvald as well. At least someone mourned him, other than her mother, who seemed to be grieving for her own choices more than for her son.

On the feast day, Thorkell came with his *hird*, his followers: ten men at arms. Three of them were his sons, none were younger than twenty, and each had far better armor and weapons than the young farm boys Olaf recruited when he needed to run off bandits.

When the men sat, Svanhild brought in the trenchers and then the cups of ale with her eyes cast down, serving the opposite side of the table and never raising her eyes to Thorkell's. Olaf took hold of her wrist when she went to serve him more ale.

"Daughter," he said, coolly, "you have not greeted our guest. I think he would like your company at his seat."

Svanhild flushed red. She had never been asked to share a man's seat at a feast before, except in her earliest memory, when that man had been her father. Now it marked her as property Olaf wished to display, and Thorkell might wish to buy. Olaf had gifted Thorkell with part of the land he had taken from Eystein, and now Thorkell was the richer man.

"As you wish, Stepfather," she said.

She walked around to Thorkell's seat, feeling awkward with all eyes upon her. Walking behind him, she could see where his hair receded from his forehead. He wore a heavy red beard, streaked with gray that hid much of his face. He was huge, and seemed somewhat misshapen from it, as though all his body parts had grown without heeding where the others stopped. His eyes were smaller and darker than Olaf's, though otherwise their shared blood marked them similarly, deep lines carved from nose down to chin, upper lip covered by a mustache, lower pouting out. Thorkell wore a silk tunic over his homespun shirt and trews, and displayed more wealth in silver rings and clasps. Looking at him now, she did not feel fear, just weariness.

"My cousin does me honor," said Thorkell, looking her up and down. Her face heated—weariness turning to anger. She sat down next to him and began drinking from his cup. He dwarfed her, blocking half the room from her view. She drank deeply; that was her job, after all, in sharing his seat. When she drained it, she felt no less angry, but less cautious. She called a thrall over to refill it.

"I was sorry to hear of your stepson's death," said Thorkell to Olaf when meat was finished, bones thrown to the dogs, and the drinking begun in earnest. "Allow me to toast his easy rest, wherever he lies." He plucked the cup from between her fingers, rough nails rasping against her skin. She tried to move away from him on the crowded bench.

Olaf's expression flickered from surprise to anger and then to a false piety that made Svanhild angrier still. He raised his cup and completed the toast, then proposed another, to Thorkell's new grandson, the son of his daughter, married off to a farmer farther south. Another of Thorkell's men gave a toast that devolved into an insult competition between two brothers who, Svanhild gathered from the weary cheers, performed this often. The insults were not very creative; the chief entertainment derived from whether they would end the evening with arms around one another in friendship, or nursing bloody noses in separate corners.

Olaf turned to talk with Thorkell's blacksmith, who he had grown up with. Since no one, not even Thorkell, was paying her attention, Svanhild again drank what was left in his cup. As she put it down, his massive hand closed over hers, and she started.

"Oh, you do like a drink," said Thorkell. "Perhaps that's enough for now, though I can see that your father—"

"Stepfather," Svanhild corrected.

"Stepfather, then. Does that mean you will not call me uncle like you used to?"

If he were her uncle, then he would be too close kin to marry with her. She did not remember that. He had not been a frequent visitor to Olaf's farm in years past, preferring to visit his last wife's wealthy family. She was dead now, and her family's favors had been bestowed on his sons, not him. Now he turned his eyes to Olaf's land, with its weak son and marriageable stepdaughter. If Ragnvald were still alive, he could prevent this—as her stepfather's first cousin, the relation might still be judged too close to hers, but with few enough prospects for her of proper birth and wealth in their district, none would voice a protest.

"My cousin did not please you by sitting you here, I can see," said Thorkell.

"I don't think he does much to please me," said Svanhild. She should be flirting and charming him. Vigdis would advise it, even if he smelled of stale meat, stale sweat. She could no more imagine bedding him than one of the cows, but from how he looked at her, clearly he had no trouble imagining it.

"Will you place a wager for me, Thorkell?" Svanhild asked. "I have no coin of my own." She tried to smile at him.

"If I had a thrall as fat as you, I—I would sell him to a minstrel to dance in his bear-show," called out one of the brothers to the other. Thorkell's men shouted their derision. They must have heard the insult before.

"What will you bet?" Thorkell asked.

"Oh no," said Svanhild. "I asked you to place the bet for me. I will wager nothing of my own."

"Not even a kiss?" Thorkell asked. Svanhild must have looked as repulsed as she felt, for Thorkell shrugged and handed his glass up to a passing thrall to refill. "No? I forgot how young you are. What bet should I make?"

"I bet they end the night drunk and peaceful. My mother brews strong ale." The brothers seemed too tired for fighting tonight. Thorkell's farm lay a half day's march from Olaf's in good weather, and today had been cold and wet for the journey.

"That she does," said Thorkell, raising his glass. He leaned over and spoke a few low words to one of his men, handing him a thin silver coin.

Svanhild watched the money change hands. "Who pays for your swords, Thorkell?" Svanhild asked. "I know you do not get enough silver just from stealing cows."

Thorkell laughed, although it sounded thin. "You do work for my cousin then, asking me this?"

"Can I not ask for myself?" Svanhild tossed her hair. "I want to know. How do you buy swords?"

Thorkell looked at her soberly. She almost liked him, then, the way he seemed to see her, not just Olaf's pawn. "I think you are wise enough to know it is not in my interest to tell you this." He glanced at Olaf. "Your father should arm himself better. Every year brings more raiders, more ambitious men from the south. Any man who does not protect himself will be swept away in the chaos."

"Are you making certain our guest is enjoying himself?" Vigdis asked from behind Svanhild, startling her.

Svanhild looked at Thorkell, putting her false smile back in place. Her mother was not the only one who could make hard choices. "Am I?" she asked lightly.

"Your daughter is a bold one," said Thorkell. "I am well entertained." Vigdis gave her a warning look before returning to her place next to Olaf.

Thorkell put the cup into her hands again, and she took another drink. "Why do you tell me this?"

"I would not see ill befall you."

"Before you have a chance to bring it to me yourself."

"I would not be so bad a husband as that," he said.

Svanhild choked on her ale again. She clung to the table edge, coughing. "And you say I am too bold," she said when she had recovered.

"I think you are just bold enough," said Thorkell, making the easy answer.

"You are a grandfather, and I am fifteen," said Svanhild, trying to be severe now. "Far too young to marry."

"Better to marry now while you still have a choice," said Thorkell in a low voice that chilled Svanhild's blood. She could tell Olaf of his words, that he meant to take Olaf's land, and Olaf would believe her if it suited him. But why should she help Olaf when she could help herself?

"You are not what I pictured when I made up a husband in my

mind," said Svanhild honestly. She glanced at Vigdis, her slanted eyes and the way she threw her head back as she laughed at the men's jokes. She put her hand on Thorkell's arm. "But if you would know me better, ask my stepfather to bring me to the *ting*."

There, she could see if she could force Olaf into getting Ragnvald's treasure for her dowry. He was greedy. He might do it. She could see what other men might like her. Ragnvald had been the rope tying her to Ardal. Now she might be anything, go anywhere. Olaf would not hunt her down if she fled him. She had nothing to offer but her beauty, whatever she had of it, her body, whatever sons she might bring. With no one to shame but herself, she might be a king's second wife, a concubine, a mistress. She could flee to the priestesses of Freya and swear to do honor to the sibling gods of fertility, to lie with kings and farmers to bring rich harvests. The thought was strange, but not as displeasing as marriage with Thorkell would be.

"I shall," he said, whispering as though they shared a secret. Svanhild flushed, pleased at what she had wrought.

Some unspoken signal passed between Ascrida and Vigdis and brought both of them to their feet. It was time for the women to clean the table, so the men might continue their drinking and dicing alone. Thorkell's men would sleep where they lay. Svanhild stood and followed Vigdis into the kitchen.

"Shall we announce a betrothal?" Vigdis asked Svanhild. Svanhild colored; she hated that Vigdis had seen her using those tricks.

"Has Olaf settled with Thorkell for me?" she asked her mother.

"It is a fair match. Thorkell is growing in power," said Vigdis, before her mother could answer.

"Yes, and he should not be," she cried. "If"—she lowered her voice—"if Olaf were half the man my father was, he would have kept his land and I would be promised to—to one of King Hakon's sons." King Hakon ruled the lands north of Solvi's and Hunthiof's fjord, and was reckoned the richest man in the west.

"Marrying with Thorkell is as much as you can expect," said her mother. "He is kind enough."

"Kinder than Olaf, perhaps," said Vigdis quietly, almost turning Svanhild from her tantrum. Svanhild shook her head. She might allow

Vigdis or her mother, singly, to speak to her like this, but both of them made her feel a little girl again, scolded for stealing honey.

"He has buried three wives," Svanhild cried. "And I would be buried too, before I am even dead."

"His wives were sickly," said Ascrida. "You are stronger stuff than that. Our family bears easily." Svanhild's mother had carried six children to birth, though none born after Svanhild survived their first year. Still, she had lived through it.

"If I am wed to Thorkell, I will—I will take a lover, and make him kill Thorkell for me," Svanhild said.

Ascrida and Vigdis exchanged another look. Vigdis stepped forward and put her arm around Svanhild's shoulder. "Wait until it's settled before you plot anyone's death," she said. "Keep charming Thorkell as you have done. Be patient. You might yet find someone better."

Svanhild scowled; she did not want Vigdis approving of her, reading her thoughts and plans so easily, not today.

"Now," said Vigdis, "try to act like a proper girl who has no thoughts beyond spinning and children. And stop looking so sad and angry."

Svanhild tossed her head. "I don't see how that's possible."

"I know," said Vigdis wearily. "But try."

5

RAGNVALD LAY ON A CURVED AND UNSTEADY FLOOR, TEETH chattering together with cold. He clenched his jaw, and the shivering moved to the muscles in his neck. He could not stop his shaking. Hands plucked at his clothes, while a low voice said words he could not understand. He was back on Solvi's ship, he must be, and this time Solvi's dagger would not slip. He fought those seeking hands, kicking out aimlessly, scrabbling at his waist for his dagger, which was still with him, sealed too tightly into its sodden sheath for him to pry loose.

"Suit yourself," said the voice, and the hands withdrew.

At length the shaking and panic that gripped his limbs subsided. The vessel did not move like a dragon ship; those were too large for the waves to buffet like this. Ragnvald sat up.

He was in a small fishing skiff, thick-planked and inflexible, rocking in the small swells. His rescuer was a sturdy man with gray hair, knuckles swollen from years plying his nets in this fjord. One of the fish in the bottom of the boat, not yet neatly clubbed like the others, jumped over Ragnvald's foot. He leapt back, nearly out of the boat, his nerves still on edge.

"Twitchy lad, aren't you?" said the fisherman.

Ragnvald gripped the gunwale. "Who are you?"

"Agmar called Agi, son of Agmar, son of Agmar son of—you see how it goes. My forefathers liked tradition." He cackled, showing a mouth missing half its teeth.

"To whom do you owe allegiance?" Ragnvald asked, still wary.

"King Hunthiof."

That was Solvi's father, the closest king to Ragnvald's land, though his family owed allegiance to no one. Hunthiof did not try to extend his power so far south, and Ragnvald's grandfather Ivar had been the last to claim kingship over Sogn.

"That is good, yes," said Ragnvald. "And he is a good king, I am told." His chattering had moved to his speech now, the worst place for it. He gripped the boat's gunwales.

Agi shrugged. "He doesn't make much bother with the fisherfolk, unless they go talking to those they shouldn't. Been a lot of fine ships full of warriors passing here these weeks." He looked at Ragnvald more carefully. Ragnvald's clothes were all wet, and before that had seen weeks of hard wear since their last washing. Still, he had a sword, a dagger, a silver clasp for his cloak, and strong teeth. Agi would not think him another fisherman.

"You're not an outlaw, are you?" Agi asked.

"I'm not an outlaw," said Ragnvald. Solvi had delivered a sentence upon him without ever telling him his crime. He might try to cover himself by having Ragnvald outlawed on some trumped-up charge at the *ting* trials, and Ragnvald would have to escape overseas, or any man might kill him on sight. If Solvi thought him dead, though, the matter was probably done with.

"Then why won't you give me your name?"

"I am Ragn—Ragnar," he said. "Thank you for saving me."

"You're a bastard, then?" Agi asked, grunting as he pulled on the oars.

Ragnvald stiffened at the insult. That would be the assumption. He had not given his father's name. He nodded.

"Noble, though," said Agi. "You talk like one of them from up at the hall. And you've a fine sword."

"Yes," said Ragnvald. He did not like the way Agi's eyes lay upon the sword, covetously. He gave some false details—a noble mother, a child born on the wrong side of the blankets. From the north, where Agi would not have ventured.

"And how did you come to be in the water, your throat half slashed?"

"A game," said Ragnvald shortly. "I fell in."

"And none of your fellows fished you out?"

"No, and they will answer for it when I see them again," said Ragnvald, scowling. They would have pulled him out if it had been just a game. He did not have Solvi's gift of making friends with everyone, but he had been respected among the men. His stepfather had sent him out raiding with Solvi so he could prove himself worthy of taking over the ruling of his father's lands, and Solvi had told him he had succeeded, that his stepfather would have a good report of him. And now it had gone wrong—Solvi had changed his mind, or never meant to help Ragnvald in the first place. The unfairness of it made his throat tight.

Belatedly he realized that the description of a man named Ragnar, rescued from the fjord with a cut throat, would be enough for Solvi or anyone from their ship to figure out he was still alive.

Ragnvald put his fingers to the wound on his throat, which bled more freely as he grew warm again. That one had not bit too deep; he could hardly wet a fingernail in it. He did not want to touch the wound on his face, which had begun to drip blood onto his trousers. He wrung out a corner of his shirt and tore off a strip of cloth to bind the cuts.

"You're not a *draugr*, then, are you?" asked the fisherman.

Ragnvald smiled grimly. He must look like one of them, a walking corpse, with his throat and face bloody, his fingernails blue with cold.

"Not yet," he said, "thanks to you." Agi was still looking at him. This man fished in waters controlled by Solvi and his father. "Though I don't know that King Hunthiof would thank you," he admitted.

Ragnvald rummaged under his tunic and pulled loose the armband Solvi had given him. He weighed it in his hands briefly. It was thick and heavy, the silver fine like satin under his fingers. The body was thick twisted wire, each strand wider than that of the heaviest chain mail. The ends were worked into boars' heads, mouths open in attack. It was a princely gift. Ragnvald had done a warrior's work to win it, and he had worn it with pride since the feast when Solvi had given it to him. It was the only wealth he had, beyond the pewter pendant he wore and his cloak clasp. The only wealth he likely ever would have, if Solvi wanted him dead.

"Thank you for pulling me out of the water," said Ragnvald, holding the ring where Agi could see it. He was warming now. His hand tingled with the anticipation of having a dagger in it. He could kill Agi now if he had to, and Agi must know that. "I would be grateful if no one knew I had passed this way," he said.

"It was no game, young Ragnar, was it?" Agi said. His eyes lit covetously on the silver, but his voice held some kindness.

"I thought it was a game," Ragnvald said. He wanted to tell Agi the truth, to try to explain himself, and the unfairness of what Solvi had done. Until he explained it to Agi, to someone, it felt as though Solvi had won. "But I was wrong. I have an enemy."

Agi looked up at Ragnvald's face and then to his right hand, tense and empty. "I am not your enemy. I'll set you on shore and be glad to see the back of you. I won't put you back in the drink, if that's what's got you fearful. You can walk to Tafjord along the cliff," said Agi. "Or away. At least you still have your sword."

Ragnvald put his hand on the wet leather that encased it. "Yes, I do," he said.

"You can still die of cold," said Agi abruptly, and started to take off his tunic.

Ragnvald was cold, but he thought Agi might mean to encumber his hands, and he refused the offer.

"Suit yourself," said Agi. He took up an oar and started rowing them toward the shoreline. Ragnvald felt shamed by his refusal. He found another oar under a folded net, and rowed from his side as an apology. His arms felt boneless. The effort left him winded, but warmer than before.

When they reached the shore, Ragnvald put the ring into Agi's hands. He stroked the silver with a cracked thumbnail. It might be the most wealth he ever held, or perhaps his hovel hid a trove of such treasure; it must sometimes wash up on his shores on the bodies of the dead.

"This is too much," said Agi. He looked more kindly now as he glanced over Ragnvald's bloody face, at wounds that still seeped. "My daughter can tend to your face."

"I must go," said Ragnvald. "Keep it."

"At least take some food," Agi quickly produced a bundle of bread and dried fish from the boat. Ragnvald accepted it mutely.

✝ ✝ ✝

AGI SHOWED HIM a way up the cliffs and left him to his climb. By the time Ragnvald reached the rim, he was too weary to go on. Above, stars had already started to wink out of the dark sky. He made a fire in the shelter of a rock scree and ate a few pieces of the dried fish Agi had given him. He had not been alone since—he could not remember—some boyhood journey into the woods, a proof of bravery.

He counted up the months he had been gone, marked in scratches on his belt. It was later in the year than he thought. The midsummer Sogn *ting* gathering would be soon, perhaps in as little as a week. Ragnvald should go there, rather than home to risk Olaf's displeasure at returning without plunder. King Hunthiof and Solvi always came to the *ting* to recruit for their raiding trips and to show off their wealth. Ragnvald could sue for his share of the bounty, and perhaps even a payment for the wound Solvi had dealt him.

He had gone often to the trials with his father, when he was still alive, and even in the years he stayed behind at Ardal to defend it while Olaf and Vigdis went to the yearly assembly, they returned with tales of how the suits had gone. Each year one of the leading men of the district acted as law speaker, and recited a third of the full body of Norse law, the third they had memorized. Then men brought their complaints, the most serious to be decided first. A jury of twenty men who were not bringing suits were selected by lot, though the Sogn *ting* was small enough most could know in advance who would be chosen. A majority decided each case, and men often voted for their friends and family and those who had paid them more than for the truth, at least if there was any margin of doubt.

Ragnvald would be one man, his word against Solvi's, but if he went now, Solvi would not have time to hear of his plans, might even think Ragnvald had died in his attack. Egil might even be there—he said he went most years. Solvi would not arrive in time to bribe the witnesses and jury, to intimidate those who would not be bought. The wound that Solvi had dealt him would serve as a witness. Ragnvald tried to keep his fingers from testing it, his tongue from probing the rent in his cheek.

He put his cloak over his head and tried to sleep, but now that he had thought of it, he could not stop imagining the trial. He would tell the law speaker his intentions to sue, and the law speaker would ask what injury or insult Ragnvald intended to sue over. There were several possibilities, and Ragnvald thought through all of them, traveling down each path, and all of their pitfalls, before coming back to the beginning again. He ran over possible testimony in his mind, picturing himself in the circle of witnesses and jurors, speaking the truth of what Solvi had done. Hilda would be there, she would see that he had grown into a man, a man who would take what was owed him, a warrior, not a coward.

Ragnvald slept eventually, and was woken by the blood throbbing in the wounds on his face. The day grew warmer as he walked. The frost that rimed the grasses of the high meadows melted as morning air touched it. Dew soaked through his soft boat shoes, chilling his feet. The curve of the land wanted to draw him farther south, and home. Home to Svanhild and his mother. Home to Vigdis, with her sighs and smiles, her glances aimed at Ragnvald alone. Home to Olaf and his disappointment. The paths to the *ting* grounds at Jostedal were harder, deer trails through forests that gave way to cairn-marked lines on bare rock.

This was the country where he had grown up: pine forests and green valleys, the sea only glimpsed in the distance on clear days. The holdings were small, the men who farmed them never venturing farther from their hearths than the midsummer *ting*. Men like Agi the fisherman, who counted on their kings to protect them from raiders, had left Sogn, a few more each year. They did not trust Olaf to protect them.

Ragnvald's father had ruled all the farms around Lake Ardal, and his grandfather had held all of the Sogn farmlands. Their bodies now lay in Sogn land, the same blood that Ragnvald shared mixing with the soil. Olaf's people had not left their bones in the land, and so they could not defend it as Ragnvald's could.

Ragnvald ate the remainder of Agi's bread as he walked, and continued until near midnight, when the sun was only a faint orange glow on the horizon, and the sky above was deep blue, studded with stars.

In the dimness, the farm before him looked like any other: a long, low hall, nothing more than a dark shape, denser somehow than the two outbuildings that flanked it. Ragnvald had pushed his hunger as far as he wanted to. He would wait for the farm to awaken so someone could feed him. He was still early for the midsummer *ting*; if need be, he would do some work here to pay for what he ate, while he planned how to get what Solvi owed him.

He walked down the valley to the farm, thinking of little but the meal he would soon have, and the farm's women who would serve it to him: proper women with long hair and swaying hips. The voyage had been long, with only ugly, half-bearded boy-warriors to look at. One of the thralls Ulfarr captured—previously a serving girl at an Irish farm—had been beautiful, until she tried to escape. Ulfarr beat her and shaved her head, and she was not as beautiful after that.

Ragnvald was not sure later what warned him; perhaps the quiet that lay over the farm felt deeper than that of sleep. He already had his hand on the hilt of his sword when he heard a woman's low moan, a despairing sound.

Ragnvald eased his sword out of its scabbard. He tiptoed between the buildings, stepping over stones in his way. The woman's crying made him want to attack immediately, but he could not advance without seeing how many he faced. As he drew closer, he heard more clearly the sounds of three people: a woman trying to hide her pain, a man's grunts, and a child's whimpering.

Perhaps it was only a marriage gone awry. But if this were going on inside the walls of the hall, he would not hear it so well that he could picture this woman, like one of the Irish thralls taken against her will by a raider.

He came upon them behind the horse barn, which stood open, its entrance a great black mouth in the dark. The man thrust and grunted, his buttocks white like mushrooms growing under a log. The woman turned her head to the side. Her assailant gripped her face to turn her toward him. A cruel man, then, wanting humiliation as well as satisfaction. Ragnvald's foot crunched on a pebble. He froze. The man did not notice, but the woman did. She glanced at the sword in his hand and blinked slowly.

Ragnvald swung hard, putting his anger at Solvi into one blow. He hit too low, and it stuck in the back of the raider's neck, lodging itself at the top of the man's spine. Blood flowed out over the woman's face. Ragnvald rushed to the man and pulled him off her. If he was not yet dead, he would be soon, Ragnvald's sword still buried in bone.

The woman screamed, then covered her mouth with her bloody hand. Ragnvald whirled toward a scrambling noise behind him, grabbing for his sword. His panic gave him the strength to pull it free, but the noise was only the woman's child, coming to investigate, eyes wide and dark. A brave child, even if he had whimpered earlier.

The dying man made a sound, and Ragnvald went to stand over him, sword in hand, in case he needed another stroke. The man held his bleeding neck, as blood pulsed between his fingers. His hand could not cover the whole of the wound.

"You fool. I did not come alone. My men will be back," he croaked.

"You're supposed to be dead," said Ragnvald, tired and stupid.

"I will haunt you," he said, spitting. "I will visit your dreams and—"

"Perhaps," said Ragnvald. "Perhaps your friends don't value you as much as you hope." He already felt the after-battle effects, the shaking, the strange lightness that made everything seem unreal. He stepped on the man's other arm, bent down and pried the raider's hand off his wound, waiting for the blood to flow out and take his life with it. It happened soon enough.

The woman sat up and pulled her skirt down to hide her nakedness. Dark blood covered her face, making her eyes stand out white. Ragnvald's hands were bloody too. He wiped them on the dead man's trousers. The woman's son still stood back from her, frightened of her appearance.

"I am Ragnvald Eysteinsson," he said. "I will look after your son while you clean up." He spoke in a low voice, trying to calm her and himself. She looked at him blankly. "You should wash your face and hands, so he recognizes you again."

"My daughter," said the woman, with a harsh laugh. "It is as well she sees what is coming for her."

Ragnvald helped the woman to her feet, then introduced himself to the child. "You are safe," he said, although he feared that the dying man was right, and his friends would return if he did not join them. How many raiders could he protect this woman and her daughter from?

"What is your name?" he asked the child.

"Hilda," she said, startling Ragnvald, though it was a very common nickname. His own Hilda was a Ragnhilda; Svanhild could have chosen it for herself. *Hild* meant battle, and this girl had seen one young.

"That is the name of my intended bride," he told her. "It is a strong and lucky name." The child only stared at him.

Strewn about the grass behind the barn, the bodies of men lay, most of them with their throats cut from ear to ear, neater than Ragnvald had managed with his man. Farmers, mostly. The few weapons clasped in dead hands were farm implements, not swords. The girl stared at them, soundless. Ragnvald worried that she might cry again, but as the silence stretched on he began to wonder if this child had lost her wits in the attack. He hoped the mother would come back soon.

She returned, as the girl started to fuss, with her hands dripping, and her face clean except at the hairline, where blood dyed her blond hair red. It was unbound now, making her look a maiden, even with her solid figure.

"Do you think they will come back?" Ragnvald asked.

The woman shrugged and scooped up her daughter, who yelled and wriggled when her mother held her too tight. "They only took what they could carry, and there is no one to defend this place now."

"I am here," said Ragnvald.

"Yes," said the woman. "You came too late to save much of anything, though, didn't you? My daughter and I are dead already. Go on, take whatever is left and leave this place of the dead."

"You are not dead yet," said Ragnvald, trying to ignore the way her words made his flesh crawl. She could not have guessed that he was half dead too, plucked from the water, with none to know if he lived or died. "The *ting* begins soon. You can bring suit against these men."

"Do you think I know who they are? What are the men of Sogn to me if they could not prevent this?"

This was what happened in a land without a king. Someone should have been protecting the shores from raiders—perhaps Hunthiof, or perhaps if Ragnvald's father had held their family's lands, this farm would have fallen under his protection. Ragnvald could have been the protection she needed, instead of coming too late. Now she had only the yearly meeting for redress, and only then if she had a culprit to name and witnesses to call.

"If I am to stand guard for you, I will need food," said Ragnvald. He could do that much. "I have been traveling and have not eaten well in a long time. Will you fetch some for me?"

He spoke firmly again, to try to cut through her anger and despair. "I do not want you to stand guard," she said. "I told you, my daughter and I are dead. We lack only a blade to make it true."

Ragnvald stood and took her arm. Her daughter shoved a hand into her mouth, her eyes wide and frightened again. "You owe your daughter better than that," he said. The child reminded him of Svanhild after their father had died, abandoned by father and mother both, as Ascrida withdrew into despair. "I will watch her while you find me food. Then we will go on to the *ting* gathering. This is a rich farm, and it is yours now. You should marry a man better able to protect you this time. As a widow, your husband is your choice."

"What makes you think I want another man after this?" she said, shuddering, but she did hand little Hilda over to Ragnvald.

"I spoke not of what you want, but of what you and your daughter need," he said. With her face clean, she was handsome enough, probably near thirty, full-cheeked, with a pouting lower lip and strong, even brows. A good catch for a man with strength at arms and little wealth. "And I need food." He was accustomed to speaking to his mother like this when she withdrew into herself, and it worked on this woman as well. She scowled at him, but went off to do his bidding.

6

"MY GUARD IS SLEEPING AGAIN." THE WORDS CAME AS A CROSS-current to Ragnvald's dream of gold and ships that passed by over his head. With the words came a pressure on his leg. He opened his eyes in a squint and saw Adisa, for that was the woman's name, standing over him, toeing his calf with her soft leather shoe. She was correct; he had been dozing in the warmth of the morning sun, where it gathered on the south side of the barn. It had seemed like a good idea to sit down and rest as he kept watch, until now.

He had been keeping guard at her farm for two days, spending the daylight hours helping her dig graves for her menfolk and piling cairns, then mumbling half-remembered words of the burial ritual, while she stared at what must have been memories, playing out in the empty air before her. Nights he passed here, or more often on his feet, waiting for an attack that never came.

Adisa was quiet and somber most of the time, and her daughter scarcely louder. The girl followed in her mother's wake without making a ripple. Now, though, Adisa's face quirked with an ironic half smile that Ragnvald answered with one of his own.

"Go inside and sleep," she said. "The dead are resting, and the living have plundered their fill."

Ragnvald did not think that was true, but he could not stay awake another full day and night without rest. This farm still had too much bounty for the raiders not to consider returning. Adisa wore copper brooches to fasten her overdress. Within empty stables, metal-worked tack hung on nails. And the woman herself—if a man kidnapped her, and made her pregnant, he could claim rights to this farm, even if she later divorced him. If she had no kin to defend her, a man who took possession of the farm and its lady would have some rights.

Ragnvald thought his fear of returning raiders would keep him from sleep when he lay down on the mattress Adisa showed him, but instead he fell into the dream of before, of the golden hall beneath the waves, as though he had never left it.

His first thought on waking was about how vilely he stank. He had not washed in weeks, and now he had spent two days burying the dead. Adisa must be more grateful to him than she could bring herself to say, to let him sleep on her clean mattress. As twilight came on, he fetched water and wood to make himself a bath. It felt as much work as burying the dead. He almost nodded off again when he finally sat within the bathhouse and let clean sweat and steam carry his grime off him. The heat loosened the clotted blood on his face, from wounds he had almost forgotten in the exhaustion of the last few days. Adisa had never even asked about them.

"Ragnvald, are you asleep again?" Adisa asked from outside the bathhouse. He did not answer at once, not asleep, but warm and free from worry as a cat in the sun.

"Not this time," he called back. "Turn around," he warned her as he rushed out of the bath to the stream behind it. He did not look to see if she had, only ran past her, through his embarrassment, into a pool that only came to his knees. He whooped from the cold as he sank down into it, and ducked his hair under, scrubbing at his scalp.

When he stopped splashing, he heard Adisa laughing behind him. "I thought all you could do was frown," she said.

"I am called Ragnvald the Serious," he replied, his back still to her. True enough—Solvi's men had called him that sometimes, and not as a compliment. Adisa's laugh took away the sting of the words, though. She had more reason to frown than he.

"Who are you really?" she asked. The pool he sat in did not feel at all cold anymore, now that he had grown used to it. It had been warmed by the sun all day.

"Ragnvald Eysteinsson," he said. "My father was Eystein Ivarsson. My grandfather Ivar was king of Sogn."

"I did not know Eystein Glumra had sons," she said. That was what his father had been called, Eystein Glumra—Eystein the Noisy, who could tell a tale, but turn none of his boasting into truth.

"So there is one thing he did not boast of," said Ragnvald. "That is good to know." He stood.

"Does Ragnvald the Serious want a towel?" she asked.

Ragnvald flipped his hair back, and bent over to splash more water on his face. Flecks of dried blood stuck to his hands.

"Not yet. I'm going back in the bathhouse." As he stood, he saw out of the corner of his eye that she turned away from his nakedness.

The fire had burned down, and the only heat left was what had soaked into the planks. Ragnvald sat and absorbed the last of that heat before steeling himself to go back outside, and face a long night's waiting. The sooner he could move Adisa on to the *ting*, the better. The peace that prevailed there would keep her safe, and then she would no longer be his problem.

"Adisa," he called. "I will take that towel now."

She did not respond. He found a towel placed outside the door, and Adisa nowhere in sight. He wrapped it around his waist and gathered up his clothes, too soiled for him to consider wearing now. Her husband or some of the dead must have left clothes that he could wear until these were cleaned.

As he walked toward the hall, he heard a cry from the child. It seemed a good sign, that her fear had passed enough that she would risk a noise. Then she cried again, a fearful, helpless cry. A warning.

Ragnvald pulled his sword from the pile of clothes. At least he never went far without that. He dropped the clothes and then, after another moment, dropped the towel as well. The only part of him it defended was his dignity, and that poorly. Perhaps a naked man with a sword would surprise whoever had caused the girl to cry and make them easier to kill.

He did not hear another sound, not from the child or Adisa. It might be nothing. Adisa might laugh when she saw him. He still held the point of his sword up. Every corner he turned, he feared he might

see her as he had first come upon her, cruelly raped by a raider. He did
not think her spirit would survive another attack, even if her body did.

He circled the main barn, rounding each corner slowly. If he had
time enough for this, then he should have taken the time to put on
his trousers. Clothes would hardly defend him, but he felt far more
vulnerable without them. Too late to go back, though. He moved on
to the hall, and on the west side found Adisa sitting on the ground
against the hall's outer wall, a man fallen over her lap, a pool of blood
spreading from his cut throat. She held her daughter to her side with
one tense arm, and held up her bloody dagger with the other.

"I dare you," she was crying. "I will serve you the same."

Ragnvald followed her sight line and saw another man waiting in
the shadows of a smaller outbuilding. He was alone, Ragnvald decided. If more than two of them had come, this one would not be so
hesitant. Ragnvald charged at him, crossing the courtyard between
them. The man hesitated, made a noise somewhere between a laugh
and a shout. Ragnvald's face heated, and he gave chase as the man
sprinted away. Ragnvald caught up with him at the fence that separated Adisa's inner yard from the outer field, and slashed his throat so
he toppled backward over it.

He waited to make sure his man was dead. He considered trying
to take some article of the man's clothes to cover his nakedness, but
it seemed like too much effort, and Adisa still sat with a man's body
pinning her to the ground.

When he returned to the side of the hall, she had shifted him off
her somewhat, and lowered her arm. She still held her daughter close
to her. The girl's eyes were round and white as new cheeses, though
she squirmed a little in her mother's grip. As Ragnvald pulled the man
off her, and away, into the shadows where his fellow had hidden, Adisa
jumped up and tore off her overdress, screaming wordlessly.

Ragnvald rushed back and pulled her daughter away from her.
"Adisa," he said, trying to cut through her shrieking, then more forcefully, "Adisa." He grabbed her by the wrists and shook them to make
her drop her dagger, then put his arms around her, holding on to her
firmly until she stopped screaming. She breathed shallowly and felt
stiff as wood in his arms. He had only meant to stop her hurting her-

self or anyone else, but now he thought she must be worried that he had turned into another attacker.

"You are safe," he said. "Think of your daughter. You must be strong for her. You were strong today." He said other things, reassurances, until her breathing slowed. Then she pinched where he had her hand pinned to him, digging her nails in hard enough to leave a swollen red bruise.

"Let me go," she ordered him. He released her, and she backed away from him, then seemed to see him for the first time, and looked up and down at him. "Why are you naked?"

"The bath," he said. He turned half away from her.

"The bath," she said. "I need a bath. Will you help me make a fire?"

He gave an abrupt laugh. "If I can borrow some clothes first."

✢ ✢ ✢

RAGNVALD AND ADISA left for the *ting* assembly the next morning. He and Adisa traded off the child for the food pack, as she grew too heavy, or wanted her mother. They found camping sites far enough off the path to risk sleeping all at once, with no one standing watch. Ragnvald needed the sleep as a drowning man needed air, and Adisa seemed the same on that first night.

The second night she was more inclined to talking after their evening meal, when the fire burned down the embers and Adisa's daughter slept, openmouthed, between them. The child was almost as warm as the fire had been, resting against Ragnvald's chest. He thought they might form a nice picture here, man and woman, with child between them, tree branches overhead. Like the first mortals, fresh carved by the gods.

"You are young, Ragnvald," said Adisa quietly. "How old are you?"

"Twenty summers," said Ragnvald. Old enough to be counted a man, young enough to be considered a young one.

"Not so young, then. I have twenty-three," she said. "Did you think me older?"

"No," Ragnvald lied quickly. Drawn as she was by grief and anger, and with her short, round figure, he had judged her older. "Is Hilda your only child?"

"Only living," she said, firmly enough that she could not have lost any other children recently. Whatever grief she carried for them was scarred over.

"You should marry again at the *ting*," said Ragnvald. He cleared his throat, and tried to sound older. "You need someone to protect your farm."

"You have been protecting my farm."

"But I am not returning with you." His answer was loud enough to make the girl squirm. "And I am betrothed."

"Oh yes," she said. "To a girl with my daughter's name."

"Hilda Hrolfsdatter," said Ragnvald. His last meeting with Hilda had been formal, Hilda wearing her finest dress as she served Olaf and the men Olaf had brought with him to make up the courting party. Ragnvald was not supposed to speak, only allow Olaf to make the negotiations with Hrolf, while he watched Hilda. They had known each other as children, for Hrolf was third cousin to Ragnvald's father. Hilda had played captured princess when he and Egil pretended to be warriors. Ragnvald remembered taking that play very seriously, for he had always known that they would be betrothed, as Svanhild would be chosen for Egil. Then, though, Svanhild had been too young to play their games, and by the time she grew old enough, their father was dead, and Ragnvald had given over play swords for steel.

At the betrothal meeting, he saw how the girl at solemn play with him and Egil had grown into the careful, serious woman who waited upon him and Olaf. She was tall and long-limbed and moved with a surety around the room, pouring cups of ale, her long hair swinging behind her. Ragnvald caught her eye only once, and neither of them smiled, the moment too freighted with promises and duty for that.

When the negotiations were done, she looked pleased, bowing her head before retreating behind the wall of all her sisters, though none of them were close to her height. She was a swan among baby chicks.

Now he lay in the forest with another woman and her daughter, who had twice come close to losing their lives in the last week. That much harm and more might have come to Hilda in the time he was away. Harm had come to him. His face was still gashed from Solvi's knife.

"Will you protect her as you have me?" Adisa asked.

"Better, I hope," said Ragnvald. "I am sorry I did not come sooner."

"They were in force," said Adisa. Her voice was very flat. "You would have died as well."

He had nothing to say to that, if she did not want to hear talk of a husband, so he made a show of yawning deeply. The child Hilda turned away from him, and toward her mother, in sleep. Adisa gathered the child in and slept as well.

✣ ✣ ✣

THEY EMERGED EARLY the next day from the forest, above the river. The *ting* assembly ground covered a patch of bare land at a bend in the Moen River. The river was cloudy with glacier-melt now, a ghostly white torrent, which added its noise to the rushing of the wind. The bright cloth of tented roofs covered open booths of turf where established families stayed, ringing the broad and rocky plain with temporary long fires and feasting halls.

Ragnvald shifted the child off his back and set her on the ground. She rubbed her eyes and yawned.

"You should stay with my family until yours arrives," she said. They came from north of the assembly grounds, and had not heard of Adisa's peril. Adisa started sobbing as soon as she saw them, stammering out what she could of her ordeal. Her mother, a stouter, grayer version of Adisa, enfolded her in an embrace, while her father scowled at Ragnvald. Ragnvald stood watching dumbly. The last time his mother had dried any tears other than her own was before his father's death.

Her father's frown grew deeper as Adisa cried. He took a threatening step toward Ragnvald, and another, until Adisa stopped him. She wiped her eyes with the edge of her shawl.

"This is Ragnvald Eysteinsson, who came—after. And saved me. Twice. Tell them."

"I came too late," said Ragnvald, suddenly tongue-tied. Adisa should tell them, not him. "I found her"—Adisa looked up at him, shaking her head—"I killed a man who was still there. And when they came back I killed one then too. She did too." He was not telling it well. He did not have the knack for boasting that other men did. He never missed it except at moments like this, when the eyes of all of Adisa's family stared at him, wanting something from him he could not give.

"Ragnvald Eysteinsson kept me from—worse," said Adisa, wiping her eyes. "And he saved me again when they came back. We must give him all welcome."

"Of course," said Adisa's mother. Her father clapped him on the back and invited him to share their midday meal, and claim a place at their camp as long as he wanted it.

He ate with them, a little apart, though, for all had news to share with Adisa that meant little to him. They pet her and let her cry, and gave sweets to the little girl. Ragnvald looked around the grounds while their talk went on without his hearing. His forefathers had once claimed pride of place and spread their tents wide on ground that never grew marshy, even when the river flooded. He could camp there and wait for Olaf and Vigdis—they would want to know he lived—but here with Adisa's family he would be more welcome than with the two of them.

On the far side of the field, the blue-and-gold banner of Hrolf Nefia fluttered as men hurried to stake down the tent from which it flew. Hilda would be there, and Egil too. Egil would have told his family of Ragnvald's fall. They would be pleased to see him living.

The wind blew fierce down the slopes, setting the skin tents flapping. In the noise, Ragnvald was able to walk close to Hrolf's without Egil seeing him. Egil's tow-colored head bowed over his sharpening leather where he worked his dagger back and forth, the scratching a thin counterpoint to the thrumming of the wind.

When Egil looked up and saw Ragnvald, his face went pale, before realization dawned and he leapt forward and embraced Ragnvald, clapping him on the back like a brother.

"I thought you . . ." He held Ragnvald by the upper arms, gripping them tightly. "You're alive." Ragnvald shook his hands off. Egil grinned and swung at him. Ragnvald threw a wide, half-strength punch at Egil that Egil ducked, and then Egil put a shoulder into Ragnvald's chest and pushed him to the ground. Ragnvald sat up, laughing.

"I'm very glad to see you," Egil said. He held Ragnvald's gaze for a moment before cutting his eyes away.

"And I'm glad to see you," said Ragnvald. He laughed, at ease for the first time since he slipped from the oars. "But I will be even gladder to see your sister."

"I could fight you for that," said Egil.

"I only meant—she must think—"

"I jest," said Egil. "I see a dunking has not improved your humor. She will be glad to see you. I don't think she much liked the prospect of—she will be glad to see you. She is here, with all my sisters. You should come have dinner with us tonight."

They spoke of Egil's journey home, how his family fared, and finding that Egil did not mean to raise the subject, Ragnvald burst out, "What did you think—on the ship?"

Egil plucked a blade of wild barley and flicked seeds off it with his thumb. "I thought Solvi was killing you. And I thought everyone on that ship had more loyalty to him than to you."

"Yes," said Ragnvald thickly, feeling an echo of that moment, the fear and helplessness. "I suppose they did."

Egil looked at Ragnvald, meeting his eyes. "They held me," he said. "Solvi's men, Ulfarr and . . ."

As he trailed off, he looked away, over the assembly grounds. Ragnvald turned to study him. Egil wore a fine festival tunic, and a silver belt buckle that looked like something they had won in Ireland together. A clasp fastened his cloak that might be the twin to Ragnvald's but was not out of place on his richer clothes. Egil came to his feet and brushed himself off.

"I would have done something if I could. The gods helped you better than I could have."

Ragnvald stood and clasped Egil's shoulder. "You can still help me," he said. "I plan to accuse Solvi. Will you stand as my witness?"

Egil took Ragnvald's arm, pulling it gently off him. "Come, let's tell my sister the good news. She didn't want to find another husband."

"Egil," said Ragnvald. Egil seemed to be slipping away from him again.

"Ragnvald," said Egil, voice pleading. "I would—I will—we should speak with my father. He will have good advice for you. For both of us." He turned, and said brightly. "See, my sister is coming this way."

Ragnvald looked. "She is not."

"Then you should come with me." Egil turned. Ragnvald walked behind him. Egil moved like a crane, his head floating above his body, his neck thin enough that a sword could sever it easily. Ragnvald shook his head to dispel the thought. Egil was a friend. Such passing fancies displeased the gods; they might turn it to truth.

Ragnvald tried once more. "Egil, you must—"

Egil turned and smiled desperately at him. "Solvi is powerful," he said in a strangled voice. "Trials are not for three days yet, after the feasting and contests. Let us talk with Father."

"You do not need his permission," said Ragnvald.

"I need his advice, Ragnvald. Leave it be." He slung an arm over Ragnvald's shoulder and walked him toward Hrolf's open-sided canopy. Ragnvald grew tense under the familiar gesture. They had been fast friends on the journey to and from Scotland—men grew close sharing a sleeping bag on board the ship—but this rang false.

"Wait," said Ragnvald. "I don't want your sister to see me like this." He gestured at the bandage on his cheek. He had not thought of it much over the days with Adisa, and it seemed as though the wound had closed, at least, when he probed the inside of his cheek with his tongue. He scraped off the edges of the bandage that he had adhered with pine pitch from the household stores at Adisa's farm. The air felt strange on skin that had been covered for a few days.

"How does it look?" Ragnvald asked.

Egil looked slightly ill when he darted his eyes to Ragnvald's face. Ragnvald put his hand to it. He did not have enough beard to cover the scar.

"That bad?" Ragnvald asked.

"No," said Egil. "It only shocked me. When it heals, it will suit you. You look fierce."

Ragnvald half smiled at that, until his fear at the wound pulling open before he saw Hilda made him control his expression. They walked toward the tent, Egil a half step ahead.

"Hilda, I've brought something for you," Egil called out. Hilda put her head around the flap, scowling.

"Egil, I'm—" Then she saw Ragnvald and her mouth dropped open.

She rushed out of the tent, toward Ragnvald, then came to a stop. Her hand hovered just above Ragnvald's arm. They were not yet even formally betrothed, only promised, and should not publicly embrace— yet that might feel less improper than this. His skin tingled where he felt the warmth from her palm. He felt bashful of looking directly at her and flushed, trying not to smile like a fool.

"You're—," she began.

"I'm alive," he said, now letting himself smile as fully as he dared.

She wore the same embarrassed grin for a moment and then scowled again, this time at her brother. "Egil, you told me he was dead."

Egil looked between them. "I should . . . I'm sure you want to . . ." He gave a small smile, before ducking into the tent.

She was very handsome, with her long auburn hair left loose and free. She had the strong hooked nose that had given her father his byname, Hrolf Nefia—Hrolf the Nose—and she wore it well. Her expression tended to sullen, but that made her smiles all the more precious. Ragnvald hesitated for a moment. Strict propriety said her father could object if they talked alone, but with all the gathered families of Sogn for a witness, who could mind? No one had cared when they were children.

Anyway, festival times brought license, even pregnancies sometimes, out of season, and hasty marriages afterward. Ragnvald's face heated. He had remembered Hilda's height, but forgotten that it meant she stood face to face with him, her eyes shining. Here was the welcome he sought. Hilda was pleased to see him.

"I am alive," he said. He pulled her hand up to his cheek to trace the path of Solvi's knife. Her fingers were warm on his wind-chapped skin. Her brows drew together as she touched his face. He did not breathe—he had only meant to show her, to have an excuse to touch her, and it had turned into something that made him feel strangely vulnerable.

"Yes," said Hilda, breaking the spell. She looked down as she pulled her hand away, though she let him continue clasping it, her fingers curled in his palm. "Egil said—he said he wasn't sure. So I still hoped." She cast her eyes down. "And made sacrifices to Ran, that she would not take you," she added quietly.

Ragnvald felt pleased and embarrassed that someone should have been thinking of him that way. "It worked," he said.

Hilda's mother, Bergdis, put her head out of their family's booth. She gave Ragnvald a dubious glance, then sighed. "Hilda, come. Everyone can see you."

Hilda smiled at Ragnvald before retreating under the tent flap.

Egil emerged a moment later. He swung his arms back and forth. "See, she was happy to see you."

"Yes," said Ragnvald. "Now, let us speak with your father, if we must. Or you can agree now. Be my witness. You saw Solvi try to murder me."

"I'm sure he's busy," said Egil. "Let's see who else is here." He started walking toward one of the other tents, leaving Ragnvald either to follow or remain standing alone.

7

RAGNVALD JOINED HROLF'S FAMILY FOR DINNER THAT NIGHT.
It was a small gathering, only a few other families besides Hrolf's own,
which was mostly daughters who stayed away from the feasting men.
Before he entered the tent, Ragnvald threw a glance at Olaf's booth.
His family's booth. Its emptiness—still dark in the twilight, as half
the booths were, this early in the *ting* gathering—had been nagging at
him like a stone in his shoe all day.

"Ragnvald," said Hrolf, when Ragnvald entered his tent. "Welcome."
He closed the distance between them with one great stride. He was tall,
taller than Ragnvald, to have made a daughter so tall. Yet after a season
warring at sea, Ragnvald could mark the difference between a farmer
and a warrior. Hrolf had a farmer's sloping shoulders, and he moved
heavily. The lines on his face came from worrying over harvests, not
outfacing enemies or the waves on an open ocean. Ragnvald stood up
straighter before he bowed, a fit greeting for his kin-to-be.

"I see you have not been so vain as my son," said Hrolf. "You have
left your hair unbleached." Ragnvald touched his dark hair. Many warriors bleached their hair with lye, to further put fear into the hearts
of their adversaries. Ragnvald had tried coloring a lock, and cut it off
when it turned a bright, foolish red.

"How did you come to survive this attack?" Hrolf asked.

Ragnvald glanced at Egil.

"Egil told us little," said Hrolf.

Ragnvald told the story again, watching to see how Egil reacted. He had not thought to doubt that Egil would stand witness for him once he learned Ragnvald lived, until they met on the field this afternoon. Now he felt foolish for not wondering further. Egil would not want to anger Solvi. Still, Egil was his friend. Surely, he would stand witness for Ragnvald. He only needed his father's say-so.

Hrolf heard him out, stroking his beard. Ragnvald waited when he was finished speaking, thinking Hrolf would have some advice for him, perhaps praise for his bravery even, in surviving the cold fjord.

But Hrolf said nothing. After a moment, his wife brought them cups of ale. "Now, let us drink to your safe return," Hrolf said, "yours and my son's."

Ragnvald drank Hrolf's excellent ale, and enjoyed Hilda's bending down close to him to refill his cup. The women brought platters of food and served the men before retreating to their own tent, leaving behind barrels so the men could refill their cups themselves.

After all had eaten their fill, Ragnvald stood and addressed Egil formally.

"Egil Hrolfsson, you were my brother and stood by my side when we fought in Ireland and won treasure together. Will you stand by my side at the trial, when I fight to win what is rightfully mine?"

Egil took a hasty swig of ale, and began choking on it.

"This is a difficult thing you have given me to think on," said Hrolf.

Ragnvald looked up at Hrolf. "I was asking Egil."

"He is my son, and will obey me, I think," said Hrolf.

"Obey you in what?" Ragnvald asked. "He was there, and he owes me his testimony."

"He owes you?" Hrolf asked. "You think yourself very fine."

"I think that I deserve a friend's loyalty and a fair trial, as all men do," said Ragnvald hotly. "You are a law speaker."

"And you came to many trials when you were a boy," said Hrolf. "You know that Solvi will buy whatever testimony he needs that he cannot threaten."

"I know that Egil is not the only one who saw Solvi attack me," said Ragnvald. "My wounds bear witness too, and with them and your son, other witnesses must follow."

"Must they?" Hrolf asked. "What cause did you give Solvi to harm you?"

Ragnvald heard a woman's inward breath, and turned to see Hilda behind him, half hiding in the tent's folds.

"He didn't—," she began.

"None," said Ragnvald, interrupting her. She had to know that her defending him would only make him look weaker. "I gave him no cause."

"You stir trouble in many pots," said Hrolf.

"I do not," said Ragnvald, darting another look at Hilda. She looked concerned. "Solvi owes me my share of the plunder and payment for this insult wound."

Hrolf stroked his mustache. "Some men's thread does not run smoothly, it is true," he said after a moment. "But it does not matter. Egil saw nothing, and he will not testify."

"If he saw nothing, it is because Solvi's men held him back—he could testify to that at least," Ragnvald said. More bitterly he added, "He owes me the truth."

"Do not speak of what my son owes you—you who would make him into Solvi's enemy. It is bad enough that you are." Hrolf stepped forward, now looming over Ragnvald.

"I need to sue for my treasure if I am to pay for"—Ragnvald glanced at Hilda—"your daughter's hand." He turned to where Egil still sat. "Egil, brother, we fought together. Your honor—"

"Kings and jarls must concern themselves with honor," said Hrolf. "My son should not throw his life away for it."

"Your daughter will be the mother of jarls," said Ragnvald.

"Your father lost his lands and his life." Hrolf stepped back. "You are no jarl."

Ragnvald clenched his teeth. Hrolf spoke only truth. Ragnvald could not change Hrolf's mind now, and any more speech would make him sound like a begging child. Ragnvald's father had lost his kingdom and then his life. Ragnvald had only good memories of him before his death, and only shame of him after. Olaf might not like Ragnvald, but at least he could not shame him.

"I will be again when I take back my birthright," he said.

"You may call a farm a kingdom, but that does not make it so." Hrolf's eyes blazed. "No. My daughter will not marry with a man who rushes headlong into trouble, and my son will not stand up for you."

"You will not say that when I rule Sogn."

"You might be king of all Sogn and Maer too, and I would not give you my daughter," said Hrolf. "You will bring grief and bloodshed to her door."

"I will not," said Ragnvald. A vision of Adisa's farm, the silence of the dead, made him wonder if Hrolf was right, if he had carried death with him from the fjord's waters, if it ran before him. "But I will not argue with you further."

He left as soon as Hrolf gestured to dismiss him.

Across the grounds, Olaf's space was still dark. Ragnvald turned when he heard steps behind him, and saw Hilda running, her hair streaming out behind her. Her cheeks were red when she stopped.

"Why do you follow?" he asked, stepping back from her. "Haven't you seen enough?" She opened her mouth to protest. "It's not my fault that Solvi attacked me—tell your father that. And I am not my father, to leave my family unprotected. You can tell him that too." He began to walk away from her. She ran a few more steps to stop him with a hand on his arm.

"Do not turn your anger on me," she said. "I too thought us promised."

He looked at her hand, and then at her face. Yes, they were promised. He did not remember a time when he had not known that she would be his bride. They had been children together, with simple dreams, and now it was his task to make those dreams true, even if the path to them was difficult.

"You still wish it?" he asked.

She nodded, blushing.

"I'm sorry," he said. "I spoke hastily." He hesitated a moment before taking her hand in his. He had frightened her with his anger. She was a big girl, but a girl still, and not as bold or brave as Svanhild. He should not frighten her. He stroked her hand until she seemed to grow calmer. She gave him a tentative smile.

"If you wish, I will—," he began, not sure what he meant to offer.

"If you make me pregnant, my father must allow it," she blurted out. Her face went red, and she frowned. "Our marriage."

Ragnvald burst out laughing and then closed his mouth quickly. This was the last thing he expected of such a solemn girl. She yanked her hand from his grasp and pulled herself up to her full height, as tall as he.

"I apologize for shocking you," she said stiffly. "Perhaps my father was right."

He abruptly sobered. "Hilda," he said, catching her hand again. "You caught me off guard. I did not mean to laugh at you. I was only surprised—that you would offer so much for me."

"I do not like to break my promises," she said, still stiff and formal.

"Neither do I," he said. "I only meant I would come back for you—you need not spend your"—now he flushed as well, and the smile from before threatened to return—"coin with me. I would not trap you."

"Would you like to be free of me, then?" she asked, and then added, acidly, "Was it only your pride that was injured?"

So she was not so young that she did not know how to wound a man with words. Still, he would not let Solvi's enmity take her from him. "No," Ragnvald said shortly. "I want to marry you. Ask of me what promises you will."

"That is what I want too. Promise to return to me, no matter what happens," she said, softening. She reached toward him, but stopped for a moment, before touching his cheek as she had earlier.

"I promise," he said. "I will bring you the bride price you deserve, and a great household to manage."

"I will wait," she promised in return, giving him a wide smile that transformed her face. "Father will not marry me off against my will, not with all my sisters needing husbands."

Ragnvald pulled her close and kissed her on the lips, a kiss she was too surprised, or inexperienced, to return. When he let her go, her smile had turned pleased and knowing. She touched her lips as she bid him good night.

✢   ✢   ✢

BY MORNING, OLAF still had not come, but news of a great procession of horses and wagons arriving at the assembly grounds distracted Ragnvald from his watch. Banners of glowing gold on a black field crested the hill before the men that bore them, and Ragnvald thought suddenly of his vision. Perhaps his golden wolf would find him here.

He watched until they came closer, and saw the golden eagle of King Hakon of Stjordal and Halogaland. His servants moved efficiently to rope off stabling areas for the horses, then began putting up tents. With the blowing wind, Ragnvald could not hear them, so it seemed a vast pantomime, too well executed to be real. Hakon coming here would bend currents of power around him like a stone in a river.

Ragnvald was still watching when a tall figure in green waved to him from across the field. Ragnvald returned the greeting, uncertainly, and then as he drew closer, recognized Oddbjorn, King Hakon's baseborn son, born of a peasant woman, not one of his vowed wives. He was a distant cousin to Ragnvald, as were all of Hakon's brood, but only Oddbjorn had ever claimed the relationship. When Ragnvald's father still lived, he and Oddbjorn had been friends. Ragnvald had not seen him in many years.

"My lord Oddbjorn," said Ragnvald, when he came within hearing distance. Oddbjorn wore his dark hair streaked with blond now. His big eyes and broad cheeks had settled into something more handsome than the wide-mouthed face of his boyhood, and warier too. He still had overlong arms, which made him a fierce wrestler, and likely now a dangerous swordsman. Then he smiled, a mischievous smile that showed the same crooked teeth he had as a boy.

"I'm still Oddi, cousin," he said, laughing. He pulled Ragnvald into a rough embrace, pounding on his back and then holding him at arm's length to look at him and his scarred face. "We heard of this at Yrjar," said Oddi, naming King Hakon's famous hall, the Hall of Eager Warriors. Once Ragnvald had dreamed of being invited there, as one of Hakon's men, but when Hakon and Solvi's father Hunthiof fell out over a border dispute, Ragnvald had turned his ambitions toward Solvi's ships instead.

"What have you heard?" Ragnvald asked, too eagerly.

"Come—if we stay here, I'll be called to work," said Oddi. "Or worse, pulled into one of my brothers' arguments."

Above the Jostedal plain stretched an ice field whose meltwater fed all the river systems of the Sogn district. They walked up to it, over a steep slope. A great mouth of ice, dark and blue in its recesses, opened where the ice field began. It looked as though a frost giant had been frozen there, about to take a bite big enough to consume a herd of cattle. Cold air issued from it, the giant's breath. Ragnvald walked along the opening behind Oddi. He did not want to turn his back on the great maw, so he tossed a pebble into its depths. It skittered for a minute, then fell into a pool of water far below.

Inhuman spirits lived in places like this. It might be the mouth of not a giant but Niflheim, one of the lands of the dead. Oddi peered in, and would have climbed in, but Ragnvald held him back.

"I do not like it," he said.

"You never used to be so cautious," said Oddi.

Ragnvald shrugged, ill at ease. He had doubtless changed since Oddi knew him. In the intervening years his father had been killed and Solvi had shown him how little men could be trusted. Perhaps he had changed into someone Oddi would no longer want as a companion. So he agreed when Oddi suggested that instead they climb over the top of the cave. Ragnvald found slim foot- and handholds, places where rocks had fallen onto the ice and melted holes. He climbed with Oddi until they stood above the cave. Below them the whole valley spread out, the tents no more than tan smudges on the green field.

"What are you doing here?" Ragnvald asked. "I had not expected to see you at the Sogn *ting* again, not while your father and Hunthiof both lived and hated each other." He paused and raised an eyebrow at Oddi. "They do both live?"

"Yes. None of our prayers are answered as easily as that," said Oddi.

"And they have not sworn a truce?" Ragnvald asked.

"Never." They walked in silence for a time. "Come, you're brooding," said Oddi.

"Egil said he won't speak for me," Ragnvald burst out, then had to tell Oddi the rest of it.

"Egil Hrolfsson is wise," Oddi said solemnly.

"Wise," Ragnvald scoffed. He could not tell if Oddi was joking or not, and did not care. "He's a coward. How could he have ever called himself my friend?"

"Calm yourself, Ragnvald," said Oddi, looking amused at Ragnvald's plight. He was joking, then. At least Svanhild would have shared his outrage. "You expect him to rush on Solvi's blade? When Solvi can probably call a dozen witnesses to name both of you a liar?"

"With these scars?" said Ragnvald, raising his chin. His wounds still smarted.

"You could have gotten them at any time."

"I am promised to his sister."

"An arrangement made between Hrolf and Olaf," said Oddi. "And Olaf has another son for one of Hrolf's daughters." At Ragnvald's glare, he continued. "You know I believe you. But you can see—"

Ragnvald brushed Oddi's hand off his shoulder.

"As you wish," Oddi said. "There's a place for you at my father's table tonight, if you want it."

"What is your news?" Ragnvald asked. "Why has your father risked encountering King Hunthiof, where the law of the *ting* means he cannot kill him?"

"You did not hear that King Harald of Vestfold came, as prophesied, to our shores?" said Oddi.

"Did he? Is he king in the north now?" Ragnvald asked in jest. At least he and Oddi were speaking more easily. Tales of young Harald and his strength at arms had been spread by skalds all up and down the western fjords.

"Perhaps he returns to Vestfold and calls himself so," said Oddi. "But no," he continued, "my father made alliance with him, married off my sister Asa to him. My father comes to the *ting* to recruit."

"Oh, so King Hakon believes Harald can do it?" said Ragnvald, trying to digest this news. "He's just a boy," he added, with a foolish pang of jealousy that this young Harald should already outstrip him, and another feeling as well, a touch of excitement that stirred his belly. Through Oddi, he might yet gain the notice of great kings.

"He is young," said Oddi, "but I do not think many of the tales exaggerated. He is tall and strong. I saw him fight our most seasoned warriors and best them, in practice at least. His mother is a sorceress, and his uncle, who raised him, is both wise and rich. If anyone can do it, he can." Then he gave Ragnvald that easy grin. "And if not, I think my father likes having Harald's name to justify his conquest. My brothers will not be content to divide Halogaland and Stjordal between them. Hunthiof's rulership of Maer will be the first thing to fall."

Hunthiof's line had been kings in North Maer, while Ragnvald's line had ruled South Maer and Sogn. Over generations, the North Maer kings had maintained their power, while Ragnvald's grandfather was king only of the Sogn district, his son a minor jarl, and Ragnvald, nothing at all. The men of South Maer and Sogn did not swear to kings anymore: they defended themselves on their own as best they could, and paid taxes to jarls, if they paid taxes at all. A king, a true king of all Norway—Ragnvald could not spread his mind wide enough to imagine what that could mean. Harald of Vestfold might look for allies in Sogn, or he might see it as a ripe prize for the followers he already had.

"Look," said Ragnvald, pointing at the field below. "I think Olaf has finally arrived. I must see Svanhild, if she is with them. She thinks me dead."

✢   ✢   ✢

WHEN RAGNVALD APPROACHED Olaf's camp, Svanhild was propping up stones around the base of the spit where her pot hung. She had all her attention focused on the task, wedging the stones tight with dirty hands, so Ragnvald was able to draw close before she looked up and saw him. She sprang to her feet. Her scarf fell forward as she rushed toward him. He lifted her up as she flung her arms around him, feeling like now he might weep for everything that had happened since he had seen her last.

When he set her down, she still clung to him. "Ragnvald," she said. "Egil said you were—and Ol—everyone—they—"

"I know," he said. "Not here."

"Ragnvald," said Vigdis, who appeared suddenly behind Svanhild, with Olaf only a step behind her. It had been many months since he had seen her too, and the beauty he had remembered was nothing to seeing her in truth. She gave him a considering look, and as always, it felt as though they stood together, alone, for a moment. His face heated. He had to force himself to look at Olaf instead.

"We are glad to hear that Egil's news was mistaken. You will stay with us, of course," Olaf said. His eyes were stony and gray.

Ragnvald steeled himself for more words, of how he had failed by coming back empty-handed, wounded. "I am staying with others for now," he said, now feeling as cold as Olaf looked. "But your welcome is appreciated."

"We must talk," said Svanhild.

"Svanhild, your help is needed to set up the camp," said Olaf.

"I thought he was dead," said Svanhild, accusingly. "Vigdis, you can spare me, can't you?"

"Of course," said Vigdis. "Dear husband, I can manage without the girl for an afternoon." Vigdis disappeared back into the tent. Olaf gave Ragnvald another challenging look, then shrugged and set out across the field toward a neighbor's camp.

"Olaf didn't mean for you to return," Svanhild said as soon as they were alone. "It looks like he almost succeeded." She reached up to touch his cheek. He caught her hand before she could touch where Hilda's fingers had been earlier.

"He didn't? How do you—are you sure?" She began to answer, and Ragnvald shook his head. He felt exposed, suddenly, here on the open plain. "Come," he said. "Let us walk." He guided Svanhild toward the sacrifice grove. Fallen logs hewn into rough benches lined the pit. It was cooler between the dark trunks of the pines, and smelled like rich soil. So Olaf wanted him dead. Olaf, who was friends with King Hunthiof, who had suggested that Ragnvald go off in Solvi's ships. It gave a reason for Solvi's attack when Ragnvald could think of none before. There had always been rumors that Olaf had killed Ragnvald's father too, rumors that his mother told him not to heed. He had believed them when it suited him as a boy, when he hated Olaf for disciplining him, for holding him back, for not being his father.

"How do you know?" he asked. "Are you sure?"

"Yes," said Svanhild. "Tell me what happened."

They sat, and Ragnvald told her of Solvi's attack, leaving aside his vision of the golden wolf. Svanhild would either make too much of it or too little. He had repeated the tale so often in the past few days that

it had settled into certain scenes in his mind. He tried to find the words
to make it real for her.

In return she told him what she suspected, and how Einar, Sigurd,
and even their mother had confirmed it, each in their turn. He tried to
imagine his mother's reaction, how she would react, but he could only
see the anger on Svanhild's face before him.

"What did she say?" Ragnvald asked.

"You know her," said Svanhild heavily. "She is dull and vague, as
she has ever been. Don't worry about her. She is not here. Are you
going to accuse him?"

Olaf wanted him dead, and had paid or prompted his friend King
Hunthiof to make it happen. His stepfather, who had raised him as
much as his own father had.

"I don't know," he said. Between the tree branches, the sunlight
still gleamed, but too far away for any warmth to reach the grove.

"I will speak for you," she said.

"You can't." His voice sounded distant to his ears, as though filtered
through water. "'A woman may only give testimony if no man can be
found.' Or 'can be brought to witness.' I don't remember. 'No man below the age of eighteen may . . .'" He had attended the trials as a boy,
with his father, and had memorized long passages of the law in hopes
of one day dealing out his own justice. Only tatters remained.

"There is no man to testify," she insisted.

"You said Sigurd knows, and he is here."

She scoffed. "You know he will not."

"You have no real words that you can swear to, only rumors. And
you are a woman."

"You don't need me, though," said Svanhild. "At least not to accuse
Solvi. Egil saw the whole thing."

Ragnvald sprang to his feet. "He told you?"

"Yes," said Svanhild. She stood as well, brushing off her seat.

"He won't testify for me, and I can't trust any of Solvi's men to
stand for me."

"What? Why not?" Svanhild cried. Then Ragnvald had to tell her
that as well.

"What will you do?" Svanhild asked.

"You cannot be my witness, but you can remind Egil what he told you, and shame him into testifying. Come with me to Hrolf's camp."

✢　✢　✢

"I SAID THAT," said Egil. He had emptied a quiver of arrows on the ground, and was inspecting the fletching on each one, to make sure it would fly true in the archery contest tomorrow.

"Yes, you said that." Svanhild stood over him, hands on her hips.

"Would you like to call me a coward again?" said Egil to Ragnvald, ignoring her. "I tried to help you."

"You are a coward," said Svanhild.

Egil flinched. "I want to live," he said. "Solvi does not forgive betrayal."

"But he has no trouble dealing in it," Ragnvald muttered. Then to Egil: "If you have no care about being called a coward in private, perhaps you will not want to be called that publicly."

Egil's jaw tightened. He would not meet Ragnvald's gaze. Ragnvald said to Svanhild, "If my friend Egil continues to lie, I will call you as a witness. But Solvi may call you a liar, or Olaf."

Svanhild lifted her chin. "Let him. I am not afraid of him."

"Please," said Egil softly. He bent over to gather his arrows in, so they would not be trampled by his or Svanhild's feet. "I will talk to my father. I will testify if I can."

Ragnvald crouched so he could take Egil's hand. It was hardly a firm commitment, but if Ragnvald treated it that way, Egil might as well.

"Your sister is still my betrothed, and you are my sworn brother. I would do no less for you."

Egil gave him a smile that might be a wince. "We were not men when we swore that."

"Do you think the gods care about that?" In tales, oaths like theirs always lasted for eternity, though Ragnvald had already seen how rarely that happened in life. Most oaths had the threat of blood or promise of gold keeping them strong. Or the certainty of shame, which was what Ragnvald could offer Egil.

Egil did not answer, but he did take Ragnvald's hand, and lean into an embrace with their shoulders touching.

"I will see you at the sacrifice tonight," Ragnvald said to Egil. Perhaps feeling the gods' eyes upon him there would give Egil more strength.

✛   ✛   ✛

AS RAGNVALD WALKED Svanhild slowly back toward Olaf's booth, she put her hand in his, as they had done as children. "Do you think he will do it?" she asked. "That he will testify?"

Ragnvald sighed. "I don't know. I think he wants to."

"I don't think Olaf will give up our father's land without you killing him," she said next. Her mind ran quickly from one subject to another. Ragnvald had been more used to that when they were together every day, when he could anticipate her words before she said them. He had not yet thought fully of what Olaf's involvement might mean, except that he had no proof, and that saved him from having to accuse Olaf in front of everyone.

"I could do that," said Ragnvald, though he did not believe it. "He is old." Not old enough to be sure, though. Duels were chancy things, and Olaf had already shown his willingness to cheat.

"Truly?" Svanhild asked. "He raised us."

"I killed for less reason in Ireland," he said quietly. That much at least was true. "I think I could." If Olaf were someone else. "He is a strong warrior, though. I would rather he only gave me what he promised."

"You could hire onto another raiding ship," said Svanhild. "Or one of the settlement ships bound for Iceland. I have heard there is land for the taking. A strong man can be a lord there."

"I was supposed to be a lord here," said Ragnvald. "Svanhild, if you do not want to testify, I can—"

"I do," said Svanhild. "Only I thought you were dead. I don't want it to become true. What is there for us here? Sogn is crowded with farmers, old feuds, old blood, there are raiders every summer. I have heard of new land. You could take Hilda there. And me too."

"Ardal's soil is richer than any icy land," said Ragnvald, though he had no true idea. He had heard the stories, as Svanhild had, of this Iceland, with its fiery mountains and broad fields, glaciers so high that clouds swallowed them, danger and opportunity. But he felt too the tug of Ardal in his blood, his father's bones, his grandfather's, the line of kings stretching back to the gods themselves. "This is home, Svanhild. It is mine, and I will take it back, for our family."

"You were almost killed," Svanhild said. "You know as I do that trials are usually decided for the richest man, not the right man. And I want to see new lands. We talked of it once."

"All I have is what you see me wearing," Ragnvald said, wishing she had not made him speak this. "Solvi even has half my armor, left in his ship. I have less than when Olaf sent me out. So no, I will not hire onto a new ship and take you on an adventure. The only way forward is to get what is mine."

He tried to talk to her of lighter things, but she did not seem to have the heart for it, and neither did he, so he led her back to Olaf's camp. She told him, as they walked, that Thorkell had come, asking for her hand, and that was how she had come here. Thorkell had traveled with them to the gathering, though with his own family, which kept him busy and away from Svanhild.

"I had thought to run away from the *ting*," she said. "But now you are alive."

✢   ✢   ✢

WHEN THE SUN dipped below the horizon, King Hakon led a procession to the pine grove for the sacrifices. At midsummer, this dark would not last long. Ragnvald found a place near Hilda and her family. Hrolf pretended not to notice him, but Egil made a space so Ragnvald could stand behind Hilda. Ragnvald caught her hand in his before the sacrifices began, feeling pleasantly foolish, the heat and pressure of her hand far more real to him than the sounds of the ceremony.

Across the circle, Olaf stood with Vigdis at his side, the firelight making her golden hair crimson. Ragnvald glanced away from her just as her eyes seemed about to find his. He did not want to think of Vigdis's beauty, her promising smiles, when he stood so close to Hilda. Next to Olaf and Vigdis stood Sigurd, looking queasy at the sight of the blood. Svanhild held herself a little to the side, standing cross with her arms folded. Even she did not support him as much as he wished.

A drum sounded, slower, coming from somewhere outside the circle of torchlight. King Hakon stepped forward. He wore simple homespun, not dyed, meant to show the sacrifice blood when it spilled. He spoke the ritual words to thank the gods for midsummer, for good weather, and good raiding. He asked them for rich harvests and successful raids and then raised the ax above his head and waited. His arms did not shake, although Ragnvald's ached in sympathy, as the thralls pulled the first sheep into position. Hakon was of an age with Olaf, broad and well fed, with thick blond eyebrows, and smile lines around his mouth. He must not have had cause to fight for some time, for he wore his beard long and braided, with gold rings glinting in the gray and flaxen hair. Had Hakon not attended, Olaf or Hrolf would have made the sacrifices and said the blessings. Or Hunthiof, but he had not come either. Hakon's show of power and wealth shifted the balance of power here, like a ship heeled over by the wind.

Finally Hakon brought the ax down on the neck of the first sheep, which died with a great gout of blood, and no sound. A goat and a cow followed afterward, these screaming and whining as they saw their fellows' blood. Hilda watched without turning her head, or moving, although her fingers tightened on Ragnvald's.

A pair of thralls pulled a reluctant ox into the pit. It stamped and snorted, scenting the blood of the other sacrifices, and pawed the ground. But the thralls had the trick of drawing it forward, alternately cajoling and beating it with switches. King Hakon's ax descended again. Blood stained his face and arms red. It dripped from his beard and the ends of his hair, and he looked like one of Odin's berserk warriors from an old tale.

When the bull finally crashed to earth, Hakon raised his hands to the sky, and spoke the last ritual words, ending the sacrifices for this midsummer. No slaves this year—the year-turning sacrifices needed only farm animals, eating animals. The gods Frey and Freya did not relish wasteful bloodshed. Thralls removed the animals from the sacrifice pit and brought them to the great cooking troughs. They would bake under hot coals all during the next day, and the next night the great feast would cover the whole of Jostedal's rocky plain.

When Hakon finished the sacrifices, he spoke more words of supplication to Thor and to the siblings Frey and Freya, who brought fertility to the fields, the gentle rains that would quicken the seed already sown this spring. His servants filled vast horns with ale, and Hakon blessed each one before passing it around the circle. As each man and woman drank, they whispered their own wishes for the rest of the year, some to themselves, others sharing tender words with those who stood close.

Ragnvald closed his eyes. He knew he should wish for success at the trials and Hilda's hand, but all he could think of was Olaf's death, if he could truly do that, when it became necessary. He drank, the smell of sacrifice blood making the ale taste sour, and said "Sogn" for no one's ears but his own. When the horns returned to him, Hakon took a mighty draught from one and roared triumphantly. The firelight made his hair gold. Perhaps this was Ragnvald's golden wolf.

Hakon called out to Odin-Alfather, speaking of slain men and corpses still to be made. A wind stirred the oak leaves overhead, and his gaze seemed to meet Ragnvald's. Blood coated his hands, and one of his eyes was in shadow. On this night, midsummer, the veil between the world of the gods and that of humans was thin. For a moment, Ragnvald could not feel Hilda's hand in his. He quailed inside—Odin's notice was a fearful thing; his heroes died young, and painfully. But Odin was the god of battle and wisdom, trickery and kingcraft. Ragnvald had need of his magic, whatever the cost. He held the gaze of Hakon-as-Odin until the king turned his head, and that fearful attention moved on.

8

THE NEXT MORNING, SVANHILD WAITED OUTSIDE OLAF'S TENT, wishing Ragnvald would visit again. He might bring her to the games and races, so she could get away from Vigdis for a time, and see the excitement. Or they could go off and talk more. She had not heard anything of his travels besides their end.

From afar, she could see two young men sparring with wooden swords, both tall, comely, and evenly matched. She watched them until Vigdis scolded her for lechery and bid her clean up from breakfast.

She looked up when she heard the horses approaching. Four men rode across the plain, mounted on horses with shaggy coats like fjord ponies, but the height and longer manes of some southern breed. Each man was a warrior. Their chests were encased in worn leather armor, and they wore marks of their skill in glints of gold at shoulder, wrist, and belt. Even the horses' bridles and stirrups showed some flashes of metal. The horses snapped at each other as they cantered, and sidled when they jostled into each other. Perhaps these were meant for the horse fights tomorrow, an event forbidden to women, though Svanhild intended to find a way to watch.

She thought they looked like something out of a tale until they came closer and she saw that one of them was old, and another had a face from a nightmare, mouth broken and poorly healed, as though it had been cloven with an ax. The foremost man, though, had clear and even features—he could still be a saga hero.

"Is your father within, young maiden?" asked the lead rider as he pulled his horse to a stop. Seeing him up close, Svanhild thought she had never seen a more handsome man, with his close-trimmed beard, the same golden red as the amber that inlaid his cloak's clasp, and his flashing, knife-edge smile.

"He's in a barrow," said Svanhild, standing. She shook out her hair. She had brushed it until it shone this morning, leaving it loose under the white of a narrow cloth band, and she was glad of it now, for the man's eyes followed it as it swayed behind her and curled around her hips. "If you seek my stepfather Olaf, I know not where he is."

"What is your name?" he asked.

"Svanhild Eysteinsdatter," she answered. One of the warriors' horses stamped impatiently. A shadow passed briefly over the man's face before the grin reappeared.

"A lovely name for a lovely woman," he said.

Svanhild waved off the compliment. "If you know mine, I should know yours," she said.

"Try to guess it," he replied, grin turning wicked.

"How shall I guess it?" she asked, tossing her hair again, glad to be invited to look him over from head to foot. "You have missed the sacrifices, so I think you do not care much for gods, and you are not from Sogn. You wear a fine sword at your belt and cut your beard close like a warrior, but there are many rich warriors in Norway. You have not enough men with you to be a king or jarl."

"Do I not?" he asked, his eyes sparkling. "Come ride with me, and I will tell you more."

Svanhild looked around. Vigdis was nowhere near. Svanhild should not do this—she would be talked over if anyone saw, and they would. But if this young man liked her, he could ask for her, and if he had wealth beyond his fine weapon, Ragnvald might arrange it for her. She stepped up onto a rock and then, taking the man's hand, climbed up in front of him on his horse. He held her familiarly around the waist, a firm grip that made her stomach jump.

"What shall I call you until I guess your name?" Svanhild asked.

"What do you want to call me?"

"You have red hair like a flame. I shall call you Loki. And perhaps when you feel insulted enough, you will tell me your name." She threw him a smile over her shoulder.

"You could never insult me, Svanhild," he said. She liked the way he said her name, as though it were a secret between the two of them. He jerked his chin at his friends, who obeyed his signal to depart and rode across the field away from them.

"Have you been up to the glacier?" he asked, pointing at the wall of ice above.

Svanhild shook her head. At night deep groans came from it, like the sounds of giants shifting in their sleep. She must have shown her fear somehow in her body, for he pulled her closer and said in her ear, "Do not be scared. I will keep you from falling."

She clung to the horse's mane as it picked its way up the rock-strewn slope above the camp. Svanhild looked straight ahead of her so she would not have to see the height they had climbed.

"Your horse is sure-footed," she said. "Do you plan to fight him?"

"Her," said the man, leaning forward as they ascended. His chest pressed warm against her back. "And what does a maiden know of horse fighting?"

"Only what I've heard," said Svanhild, now worried that she had steered the conversation where a woman should not.

"Then I've some advice you might not have learned: never fight your own horse, only bet on others'." He laughed, and she smiled, though he could not see it. "Anyhow, this mare is too sensible to fight. It is only the stallions that can be provoked."

"Horses are not so unlike people, then," she said, though she herself often wanted to fight. When they reached the summit, he climbed down first and helped her down. In the short time it had taken to reach this place, clouds had come in to cover the sky. A wind started to blow, carrying the cool breath of the ice cave toward them. Svanhild regretted not bringing her coat.

"You are short," she said when he stood next to her. He was still so handsome, and with a knowing quirk in his smile, so that she could only dart glances at his face, now level with hers, before looking away, blushing. "And wealthy enough to have a good horse, and a gold clasp for your cloak. Your armor is much scuffed, though, so I think if you are a king, it is of a very small place." She smiled at him on that last, and found an answering smile from him.

"Perhaps this armor has saved me many times, and I would not part with it for prettier," he said.

She had to look away from him again, and looked instead into the ice cave. The blue was brighter than the clearest jewel.

"Tell me more so I can guess," she said.

"Tell me of yourself, fair Svanhild. All I know of you is your name."

How little there was to tell. "My father was a boaster, my grandfather was a king." It sounded to her like it could be a rhyme. "My stepfather wants to kill my brother, and he may yet do it." Her throat grew tight, and she stopped speaking. The cool air from the cave made her face feel all the hotter. She tried to remember some of what Vigdis had taught her of how to catch a man's attention. It was not with tears; she could remember that much.

"He wants to kill your brother?" the man asked. "How do you know?"

"He sent my brother Ragnvald out raiding to be killed by Solvi Klofe, who tried to do it, but Ragnvald survived."

"He survived," said the man slowly. Svanhild turned to look at him. "That is good," he added, "but I did not ask about your family. I asked about you."

"I am a girl raised on a farm," she said. What else could she tell him: that she spun poorly, that she hit her stepbrother with his own sword? "I think my brother should sail away across the sea and take me with him. I have only ever seen these same mountains."

"Where do you want to go?"

"Anywhere—everywhere." She had thought of this often. Ragnvald was supposed to find her a warrior to marry, one who might go raiding to Scotland or beyond, and bring her with him for the long winter sieges. Or settle in Iceland or the Orkney Islands, as she had tried to urge him. "Why should he be the one to decide? Why should he be the one who gets to go?"

"I could take you there," he said. He stood close behind her, looking into the cave with her. He did smell more of sea than of earth.

"Should I have called you after a sea god rather than a trickster? No,

I think you are still Loki, full of fire and guile." She had said it to be flirtatious, but she could see, or sense from the way he shifted, that her words made him uncomfortable.

"Come," he said. "We can walk a little ways into the mouth." She looked up at the blue maw of the glacier, into the recesses where it turned to blackness. Svanhild would have hesitated to go in with someone she trusted as much as Ragnvald, and told herself she would not plumb those depths with this man, whose name she did not know.

He extended his hand. "Do not fear me," he said. He looked away from her almost shyly when she took it. She should not have come even this far with him, and now that she had, she would not be a coward. On the sacred *ting* grounds he would never do her harm, even if he had it in him, and that last look had done more to earn her trust than any words he could speak.

Someone had been here before, tramping a dark, rough path into the ice that was easy enough to walk on. They could not remain holding hands, so he placed her hand on his shoulder and led the way, past wet blue walls, until the gray sky only showed a small glimpse behind them. Here a narrow stream of water cascaded into a pool far below, passing every shade of blue from white to midnight before plummeting into darkness.

"Is this another world?" she whispered.

"It might be. See, I have already taken you somewhere else," he whispered back.

"Yes," she said.

"Do you not think you would fear the long sea crossings? The wind would tangle your hair." He touched her hair where it lay over her arm. She shivered, more from the sensation than cold. He took the excuse, though, and draped a part of his cloak over her shoulder.

"The wind tangles my hair in Ardal as well," she said, "and I see nothing but cows and sheep." The longing hurt her chest even as hope made her heart beat faster. If it were as easy as this, to find a husband who would take her away—she would have to leave Ragnvald, but she would have to leave him anyway, one day. He wanted Ardal, to follow the duty of generations before. He never wanted to leave.

"I would take you with me," he said, with a fierceness that surprised her. "I have ships, men, wealth. I am not a king, but my father is."

She thought for a wild moment that she would, she would do it, even if she had to be his concubine. She would leap with him, if he could make her feel like this even sometimes.

"A king's son," she said. She looked at him again. There was something familiar about him: this short king's son with the red hair and beard. "You are quite short." She stepped away from him. "You are Solvi Klofe, Solvi the Short, Solvi who tried to murder my brother." She backed away, her voice rising. The expression on his face told her she had guessed right. "And now you take more revenge on me? Or make me look foolish?" No, that had been her doing. "Take me back to my tent."

He looked stricken and reached for her. "I would never hurt you."

"You would never?" She pulled away in horror. "You already tried to hurt me worse than anything you could do to my body. Ragnvald is my brother. I hope he kills you."

"I did not want to—" He seemed to cut himself off. "I am glad he is alive. I promise—," he began again, spreading his hands.

"Don't promise anything," she cried. "Your promises are worthless."

"No man could say such a thing to me and live," he said, his voice suddenly hard. "You know who I am now, so stop this foolishness."

"A man will say that to you, at the trials."

"Are you a seer, then?" he asked, stalking toward her, no longer trying to placate her. His changeability frightened her—this man could turn from playful to deadly in an instant. No wonder Ragnvald had not seen his betrayal coming.

She backed away farther, trying to stay on the path through the ice without taking her eyes off him.

She took a false step, though, and slipped, so he had to lunge and catch her. She crouched for a moment before standing again, blinking away her tears. Her ankle hurt, although she did not think she had damaged herself too badly. She turned away from him and began climbing back to the daylight world.

"Let me take you back," he said when they reached the edge of the cave. His horse was still beneath the trees, nibbling at spring buds.

"If Ragnvald sees you with me, he will kill you," said Svanhild.

"He will not," said Solvi. "He would not bring a blood feud down upon his family." He looked rueful, and Svanhild read something there: Solvi's true strength was to do what others would not. He would not fear a blood feud. He would sow discord and go off laughing. Svanhild banished the thought—she did not want to see anything to admire in Solvi. She already enjoyed his looks too much. "My men would kill him before he could do it," he added.

"You tried." Svanhild's voice rose to a shriek. "Maybe he can't be killed by you."

He smiled then, for no reason she could see. "You don't want me dead, fair Svanhild."

"I know my own mind," she said.

"I do not want you to hate me."

Svanhild did not know how to respond to that. "Take me back, then," she said haughtily. Her ankle throbbed.

He helped her mount in front of him again. As they picked their way down the slope, she tried not to slide over the horse's neck, but also to keep a gap between herself and Solvi. How embarrassing that she had let him press himself against her.

She held her head high as they rode back to Olaf's camp. Olaf and Vigdis stood there watching her. "I would speak with you," said Olaf coldly, and it took Svanhild a moment to realize that he was talking to Solvi, not her.

Solvi ignored him, swinging off his horse and down to the ground before extending a hand to help Svanhild. She accepted his hand without thinking, and he gave her another of his grins, which grew broader when she scowled at him. He must think that the ride back had somehow reconciled her to him. Well, he would not find her favor won that easily.

"We had an agreement, Solvi Hunthiofsson," said Olaf.

"Is this the place you'd like to discuss our agreement?" Solvi asked, looking around. Members of Olaf's household had gathered, as well as others who had come to greet Solvi.

"No," said Olaf between gritted teeth. "Come into my tent and drink with me." He looked at Svanhild, then back to Solvi again. "My daughter will wait on you."

"She was sure to tell me she was not your daughter," said Solvi. His eyes lingered on Svanhild for a moment, and try as she might, she could not look away, or cast her eyes down. "But yes, have her wait on us, and I will accept your hospitality."

Svanhild stared at the two of them: Olaf, tall and stony; and Solvi, smaller, but still holding the reins of power here, by force of personality and blood. The arrogance of kings, the strength of a warrior—even a very short warrior—in his prime.

Vigdis beckoned to her, drawing Svanhild to the kitchen area, where she produced two pewter cups and a cask of ale. "Listen, but do not speak," she said in an urgent whisper. On the ground behind her, little Hallbjorn patted his hands on the dirt. "You have done well. This Solvi is smitten with you, I can see it. If you would not marry Thorkell, make Solvi love you more."

"Solvi tried to kill—"

"I said listen," said Vigdis. "Grudges are for men to hold. Think what you could do for your brother as Solvi's bride. And bring them ale. Let your hair fall on Solvi's shoulder. Do not be over bold, but stay close when you serve him and"—she paused and smiled—"go. You have already done well. You don't need my advice."

Svanhild felt like a block of wood as she took the few steps toward Olaf's tent. She had no intention of flirting with Solvi any further. Her face flamed as she thought of how much of that she had already done. And if Solvi asked for her—she shuddered at the thought—Ragnvald would never forgive her if she consented.

"Your agreement was with my father, not me," Solvi was saying when Svanhild entered with the ale. He sounded disdainful, and Olaf's face looked like a thundercloud, which made her want to cower. Olaf's rages ruled Ardal. Solvi looked unconcerned.

"It was your error that brought us here," said Olaf, ignoring the ale Svanhild set in front of him. "If you'd done what you were supposed to, that upstart wouldn't be bringing suit against us."

Svanhild's hand shook when she put Solvi's cup down in front of him. He caught it before it spilled, his hand over hers, which she plucked away as if his touch burned her. He raised his brows, mischief in his eyes, then turned to Olaf again.

"As I said, your agreement was with my father, not me. Ragnvald was a good warrior, but if he brings suit, he has nothing but words. No one will bring swords to defend him. No one will stand witness for him. And when he's done, he will have falsely accused a king's son."

"He is still alive," said Olaf.

Did Olaf really not care that Svanhild could hear this? Did he think her as much a coward as he was? Or did he imagine that his rages would keep her from telling Ragnvald what she had heard? She stayed still, holding the cask of ale in case they should call for more, but neither had drunk more than a sip.

"That is as I meant it," said Solvi, looking up at her.

"You cannot be that stupid," said Svanhild, "or think I am."

"Say the gods stayed my hand, then," he said, still to her. She could believe that, though it changed nothing.

"Did they?" Olaf asked, looking concerned. "How am I supposed to govern Ardal with that troublemaker still around?"

"That is not my concern. I have no interest in your little farm's business," Solvi said scornfully. Then he glanced at Svanhild. "Except this—give me this swan girl as a concubine, and I'll lend you men to defend your land. I've heard you need it."

Svanhild gasped. This must be why Olaf had allowed her to hear him. He might do it, even with the insult of Solvi asking for her as a concubine—warriors would make Olaf an important man again, more so than his cousin Thorkell. "I would never," she cried. "I've heard what you said. I'll—I'll tell Ragnvald. I'll testify against you."

Solvi laughed. "A girl's testimony? And what would that be worth?" he asked her, and then, not expecting an answer, got to his feet and said to Olaf, "She's a wild one. My offer stands. Send the girl to me if you agree."

"Never," said Svanhild.

As soon as he left, Olaf grabbed her arm in a bruising grip. "You worthless girl," he said, shoving her forward. "I ought to beat you black and blue."

"You wouldn't want to damage me before you sell me to someone," she said, shakily.

"If you testify against me, I'll make you worthless even as a concubine. No man will want to look at you when I'm done." He dragged her from the tent and brought her to Vigdis in the kitchen tent. Vigdis looked mildly shocked to see them like that, Svanhild kicking, Olaf holding her up by the arm.

"Keep her tied up," he said to Vigdis. "I don't want anyone but you to see her until after the trials are done." He flung Svanhild against a sack of grain, knocking the wind out of her. Her scream was muffled by the sacks as Olaf turned her over and Vigdis tied her hands behind her back. Olaf yanked her wimple forward and tied it around her mouth so she couldn't cry out again. He turned her over onto her back again. "Don't try anything," he warned. "Things can go much worse for you."

The child Hallbjorn watched this with big, round eyes and then began to cry. Vigdis scooped him up and held him on her hip, bouncing him until he stopped, though he still watched Svanhild warily.

"She'll be a chore to take care of," said Vigdis to Olaf before he left.

"I'll give you a new brooch," said Olaf. Vigdis nodded. Olaf left, and Vigdis knelt next to her.

"You are a foolish child," said Vigdis, almost kindly. "You've angered all of the men who would help you." Svanhild glared at her. "Ragnvald—I suppose he would, but he can't, can he? And he will hear of your ride with Solvi, and wonder if he has any friends left in the world."

With that she carried Hallbjorn outside and bid Sigurd watch him for the afternoon. When she returned, Svanhild kicked and cursed at her from behind the gag until she grew too exhausted to move.

She slept, and when she woke, Vigdis was gone. She fingered the knots behind her back. She could not gain purchase on them, and could barely move her wrists. She struggled a bit more, then flopped against the grain sacks, saving her strength. Everyone would be gone during tonight's feasting; perhaps she could make her escape then.

9

THE MORNING AFTER THE SACRIFICES, WORD SPREAD AROUND the camp that Solvi had come. Ragnvald's nerves were stretched thin during his archery contest with Egil. On the sidelines, Solvi laid bets and talked loudly. Ragnvald could think of little but his upcoming trial, and his arrows hit the ground more often than they struck the target.

At least his anger at Solvi's presence spurred him to win a footrace later in the afternoon. Ragnvald looked to see if Solvi had noticed this triumph, so similar to the race on the oars, but he was lost in the crowd of taller men.

Ragnvald had heard that Hunthiof had not come with his son. As he walked off the exertion from the race, he tried to think of what that king's absence might mean for him—at the least, Solvi would have fewer men to help him intimidate the trial's jurors.

After the footrace, grizzled old warriors competed in ax-throwing contests. King Hakon himself took the prize there. A troupe of wanderers arrived at midday with a tame bear, which did tricks, turning somersaults and balancing an inflated pig's bladder on its nose. Hakon gifted each of them with a handful of hacksilver. Ragnvald wondered that Svanhild had not come to see the troupe. She loved dancing bears.

That night, King Hakon feasted all the men of Sogn. Hakon's steward seated Ragnvald far down the table, above the free farmers, and below all of his warriors and most of the merchants. Ragnvald could not see Olaf and Vigdis, but that was not so strange. Each table sat in its own pool of firelight, faces shadowed in the dusk.

Hakon had brought two of his wives to host, and a few of his daughters to share cups with the most favored of his guests. Hakon's wives set a good table, a first course of huge wheels of cheese, honey for the bread, followed by salted fish simmered in milk, sweet fruit both fresh and stewed. The sacrifice meat came next, cooked so long in its own fat that the beef fell apart when he pushed it onto his bread with his dagger. Since he sat lower on the table, the ale did not come until Ragnvald had finished half his meal, but when it arrived it tasted strong, sweet with the apples of the summer before.

Hakon's trueborn sons had come as well. Heming the Peacock decorated the upper table in his blue silk tunic and the broad, gold-buckled belt won roving into Rus and trading with the Swedish king at Kiev. He and his younger brothers joked and chatted on the dais, Oddi dark among all the bleached heads. Their talking, overloud, seemed to Ragnvald a self-conscious performance.

Hakon put his arm around Heming, who said something to him that caused Hakon to throw back his head and laugh. Ragnvald's food was suddenly hard to swallow. He would never be as favored as these men, even had his father not lost their land, but he could have started with something, not just Olaf's enmity.

He should have asked to be seated with Adisa's family. They made him welcome each night as though he belonged to them, and had cheered him in his footrace. When he came to Hakon's feast, though, he had wanted to see where Hakon's steward would place him, and learn something of his status.

Ragnvald turned his attention back to the merchants who sat near him. Some of them were known to him from *tings* years previous, and he listened as they spoke of places they had traveled. After one who had journeyed as far as Constantinople had his say, talk turned to matters closer to home.

"I can hardly sail down the coast of Norway anymore without losing all my wares to sea kings," grumbled the man who had been to Constantinople.

"Why return?" asked another. "The weather is far better in England."

"They're poor from the war," said a third. "But Paris can still afford good Norse furs and slaves."

"And Solvi is the worst," said the first merchant again. "Next summer, I'll buy my furs in Vestfold, even with the added cost. King Harald promises to rid Norway of these sea kings who strangle commerce."

That drew Ragnvald's attention, and the other merchants suddenly became very interested as well. As king, Harald aimed to set up centers of commerce, like the Danes' Hedeby, at various locations along the Norse coast, and protect them from rovers. No wonder King Hakon wanted to be Harald's ally—whatever king had such a center in his lands would grow wealthy from tax and trade, and Harald could not hope to administer it all by himself. Ragnvald listened until the conversation turned to boasting again—the merchants now comparing their greatest sales. This talk made Ragnvald weary. He measured his own wealth in only a few ounces of silver, and the foundation of his father's old hall, which now Olaf meant to take from him.

The men who sat below Ragnvald were farmers from Sogn, men he had seen at every *ting*, men who blended together in his memory. They talked over the day's rumors: Solvi had taken an unmarried woman of fine family for a ride across the plain. Try as he might, Ragnvald could not catch the name of the woman in the gossip that flew, and when he asked, the farmers all had other news to tell him. Well, it could not have been Hilda—Solvi would never have chosen a woman so tall.

Next to Ragnvald, a man fell to his knees and vomited up the rich sacrifice meat onto the grass. At the head of the table, two men drew swords on one another. Hakon's guards made no move to break up the fight, but herded them into the proper dueling perimeter. The benches emptied as men rose, of one mind, to watch the fight.

The crowd caught Ragnvald and pulled him along as it spread out around the edge of the dueling ground. He watched as the two men, one dark and one blond, matched in height and coiled tension, circled each other, swords drawn, shields strapped to their left hands. The sun had set and the long twilight lingered, leaving the sky a grayish pink, making the fighters look like a shadow play, their features indistinct. No torches lit the fight, so not until they turned did Ragnvald see that the lighter man was Heming the Peacock, Hakon's eldest son, handsome and haughty. He kept his blond beard clipped close, to better show off the straight line of his jaw. He dressed his hair long and bound back with a leather thong, brushed smooth as wood. Where the darker man wore wool homespun and large-ringed mail that weighted down his movements, Heming's sleeves billowed in the wind, imported silk. His mail shirt was fine and light as well, silver like birch leaves.

The fight's first spasm of violence had given way to measured pacing, as Heming and his opponent circled one another, feinting as much with shields as swords. The dark-haired man moved slowly until he decided to strike, and then he lashed like a bolt of lightning. Heming moved like liquid, never long in once place, never providing a steady target.

Ragnvald found himself hoping the dark-haired man would win. He reminded Ragnvald of himself: brown-haired and serious-faced, here among all these fair heads. The pace of the fight quickened. Heming and his opponent hacked at each other's shields in grim silence. The chatter of the feast quieted so all could watch. For a time, the contest looked even, until Heming's shield gave up its last piece of linden, leaving him with only the iron boss held in his gloved fist. This he hurled at his opponent, snarling an insult Ragnvald could not make out.

The dark-haired man tossed what was left of his shield aside as well—the honorable thing to do, but not wise. Now the sound of blade on blade rang out over the plain. Uneasy whispers flew. This was not the sort of battle men liked to see at the *ting*, a fight to the death. Far better first blood or injury, leaving the loser to buy back his life. Ragnvald made his way through the crowd to stand next to Egil.

"Who is Heming's opponent?" he asked.

"King Hakon's favorite jarl, Runolf," said Egil, sounding eager. "My father tells me this fight has been brewing for a long time."

"How can Runolf win? Even if he kills Heming, Hakon will be against him."

Egil took a swig of his ale. "He cannot win," he agreed.

Ragnvald examined Runolf more closely. The strain told on his face. A muscle pulsed in his jaw. The tendons in his neck stood out like ropes. Heming fought with freedom and grace, Runolf with grim purpose, trapped in an impossible situation where the only escape was death or outlawry. Ragnvald stole a glance at Hakon. The king watched the contest, intent as a falcon, his heavy brows drawn low over his eyes. Ragnvald wondered what outcome Hakon hoped for. Men did not always love their sons best.

Runolf stumbled, and Hakon started forward and then checked himself. "His fate has put him in this place," said Egil. "All he can hope for is to die with his sword in his hand."

Egil was right. Runolf fended off two more blows from Heming and then stumbled again. Ragnvald took a step toward him without thinking, as though he could take Runolf's part—but who was Runolf to him? A wise man would stay out of an impossible fight.

Runolf's knee hit the earth. He scrambled to his feet again and tried to bring his sword up, but Heming's was there first, a hard stroke against the side of his neck that went foul and sliced down into his shoulder. Heming worked to free his sword as Runolf fell. He raised his shield arm one last time even as death claimed him. The blood on Heming's hands was black in the deepening dusk.

"Does Runolf have family to avenge him?" Ragnvald asked Egil, shaken. He glanced at Egil, whose eyes were still fastened on the dark wound. A woman came forward, her face like a crumbling cliff, and placed her veil over Runolf's eyes.

"Who would challenge a king's son? They will take the wergild instead," said Egil. Ragnvald watched Runolf's woman, whose hair trailed over the fallen man. She looked like a woman who would rather have blood than a payment from Hakon. Wergild would not take away her pain or let her husband's spirit rest.

"We will see tomorrow," said Ragnvald. Tomorrow when the trials began, and Ragnvald would also see if Egil would testify for him. Ragnvald looked back up the length of the table to where Hakon's sons sat. They joked and postured for one another as though nothing had happened, even as Heming called for a rag to wipe the blood from his hands and face. Slowly, men returned to the feasting tables. Ragnvald watched Hakon's sons on their carven chairs, trying to read their personalities from how they ate. Heming took bites when it pleased him, gesturing with his dagger more often than he used it to spear a piece of meat—already boasting of his victory tonight. The middle son, Geirbjorn, tried to imitate Heming's manners, but he had not the trick of it, and the hungry way he watched his brothers and father gave his jealousy away. The youngest trueborn son, Herlaug, was sour of face, and ate as little as his brothers, without their enjoyment or showmanship. Perhaps Ragnvald had been wrong to be jealous—he might wish for a father like Hakon, but brothers like his sons would be far more trying than Sigurd. Oddi alone ate with great appetite, more intent on eating than on his kin's words, though he still laughed when it was required of him. Ragnvald wondered how he felt about Runolf's killing. Before the duel his eyes had sparkled; now they seemed troubled.

Ragnvald shook his head. It mattered little to him that Hakon had ambitious sons—they only followed their father's example. Hakon's father Grjotgard had held far less land than his son did. Hakon had spent his youth conquering more lands, and now they stretched far into the north, where the lights in the winter sky touched the ground, where the elves and *hulda*-people lived, in lands eternally swathed in mist. Some men still managed to outshine their fathers.

✢ ✢ ✢

BLOOD RAN THROUGH Ragnvald's dreams that night. He woke in the dimness of midnight, feeling hungry and feral, a wolf outside a crowded hall. He wanted to rise and walk across the assembly grounds to Olaf's tent and finish it then and there. Instead he sat in the entrance to the tent he had borrowed from Adisa's family, picking the worst of the dirt out of his tunic, and the wild feeling gave way to nervousness that knotted his stomach. Solvi should at least give him a share of treasure today, more if Ragnvald could use the threat of Svanhild's knowledge to force Egil to testify. Solvi might even turn the accusation upon Olaf—the best outcome, for Ragnvald would then have leverage to force Olaf to give him the lands he held in trust for Ragnvald. Perhaps even his own lands.

As he waited for sunrise, a deer wandered close. Ragnvald did not have spears or a bow, so he only watched it pick between the saplings on dainty feet, putting its nose down to eat. It was a young buck, with fuzzy points of antlers on its forehead. He wondered that the animal was alone; perhaps he had been driven off by the lead stag, although it was not yet rutting season. The deer lingered as the sky lightened, eating tiny tree shoots bare.

He remained near his tent until he could not stand waiting any longer, and then walked out to the trial ground. Log sections on end stood in a circle for spectators' seats. Men sat with their sons, teaching them who was admirable, to be emulated, and who was not. Ragnvald had sat there once with his father, who thought that men should settle issues by dueling, not by suit. Olaf, however, said that feuds destroyed great families, and the land was more peaceful under the law courts. And anyway, a duel could still be fought if the litigants did not find the verdict fair.

The men who formed this year's jury sat in true seats on one side. Twenty men were chosen by lot to serve as the jury, and they could ask questions and demand witnesses. Of course, the audience shouted out questions too, and the jury could be sure to know which way the wind blew before they voted.

Solvi and his men stood to the outside, behind the crowds seated around the circle. They seemed more dangerous than the other men there, aloof from the farmers' conversations, the small concerns of sheep and meadow. Solvi's smile was mocking.

Ragnvald paced near where the other petitioners gathered; his face must have warned people off from approaching him, for few did. At length Hrolf Nefia held up the speaking stick and banged it on a rock for silence. Hrolf had taken the role of law speaker this year. Each year someone must speak a third of the law, so every man who did his duty and came to the trials would know it complete in three years.

Hrolf invoked Tyr, the giver of laws, asking him to witness the jury's fair judgment. Once he finished reciting the law, the trials began. Jarl Runolf's family brought suit against Hakon's son Heming for Runolf's death. Runolf's uncle made his case, and each side called witnesses to attest to the fight between king's son and jarl. Runolf had, Heming's men swore, insulted Heming's manhood, which lessened the amount of wergild that could be paid. The jury awarded the payment, meager and ungenerous for a jarl's death, and Runolf's family took it, rather than continue a blood feud with a family as powerful as Hakon's. A murmur went up from the assembly. Accepting wergild over feud might bring peace, but it was not the stuff of poetry. The crowd wanted more blood.

More death suits followed, and it was not until afternoon that less serious suits were allowed.

"I call plaintiffs with cases of insult wounds, disfigurements, maimings, to come forward."

Ragnvald stepped forward into the ring of onlookers. He had tried to eat some bread and cheese for his midday meal, but it stuck in his throat, and now his stomach roiled, a stew of hunger and nerves.

"Are you calling this an insult wound?" asked Hrolf, before Ragnvald could even speak the words of accusation. "Or disfigurement?"

"Can I not let the jury decide?" Ragnvald asked.

Hrolf nodded. "You may."

Solvi stood on the other side of the circle, behind an empty seat. He wore an amused expression, as though Ragnvald accusing him was a joke. Ragnvald could not see Svanhild.

Olaf sat a third of the way around the circle from Ragnvald. With him was Vigdis, her face pale. She looked as beautiful now, with haunted eyes, as she did when her lips curved with satisfaction. He wondered if she feared for her place if Ragnvald accused Olaf, or for her child Hallbjorn. Ragnvald had no intention of hurting his young stepbrother.

Hrolf handed him the speaking stick.

"I accuse Solvi of wounding me on the face. I sue him for payment of that and for the raiding treasure he has denied me." Ragnvald's voice rang out across the plain, just as he had imagined. He faced the jury, although he could not bring himself to look at their expressions, for they had appeared stern and unbending during the other cases. He looked instead at their stomachs as he began his tale, the well-fed bellies cinched tight by their best bronze belts. Ragnvald's feet crunched in the dry grass as he paced and spoke, telling of the raiding, and how Solvi had come to wound him.

"Do you have any witnesses who will stand for you?" Hrolf asked.

"Yes," said Ragnvald, holding Hrolf's gaze. He would not let Egil escape this—calling his chosen witnesses was Ragnvald's right, whether Egil's father liked it or not. If Egil would lie, he must lie to everyone.

He only wished Svanhild were there to remind him that any time she could tell the truth, even if she would not be accepted as a witness. It unbalanced him not to see her there. "I call Egil Hrolfsson to witness."

Egil stepped forward, his eyes cast down, refusing to look at Ragnvald. "You took this journey as well," said Ragnvald, walking close to Egil. "Afterward, you went to Ardal and told my family, told my sister—who will swear to it—that you saw Solvi kill me, and throw me in the water."

"Do you wish to call your sister as a witness?" Hrolf asked.

Ragnvald glared at him. "No. I am questioning your son." He should not have mentioned Svanhild. She could not be a sworn witness to this, not when a man—Olaf—had witnessed it as well. Unless Ragnvald accused Olaf too—then Hrolf should allow Svanhild's testimony to balance their stepfather's lies. But Ragnvald feared he did not have enough evidence to accuse Olaf.

"She is a woman," said Hrolf. "She may not testify unless no one else was present to hear my son. Is that the case?"

"Let us hear what your son says first," said one of the jurors. Ragnvald looked up, surprised, and saw Adisa's father. Ragnvald had not told him of his suit before. He should have, he saw that now. He could have used that friendship better.

"Do I speak the truth, Egil?" Ragnvald asked. "Did you see what happened?"

Egil turned to face the jury. "I saw Ragnvald dance on the oars. I saw him win the first race. I knew that he fell. I did not see more."

"And how did I get this wound on my face? You can see it is no more than a week old," said Ragnvald.

Egil glanced first at his father, who shook his head slightly, then at Solvi. "I don't remember," he said. Ragnvald felt a small thrill of triumph. No one could believe that, not the way Egil spoke.

"Why did you tell my family that Solvi stabbed me?" Ragnvald asked.

"I—I don't know what I said to them," said Egil. "I don't remember."

"Svanhild does," said Ragnvald. A part of him was enjoying this: Egil bending, Egil faltering. He had thought Egil his equal, but Ragnvald would not have lied in front of the gods.

Adisa's father raised his hand. Ragnvald pointed to him. "Where was Solvi Hunthiofsson when Ragnvald was on the oars?" Adisa's father asked. It was a juror's right, to clarify anything he had questions about.

Egil glanced at Ragnvald and then at his father. "I don't know."

"Why were they dancing on the oars?" asked another juror.

"Solvi said he'd give a gold ring to whoever could run up and back on the oars," said Egil.

"Who won? Who ran up and back?" the juror asked.

"The pilot's son. And Ragnvald," said Egil miserably. "Until he fell."

"He fell? Did you see it?" the juror pressed.

Hrolf stepped forward. Egil was very close to being called a liar, and in front of a jury lying was a grave offense, for which Egil might stand trial later. "He said he didn't see it," said Hrolf.

Adisa's father spoke again. "Ragnvald Eysteinsson, do you believe that Egil saw you fall?"

Ragnvald glanced at Egil. He still did not wish to call Egil a coward in front of the men of Sogn, and that was how this story would sound. "Solvi pulled his dagger. Egil saw—something. I think he moved to help, but too many men stood in his way."

"Is this true?" asked the juror. "Did you see the dagger?"

Egil nodded, then spoke tremulously. "I saw Solvi's dagger."

"Did you see him stab Ragnvald?" Hrolf asked.

Egil shook his head no.

Hrolf turned to Ragnvald. "Has my son lied today? Do you accuse him of that?"

"No," said Ragnvald. If he accused Egil, Hrolf would be against him, and if he could not prove that accusation, he would owe Egil payment for the insult. Slowly, measuring out the power he held, he said, "I do not accuse him."

Another juror spoke. "Egil Hrolfsson, is it possible Ragnvald could have received this wound after falling out of the boat?"

Egil nodded.

"You must speak an answer," said Hrolf.

"It is possible," said Egil.

"Does anyone wish to question Egil further?" Hrolf asked. The jury stayed quiet. Ragnvald looked around the circle, trying to find faces that looked sympathetic to him, avoiding the faces of anyone he knew.

"No," Ragnvald said, finally.

"Do you wish to call any other witnesses?" Hrolf asked.

Ragnvald looked around the circle slowly. He still did not see Svanhild anywhere, and he began to grow worried. She would not have missed this moment. She should have been clamoring to speak.

"Do you have any other witnesses?" Hrolf asked.

"I see a few other men from my voyage standing with Solvi Hunthiofsson," Ragnvald said. "Would any of them speak for me?"

Solvi's men betrayed even less with their expressions than did Solvi. Ragnvald was not surprised; he had only mentioned them to make sure the jury knew that any other men who might speak for him today stood with Solvi. Two of them had, indeed, stood behind Solvi when he had stabbed Ragnvald, keeping any of the other men from rushing to his aid. They would be no help.

Ragnvald waited, watching them. The crowd looked to Solvi too. "They do not speak," said Ragnvald finally. He handed the speaking stick to Hrolf, who banged it on a stone until there was silence.

"Solvi Hunthiofsson," said Hrolf. "You have been accused of wounding this man, Ragnvald, on the face, with the intent to kill him. You may now defend yourself." He held the stick out to Solvi. Solvi leapt up on one of the log seats, waving off the stick as though he did not need its authority. He grinned at the assembled crowd. He had ever been their favorite, from when he was a small fierce boy, made doubly fierce by surviving his burning. He had been the first into any trouble and the last out of it. He could turn them back to his cause now, Ragnvald knew, with little more effort than it took to flash his teeth at them.

Solvi had opened his mouth to speak when a commotion from beyond the circle drew all eyes. Ragnvald saw a woman run up and for a moment did not recognize Svanhild in such disarray. Svanhild bent over to catch her breath, her hair barely restrained by a soiled wimple, her mouth reddened.

"Solvi Hunthiofsson speaks now," said Hrolf loudly.

Ragnvald looked back at Solvi and was surprised at what he saw.

Solvi looked stricken, pained at Svanhild's appearance. Ragnvald did not know why, but he realized suddenly that Svanhild had been the woman Solvi had been riding with, and that was why no one had spoken her name to him. Solvi must have said something to her that he would not want repeated—which was why he looked so shocked. Ragnvald would scold Svanhild later for her rashness; now it seemed as though it might help him.

Solvi glanced around, more ill at ease than Ragnvald had ever seen him. Then he seemed to make a decision. He smiled again, a little abashed.

"Ragnvald sailed with me," he said. The voice that commanded warships rang out over the plain. "And yes, I gave him that wound."

IO

SOLVI SMILED AS A SHOCKED ROAR ROSE FROM THE CROWD. HE glanced at Svanhild, who planted her hands on her hips. Ragnvald looked as though he had been rooted to the ground.

"I wish I hadn't, now," Solvi continued. He turned his gaze to the jurors; he could not keep his tone as light as he must if he continued watching Svanhild. He could still hold them, charm them, hope they would see him as a mischievous boy too bold to stay out of scrapes but too honest not to own up to them.

"Ragnvald deserves his share of the treasure we raided. And I'll pay the wergild." He looked down at Ragnvald from his perch. "But if you try to fight me . . ." He grinned again, this one sharp-edged. "Your family will not like to pay the cost."

Svanhild's eyes narrowed. "He admits it," she said, only loudly enough so those nearest Solvi and Hrolf could hear. "But there is more. I heard him talking to my stepfather, Olaf Ottarsson. Olaf paid—"

Ragnvald stepped forward eagerly.

"Quiet, girl," said Hrolf. "No one asked you to speak."

Ragnvald held up a hand. "I must talk with my sister. She knows more." He looked around, as if for support. "She will testify against Olaf. It is not only Solvi who compassed this."

"No," said Hrolf. "You have made suit against Solvi, and you have won." He banged his stick on a rock for silence. "Since there is no argument about what happened, if the jury does not object, I will set the sentence."

"There is an argument," said Svanhild. "Ragnvald, this is your chance."

Ragnvald hesitated.

Be a clever boy, Solvi thought, take what is offered, and wait to take more later.

Hrolf named the price for the injury, a double handful of silver, a price both high and fair. Solvi voiced his agreement. He could afford the injury price with treasure he had brought.

"Are you satisfied with this?" Hrolf asked Ragnvald. "Will you consider the matter closed?"

Ragnvald took a deep breath and drew his shoulders back. The look on his face made Solvi nervous. This should be enough. Ragnvald had been a cautious warrior when he fought for Solvi. He would not overstep now.

"Ragnvald," said Svanhild again. "I can help you. Please. We must."

Ragnvald glanced at Solvi, a moment's indecision in his expression, before he frowned and set his jaw. "No. I say that Solvi did not act alone," he said. "I say that my stepfather Olaf threatened, bribed, or otherwise compassed my murder with him. I say that he did this to keep my father's land from me, and now that I am old enough to be counted a man, he should turn my land over to me. I say that my sister Svanhild will testify to what they plotted." He looked at Svanhild, who nodded.

Solvi stepped forward and said quietly to him, "Be warned, I will not let that accusation stand."

"Why not?" said Ragnvald angrily, stepping back and speaking so the whole crowd could hear. "I thought you were in a truth-telling mood."

"Leave it be," said Solvi, still under his breath. "You will not like what follows."

"Oh, are you a prophet now?" Ragnvald asked.

"An accusation has been made, unless you'd like to withdraw it," said Hrolf.

Ragnvald turned to the crowd and said, "No, I do not. Why deal me this wound? Why throw me in the water?"

Solvi took the speaking stick, too aware of Svanhild watching him. "Who said anything about killing?" he asked. "Is it not the duty of a captain to lesson his men?" He punctuated his gestures with the stick. Men around the circle nodded in agreement. "This boy, Ragnvald, fell, injured, without his treasure, and I thought to make him whole again. Now he levies baseless accusations against me and his honored stepfather. I demand payment for this insult." He passed the speaking staff to Hrolf.

"Solvi Hunthiofsson is not the only one insulted here today," said Hrolf. "Does Olaf Ottarsson wish to respond to these charges?"

"It's not an insult if it's true," said Ragnvald.

"You've had your turn," said Hrolf in an angry undertone.

Olaf paced across the ground slowly, deliberately. He took the stick from Hrolf, frowning, every inch the disappointed parent. Solvi would have admired his acting skills under other circumstances. "I would take responsibility for this," said Olaf, "but Ragnvald has seen twenty winters now. He must take responsibility for his own choices."

"Do you deny these charges?" Hrolf asked.

"Of course I do," said Olaf. "If my honor is in doubt, surely no one could doubt the son of King Hunthiof."

"Then it is decided," said Hrolf.

"I have made a new accusation," said Ragnvald. "You must allow me to call and question my sister."

"She is a girl-child," said Olaf scornfully. "She cannot testify."

"A woman may testify, if no men were present to witness what she testifies to," said Ragnvald. "Were any men present to witness what you saw?" he asked Svanhild.

"The only men present were those accused," Svanhild's voice rang out, high and girlish. "They spoke of what Ragnvald says. I will swear to it." Her eyes blazed at Solvi.

Solvi edged closer to Ragnvald. "And I will deny it, and so will your stepfather. Your sister will be shamed, and you will owe a greater amount than you can ever repay," he said quietly. "Do not make her do this."

Ragnvald drew away from him again. "Surely you know already that no one can make my sister do anything."

"Yes," said Solvi. "But for a brother she loves . . ." He wanted to shake Ragnvald. He had seen a chance of winning Svanhild's affections again. She had liked him very well the day before, without disdaining his height, or the scarred legs that made him so short. She could like him again, this bold and pretty girl.

This would not go well for Ragnvald, and Svanhild would never forgive Solvi if he called her liar in front of all the men of her district. Ragnvald looked like a ship's pilot caught between rocks and a heavy sea. His brows were drawn together; under them, his eyes were worried. He stepped toward Hrolf with his hand outstretched to take the speaking stick from him, but stopped. He glanced at Solvi, then Svanhild, then back to Solvi again. Svanhild opened her mouth to speak, and Ragnvald stepped forward.

"I withdraw my accusation," said Ragnvald, finally, to Solvi. "I accept the payment Hrolf set." He turned to Olaf. "I will still have my land. Unless you want to withdraw the promise you made to my father."

Solvi breathed out a sigh of relief.

"I do not accept," said Olaf. "Let the lying girl testify, let all know what a worthless son Ragnvald has been to me. I want payment for this insult. The land will never be yours. It will belong to my sons, Sigurd and Hallbjorn. I was the one who held the land when your father could not."

"My father's bones lie in that land. It is mine," said Ragnvald angrily.

"Let the land be forfeit, then," said Hrolf. He was friends with Olaf, Solvi remembered. He and Olaf had arranged the betrothal between Ragnvald and Hilda, and now they would both want it called off.

"I withdraw my accusation," said Ragnvald again, his eyes blank with fear.

"It was spoken," said Olaf. "I demand payment."

"It was spoken," said Hrolf. "Let Solvi's payment for the injury go to Olaf Ottarsson, and let Olaf keep his land for his sons. He has earned that much."

"I do not agree to this," said Solvi. He had already regretted his father's alliance with Olaf, and this was too much, that Olaf should be paid for being too cowardly to kill Ragnvald himself.

"It is true that a spoken insult is not the same as an insult wound," said Hrolf. "Let Olaf be paid a third of Solvi's price, and Ragnvald be paid nothing. Does that serve?"

Olaf looked like he did not know who he hated more, Ragnvald or Solvi, and Ragnvald appeared to have a similar conflict of mind. Solvi had not thought they looked anything alike until that moment of offended dignity.

Solvi glanced at Svanhild. Hrolf had overstepped himself; this was needlessly cruel to Ragnvald. "Ragnvald deserves his payment for his injury," said Solvi. "And I have nothing to say about this business of land. It seems ill-done that a boy should lose his father's bones over a hasty accusation." The time for winning grins was over, even if he could muster one. "Property disputes are heard tomorrow, are they not? You are law speaker here." A murmur of agreement sounded from the assembly. "Is this done now?" he asked wearily.

"Then let these be the terms," said Hrolf. "Ragnvald must render to Olaf a third of the payment he receives from Solvi. The rest he may keep." Ragnvald clenched his teeth so tightly Solvi thought he might break one.

"Do all agree?" Hrolf asked again.

The jury all raised their hands in agreement.

Ragnvald and Olaf nodded, each wearing the same sullen expression.

"Are you satisfied?" asked Hrolf again, in a tone of voice that said Ragnvald had better be.

"I am," said Ragnvald. He bowed his head and spoke the formal words: "I swear to accept this verdict, in the name of Tyr, the giver of laws. I will seek neither blood, nor further payment in recompense for this crime." He gestured to the red seam on his cheek.

Solvi's sympathy swung briefly back to Ragnvald. At least he had a reason to feel wronged. And had the dignity to employ the proper formula, while Olaf still looked angry enough to spit nails.

"What of my father's land?" Ragnvald asked Hrolf. "You do ill to try to give that away."

"We will settle that tomorrow, when disputes of property are heard," said Hrolf.

"Come," said Solvi to Ragnvald. "I will discharge my debt." Ragnvald followed him out of the ring.

✣   ✣   ✣

SOLVI WALKED AHEAD of Ragnvald, self-conscious about his limp, until his men fell in around him, forming a protective wall. They could keep physical threats off him, but could not advise him how to proceed here. Solvi bid his men stay outside the tent to give him privacy.

It was a small tent, the same one that he pitched against his ship's mast to keep out of a storm. It could be carried by a single horse. Inside was tall enough for him to stand up, while Ragnvald was forced to stoop. If Solvi had come as his father's representative, he might have brought a larger one, but he came for himself, because the trials entertained him. And, it seemed, because his fate, his *wyrd*, had drawn him here, to Svanhild Eysteinsdatter. Or Ragnvaldssoster, he thought, smiling to himself.

"I have a ring like the one you should have won in the race," said Solvi. "It is worth more than the weight of silver imposed in Hrolf's sentence."

Ragnvald had been shifting from foot to foot. Now he burst out, "I don't understand you."

Solvi suddenly felt ages older than Ragnvald, though only five years lay between them. Ragnvald had behaved like a fool today. Solvi wished he had never heard of Ragnvald or his stepfather.

"Understanding was not part of your payment," he said. Here was an opening. "But if you like, consider my . . . generosity a payment for your good opinion. Tell your sister you and I have come to an accord. Tell her she has nothing to fear from me."

"You think you can buy her acceptance? Of you?" Ragnvald asked.

Solvi pulled the thick band of yellow gold from his own arm and tossed it to Ragnvald. "Will that do?"

"It's enough for me. I had not that much beauty to lose." Ragnvald held the gold, and stroked it with his thumb. "I will tell my sister what you've done, and why," he said, quirking the unwounded corner of his mouth. "That is all I can promise."

Solvi bristled at Ragnvald's expression. He had been generous to Ragnvald, when his choice to speak had changed Ragnvald's fate in the trial circle. Ragnvald was fallen and disgraced from an already fallen family, and still he kept his sister from Solvi. Few of Solvi's warriors did not have a king of some small district among their forefathers, yet Ragnvald thought his grandfather still made him exceptional.

"No one will respect you after today," said Solvi. "Do you truly think tomorrow will bring you your land back? You will not win that one with words, and you will not hold that land without killing him. Bring a sword next time." He spoke to anger Ragnvald, who had always been quick to defend his dignity. Ragnvald should not smile at him, as though he knew a secret Solvi did not.

Ragnvald laughed out loud, not happily. Solvi's words had found their mark. "You accuse me of wanting impossible things, when you ask for my sister's good opinion?" he said. "There is nothing I could tell her to make her love you any better. Svanhild makes up her own mind."

"She would defy her brother?" Solvi asked.

"Easily," said Ragnvald, "even if I ordered her into your bed." Solvi had to revise his opinion of Ragnvald again. Ragnvald, usually disdainful and touchy, seemed unconcerned about his sister's defiance, seemed even to take pride in it. Solvi, who had been raised with few women about him, and none of noble birth, could not understand this, but he risked looking even more ridiculous if he asked Ragnvald to say any more on his behalf to Svanhild.

"What will you do now?" Solvi asked.

"I still mean to take back my land," Ragnvald said.

"You have a strong arm, and a good head, Ragnvald Eysteinsson," said Solvi. "If you fail in that, one of my ships would have you."

Ragnvald laughed at him again—for the last time, Solvi promised himself. "No, thank you," he said. "This head suits me better attached to my shoulders."

"It wasn't your time to die. And when it is, it will not be at my hand."

"Don't make promises you cannot keep."

"I thought you swore not to hold a grudge," said Solvi. He put his hand to his sword, and Ragnvald did the same.

"Did I?" said Ragnvald. He pulled his hands away and held them up, empty. "I swore not to take revenge." He waited a moment, then touched the scar on his cheek again, as though it were a talisman. "For this, at least."

II

ALL RAGNVALD COULD THINK ON LEAVING SOLVI'S TENT WAS
how foolish his decisions had been at the trial. He had seen Svanhild
rushing across the plain, heard her brave words, and seen the hope in
her eyes that he would be as brave. He thought of the stories they had
told each other as children, learned at their father's knee. In none of
these tales did a hero back down from a challenge, choose gold over
blood, or take a prudent course when a bold one beckoned.

Ragnvald had been too much a boy in that moment. He wanted
to follow where Svanhild's certainty led, even into destruction, and
when Solvi offered a fair deal—insult payment and treasure restored—
Ragnvald had rejected it. Solvi was certainly correct; none would wish
Ragnvald to hold Ardal now, not after he had acted like the young
hothead Hrolf feared joining his daughter to.

"He let you go this time?" Oddi asked, falling into step beside
Ragnvald. He looked relieved. Ragnvald had not been as alone as he
thought. "Be cautious now," Oddi said. "You know who retaliates at
once." The saying ran: Only a slave retaliates at once.

"Yes, and a coward not at all," Ragnvald said testily, capping the
proverb. He scowled at Oddi. He did not need reminding of his folly.
He gripped the ring Solvi had given him, now wrapping around his
arm—he had shown his hand, angered Solvi, angered Olaf before all
the men of Sogn, and lost himself his true prize.

"Were you waiting here to tell me that?" he asked.

"Yes," said Oddi. "And to tell you that we brought a goldsmith with our household who will divide that for you. You owe Olaf a third of it, do you not?"

"Let your man weigh it first," said Ragnvald. He touched the velvety gold. "I have to see if Svanhild is well. She did not look—" He shook his head.

"Your sister is a bold one," said Oddi.

"Yes, she is," Ragnvald agreed, and now it did not make him glad. "It's going to be dangerous for her in Olaf's household after this." He should see her married off as soon as possible, and not to Thorkell. Solvi was a terrible choice, even had he proposed marriage and not concubinage—a man with no honor would make a poor ally.

Ragnvald kept his head down among Hakon's tents. Being scolded by Oddi was bad enough, but now everyone would find a way to tell him how he could have prosecuted his case better, and how he should proceed tomorrow, when he sued for his birthright.

The goldsmith weighed the armband, and snipped off a piece of it—larger than Ragnvald had hoped—with big steel shears. He offered to remake it into a more slender armband for Ragnvald, but Ragnvald declined. He would decorate Svanhild and Hilda with gold first, take back his father's lands and field a raiding ship. Then and only then would he show off his wealth in jewelry. He shoved both pieces into the pouch at his belt.

"Where are you going?" Oddi asked when Ragnvald began walking across the field to Olaf's camp.

"To give Olaf his 'insult price,'" said Ragnvald acidly. "And to see Svanhild."

"Let me walk with you," said Oddi.

"You think Olaf would do me harm in broad daylight, after the decision?" Ragnvald asked.

"I think he'd wait until your back was turned," said Oddi. "You were too busy losing yourself in that mire of accusations and whispering with Solvi to see how he looked at you."

"How?" Ragnvald asked.

"Like he wanted to kill you," said Oddi.

"He does want to kill me," said Ragnvald.

"Don't make it easy for him," said Oddi, "even if you are angry with yourself."

"Why do you care?" Ragnvald asked. Oddi's advice annoyed him for being so sensible. He should have thought of all these things.

"I want my friend living," said Oddi mildly.

"I'm sorry," said Ragnvald.

"I'm the baseborn son of a man with too many sons already. I need friends as much as you do," Oddi added as they reached Olaf's camp, too late for Ragnvald to find out more. He wondered if Heming Hakonsson was any less willing to take the life of a half brother than his father's favorite jarl.

Some commotion was taking place, involving too many people for Ragnvald to see what was going on at first. A crowd had gathered to watch as Olaf dragged a small figure—Svanhild—across the ground, shouting at her, and hauling her up by the hair to cuff her face as she struggled.

Ragnvald ran forward, hand on his sword, Oddi at his heels. He shouldered the crowd aside and stepped in close to Olaf before he could hit Svanhild again. Her cheek was reddened and swelling, her expression dazed from the blows.

"What is this?" Ragnvald yelled. "You have no right."

"She's my daughter, I have every right."

"Stepdaughter," said Ragnvald. "She's my sister. Until she is married, no one may punish her without my leave, now that I'm a man."

"You are no man," said Olaf, moving to strike her again.

Ragnvald pushed Olaf, hard, and he stumbled back. "I came to bring you your insult payment," said Ragnvald. "But since now you've insulted me in return, I think we're even." Indeed, Olaf's words were grounds for any man to duel.

"Would you like to bring that to trial too? Can't you settle anything yourself?" Olaf taunted.

Ragnvald began to draw his sword. "I can settle this," said Ragnvald. The circle of onlookers moved back, giving him room. Svanhild scrambled to her feet and caught Ragnvald's elbow.

"Don't do this," said Svanhild. "He is unarmed. It would be murder." She was right; Olaf did not wear a sword, only an eating dagger on his belt.

"Would you duel with me then, stepfather?" Ragnvald shouted. "Is that how we shall settle this?"

"You cannot even afford shields for a duel," said Olaf.

"My father will provide them," said Oddi from behind him, voice low and certain. "And I will stand as his second."

"We can move to the dueling ground now," said Ragnvald, anchored by Oddi's support. "Fetch your sword."

Olaf smiled in a way that made Ragnvald's skin crawl: crafty and self-satisfied, for no reason Ragnvald could guess. He looked over at where Vigdis stood at the edge of the crowd.

"The girl is bleeding," Olaf said to her. "See to her."

Vigdis walked toward them, tugging her hair over one shoulder to keep it from tangling in the wind. Even in the midst of this, she transfixed Ragnvald. She seemed to look through his skin, seeing all his doubts, even as he pressed ahead.

"No," Ragnvald muttered, looking at the ground. He was on less firm footing here. He hardly knew what he was going to do with himself, never mind Svanhild. "No," he said again, raising his eyes to Vigdis's. She was beautiful, but she was Olaf's creature. "Svanhild comes with me."

"With you?" Olaf scoffed. "Do you want her to follow you to Hel?"

"I would," said Svanhild, standing up straight, letting her hand fall. Her jaw was swollen from Olaf's blow, puffed out of true, and her eyes were red. Ragnvald should not have left her with Olaf for even a moment after the trial.

"Do we duel, stepfather?" Ragnvald asked.

Oddi cleared his throat. "My father will oversee the dueling ground," said Oddi. "I must speak with him about it." He put a hand on Ragnvald's left arm, the one that did not hold his sword. The right was growing weary. "I cannot procure shields immediately either, cousin," he said quietly.

"Tomorrow then," said Olaf to Ragnvald. "We duel."

"For my father's land," said Ragnvald. "Agreed?"

Olaf nodded. "Agreed."

✠ ✠ ✠

AS HE WALKED away from Olaf's tent, with Svanhild in tow, the import of what he had done settled on Ragnvald. He had taken responsibility for Svanhild, and now she walked with him, a half-grown child who needed protection, who needed a place he could not provide. She was the bravest of girls, but she was still a girl, and he had no idea what to do with her.

"You can stay with Hrolf Nefia's family for now," he told her. "They may not want me to marry Hilda, but they must have some kin feeling left."

"I must tell you," said Svanhild. She repeated what had passed between Olaf and Solvi, nothing Ragnvald had not suspected, but it still made him angry now to hear that they had discussed it so openly, and Solvi's lies at the trial. "You should have let me testify."

"No," said Ragnvald. "I should not have let you speak at all. They would have called you a liar. No one would believe a woman's word over Olaf's and Solvi's."

"That is not fair," she said in a low voice.

He stopped stamping across the field to turn and look at her. "I should have been satisfied with Solvi's payment. So should you."

"It is your birthright." Her voice rose. "You can't let him win."

"You cannot have everything as you will it." He wished he believed as strongly as she did, that events would turn out for the best, that the most honorable man would always win. "I will kill Olaf tomorrow," he promised her, "and he will suffer for what he did to you." Svanhild gave him a look he knew was her trying to be brave for him, to keep her doubts to herself. He wished he had comfort and certainty to offer, but having none, kept silent.

Such was the speed of gossip at the *ting* that the news of the duel reached Hrolf's camp before Ragnvald did. He had meant to tell Hilda of the trial and the duel, but Hrolf barred the way, with Egil glaring at him.

"I suspected you were a fool before," said Hrolf. "And now you have proved it." Ragnvald did not have much defense, since he could not think of the trial without cringing. Hrolf had been right; it was only Olaf's anger, and the duel Ragnvald had provoked, that gave him any hope now.

"I have come to speak with Hilda," he said instead.

"You and my daughter have nothing to say to each other," said Hrolf.

"We have promised to each other."

"She cannot promise herself to anyone."

"Stop it!" Svanhild shrieked. "Stop arguing, for once." Hrolf and Ragnvald both looked down at her. A few girls popped their heads out of the tent behind Hrolf, alert to the sound of any kind of domestic drama. Hilda pushed past all of them, giving them a withering look. She met Ragnvald's eyes before bending down and dabbing at the blood on Svanhild's lip with the corner of her apron.

Ragnvald took a deep breath. "Olaf was beating her for trying to testify against me," he said.

"And he tied me up for the last two days," Svanhild said, half gulping the words.

"She needs a place to stay for the rest of the gathering," said Ragnvald. "May we rely on your hospitality?"

"Of course," said Hilda.

Hrolf's face looked like a thundercloud for a moment, but then he sighed and said, "Of course. You and my daughter have already dragged us into your quarrel with Olaf. The home of Hrolf Nefia is open to the needy."

Ragnvald ducked his head. He had done ill to bring Svanhild into his quarrels. Hrolf had accepted her churlishly, and cast Svanhild as a beggar, but at least she would be safe tonight.

✛   ✛   ✛

ODDI OFFERED TO let Ragnvald sleep in Hakon's camp that night, within the circle of their guards and wealth, rather than out in the forest, and Ragnvald accepted, though he insisted on setting up his own tent. He might not sleep, and he did not want to annoy anyone of Hakon's retinue with his wakefulness.

He was not scared of Olaf, though nerves did keep him up into the darkest part of the night. He had never dueled before. It would be more formal than daggers in the dark, the stealthy raids he had led for Solvi. He had practiced dueling, of course, but it was different with sharpened blades. Tomorrow all would be settled, and more finally than a trial could do.

He ran his hand over his sword arm as he lay in the darkness. The muscles were hard when he flexed them. He was strong—a year's raiding had made him so—but Olaf had twenty years' experience on him, and was probably no less strong. Ragnvald thought himself clever enough; still, in contests past, he had seen how the young and strong could fall to the old and crafty. He would need to be both bold and watchful tomorrow, to dance as carefully as he had on Solvi's oars. More carefully.

And he would need his sleep. He breathed deeply, trying to think instead of pleasant things. Hilda, in her tent, patient and steady. A good wife for bearing sons and running a farm. She shared that tent now with Svanhild. No, thinking of Svanhild would not bring him rest, only more worry. He thought of Ardal, of the broad lakes and high green pastures, as green in summer as the fabled green of Ireland. Of Sogn Fjord, the site of his father's barrow, and the foundation of his father's hall, now burned. His great-grandfather had fought giants that came down from the Keel to try to take their land, and driven them back with a magic spell, or so Ragnvald's father had told him when he was a boy. Even allowing for some exaggeration from Eystein the Noisy, the blood of Ragnvald's forefathers had watered the ground of Sogn and Ardal, where they had made their home since the gods made the first men. He would think of that when he fought tomorrow. He thought too of the golden wolf that waited for him, in life or death. The fates had already decided if he would live or die tomorrow, and waited only for him to choose how he met his fate, bravely or poorly.

He had almost drifted off when the snap of a twig made him tense. He put his head outside his tent and saw Vigdis standing there in her shift, a shawl wrapped around her shoulders against the cold. The shadow and folds of the fabric around her body in the moonlight made her look like a temptress spirit.

Ragnvald stared up at her for a moment, then came to his feet and said with a dry mouth, "Stepmother."

She made a face, as he knew she would. She never wanted him to call her that. He had tormented himself on long nights on the open sea, thinking that he had imagined every heated look she gave him. She turned none of those glances on him now. She looked frightened.

"Ragnvald, Olaf means to kill you," she said.

"Yes," he said. "Tomorrow we duel. Or does he plan to cheat?"

"No, he plans to do it tonight," she said, gripping his shoulder. "You are exposed here."

They spoke quietly. A shout would rouse Hakon's men, though perhaps not quickly enough.

"Why are you telling me?" He took her arm. He had never touched her purposely before, only suffered burning from her fingers since the day Olaf brought her home as a bride, only a handful of years older than himself, though far older in experience. "Should I follow you somewhere even more exposed?"

"Why do you think I bear you ill will?"

He laughed shortly. "Many, many reasons." Ending with her imprisonment of Svanhild. "You have been setting me against Olaf since you came."

"He hated you before that," she said. He noticed she did not deny the charge.

"What should I do?"

"Go inside with Hakon, before they come. Olaf is a coward. If he fails tonight, he will leave without dueling."

"Why are you telling me this?"

"Because one day you will come to make me a widow, and I will welcome that day and welcome you." She stood on her toes and kissed his lips lightly. He let go of her, surprised, and she turned away, her footsteps falling soundless on the soft grass.

"Wait," he called after her. She did not stop.

He turned back to his tent, pitched only a few feet from the edge of Hakon's huge feasting tent. It billowed and then caved inward. Ragnvald saw Olaf, his sword stuck into the puddled canvas. Sigurd stood behind him, his hair blue in the dimness of midnight. Olaf charged toward Ragnvald, over the fallen tent.

Ragnvald sidestepped, but a rope securing Hakon's tent blocked his way, and Olaf's sword went through the meat of his upper arm, his sword arm, a strange hot and cold sensation that brought no pain with it. Sigurd followed a half step behind him, his sword tip wavering.

"Finish him," Olaf commanded his son. "You must do this."

Sigurd gamely took a step forward, but he hesitated before attacking, and Ragnvald parried his thrust, pressing him back. As Ragnvald attacked Sigurd, Olaf lunged again, slicing a shallow cut along Ragnvald's flank. That one hurt immediately, as every breath opened it further.

"You didn't think you could win a duel?" Ragnvald asked loudly, edging along the tent. Someone must hear this soon. He kept most of his attention on Olaf; Sigurd looked as though he would attack only on Olaf's command.

"You're not worth dueling," Olaf said.

"Yet you didn't think you could murder me alone?"

Olaf lunged again. Ragnvald's sidestep brought him within Sigurd's range. He parried a clumsy slash from Sigurd without much difficulty.

"I only wanted my son to see what a coward you were," said Olaf.

"He can already see one coward here tonight." Ragnvald glanced at Sigurd again. Sigurd wore a lost expression on his face, visible even in the dim midsummer night. He did not want to be here. That could work to Ragnvald's advantage, and he would need every advantage now. The muscles of his arm throbbed from Olaf's lucky first slash, and moved sluggishly. Soon he would not be able to lift his sword, and Olaf could do what he liked with him.

One more lunge would do it, though. He probably had that in him. Ragnvald took a few more crabwise steps. He put a tie line between himself and Olaf, then made a feint forward, hoping to invite Olaf's attack, while keeping half an eye on Sigurd. Olaf did take the step toward him, but not far enough to come inside Ragnvald's guard. Ragnvald moved sideways again.

"Now who's the coward?" Olaf hissed. "Come and fight."

Ragnvald tried not to react to Olaf's words. Anger would avail him little now. Another step, and Olaf would find himself tangled in the tie lines if he attacked in any other way than a straight thrust. Ragnvald stepped over the rope and swung his sword with both hands. A half second faster, and it would have taken off Olaf's head, but Olaf threw himself to the ground and only lost a patch of scalp, while Ragnvald lost his balance from the too forceful swing.

Olaf stabbed upward, through Ragnvald's thigh. Ragnvald shouted. Blood wet his trews. His grip on his sword was failing. He let go of it and reached for his dagger with his left hand. If Olaf killed him, at least they could die together.

On the ground, Olaf scrambled backward, out of the way. Ragnvald took another step back and stumbled against the tent. His vision was a black tunnel now that contained only Olaf, trying to stand, and a pair of embroidered shoes on the ground next to him. He looked up to see Oddi.

"Enough of this," said Oddi, sounding just like his father. "The duel is not until tomorrow."

"They came to murder me," said Ragnvald, sagging back against the tree. Other men of Hakon's court gathered around them.

"This man is wounded," said Oddi to his fellows. "Someone see to him."

A young man rushed forward and bid Ragnvald sit. He tore bandages from Ragnvald's shirt and tied them around Ragnvald's wounds, over his clothes. The pressure made Ragnvald cry out, as his vision narrowed further.

"They came to murder me," Ragnvald repeated thickly. The pain crested and then receded, a tide moving with his blood. He could manage the worst of it now, he thought.

"That much is clear," said King Hakon. Ragnvald looked up at him stupidly. When had King Hakon arrived?

"I only wanted redress for today's insult," said Olaf. "This—boy has insulted me, and stolen my daughter—"

"Stepdaughter," said Sigurd, under his breath. Olaf gave him a dirty look.

"We planned to duel tomorrow," said Ragnvald. "Did you fear me so much?"

Olaf pulled himself to his feet. He was still breathing hard. "He does not deserve the honor of a duel."

"You have attempted murder," said Hakon, implacable.

"It was not murder—it was my right," said Olaf. "Solvi Hunthiofsson will speak for me."

"I cannot think what he could say to change what I have seen," said King Hakon, "but someone fetch him anyway."

It seemed like little time passed between Hakon speaking the words and one of his men reappearing with Solvi in tow, but it must have taken several minutes. Ragnvald was very thirsty.

"Why did you call on me?" Solvi asked Olaf, before anyone could question him. "I want nothing more to do with you."

"I was only finishing what you started," said Olaf. "What you could not do."

"You will not put this on me."

Dimly, Ragnvald was aware of someone slapping his face. His bandages were tightened, sending more pain blooming up from his thigh through his groin. "You may duel with Olaf tomorrow," said Hakon to him. Hakon's face was right in front of him. Was Ragnvald standing, or was Hakon sitting? Ragnvald could not tell.

"He is not well enough to duel," said Oddi. "I will stand for him. I will gladly kill Olaf for him."

"No," said Ragnvald. No, he could not let Oddi do that. Ragnvald was not aware of much at this moment, but he clung to this. Olaf was his. "No," he said again. "I may die of my wounds. Olaf is a coward, but he holds my lands for me now. I will kill him, if I recover. And if I do not, may the gods deal with him as he has with me."

Hakon's face retreated away from him. "Ragnvald Eysteinsson has spoken," he said, "and I judge it good. He may have his own revenge." To Olaf he said, "I declare you outlawed from my lands. Any man may kill you on sight and come to me for reward."

Olaf paled, and squared his shoulders. "You are not my king," he said, showing the first bravery he had since coming to the assembly.

"And young Ragnvald wants you to live so he can kill you himself. Go back to Ardal, tonight, or I will let my sons make what sport of you they will."

He might have said something else, but Ragnvald slumped forward. He breathed in the dust of last year's leaves, and then he knew no more.

12

WHEN RAGNVALD WOKE UP, HE FELT DRUNK. HIS MOUTH tasted of spirits, and his arm, side, and thigh ached and burned by turns. He sat up, his head spinning. He was in a well-decorated tent, on a raised bed, with Svanhild sitting by his side.

"Ragnvald," she said, sounding relieved. "I'll go get someone."

Ragnvald lay back down again, but it did not stop the tent walls from shifting around him, as though he were rolling down a steep slope. He wanted to throw up.

Oddi and King Hakon appeared next. Ragnvald sat up again—he would not lie down when a king was talking to him. "I know you feel terrible now," said Hakon, "but my healer says you are very lucky. Your wounds are in muscle only. You will heal quickly."

"Thank you," said Ragnvald, his voice scratchy as though he had not used it in some time.

"Olaf and his household have gone as my father ordered," said Oddi. "A few other families left as well—I think some of his kin?"

"Thank you," said Ragnvald again. He did not know what else to say.

"I knew your father and grandfather," said Hakon. "Your grandfather Ivar was a mighty king in Sogn. His brother was the most feared sea king of the northern coast. Do you know that fishermen still look for his treasure caches in the barrier islands?"

"Yes, my lord," said Ragnvald. He had learned the tales, been proud of them, to come from a line of kings who protected their people and their lands, and to be descended from fierce raiders as well, who conquered wave and rock so that they were called sea kings, kings with no land, only plunder.

"Eystein Glumra, we called your father," Hakon was saying. "Eystein the Noisy. All bluster and boasting, no action."

Ragnvald felt distantly angry, but the pain in his body was more immediate. And there was no use for this anger; Hakon spoke the truth.

"But you are not like that, are you?" Hakon looked at Ragnvald curiously, as though he actually wanted to hear Ragnvald's answer.

"I hope not," said Ragnvald. He wished Hakon would get to the point and let him rest.

"You are a rare one, to let Olaf live," said Hakon. "You would rather kill him yourself than have his land pass easily to you."

Distantly, Ragnvald remembered that Oddi had offered to kill Olaf for him, and Ragnvald had declined. At the time, he had not wanted anyone else to take his revenge.

Hakon looked at Ragnvald, stroking his beard. It was thick and long enough that Ragnvald wondered if Hakon counted his personal fighting days over. A sprinkling of gray hairs dulled the golden strands, and the skin around his eyes was heavy. Jarl Runolf had been Hakon's friend, Ragnvald remembered. Hakon would wish to mourn for him but could not, not when his own son was the killer.

"What will you do now?" Hakon asked.

"I am wounded," said Ragnvald. It was as well that Olaf lived. He did not regret that decision, though he had hardly been conscious when he made it. Let Olaf hold Ardal until Ragnvald knew if he would live or die, if he would heal maimed or whole. He owed it to the land of his forefathers. No one would acclaim him jarl or king if he could not fight. He would rather die unknown than let his name live on like his father's.

"You will be well enough soon," said Hakon, cutting through Ragnvald's self-pity. "There are those who would take you for your strong back and stout sword when you are recovered."

Yes, men like Solvi or worse, raiders who would demand a tithe in blood, terrible oaths and rituals to give him a place on a ship when he did not have silver to buy a spot. Ragnvald had seen the scars, the marks of brotherhood that bound some of Solvi's warriors to him. Ragnvald had enough respect for Solvi himself, mixed with an equal helping of fear, but did not want to become one of his sworn men. They renounced their ties to land and family, and had no children besides those they got on thralls and unwilling captives, children who would never know their father's names, unless their mothers named them in hate.

Hakon must have read that in Ragnvald's face, for he laid a hand on Ragnvald's shoulder and said, "Not that, not the sea brethren. I offer a place in one of my ships."

A glimmer of hope flared up, even through Ragnvald's haziness. "My sister Svanhild," he said, glancing at where she sat by his side. "I cannot send her back to Olaf."

"Who has her keeping now?" Hakon asked.

"She has been staying with Hrolf Nefia and his family," said Ragnvald.

"The father of your betrothed," said Hakon. "Yes, that is a good place for her. I will speak to him and make sure he treats her well."

"I want to go with you," said Svanhild, jumping to her feet. "I could care for you until you're well."

"That is generous," said Hakon, "but my whole household is on the move, now. There would be no place for you."

"Take me on your ships," said Svanhild. "I could cook and mend sails."

Hakon laughed. "She has a good spirit," he said. "If young Ragnvald fails," he said to Svanhild, "will you avenge yourself on Olaf?"

"Of course."

"I will speak to Hrolf Nefia myself. You will not lack for comforts, my dear."

"Thank you," said Ragnvald, and Svanhild echoed him.

"Should I ask Hakon to set a guard on you so Solvi doesn't carry you off?" Ragnvald asked Svanhild, after King Hakon left.

"I don't think he will." She looked faraway for a moment.

"What do you think people will say of that?" he asked. The farmers who had spoken of Solvi's ride had surely been laughing at him as they hid the woman's name.

She stood swiftly. "Little enough, I think, when you have given them so much else to speak of. If your leg pains you so much that you must be cruel to one who has done nothing but stand by you, I will send for the healer."

That seemed unjust. If he were maimed, he would be at the mercy of women for the rest of his life, like this. Better to die.

"I had thought to send Hilda to comfort you, but not now," Svanhild added, not above using her power over him at this moment.

"Why did you ride with him?" Ragnvald asked, reaching over to pat the seat. He would not apologize, but he could, he supposed, be kinder, or she would leave him alone, and soon they would be separated for many months again.

"I did not know who he was," she said, looking away. "And I wanted some other prospect besides Thorkell."

"I will find someone better for you, I promise. What of Oddi? You could do worse than a king's son."

Svanhild made a face. "He looks like a frog. A handsome frog, though." Her look turned pensive. "Find me someone, though. I do not think I will be welcome with Hrolf for long."

✛   ✛   ✛

THE NEXT TIME Svanhild came, she brought Hilda with her and left them alone together, giving Ragnvald a conspiratorial look on leaving. Hilda wore light festival fabrics—her best dress, Ragnvald judged, in a bright blue that made her hair look like fine, polished wood.

"I'm glad you are well," she said. "I brought a tafl board so we can play." She unrolled it on the small folding table next to his mattress. Ragnvald wedged himself more upright, sending a bright splash of pain through his leg. She set up the pieces, the king and his defenders in the middle, the raiders on the outside. "Which position do you want?"

The raiders had the easier role—they had only to surround the king with four pieces anywhere on the board—while the king had to escape them to the corner squares.

"The king," he said. "Since Hakon has given me a place here."

"Making me the raiders," she said, smiling shyly at him. "That hardly seems apt."

The game played out predictably. Hilda was not a very skilled player, and did not know the tricks that Olaf had taught Ragnvald for winning on the king's side. A few moments occurred when she had an advantage she did not know enough to turn into a win. Then Ragnvald reached the corner of the board and finished the game.

"We can play knucklebones when you're feeling better," she said. It was not a very athletic game, but he did not want to have to move quickly right now.

"Hilda, your promise to me—if I am maimed . . ." Hakon's healer had good to say of Ragnvald's wound when she came to check on it, but without testing it, Ragnvald could not be sure.

"You will heal whole," she said. "Everyone thinks you will."

"Svanhild thinks that everything will always come out as she wills it."

"I think she is right this time. Or are you trying to escape your promise again?" Hilda asked, with a smile that did not fully hide her hurt.

"Never," said Ragnvald. "I keep my promises, and this is one is no hardship to keep. When I take back Ardal, you will be its mistress." She looked pleased at that, so he continued. "And my grandfather was king of Sogn. I mean to take that back, and you will be queen."

Her smile disappeared. "I wouldn't know how to be queen."

She showed proper modesty with those words, the modesty often praised in proverbs. Yet the women of Svanhild's favorite tales rarely displayed that virtue. He could not picture Hilda as the princess Unna, whose husband lay long abed one winter when he should be avenging an insult to their family. She had threatened and berated him until his blood was up and he did his killing. He died on the sword of his enemy's son, yet that did not make Svanhild like Unna any less.

"It will be a long time from now," said Ragnvald. First he must get up from this bed for more than just pissing in a pot. "Let us play another game. You could have beaten me last time. I'll show you."

✢   ✢   ✢

A WEEK AFTER Ragnvald's trial, Hrolf's camp began packing up. Svanhild had not felt welcome there, and spent as much time as she could with Ragnvald. She and Hilda tried not to let him grow too bored, trading off visits, playing rounds of tafl with him, sending Oddi to amuse him when that paled. His wounds healed swiftly with the attention of Hakon's women, who knew more of healing craft than Svanhild did. By the end of the week, he could walk without support.

On the day of their leavetaking, Ragnvald walked Svanhild over to Hrolf Nefia's camp and left her there with her bundle of clothes gifted by Hakon's women. She had left a few things behind at Ardal—her favorite spindle, which no one else liked to use, and some of her well-worn underthings—but she had worn all her jewelry here, and she comforted herself with the thought that when Ragnvald killed Olaf, all of her possessions would be returned to her.

She only hoped her mother would not be too mistreated by Vigdis and Olaf now that neither of her children were there to bear witness. Svanhild could not let herself worry too much, though. Her mother had made her choice when she married Olaf rather than take her children back to her family. That she had done it to help preserve Ragnvald's inheritance only excused her so much, especially now that Olaf had proven himself not to have enough honor to uphold Ragnvald's right to the land.

Ragnvald bid his good-bye to Hilda with Hrolf frowning at them, kissed Svanhild on the cheek, and walked back across the field. He walked slowly and stiffly with his wound, but Svanhild thought he would be whole enough soon. He held his shoulders back as he walked, and if he felt much pain when he bid her good-bye, he kept it from his face. Svanhild could tell he was glad to have her gone, no matter how much he loved her. She was a burden for him now.

After they watched Ragnvald leave, Hilda engulfed Svanhild in a sisterly hug, and immediately set her to work packing up the family's tents. As she rolled up a leather tent, a shadow fell over the weathered skin. She looked up to see Solvi standing over her. He was dressed for travel as well, in the armor and cloak that she had first seen him wearing.

"You could come with me instead," he said without preamble.

He would have heard all about Olaf and her disposal with Hrolf's family. Gossip traveled quickly around all of the Norse lands, and never faster than around the tents of the *ting* gathering.

"And be your concubine?" Svanhild asked acidly.

Solvi shrugged and then grinned. "Say wife, if you like."

Svanhild tried not to be flattered by that. She had felt uncomfortable as Ragnvald's hanger-on in Hakon's tent, and she was still uncomfortable now as an unwanted burden for Hrolf Nefia's family.

"I have heard nothing in Hakon's camp but how King Harald came to promise your father's doom," she said. "Why should I make my home in a hall with a wolf already at the door?" It was not the reason she meant to say. She had far better reasons not to go with Solvi, beginning with the enmity between him and Ragnvald. She forced herself not to look away from his handsomeness. He had a fine face, and a smile she wanted to answer with her own, and if she looked at him long enough, she might grow accustomed to it.

His eyes grew shadowed for a moment, but then he smiled wider. "If we went elsewhere, to another land, you would say yes?"

"Another land, another life, another girl—woman, whose brother was still unscarred? Then perhaps."

"You cannot forgive me that? I gave your brother his treasure. I did it for you."

She laughed. "Only out of fear of what I'd say," she said, to bait him. "That kind of favor is not the sort of thing to set a maiden's heart ablaze. And you didn't tell the whole truth."

She turned her eyes back to her packing, although she wanted to stand up and confront him. There was something undignified about kneeling on a rolled-up tent while they spoke.

"I got Ragnvald what I could. I couldn't—"

"You couldn't admit to being a murderer for hire? No, I think not."

"I couldn't call my father a murderer for hire," said Solvi. Svanhild looked up at him again. She expected to see him still wearing his customary grin, disarming, false, but instead he looked troubled. "What would you have done? For your father?"

Unwillingly, Svanhild thought instead of what her mother had said, about the choices she made to protect her children. Wrong choices, perhaps, choices that brought Olaf into their lives, but choices made for the right reasons, which could not be undone.

"I?" Svanhild asked. "I am just a woman. What do women know of honor?"

"I think you know a great deal," said Solvi. Now he smiled, and Svanhild grew angry that she had believed his show of sincerity.

"When Ragnvald returns, my stepmother will be a widow. She might like you," said Svanhild waspishly. "She's looking to trade up from Olaf. A king's son, perhaps."

"I know the type," said Solvi. "I want you. And you like me, a little, I think. Or did, before you knew my name."

"I did," said Svanhild honestly, then scowled at herself for admitting that. It did her no good to tell him. Now he might think she would actually agree to his request. "I know who you are now. And you know what your actions have wrought." She gestured at the bruised flesh of her face. Hilda's sisters told her that her jaw was green, though the swelling was gone now.

"I'm sorry you were injured," said Solvi. "Truly."

"I will not be your concubine or your wife," she said evenly, "but I thank you for the offer." Somehow she thought he deserved that much. "Now leave me be."

"You will not be happy as a farmer's wife," said Solvi. "You told me that."

"I will not be happy in the household of men who tried to compass my brother's death. You do not know me. I will be happy enough as a farmer's wife."

"Perhaps I do not know you," he said. "Perhaps you do not know yourself yet. If you are unhappy in the household of Hrolf Nefia, send me a message, or come to me, Svanhild Eysteinsdatter. If Tafjord falls, we will find a home across the seas, or make the seas our home." It was as if he did not hear her rejections, or did not care about them, and now he used her words against her, voicing her dreams. If only it was someone else that spoke them. If only he had chosen to disobey his father earlier.

"Farewell, Solvi Hunthiofsson," said Svanhild. She stood and watched him with her arms crossed until he finally gave her a faint smile and walked away.

Svanhild continued her work with ill humor. She knew she had not gotten the better of that meeting. She should have made him understand how she loved doing farm work at Ardal, managing the dairy at the shieling, the high mountain pasture, herding the sheep out to graze in the morning and back to the barn in the evening. She loved the long days spent under the sun and clouds, the endless beauty of Ardal's land. She loved the winter less, trapped inside with Vigdis and Ascrida, but when she ran a farm of her own, she would surround herself with the daughters of local farmers, pleasant girls whose company she would enjoy.

And if her husband brought in another wife—well, that could not be worse than being concubine to a sea king. When would she see one such as Solvi—every half year, when he came home from raiding? And the rest of the time she would be trapped in his dank hall, raising his brats, awaiting his return. Even if she wanted that kind of life, wanted him, Solvi was a man without honor, a man she could not consider.

She glanced around at Hilda and her sisters, each working at her task. She could not imagine any of them, even the headstrong Hilda, being tempted by an offer such as Solvi's. She flushed and put her head down, working until her arms ached.

✣   ✣   ✣

HROLF'S FARM WAS only a half day's walk from the gathering grounds, though mostly uphill, so they did not leave until after the midday meal. Egil walked with the mule, who was prone to fits of sulkiness, and needed his cajoling to continue the upward march. Hilda and Svanhild went first among the women, just after Hilda's father himself. Svanhild hurried to match Hilda's long stride. She was so tall, it was like trying to keep up with Ragnvald again.

Hilda had other qualities that reminded Svanhild of Ragnvald as well: her quiet watchfulness, the way she kept her own counsel. Svanhild had wondered if Hilda would abandon Ragnvald when his luck was at its lowest ebb, but she had visited Ragnvald's side as he healed, and the words they exchanged, in quiet voices, seemed to bring both of them contentment.

"Now you're walking too fast," Hilda called out to Svanhild, who looked back and saw that Hilda now carried her littlest sister, Ingifrid. "She can't keep up." Svanhild smiled ruefully, and slowed her pace. She looked behind her, memorizing the slope of the land, the path markers on the cairns they passed. "What do you seek?" Hilda asked. "Do you fear pursuit?"

"No," she said. "My stepfather is too much of a coward." Then, more diffidently, "I want to know my way back."

"Do you expect to be traveling here alone?"

"I don't know what to expect," said Svanhild. Ragnvald had taught her to be always prepared, in the woods around Ardal, in which he knew every stump and fallen tree, and had showed her hidden hollows and groves where snowdrops bloomed in the spring in shafts of sunlight when all else was frozen still. She could see why he would not want to leave it.

In the late afternoon they stopped for water and a small meal. Svanhild did not know how to react to Hilda's sisters, whose conversation seemed composed entirely of little barbs, and she could not tell which ones would produce a stony silence and which gales of laughter. They tried with Svanhild as well, needling her about her height—shorter than Hilda's next three younger sisters—about Solvi, calling him crippled and twisted; about Ragnvald, which made Hilda scowl as much as Svanhild did.

"There it is," said Hilda when they first caught a glimpse of Hrolf's hall. It stood on the edge of the forest, a border space that looked half in another world, a haunted world of more gray than color. The vegetable garden was shaded; stalks straggled along the ground, seeking light. The hall's planks were weathered, rather than gleaming with fat rubbed into the wood, as fine halls were. Ardal was not so different from this building now, even if Ragnvald said it had gleamed when he was young. All but the richest farms needed all of their fat for light and cooking.

Hilda made room for Svanhild in her sleeping chamber. Svanhild did not feel tired, though, not even after the long walk from the assembly plain at Jostedal.

"I'm glad you're here," said Hilda to Svanhild. "Do you think you'll be able to sleep?"

"It's much quieter than the hall at Ardal. Olaf keeps more men than your father does," said Svanhild. Hilda was silent, and Svanhild worried that it might sound like a reproach. "I shall be glad not to hear their snores," she added.

"Where do you think Ragnvald sleeps tonight?" Hilda asked.

Svanhild sighed. Hilda had lost no opportunity to bring him up whenever they spoke during the day, clinging to that one subject they held in common.

"On some shore," said Svanhild. "I wish I were there with him. Not that your family is not . . . kind to take me in, but . . ."

"I know," said Hilda. "I would like to be where he is as well. But it is not our place."

No, Hilda would not think so. She rolled over on her side, making a warm tent of blankets between the two of them, and slept, while Svanhild imagined that the sound of the wind through the rafters of the hall was the sound of waves instead, that Hilda's snores were a sailor's, and that this solid bench swayed because it carried her somewhere far away.

13

HAKON'S GREAT TRAIN OF FOLLOWERS MEANDERED DOWN THE slope toward the fjord. Horses pulled carts over rough ground where they frequently became stuck, making the animals balky. Ill-tempered thralls carried heavy loads down steep hills, and stopped to rest every hundred steps. If Ragnvald were at his full strength, it would be less than a day's walk to the shore where Hakon left his ships, but now he was grateful for the slow pace.

Hakon's ranks had been swelled by men from the *ting*, all hoping to win gold fighting at his side—farmers' younger sons, newly freed slaves, men who to Ragnvald, his every step tinged by pain, seemed either too young or too old, untrained in all but the most rudimentary fighting techniques.

They spoke of meeting the legendary Harald at Yrjar, and fighting for him as well. Ragnvald wondered at that. He could not imagine a sixteen-year-old boy king, no older than Svanhild, as anything but a figurehead. Hakon was a true king, grown mighty in wisdom, riches, and land. Ragnvald was content to follow him, lucky that Hakon had chosen him.

Their path overlooked the river Moen, whose waters passed the *ting* grounds, and which now plummeted over boulders, flying into the air and catching the sunlight. Wildflowers dotted the banks. The sound of rushing water and the wind flowing down the mountains was louder than the clanking and grumbling of Hakon's train.

"How do you fare?" Oddi asked, coming up alongside Ragnvald, who resisted the urge to answer curtly. He had been grateful to spend a day without anyone's solicitude, but he supposed this was better than being ignored.

"Well enough," he said.

"Heming's badgering Father for a fleet to sail against Solvi. Now, rather than in a year as we planned."

"I'd go with him," said Ragnvald, smiling wolfishly.

"Of course Father won't do it—he's still wroth with Heming over the duel."

"Why did he do it?" Ragnvald asked.

"There was no insult, I'll tell you that much," said Oddi. "Heming is spoiled and jealous and—hello, brother."

Heming's horse stamped on the packed earth of the trail. "Have you walked enough, young Ragnvald? Would you rather not ride?"

Ragnvald turned and greeted Heming with wave and a bow. He rode a tall and sturdy-looking horse that must surely have had some Spanish blood to make its coat shine like that, coal in the sun. In his hand he held the reins of a mare, shorter and shaggy-haired, wearing a saddle with stirrups.

"Do not fear for my healing, my lord," said Ragnvald, although he was sure Heming did not care about his wound at all.

"Are you refusing a chance to ride this fine mare here?" Heming asked.

He seemed in good spirits, and if Ragnvald had not seen him kill Runolf, perhaps he would not have been so suspicious. When Ragnvald did not respond, Heming added, "True, her dam was a fjord pony, but I do not scorn to ride her, and neither should you. She will keep walking after this high-spirited boy has fallen asleep."

Ragnvald turned to see what Oddi would say. He did not merit a horse, or had chosen not to ride, but he had fallen back into the stream of people and cards.

"Thank you, my lord," said Ragnvald to Heming. His ascent to the mare's back was more laborious than he wanted it to be, but once he sat atop her, his leg began to ache, as though it had been waiting until he stopped to show how much it hurt.

"Thank you, my lord," said Ragnvald again, with more feeling. "I do not mind the rest."

"I thought not. I will still keep the pace slow—you do not sit as one long accustomed to the saddle."

"No," Ragnvald agreed. Before his father's death, he had ridden a fjord pony all over Sogn with him; since then, he had sat upon the farm's horses rarely.

"Your stepfather did not do well in that," said Heming. "Among many other things, it seems."

"There was a time when I would have argued with you," said Ragnvald, "but no more." Olaf had not judged the keeping of many horses to be worth the expense. One for his own pleasure was enough for him. Let oxen pull plows, and be made into stew meat when they grew too old.

They rode without speaking for a few minutes, the noise of Hakon's procession filling the empty air. Even though they did not seem to be going very fast, every few minutes they overtook another foot traveler, until they reached the front of the procession, with only a few of Hakon's guards riding within shouting distance.

"My father likes you," said Heming.

"I am grateful for it," said Ragnvald. "He does me honor."

"Yes, he does," said Heming, his tone implying that he thought it might be too much honor. "Why did you not want my baseborn brother to kill your stepfather?" So Heming wanted to remind Ragnvald of Oddi's place in Hakon's family. Oddi would not automatically inherit on Hakon's death, since he was illegitimate, but he might still win acclaim, and his father might gift him with lands. When Ragnvald did not answer immediately, Heming added, "I have not seen Oddi so concerned about anything in a while."

"I am honored to count him among my friends." Ragnvald glanced at Heming, who was sneering slightly.

"I think you must have been fevered when you refused his help. Are you so bent on revenge that you must do your killing yourself?"

Ragnvald hesitated. What he said to Heming would be carried to Hakon, in one form or another. The slope their horses walked down steepened and grew slippery.

"Revenge is part of it," said Ragnvald. "But what would have happened after your—after Oddi killed my stepfather? Either I would have had to go to Ardal, wounded, and contend with Olaf's son Sigurd, or follow your father and leave Ardal in Sigurd's hands." A king, a jarl, even a simple farmer, owed his land his best protection, even if that came from someone else. His face felt hot as he spoke, but he did not want to stop speaking and have Heming think him dimwitted. "Our neighbor, Thorkell, is also Olaf's cousin. It's possible peace with him might be bought with Svanhild's hand—he is canny and lazy, but I would not want to risk it."

"If your sister would agree," said Heming. "She seems too wild to buy anyone with." Ragnvald looked at him sharply to see if the words carried insult, but instead he saw that Heming wore a thoughtful expression.

"I would not force her into a marriage, even were I in the position to do so," said Ragnvald, even stiffer than before.

"You will need to show her she must obey you, soon or late," said Heming, laughing. "Women need strong handling."

An angry retort sprung to Ragnvald's lips, and he suppressed it. "Well," he said, after a moment, "how does that work with your sisters?"

Heming laughed, more good-natured this time. "I have not tried it," he said. "My father directs their marriages, and my younger sister Asa was happy to marry Harald."

"King Harald?" Ragnvald asked.

"Yes," said Heming. "Do you not know the story?" Then, without waiting for Ragnvald to answer, he continued, "Before he was born his mother, a sorceress of renown, had a great dream, in which she saw him as a tree with bloody roots and green leaves, which meant that he would soak Norway in blood before bringing it prosperity."

"That is what conquerors do, I suppose," Ragnvald said.

"And," said Heming, "he hasn't conquered Norway yet, but he's promising to do it, and in the meanwhile marrying every woman who takes his fancy and can bring him an ally."

"Well, your sister Asa has grounds for a fine divorce," said Ragnvald lightly. "A princess should be a first wife."

Heming made a noise. "So you would not marry your sister to this Thorkell?"

"No, I would not. She is a brave girl, and would do what is necessary, but I would not like to ask it of her." He returned to his grim view of the future he had avoided by joining Hakon. "Thorkell might find it a good time to attack, take Svanhild if he wanted. Wounded, still fighting Sigurd, we would be easy pickings. Now Olaf can guard my land for me, and whatever his shortcomings, he is competent enough for that." He said this last hotly, daring Heming to question him.

"That seems like a good reason," said Heming. "I can see why my father likes you. If he gives me permission, I would ride out and help you kill this Olaf. He's a man who shouldn't be left alive longer than he's needed."

Grudgingly, Ragnvald found himself warming to Heming. Perhaps he was nothing worse than a handsome and spoiled king's son, no crueler, no worse than any other man with his birth and wealth.

"I mean to sail against Solvi," said Heming abruptly, when they were side by side again. "Would you come with me?"

"With pleasure," said Ragnvald. "If that is where your father sends me."

"I mean to go whether he wills or no. And you can tell him that, if he asks."

"Do you want me to?" It seemed now that this was what Heming wanted from him: if he could not have his father's approval, Ragnvald's might do.

"I don't care," said Heming. Ragnvald did not respond. "He defied his own father when he went to conquer Halogaland," Heming added. "He forgets that." He turned and looked Ragnvald up and down, the sneer returning. "You may keep the horse for the rest of the day," he said. "Return it to me when we camp for the night."

✠ ✠ ✠

THAT EVENING THE procession reached Hakon's ships where he had left them beached on the shore of Lustra Fjord. Hakon's stewards directed men in their loading until the sun dipped below the horizon at midnight.

In the morning, Oddi invited Ragnvald onto Hakon's flagship, with all of his brothers. It was the sleekest ship, and would sail first, camp at the farms and halls of Hakon's allies, while the others stayed on barren islands and wallowed in heavy seas.

The day was chilly and damp, without much wind. Ragnvald took his turn at the oars, until it troubled his wounded shoulder. The wind picked up as Lustra Fjord joined the great Sogn Fjord, whose high walls were lost in fog. He watched the farms go by, high atop cliffs. Near noon they sailed past the market town of Kaupanger, where houses ringed a broad beach. Ragnvald had been there once before, with his father, and seen slaves of all races, men and goods from all corners of the world. The town was rich enough that its elders could hire warriors, and not pay taxes to any king for protection. This Harald might change that.

While they traveled, Heming put aside the clothes that caused him to be called Peacock, and instead wore homespun and leather like any common sailor. That these were of a fine make and hung in some indefinably perfect way from his frame did not escape Ragnvald. At least Heming was practical enough not to wear his silks shipboard.

Hakon's younger sons were near to Ragnvald's age. The middle son, Geirbjorn, seemed to be a slightly more winning version of Ragnvald's own stepbrother. He was stout and brown where Sigurd was skinny and pink, but had that same ingratiating, hesitant quality. He joked with his father, and after each witty phrase he looked around to see what effect his words had made, who smiled, and who ignored him. The youngest, Herlaug, was quiet and sullen, with a colorless face: eyes, lips, and hair all blending into one sandy sameness.

Travel to Yrjar could take as little as two long days in fine weather, but the wind turned fitful when they left Sogn Fjord. As they traveled north, the light grew thinner and paler, like the whey that ran off the fat cheeses Vigdis made in the summer. Oddi told Ragnvald that at the farthest reaches of his father's territory, during the depths of winter, a night came that lasted for a month, and the stars turned a different way than they did to the south. He said also that ghosts and spirits walked those flat, cold lands in the long night. Ragnvald could not work out whether Oddi was jesting with him or not.

Hakon pointed out fjords and islands where he had fought as a young man. He expected his sons and Ragnvald to listen to his stories, and learn from the lessons he would impart. Ragnvald could see from the expressions on their faces, even Oddi's, that they had heard these tales before, but to Ragnvald they were new.

Also new was the way Oddi and his half brothers joked with their father, finishing his tales for him, pointing out that the last time they had passed a particular rocky strand, he had fought a hundred men there, and now it was five hundred.

"See, Ragnvald respects me, at least," he said, laughing, and cuffing Oddi.

Ragnvald smiled, forcing a broad grin, wishing he could be part of their play.

✛ ✛ ✛

AT THE MOUTH of Trond Fjord, two days after they had left the assembly grounds at Jostedal, Hakon's ship stopped at a farm on the island of Smola.

"I spent summers here as a boy," said Hakon, "learning the ways of the sea."

Ragnvald stood near him in the prow as they approached. The island was low and green, with few trees. "It looks a fair place for riding, as well, my lord," he said.

"Yes," said Hakon. "I used to cause a horse fair to be held here in the summer, within easy reach of horse merchants from Frisia. Perhaps I will one day again."

The hall at Smola was constructed in the old style, with a low ceiling and walls of turf to withstand the harsh winds. The steward's wife fed them around the central long fire that night. They drank fermented mare's milk rather than ale, for Hakon said that grain did not grow well under the constant sea winds in this exposed place.

"How does my mare, Erna?" Hakon asked his steward Rathi as they dined that night.

"Her last foaling was difficult on her," Rathi said. "It may have been her last." He was a stooped, bald man with a protruding chin that gave his face a petulant expression.

"Her get is ridden by kings all over Norway," said Hakon. "Let us try for one more."

They spoke of other farm business. When the women were clearing the trenchers away to feed to the pigs, Ragnvald heard Rathi say, "There is a more pressing matter I would trouble you with. You remember Helgunn, the wise woman?"

Hakon nodded.

"Her son was lately killed in a raid upon our coast."

"A raid?" said Hakon. "I had not heard—"

"Some old rovers of Hunthiof's," Rathi continued, "without enough to do. I'm told that king keeps his men too close this summer, for fear of Harald's attack, and they chafe at it."

"Hunthiof and his son must fall," said Heming. "Young Ragnvald knows this is true."

"We sent them off smarting," said Rathi. He gave Heming a baleful look. "Only Helgunn's son was killed."

"And?" Hakon asked.

"And now he will not stay dead," said the steward. A thrill of fear traveled up Ragnvald's spine, and made him shiver where he sat, warming his boots by the fire. He remembered the man at Adisa's farm who had lived with his throat cut, long enough to say words that chilled Ragnvald's blood.

"Helgunn would not consent to have him burned," Rathi continued, "and instead put him in a barrow as though he were a king. Now this wight walks at night, and the peasants are frightened."

"Kill the sorceress, and have done with it," said Hakon. Ragnvald flinched. He had slept poorly since his trial. Now his imagination showed him a vision of a bloodied sword through the throat of a woman whose black hair was streaked with gray, who had only tried to save her son. When she died, she did not cry out in vain but spoke Ragnvald's name. He shook his head, and it wobbled from ale and fatigue.

"We did, of course," said Rathi, his voice sounding to Ragnvald as if it filtered to him through sea water. "But the wight still walks. The sorceress has a daughter, whom we have not found."

Ran was drawing Ragnvald down into her darkness, the fjord waters closing over his head, to whisper things in his ear that he did not wish to know. He felt he could not allow the killing of this daughter, the wight's sister.

"Has the wight killed anyone?" Ragnvald asked. Rathi looked at him for a moment, then to Hakon, who nodded.

"No," said Rathi. "But he is armed. And these creatures, first they feed on the blood of animals, and grow monstrous by it. Then it will kill our children, women, and when it is strong enough to kill our grown men, it will be too late for any but a god to stop it."

Hakon looked worried. "How was the man killed?" Ragnvald asked.

"He took an ax to the skull," said Rathi. "The sorceress Helgunn packed the wound with moss and cobwebs and said mighty spells over him, and though he should lie still, the dead man walks. She said she was only trying to cure him, when we put the question to her."

That was how the tales said it was done, though Ragnvald had a feeling that this wight was not so murderous as the ones in the tales. Or else he just did not like the idea of these women whose protector was dead now condemned by the men of Smola.

Rathi laughed, a mirthless sound. "As though a man can be cured of being dead, once the thread of his life is cut."

"Someone should kill the wight," said Ragnvald without thinking, "not the sister. If the magic lives beyond the mother, then killing her will only make it angrier."

"You?" Rathi asked, rudely.

"Not me," said Ragnvald, though his protest was lost when Heming began talking over him.

"Not Ragnvald alone," said Heming. "I will kill this thing, Father, and if I fall, Ragnvald can stand in my stead."

"No," said Ragnvald, though quietly enough that anyone could ignore him, and they did. It was a fine compliment that Heming should choose him for this honor.

Hakon shook his head. "I would not risk you," he said to his son. Heming looked lost for a moment, and Ragnvald pitied him.

Then Hakon gave Ragnvald a considering look. "It is a brave suggestion. You may go and see to the wight, if you take my son Oddi with you."

"I did not mean to . . . ," said Ragnvald, then trailed off without refusing. He stood to rise or fall in Hakon's eyes by his choices tonight.

He should have stayed silent before; now, between Rathi's ill temper and Heming's ambition, they had volunteered him for this task. He was one of Hakon's men, and Hakon protected Smola. Oddi put on an expression that might have made Ragnvald laugh under other circumstances; he could not seem to decide whether to be glad of his father's notice, or scared of what they must do.

"The wight comes out on cloudy nights," said Rathi. "Perhaps you shall see him tonight."

✢   ✢   ✢

THOUGH IN HIGH summer the sun barely dipped below the horizon at midnight, a gathering storm lent a false darkness to the heath where the wight's barrow stood. Oddi walked a half pace behind Ragnvald as he circled the mound, examining it. The earth had been dug up, though whether the creature had done that or his hunters, Ragnvald did not know. The clouds hid the twilight glow from the sky, and illumination seemed to come from everywhere and nowhere.

"You do get yourself into trouble," said Oddi. "Why did you agree to this?"

"I did not," said Ragnvald.

"You did not object, either. And now this brute is going to kill us. I hope some of Rathi's thrall maidens weep over our terrible fate."

"It's too late for me now," said Ragnvald. "I'll look a coward if I go back." He had ample time to regret opening his mouth since dinner. "You might not," he added, dryly.

"You know that is not true," said Oddi. Ragnvald had been counting Oddi as bolder and wiser than him up until now, but the tenor of Oddi's voice, brittle with fear, made him reconsider. Oddi tried to avoid notice; it might be a wise tactic for him, but it was not the stuff skalds made songs upon.

"This is like the trial," Oddi persisted. "You're plunging ahead out of pride."

"Your father thinks we can do this," said Ragnvald. Or Hakon did not much care if Ragnvald lived, and he was a convenient offering to keep the steward Rathi happy. Still, in the tales, the monster killed the band of men, and fell to a hero's blade. Ragnvald felt a stir of hope that his earlier brushes with death might have given him an advantage here. A breeze fluttered the heads of the wildflowers in the field, the small white motes closed up in the dark. The strange, low light made every blade of grass on the mound stand out in sharp relief. Ragnvald touched his sword.

"I don't like it here," said Oddi.

"You don't have to be here," said Ragnvald, irritably. Oddi's fear could infect him easily, he knew that, if he listened to Oddi rather than focusing on the task ahead. Oddi did not answer. "Maybe I'm supposed to do this on my own," said Ragnvald.

"What does that mean?" Oddi asked, stamping his feet. Ragnvald felt the cold as well, penetrating his leather jerkin and making his skin shudder. "Have you turned prophet?"

Ragnvald did not answer. His vision, or imagining, of the sorceress, who did not deserve death for trying to heal her son, seemed like a fancy now that he was out in the cold. He was no hero, simply because a fisherman had saved him from drowning. He could be sleeping, finally, in a bed that did not sway with the sea's currents. Although he would probably be thinking of the wight tonight anyway. As well he was out here to face it.

"What now?" Oddi asked after Ragnvald was silent for a time.

"We wait," said Ragnvald. "It will come."

He could not count the time, for they had no torches with them, but it seemed like an hour had passed since midnight, perhaps two, when the wind began to rise. It lashed Ragnvald's hair around his face, carrying moisture to his lips that tasted of salt, as though it had been whipped off the sea, not come down from the sky. Ragnvald began to shiver and could not make himself stop. Sorceresses commanded the sea, he knew; perhaps he had been hasty to sympathize with the wight's dead mother.

. Out of the wind and driving rain, it came. A silhouette at first against the charcoal sky, it lurched over the uneven ground. With every step it stumbled, only to recover its balance just before falling. Its clumsiness made it seem more implacable, as though it would plow over and through anything that lay in its path. It had been a big man in life, broad and bearded. Now the face seemed dark, the beard matted.

Far-off lightning crackled behind it. Ragnvald stood staring at it for a moment before recovering enough to draw his sword.

"It is real," said Oddi. Ragnvald fancied he could hear Oddi's nervous swallow, even over the sound of the wind. "A *draugr.*"

"Yes," said Ragnvald with a bravado he did not feel, "and I'm going to kill it."

Ragnvald advanced on the *draugr*, sword in front of him. As he drew closer, he could see that it carried a knife in one hand, and an ax in the other. It moved slowly, yet with a terrible purpose, as though it did not even see Ragnvald and Oddi. Ragnvald approached close enough that he could touch it with his sword, and smell its terrible stench. It made small, animal snuffling noises, and had the heat of a man. It still seemed unseeing.

Ragnvald put his sword to the *draugr's* neck—would it do anything if he cut the throat? Or would it only continue? Its journey had not been stopped by its first death. Fear stayed Ragnvald's hand.

The wight finally turned its head and regarded Ragnvald with bloodshot eyes. It raised the arm with the knife and hurled it. Ragnvald ducked. The blade parted the fabric of his shirtsleeve.

Ragnvald tried to summon from within himself the anger of battle, the single-minded focus that would banish nerves and give him the strength to kill this thing, but found only cold, and fear. Fear that this was not his fight, that he should not be here, that this was folly and he was no hero out of legend.

He stood and looked at it again, into unseeing eyes. The *draugr's* forehead was nearly split in half by the ax blow that had killed it. Black blood stained its cheeks. It pawed at its face, as if trying to wipe the marks away. Ragnvald's stomach twisted when he saw the white of skull through the layers of clotted blood and leaves. He knew he should not be moving this slowly—he should fight, kill, do something—yet he paused and looked at it more carefully, as it stood there. Its skin bore the marks of a hasty washing—someone living had cared for this creature, and recently. The sister.

With that same ponderous slowness with which it walked, it raised its ax. Ragnvald could easily dodge the blow, yet fear and a strange fascination rooted him where he was until the blade whistled near him. The ax glanced off a rock. The wight made no sound beyond its footfalls. It swung arm and ax as if they were both stone, insensible to pain.

A blow from its fist caught Ragnvald on the shoulder, and he stumbled back. It swung again, and this time Ragnvald raised his sword to block the blow. Its movement did not slow. Instead it drove the flesh of its forearm onto the blade. Now Ragnvald moved quickly, recoiling in horror. The *draugr* did not feel pain; it could grab him, could use him to feed its terrible hunger. But it did not grasp when it touched him. It stared down at him, tilting its head like a raven about to rend carrion.

Ragnvald froze. It might not be hungry, but it could still kill him with its terrible strength. It could not feel Ragnvald's sword when it swung its arms—how could Ragnvald kill it?

The grass crunched behind Ragnvald—Oddi coming forward to take up Ragnvald's fight if he fell. He could not let Oddi die in his place. He found his feet again, but stayed in a low crouch. He clenched his sword in his hand, hard, as Olaf had warned against when he had trained him. Hold the sword too tightly and it could be knocked from his grasp. The grip must be gentle and strong.

The wight was still above him, swaying where it stood. Ragnvald raised his sword and drove it up into the creature's throat.

It fell just as a man would, hands scrabbling at the weapon, although unlike a man, it closed its hands around the sword, cutting into its palms, sending blood showering down on Ragnvald. Ragnvald tried to avoid it, for the blood of a *draugr* was cold bile, cursed. It sprayed everywhere, from the creature's mouth, the wound at its throat, its hands. Blood covered Ragnvald's face, and his hands where they were stuck with fear and shock to the hilt of his sword. The *draugr*'s limbs shuddered one last time, and Ragnvald scrambled out of the way so it would not fall on top of him.

Ragnvald breathed heavily for a moment, his hands shaking, and then stood up. His legs could hardly hold him. He felt weak, as though he was bleeding from some great wound. He knew this sensation, though; it was when the touch of Odin, the battle madness that any warrior must partake in, retreated, leaving mere humanity behind. Ragnvald knelt next to the body. A great warrior would probably have spent less time on his rear, he thought sourly. The half-healed cut in his thigh ached.

He had no fear of contagion now; indeed, all his fear had drained away, leaving only weariness behind. He began the bloody work of cutting the head from the body, severing tendon and muscle. He grew tired halfway through the neck bone, sick of the gore, and too weak to do it neatly, so Oddi came and helped him with the last cuts.

"I will tell my father of your bravery," Oddi said, a hint of awe in his voice.

"You would have done it too," said Ragnvald. The wight's blood had started to become tacky on his skin. Perhaps Rathi's thralls would heat some water for him, feed him spiced wine, and wash him clean. Perhaps a comely thrall would warm his bed tonight. Ragnvald tried to feel excitement at that idea, but he was too slicked with blood and his own fear-sweat to imagine touching a woman now.

"No," said Oddi. "I would not. I do not seek fame." He looked at Ragnvald as though he expected a response, perhaps for Ragnvald to recoil in horror at his unmanliness. Ragnvald did not feel like judging any man tonight. He was no braver than Oddi. This wight was not so different than he had been, when Solvi slashed his face and sent him to die. The fisherman had called him a *draugr*.

✢   ✢   ✢

WHEN RAGNVALD AND Oddi returned to the hall, so many lamps were lit, it looked like golden day within. Ragnvald placed the head at Hakon's feet, and tried to keep at bay the hysterical laughter that wanted to bubble up. He could think of nothing so much as the farm cats back at Ardal, laying their tributes of mice and sparrows before Vigdis, their queen.

While Oddi told Hakon what Ragnvald had done, one of Rathi's most beautiful thralls washed the blood from Ragnvald's hands. "We must still burn the corpse in the morning," said Ragnvald, without looking up from this thrall's face. Hakon gave him a flagon of wine to share with Oddi and told the thrall girl to pour it for them.

"Should I toast you?" Oddi asked, as Ragnvald drained his first cup in one draught, and held it out for the girl to refill. She was lovely, with a cap of dark hair, cut short as a thrall's should be, yet Ragnvald looked on her and thought of the *draugr*'s sister, in hiding, of the *draugr* itself, its black blood wetting Ragnvald's hands and face. He wanted to vomit up the wine he had just swallowed.

"I see not," said Oddi, when Ragnvald did not answer. He drained his glass as well. The wine did not taste like much, sour and clay-flavored from its long storage, but after a few glasses, Ragnvald started to feel it in his head, and the horror of the night's work receded somewhat. He had killed before, but this felt different. That had been in an ambush, silent in the night, or even better, surrounded by all of Solvi's men, yelling and screaming to frighten monks who ran away.

"What do you think it felt like, to be half dead like that?" Ragnvald asked.

"You would know, Half-Drowned," said Oddi. Ragnvald did not like this new name Oddi had for him.

"Do you think that—do you think me half dead?" Ragnvald asked. Perhaps he was; perhaps that was why he could not feel pride in this killing, as he had when raiding with Solvi. Perhaps Solvi had cut out that part of him when he fell, or Ran had stolen it in the water, and what emerged was half a *draugr* already.

"No," said Oddi. "I jest . . . when I should not. You did a brave thing tonight."

"Do you think he knew—do you think he was sensible of anything? Do you think he had pain or fear when he died?" He should stop talking; Oddi could not know the answer to these questions. No one could.

"I don't think he felt fear or pain," said Oddi. "He did not seem to. That is why—why I was frightened."

"Do you think he went back to his sister during the day?" Ragnvald persisted.

"Stop," said Oddi. "I do not know why you ask these things, but it cannot help to know. It was an evil creature, and you killed it. Nothing else should matter."

Ragnvald took another drink rather than continue to ask, and when the thrall would have poured him another, he took her wrist instead, and took her into a darkened corner of the hall. Under the blankets, she spread her legs for him, and let him sleep and forget.

14

SOLVI DEPARTED FROM THE GATHERING GROUNDS NOT LONG after Hakon did. He had won enough gold on horse fights and other races to make up for what he had been forced to pay Ragnvald, but he still felt he came away a loser.

There was not a man leaving the *ting* assembly who would not think that Olaf had paid Solvi to kill Ragnvald. Solvi's father would not be pleased about that. Some might even suspect the truth—that it was Hunthiof who had brokered the murder—and he would be even less pleased about that. The longer Solvi delayed, the more likely someone else would carry the news to him, and Hunthiof would have time to burn out his anger before Solvi saw him again.

The men Solvi had brought with him—Snorri, Ulfarr, and Tryggulf—had been his companions since boyhood and followed him in everything. Hunthiof had assigned them to be Solvi's minders when he first decided as a boy not to die from his wounds, not to sit in the corner and be a cripple all his life. He did not remember the fire that cost him his height, and nearly cost him his life. He had a nurse, who said that he passed a year between life and death. He remembered the next year, watching other children walk when he could not, learning to crawl and then dragging himself along on sticks, and finally walking again. He remembered his mother, who had loved him and wanted him to live, but who had been too horrified by his injuries at first to spend much time with him. Then she died of a fever before he could walk again.

Hunthiof had given these men the task of making Solvi into a man and keeping him out of trouble, and when he reached majority, the first thing he asked was for his father to release them from their oath to him, and to ask them to swear loyalty to Solvi instead. He kept them by him now, for not only were they loyal but they reminded him that he could win men to him even as a crippled boy.

They passed a few weeks visiting Solvi's scattered men on the islands that guarded Norway's shore. This one supported only one hut, and enough grass for a family of small, shaggy goats. After enduring the scolding of their host's wife after Ulfarr half knocked down their hovel in a wrestling match, Tryggulf asked, "Are we going back to Tafjord?"

"Yes," said their host, Vathi, scowling at his wife, "go, and then come back with more ships and men." Solvi only traveled in a small skiff with his companions. He had left the horses with a friend on the mainland. "I want to go raiding this summer. You can see my welcome here is piss-poor."

Solvi had been enjoying passing news and gossip with his men who lived here, half in the sea, his true men. They dwelt in rude structures, thick-walled—except Vathi's, it seemed—hardly tall enough for even Solvi to stand up in. They spent their days fishing, harassing other fishermen, or occasionally banding together to take tax from passing merchant ships, if the timing and wind were right. They grew restive quickly, quarreling with their wives and each other, and each asked Solvi when he might put together another raiding party. They had heard that Vestfold grew fat on conquest, and undefended, while Harald's war took him away.

"Maybe if you brought me something pretty next time," said Vathi's wife, "your welcome would be warmer."

"Are you going to impress seagulls with it, woman?" It was clearly an argument they had fought many times before. "I'm saving it."

"Saving it for what? Are you going to be a prince some day?"

"Saving it for a better wife," he muttered.

"Ha, who'd have you?"

"At least I could find a wife who'd give me children." This shut the wife up, and she went into her half-fallen hut. The sounds of her moving heavy cookware issued from within.

"I don't know yet," said Solvi, both amused and discomfited by this display. He had a wife at home, a wife who would be only slightly happier to see him than his father would. If Svanhild were there, she might give him a warmer welcome, and want to hear of his adventures. Or even go on them, though he could hardly picture her here with Vathi and his wife, who stank of fish and sweat, and could do nothing but argue.

If only he could sneak into Tafjord and sneak out with a few ships, he would never need to face them.

"Might be best to stick close to home. I've heard things. Kings' doings," said Vathi. Things Solvi had just finished telling him—most of these men were none too bright. Solvi tried to look patient and interested as Vathi continued, "Well, if you need a good soldier, you know where to find me. I'll make muster, for a little treasure." Vathi looked troubled, though, as well he might, for Solvi had also told him the rest, that standing with Hunthiof might put him on the losing side. Solvi could see no way out of that. If all of Vestfold's armies and all Hakon's lands of Stjordal and Halogaland stood against them, there was nothing to be done.

Or Vathi might only worry about leaving his wife alone again. Perhaps he did not hate her as much as it seemed.

Later that night, Snorri pulled Solvi aside. He did not like to speak much through his ruined mouth, and like many men of few words, those he did trouble to say were worth listening to.

"You cannot avoid it forever," Snorri said to Solvi. Because they had been sailing together for so long, Solvi had no doubt what he meant. He sighed. Of course, Snorri was right. He would have to face his father, and Harald's and Hakon's threat.

"Or is it the girl?" Snorri asked, when Solvi failed to respond.

"What about her?" said Solvi. "She's not here." Sometimes it seemed as though Snorri could read his thoughts. He had dreamed of her last night, and woken up happy, then grown sour as he realized that she was only a dream, that she was far away from him, and if she thought of him, it was with some mixture of dislike and amusement. If he had taken her away before the trials began—but what was done was done.

"She doesn't matter," Solvi said. Though she had liked him, he was sure of that.

✢   ✢   ✢

THEY APPROACHED TAFJORD on a day of pure calm, and had to cover the last leagues by rowing. A dense fog hid the halls. A mass of arguing voices reached their boat before they drew close enough to see anything. No violence, it sounded like, but a crowd had gathered. Solvi saw to the horses and sent Snorri ahead.

When Solvi was finished stabling the horses, he found a great confusion of farmers milling around the kitchen door. Snorri stood on a log, calling for order in his broken voice. No one heeded. Solvi waved his arm over his head, and Snorri leapt down and walked over to take the reins of Solvi's horse.

"It's the delivery of spring vegetables," said Snorri, a thread of panic in his voice. He could pilot a ship through the worst of storms, but a simple household transaction left him floundering.

"Where's Geirny?" Solvi asked. His wife was housekeeper at Tafjord—she should manage this delivery with her steward, Hunvith, and make certain that each farmer had delivered according to his requirements.

Snorri shrugged. "She is sick, I have heard."

Solvi was tired from his journey, but would rather handle this than have to see his father or Geirny. He took Snorri's place on top of the stump, and called for silence. When he exerted himself, his voice could be heard ship to ship in a gale, and he was proud of it. On the post, he was only a hand's breadth taller than the surrounding farmers— and they grew up shorter than well-fed warriors. They knew him for Hunthiof's son, though, and the muttering stopped.

Solvi had grown up riding all over these men's farms. He began calling out their names according to their distance from Tafjord, according to the memories he had of riding to greet them in the days when he had dogged the footsteps of his father's old steward Barni. Now Barni stayed in the hall, for his joints always ached, and played endless games of tafl with Solvi's father. Know their names, Barni had told him, when Solvi wanted nothing more than to adventure across the sea as his father had done. The names of farmers held no excitement next to that.

"Humli, what do you bring this year? How do your shaggy cows?" Humli farmed the upper slopes, and had bred his cows for their thick coats, which he tanned into rugs and wall hangings that made his home the warmest, if strangest-looking, dwelling within walking distance of Tafjord.

"Warm as always," said Humli, bringing forward a sack of spring onions, fragrant through the soiled homespun.

Solvi called out a few more from his perch, then climbed down to walk among them, shake hands, and give out silver to those who had done well this year. He talked with each of them to hear the state of their lands, and who had sheep carried off by wolves. Solvi gifted one wolf-plagued farmer a puppy from one of his hunting dogs.

The farmers lined up their tributes along the outside kitchen wall, except the living beasts, including a calf that would make a kingly roast this fall. These Solvi bade them lead into the byre, where one of the thralls could see to their provisioning. Except for horses, animals did not live long at Tafjord—there should be plenty of space for them.

The last farmer showed Solvi his cart's burden: sacks of turnips from the last season. It was not much, but Solvi recalled that this man's farm stood on the very edge of the arable land, near where the ground became too rocky to farm in the high mountain passes. He could be forgiven. Solvi gave the farmer his tally stick, showing that his tax had been approved, and sent him to the kitchen for some lunch.

Finally Solvi had accepted all the tribute, the cheeses, cabbages, eggs, dripping leather-lined baskets of *skyr*, the skins of ale, all the things that would feed Hunthiof's court over the summer. He invited those farmers that lingered to stay the night for feasting, although he did not know if anything would be prepared for them.

Two large halls stood higher than the sheds and outbuildings that made up Tafjord: the high-roofed drinking hall where Hunthiof feasted his warriors, where tales were told, and feuds began, and the longer, lower-roofed living hall. Solvi entered his home through the kitchen, and found Geirny sitting with his father, playing knucklebones. Geirny giggled when Hunthiof caught her wrist in his hand and prevented her from scooping up the bones before the clay ball bounced again.

"The farmers have brought in their tribute," said Solvi. Geirny tossed the ball again. Solvi threw the tally sticks down onto the table, among the bones. "This is your duty, Geirny."

Geirny tossed her hair. Solvi remembered when he had first seen her, and wanted her. When his father had paid her father, King Nokkve, a steep bride price to buy this beautiful woman for his crippled son.

"I thought my duty was to give you a son," she said.

"Yes," Solvi answered. "And you have failed at that too." He regretted the words the moment he said them, for he could predict what would come next, and it would set servants' tongues to wagging.

"Whose fault is that?" Geirny asked, her voice rising shrill. He should have divorced her long before this, before their relationship had soured so much she would question his manhood before witnesses, but their marriage had also bought peace between Hunthiof and King Nokkve. Solvi's mother had been Nokkve's sister, which made Geirny his cousin. That family connection alone should have bought peace, and would have, if both kings were not so quick to anger.

He had been down this road with her before. If he reminded her that the law gave him the right to divorce her for barrenness, she would cite his twisted legs as the reason none of their sons had lived to take breath. Would Svanhild attack him thus? Probably, he thought, but she would not shirk her duty with the farmers either. Ragnvald had spoken of her on their journey together as the most spirited of women, and Solvi had found her so, spirited and charming.

"Call your steward to bring the tributes into the kitchen and have dinner prepared for the farmers who pass the night here," Solvi commanded Geirny. She looked from him to his father, and brazenly held his father's gaze until he nodded his permission. Solvi thought of Svanhild, and of the ocean, and the men who looked to him for instruction, leadership, life, everything, so he would not rage at his father and Geirny.

"You should let me rule my own wife," said Solvi when she had left.

His father looked slowly up at him, as though Solvi were not worth the effort of turning his head.

"You should be able to rule her," Hunthiof replied.

✣ ✣ ✣

SOLVI KNEW THERE would be no speaking with Geirny until she was out of view of his father. He had built her a separate chamber when they were first wed—such privacy was rare, except for the richest of kings, and he wanted her to feel special, and to boast of his generosity. He found her there, when any halfway competent housewife would have been overseeing the evening's meal. She had a candle lit, though it was daylight, and brushed her hair slowly with a walrus-tusk brush he had bought for her in Dublin.

"Geirny, why did you not manage the farmers today?" He spoke quietly, as he would to a skittish horse. If Geirny became upset, she might not speak for days. "You are housekeeper here, as your mother trained you. You told me before I left that you were bored, and so I gave you more to do."

"Your father bid me play knucklebones with him," she said, not looking at him. "I told him I had work to do, but he insisted."

"Did you argue?"

"He is king here, not you."

"Is that what he said?" Solvi asked, his voice rising.

She rocked back and forth on the bed, a subtle movement he was not even sure she was aware she made. He took a deep breath to calm himself. Geirny was difficult, and had been since her arrival, but she was not at fault here. Hunthiof played games with more than just the sheep's bones, games to remind Solvi who ruled here, and who did not. Games like setting Solvi to kill Ragnvald for Olaf.

"Geirny, if you want a divorce, tell me so. I would not have you stay where you are unhappy."

She looked at him, her eyes focusing on a spot just to the left of his face. "I want a son, husband. Give me a son."

He came to her that night; with the lights out, he found her less disconcerting, only a warm body in the dark that did his bidding. She made few sounds—she did not find pleasure in their coupling, and once the early days of their marriage were past, Solvi no longer tried to give it to her. He lay next to her for a time after his duty was done, listening to her quiet breathing. He could have loved her once. Not, perhaps, with the terrible passion that his father had for Solvi's mother, the kind that burned all in its passing, and had burned out any love his father might still feel, so now he must play games with everyone around him. But love enough for a man to feel for his wife, the mother of his children.

He doubted his seed would catch tonight. He knew of no woman who had borne him a living son. Some few daughters, in Ireland and at other courts, the daughters of thralls, who would grow up to be thralls themselves. Geirny might have been correct—he was not able to make his own sons. Let his father acknowledge another heir. Solvi had men enough to follow his banners, treasure cached in island caves; he did not need his father's kingdom. But he would not leave while his father still wanted him here. His father needed him to defend Tafjord and his right to Maer's land tax from Hakon's grasping sons.

He lay back on the mattress. He would rather his shipboard tent than this, the waves moving underneath him. There was plenty of time to go raiding across the great sea again this year. Or back to Frisia. In previous years he had harried that coast well, but none had followed the Rhine inland past Dorestad to see what riches the deeper country held: Frankish wine, Frankish swords, Frankish beauties, lovely small women who would not look down on him. Or he could go raiding up into Halogaland. The Saami brought in reindeer hide and dried fish that King Hakon sold south, and made him rich. Solvi could skim a little of that bounty. If Hakon went to Vestfold with all his warriors, Halogaland would be undefended.

✢   ✢   ✢

HE HAD THUS far avoided talking with his father about the *ting* trial, but he could not for long. He had grown tired of dreading the conversation, so he lingered in the kitchen the next morning until his father came in and joined him at breakfast.

"I have heard many tales from our farmers," said Hunthiof. The woman thrall who attended the fire grew tense at his tone of voice.

"Olaf is a fool," said Solvi. "He tried to murder Ragnvald outright after the trial."

"And you told everyone that he had asked you to kill Ragnvald. Worse than a fool is the man in the service of a fool."

"I am not the one who made that choice," said Solvi. "You judged poorly there."

"Olaf and his cousin Thorkell are the closest to rulers that Sogn has. You know we needed his goodwill."

"He is a weak and foolish man. His actions at the *ting* proved him so." Ragnvald had been a fool too, but Olaf had proven himself the bigger fool.

"It is not your place to judge me," said Hunthiof, coming to his feet. He towered over Solvi, but most men did. It was not his father's height that cowed him, but years of reminders that Hunthiof could throw him over for another son, a better son, one who would grow as tall as him. He never had, though, for Solvi was the only living child of his beloved wife, and he had promised her.

"Ragnvald will be jarl in Ardal with Hakon's backing," said Solvi quietly. "If we can make peace with him—"

"If this was your thought, why did you not kill Olaf for Ragnvald?"

"I—"

"Because you didn't think, because you wanted the middle route. You have to commit to a course of action, or you'll never make a good king." Hunthiof did not sound that angry, only tired and sad. He had been training Solvi to take his place, when the whim struck him, for as long as Solvi had been alive, and always seemed to find Solvi wanting.

"I'm not sure he would have wanted that—he wanted his own revenge," said Solvi uncertainly. "And he's allied with Hakon."

"He would have owed you," said Hunthiof.

Solvi thought that Ragnvald might not see it that way, not if he was determined to hate Solvi. He might as easily use it as an excuse to take revenge for a kinsman, no matter how much he had hated that kinsman. It was easy to forgive a man who was dead.

He started to say this, but Hunthiof held up his hand. "Done is done. We must speak of Geirny."

"I wish to divorce her and marry someone new," Solvi said. Hunthiof could declare another heir, one of his unacknowledged bastards fostered out to other kings and jarls. He did not seem to ever think of those boys, though, sending them out of sight and never asking of them again. So Solvi, because he wore his mother's face, must live up to all of his father's hopes for an heir. He should have disappointed his father more—then he could raid as he desired, perhaps even take a few ships past England, to see what lay along the west coast of France. Or even into the Mediterranean to Constantinople and beyond. A man with a stout ship had no limits.

"No," said Hunthiof. "Her father would not stand for that."

Solvi had let himself forget that. Divorcing Geirny would probably be insult enough to reopen hostilities with Nokkve. "I should at least take a second wife," he said.

"Do you have someone in mind?" Hunthiof asked. "She cannot be so highborn as to give insult to Nokkve's daughter."

"Svanhild Eysteinsdatter—Ragnvald's sister," said Solvi. He had not spoken of her out loud to anyone except Snorri, Ulfarr, and Tryggulf, and they might as well have been extensions of himself. He hoped his father would not see how much he wanted this.

Hunthiof only laughed. "That's one way to make him an ally, I suppose. If you can do it, then make it so."

"You think?" Solvi asked.

"You need sons, and you need a good housekeeper. You still ought to have killed Olaf, but this may help smooth things, no matter whether Olaf or his stepson survive their battle."

"Then I will return to Sogn," said Solvi, feeling lighter than since he left the *ting* grounds. If Svanhild refused him again, at least he had an excuse to be away from Tafjord for a time. Perhaps he would take a quick raiding trip up the coast before the overland trek to Hrolf's farm. Time might make her bored and soften her anger against him. Svanhild had said no, more than once. Solvi was in no hurry to be refused again.

15

RAGNVALD MARCHED WITH HAKON AND HIS SONS TO BURN THE
body at the barrow and inter the wight's bones next to his mother's.
The villagers came as well to see the creature put to rest. Hakon said
the prayers for the dead. Ragnvald echoed them, and added a few of
his own: for this wise woman he had never met, who had reached past
death to ask Ragnvald to bring her son rest. Ragnvald watched the
wight's skin blacken and blister, and tried not to think of how its flesh
smelled like sacrifice meat roasting at the midsummer feast.

At the margins of the crowd a woman stood, her face almost covered by her scarf. Her bearing was erect and stiff with fright. When
she turned, her scarf exposed a fringe of black hair at her waist. As
the fire died down, the spell of silence holding the witnesses lifted.
The villagers spoke of this evil, and of others that had come before it.
Strange things came out of the sea mists here; this story would join all
the others, until no one remembered the truth of it.

Ragnvald escaped the men who wished to offer him congratulations and chased after the woman. "The sorceress's daughter," he said,
when he caught up to her. He grabbed her arm and spun her around.

She flung the cloak off her head. "Will you kill me now, Ragnvald
Eysteinsson, killer of the dead?"

"Are you dead?" he asked. "I know that—thing—was none of your
doing."

"He was no thing," she said, raising her chin. Her eyes blazed with fury, where her mother's in his vision had been pleading. "He was my brother."

"You know what he was," said Ragnvald.

"He was not a *draugr*," she said, her voice trembling. She was young, younger than Ragnvald had thought. Ragnvald hoped she would not die like her mother had.

"What was he, then?" Ragnvald asked, more gently than he intended.

"He was struck with an ax while defending us. He should have died from the blow, but he did not. My mother tried to heal him." Her eyes met Ragnvald's, pleading this time. "She tried to heal him. He would not be healed. He would have died eventually. He could not even feed himself. But he tried."

"Nothing more than a man trapped between life and death?" Ragnvald asked, angry now that this girl should have lost both mother and brother to foolishness. Foolishness from Hakon and himself, foolishness from Rathi and the men of Smola, too blind to see what the *draugr* really was. "That is a terrible spell. Your mother—" He closed his mouth on the words. He could not tell this beautiful, bold girl that her mother had deserved her death. "She should have let him die. She should have told Rathi what she did."

"She did, but who would believe her?" the girl asked angrily. "And what mother would let her son die? She thought he might live."

"I killed no more than a dead man. He died easily," said Ragnvald, half to himself. It had not been heroism, this killing—he had felt that last night, in his cups, with Oddi. Any child with a sharp stick could have done the same.

"I will tell no one," she said, misreading his words. "You may have the tales sung of your glory."

Ragnvald laughed shortly. "There are many saga heroes who were robbed of their songs today as well," he said. "I will tell Hakon the truth." He looked at her again. Her beauty was like a rock a man could break against. "Will you be safe here?" he asked.

She shrugged. "As safe as I ever was."

"I will tell Hakon it was none of your doing," he said. "And if you are in danger, you can come to me at Ardal. I will protect you. Give me your name, so I may tell all you are under my protection."

"My mother named me Alfrith," she said.

"Wise-beauty," said Ragnvald.

Alfrith nodded. "Men call me Groa, though," she said, and Ragnvald knew her for a warmth-woman as well as a sorceress, who took lovers to keep herself fed, and kept herself barren through her sorcery. Well, women without protectors must make what paths they could. "It only means 'wife,' so it tames men's fear of me."

A wife to many, Ragnvald thought. "Men should fear you," he said. If he were rich, he could keep her as a concubine, for himself alone.

"You flatter," said Alfrith, "but you are right, they should."

⨯   ⨯   ⨯

RAGNVALD WALKED WITH Hakon back to the hall, pulling him away from his sons and retainers to walk along the shore. Seabirds dug for clams in the sand. The waves lapped the shore gently here. Ragnvald took a deep breath.

"It was not a *draugr*," he said. "It was a man, struck in the head with an ax. His mother was only trying to heal a wound she should not." He frowned. "I should tell Heming, and your other sons." Heming's slight, indifferent friendliness had turned cold that night, and Ragnvald could not blame him.

Hakon did not speak for a time. "That is a *draugr*," he said eventually. "What is the difference? He walked, yet he was dead. He did not feel pain. Do you think less of yourself because he could die on your sword?"

Ragnvald did not answer. The *draugrs* in the songs had strength and size beyond mortal men. It took a true hero to kill them, not just luck and a willingness to pursue them. He wondered that the men of Smola had not been able to kill it until now, and said so to Hakon.

"Because they did not do as you did, and go out to try to kill it, fearing they might die in the process."

"I did not want to go," said Ragnvald. He had less desire to admit that than the *draugr's* true nature. "I only—once I spoke, I did not think I could refuse."

"I know that," said Hakon. "But there is no need to worry. You are still the hero my men believe you to be. If you tell them this, they will think it false modesty. Your stepfather did not do well to lead you to question every move you make. It will make you look weak when you are stronger than you think."

Ragnvald thanked him for that. Though he could not see the heroism in it, he liked Hakon for saying so, even as he mistrusted his craving for praise. It must have been this hunger that led his father to earn the name "Noisy" and men's mockery for his boasting.

Though Hakon advised him not to, Ragnvald still told Oddi the truth about the *draugr*, for he could not bear the strange looks Oddi gave him, as if Ragnvald were more than mortal. Oddi said much the same thing as Hakon.

"You still fought it. I feared to." He did not look Ragnvald in the face. "I feared to."

"You would have done it, though," said Ragnvald. He admired Oddi, his prickly humor, the fine line he walked between his brothers. He wanted Oddi for the friend Oddi had named him, before this new constraint.

"You told my father this?" Oddi asked. Ragnvald nodded. "And he said—"

"The same thing you did," Ragnvald replied brusquely. He wanted nothing more to do with this conversation.

"He values you now—now is the time. Ask him for men to take back your father's land. You need not come to war with us, not when you have done him such a service."

"I have done him no service. Had I known—it was no harder than killing a child, and no more honor either."

"You insult my father," said Oddi. "You do not need to ask him for a gift, but do not throw his words in his face."

Ragnvald was taken aback. He bowed his head. "Thank you," he said. "I value your advice." Oddi looked at him curiously. Ragnvald could not read the expression, but at least that strange touch of awe was gone now.

"Do you always make things so difficult for yourself?" Oddi asked. Ragnvald shrugged. He did not like this kind of attention. "Well," said Oddi, "part of me is glad you will not ask him, for I would miss your company on our journey."

"You shall have it," said Ragnvald. "I would not miss the excitement."

They feasted that night, in celebration of Ragnvald's victory. They would sail to Yrjar on the morning tide. Hakon bade Ragnvald sit next to him, and share his fine Frankish wine.

Soon Ragnvald had toasted enough times with him so that he did not worry at Rathi's glares or his own lingering sadness at the deaths of the sorceress, or healer, and her son. The skald who traveled with Hakon sat down by Ragnvald's side to hear him tell the tale again, so he could make it over into poetry. Ragnvald told it as best he could, with his head swimming from exhaustion and drink. He kept to himself what Alfrith had told him, that perhaps a spell held the young man in life, but he was no *draugr*, just a man whose wits had been riven from him with an ax. He told of his fear instead, of the wind that rippled the grass, how the *draugr* came, and how it felt no pain, how its breath stank, how its blood burned. The skald seemed well satisfied.

When he found his bed, he dreamed that he slew the creature again, and it spoke to him, words that Ragnvald could not recall on waking. He lay on his bench, looking up at the earthen ceiling, and wondered if Odin collected those slain as the *draugr* was, doubly slain in battle. Perhaps that was a riddle the hanged god would like.

✣   ✣   ✣

THE WEATHER TURNED fine as Hakon's ship approached Yrjar, home of Hakon's fort. Hakon's younger sons, Herlaug and Geirbjorn, sought Ragnvald out to share watches with him, and asked him to judge who reached the bow first when they ran along the gunwales. The flotilla sailed into Yrjar in late afternoon five days after they departed Smola, to find the small harbor swelled with ships.

"Is it not too many ships for raiding?" Geirbjorn asked his father. He leaned forward over the gunwale next to his father.

"How many ships did you go to Ireland with?" Hakon asked Ragnvald.

"Ten," said Ragnvald shortly. He was beginning to see how Jarl Runolf had run afoul of Hakon's sons, for Hakon liked to set Ragnvald against them in conversation, putting up Ragnvald as an example that his sons should follow. No wonder they had grown to hate Runolf, if Hakon had used him thus.

"And was that too many?" Hakon asked.

"Sometimes yes, sometimes no," said Ragnvald. "Some harbors were too small, and it was hard to feed so many men. But when we sacked the monastery, they could not resist us." A few monks had wielded axes. Most had died without ever raising a hand to defend themselves. The berserks who accompanied them had made sport of the ones who lived in ways that Ragnvald did not wish to remember.

"We will divide our forces when necessary," said Hakon. "You will see. But more is"—he spread his hands—"more. We go to war now. Everything will be different."

He pulled Ragnvald in for a private conference near the bow. "You have pleased me," he said.

Ragnvald bowed his head, and said his thanks. He had been pleased with Hakon as well, although that would matter to Hakon less.

"I wish my sons were more like you, and I wish to keep you close as an example to them." Ragnvald had imagined what it might be like to be one of Hakon's sons. Perhaps he would be as proud and boastful as them if he had not his father's memory to compare himself to, and a living stepfather who had been ever harsh and critical.

"I think you will go far," Hakon continued. "I would have you swear to me, at the welcome feast." A king's sworn man—it was an honor, even if Oddi was right, and Hakon owed this to him after the killing of the *draugr*. He would give Ragnvald gold rings, and a share of their plunder, and in return Ragnvald must praise his king's name and fight for him. If he failed in his loyalty, he would be known as an oath-breaker, and no other man would trust him.

"I thank you," said Ragnvald. "I will swear."

✜ ✜ ✜

YRJAR WAS A masterpiece of earthwork. A moat skirted the sloping walls of turf that surrounded the hall and outbuildings, enclosing enough space to hold many families and their livestock. Four entrances cut through the earthworks—choke points for any attack.

After they beached the ship, Ragnvald followed Hakon's procession in through the western entrance under the watchful eyes of Hakon's sentries. Inside the walls another ditch lined with sharp stakes protected those within from attack over the top of the walls. Even with the help of draft animals and iron tools, this fort must have taken generations to build. The hall it protected was finely made too, in the new style, with supporting posts set as close to the outer walls as possible. Ragnvald had not been inside such a hall, but he had heard the proportions were far more graceful, more suited to men standing upright than an old-fashioned hall with its low beams. In Olaf's hall the space was so subdivided that three men could not stand abreast anywhere within.

The great doors of the hall opened, spilling light from dozens of torches and oil lamps out onto the shadowed ground. Within, the hall was packed with men, lining benches and tables. Dogs squabbled between them. Men urged them on with bones and taps on curly flanks. Ragnvald followed in the wake of Hakon and his sons to the front of the hall.

On the dais stood two imposing men. One was old, with blond hair fading to gray, still rangy like a warrior, with long mustaches that fell on either side of a dour mouth. Tangled golden hair crowned the other; a half-grown golden beard hid half his face, though not his blue eyes and brilliant, gap-toothed smile. He still carried himself like a boy, not a warrior, long limbs held loosely as he bounced on the balls of his feet. These would be Harald and his uncle Guthorm, the prophesied king and his trusted adviser.

Ragnvald thought of his dream, for this boy's hair held the brightness of youth, the brightness of gold glimmering in sunlight, while Hakon's gold had faded with time. Still, Heming was another blond head—any of them might be his golden wolf, or none of them.

A woman who might have been twin to both of them stood a half step behind—this would be Ronhild the Sorceress, clothed in blue and scarlet. Songs had named her the most beautiful woman in all of Vestfold when she was younger, and she was not too old now to hide the truth of those words. Blond hair swept back from her high brow. She had finely shaped cheekbones, and a full lower lip. She could take any man as a lover she wanted still, even as she grew into those virtues reserved for men and women in middle age: wisdom, far sight, shrewd bargaining.

"Well met," said Guthorm. He and Hakon exchanged bows.

"How many men did you get?" Harald asked eagerly.

"Another hundred at the Sogn *ting* and surrounding areas," said Hakon.

"Our force betters yours now," said Heming.

Harald bristled. His uncle shouldered in front of him. "The bigger the force, the faster other kings will fall to us," he said.

"Yes," said Harald. "Like the seven kings in Hordaland."

"We will discuss it more later," said Hakon. "Tonight we feast, to bid welcome to the new warriors."

Ragnvald was seated near the dais, among Hakon's richer warriors, where he felt the shabbiness of his patched leather armor and bog-iron sword. He had not reckoned up how many fine young men Hakon had gathered for his war-making, until he saw those already gathered to feast. He would have to fight bravely to distinguish himself from them.

How motley Solvi's crew had been in comparison. Now Ragnvald did not doubt Hakon's power, for those he had already gathered looked like warriors out of legend, broad shouldered and well armed. The men of Solvi's crew had been tough, yes, but grown old too soon, sword-bitten, gripped by the knowledge that each battle could be their last. Hakon's men were in their prime, few maimed or disfigured yet from fighting. What farmers' sons swelled their ranks would soon be turned into warriors, with these men for company.

At his table he introduced himself and met in turn: Dagvith, a younger son of a jarl from the east; Dreng, a Danish adventurer, who spoke Norse with an accent that Ragnvald had to work hard to understand; and Galti, eldest son of a coastal jarl slain by Solvi Hunthiofsson. After giving his name and homeland to a slew of new faces, Ragnvald accustomed himself to saying he was from Sogn. Near South Maer, if the man asked further. No one had heard of Ardal, as they had on Solvi's ship. Men here came from far away, from Vestfold or even across the Baltic Sea, from the settlements of Danes and Swedes on those far shores.

"I mean to kill Solvi," said Galti when he heard Ragnvald's name. He said it with a snarl, and Ragnvald knew he was expected to argue that Solvi was his to kill. Ragnvald did not know whether to be pleased or not, that people knew his story when they heard his name.

"I wish you every chance," Ragnvald said, reaching toward the center of the table to break off a chunk of barley bread. "You could have done it at the Sogn *ting*. He traveled with few men." Galti scowled—it seemed he had hoped to bait Ragnvald. Ragnvald did not let this trouble him; his stomach commanded more attention, growling at the rich scent of meat that filled the hall. Steam from the tureens on the tables carried foreign spices to his nose. Hakon must be richly provisioned that he could keep these warriors at his table, week after week.

Galti pared a scrap of something from under his fingernails with his dagger and, after examining it, worried it between his teeth. Ragnvald ladled a generous serving of the meat and cabbage stew onto his bread with a wooden spoon.

"I heard you had reason to avenge yourself on him," said Dagvith, the jarl's son, his eyes wide and guileless. He was a young giant with plain, oversize features, and wore his size as if he had not yet accustomed himself to it. His hair was a natural sun-streaked gold, as were the uneven strands of beard dusting his chin.

Ragnvald touched the scar on his cheek. It hardly pained him at all now, but he could feel the difference in every movement of his face—a constant reminder of the cold end of every life. "What?" he said, "You do not think Solvi made me prettier?"

That drew a laugh from Dagvith. Ragnvald dug into his food with pleasure. It was goat—Hakon's generosity only extended so far. Golden fat studded the broth, and the well-stewed meat melted between his teeth and tongue.

Galti still looked at Ragnvald suspiciously. "No, he did not," Galti said. Ragnvald resolved to keep a careful eye on him. A man who could not laugh made a dangerous foe—Ragnvald knew that much from Olaf.

"Solvi Hunthiofsson tried to kill me, but he failed," said Ragnvald. "And I have reason to believe he held the knife for my stepfather. He is my true enemy."

"This Ragnvald is a thinker," said Dreng the Dane, "not a hammerheaded know-nothing like you, Galti." The men scowled at each other, but Ragnvald had the feeling that they knew each other well, and these words counted for little between them.

The hall fell quiet as Hakon's lead skald stepped forward. He was young for someone of that profession—usually they were old or crippled men, useless for farming and war-making. Then he took up the small harp that sat by his side, and Ragnvald noticed the perfect care in his movements, and the way his eyes followed behind his hands. He was blind, probably from birth or some childhood fever, rather than injury. He could not be a man, could not be a warrior, so he chose this instead.

The harp too was unusual—no Norse crafted them. Ragnvald had only seen their like among the treasure pillaged from Ireland. The skald gave his name, and those of his ancestors, then began his tale. He spoke in the kenning-rich phrases of poetry, with a riddle in every line, accompanying himself by strumming his harp. He told the tale of Hakon's father, and how he expanded his territory to pass it to his son, then how Hakon had further expanded it.

Few sitting at the feast would not already know this story, and still they listened intently. There were lessons here, buried in the alliteration, lessons of vengeance and generosity, punishments for those who erred and rewards for the brave. And lessons too in how Hakon saw himself and wished the world to see him. The Hakon in the tales was wise and thoughtful. The Hakon sitting in his chair at the head of the long tables nodded when some clever phrase was put in his mouth, and frowned at the moments that illuminated his hastiness.

The tale held equal measures of both. Hakon had been exiled for three years to Orkney for killing his uncle, his mother's brother. The tale made much of the insults that had passed between them, for if it had not, Hakon would come out of the story as a kin-slayer. Three years of exile were not enough to pay for such a sin. Hakon's face grew easier when the tale passed from the insult pole his uncle had raised to him, past the duel, during which Hakon had cut off his uncle's legs and left him to crawl out of the dueling circle to die, finally to the years of Hakon's exile. Hakon had won great fame in Orkney, making daring raids against Scottish settlements in the Hebrides, and winning more land for Norse settlers.

Ragnvald watched Guthorm and Harald as the skald spoke. Harald looked attentive for the first few minutes, then bored, then started flirting with the woman who shared his cup. Her looks reminded Ragnvald of Heming—this must be Hakon's daughter Asa, whom Harald had lately married.

Against his will, Ragnvald felt a little pity for Heming—in the shadow of such a great father, he must hunger for glory, some way to make his own name remembered. The powerful men of the district leaned their heads close to one another and spoke in low voices. Dagvith had some familiarity with them and told Ragnvald their names and relationships. When the song ended, Heming walked behind them, speaking words in one ear and then another. Some were pleased by what he said, some discontented. Ragnvald thought perhaps he was trying to gather support for his attack on Solvi. Hakon could not but know of it, not when Heming spoke so boldly.

The final stanzas of the song were standard praise-words for Hakon, and then it wound to a close. Members of Hakon's court stood to give toasts to his greatness. Hakon accepted a few of these and then raised his hand to end them. At some unspoken signal, thralls and servants came into the hall with casks of sweet summer ale. The skald sang the first few words of a drinking song in his loud, pure voice, and the assembled warriors took it up.

Hakon caught Ragnvald's eye and beckoned him to join the fine lords at the head of the table. "Drink with us, Ragnvald," said Hakon. Heming flashed Ragnvald a look he could not read, and Ragnvald thought again of Runolf's fall at the *ting*, the contest he could never win.

Ragnvald thanked him uncertainly. Hakon's hall was filled with men who could call themselves Ragnvald's betters. His grandfather had been a king who could stand with any of them as an equal, but his father Eystein had thrown that away.

"You must take the place you desire, Ragnvald," said Hakon, seeming to read Ragnvald's uncertainty in his face. He put a hand on Ragnvald's shoulder and turned him so Ragnvald looked down the length of the hall. The soapstone lamp overhead swung slightly on its chain, and the shadows of the assembled men moved with it, making them look for a moment as if they were under water, in Ran's chilly hall. Ragnvald shivered, even in the heat of the crowded room. He sat down next to Hakon.

"I see you watching everyone so carefully," said Hakon in a voice too quiet to be heard by any but Ragnvald, "and I think: I do not know if this man can be trusted."

"I meant no—," Ragnvald started, too loudly.

"It is good to look, to see how things stand, but guard your face better," said Hakon. Ragnvald nodded, acknowledging the advice. It was a great compliment that Hakon chose to lesson him. "Tell me what you see in these men."

Ragnvald saw heads bowed over drinking horns and dishes of food. Galti looked around at the other warriors jealously. Dagvith—the son of wealth and nobility—his expression held nothing but pleasure at good food and strong ale. Dreng the Dane smiled cruelly at something Ragnvald could not hear. He would sow discord wherever he went, and blame it on Galti if he could, or anyone else unfortunate enough to be near him if he could not. Behind them two dogs fought over a bone, while a larger one circled the fight, growling and raising the fur on the ruff of its neck.

Closer by, he saw men caught up in drinking and dicing. One warrior past his prime, a voluble drunk, spoke urgently to his companion, who ignored him.

"I see many things," said Ragnvald. "What do you want of me?"

"You can do better than that. Who will lead, and who will follow? Who will the skalds sing of tomorrow?"

Ragnvald sighed. "Dreng the Dane is sly as Loki, and will find nothing but trouble, no matter how clever his schemes. Galti envies every man everything he owns and will die on some sword or another." He glanced at young Harald and his uncle, at Hakon's jarls, sitting close by. He had opinions of them too and dared not speak them.

"Tell me what else," said Hakon. "You will not anger me."

"Jarl Ingimarr is concerned about something that is not the coming war, something that does not bode well for your son Heming," said

Ragnvald slowly. Ingimarr, as if in answer to Ragnvald's low-spoken words, glanced at Heming Hakonsson and then again at his hands, tracing sword calluses with his fingers.

"Jarl Hafgrim is eager for wealth, and wishes not to tarry long in your hall." Ragnvald tilted his head. "Perhaps he is even more eager for bloodshed."

"And Jarl Vekel?" Hakon prompted. Ragnvald saw a young man, scarcely older than himself, nervousness making his eyes shift and fingers dance.

"Between those two wolves, Vekel will not long hold his lands, will he?" Ragnvald asked, purely a guess this time.

"And what do you think of young Harald and his uncle?" Hakon asked, very low.

"Harald is young and ruled by his uncle," said Ragnvald. "His uncle is ambitious. This is no more than any man will have seen, though."

"Which of the men would you follow?" he asked Ragnvald.

"I've chosen who I would follow." Ragnvald inclined his head slightly toward Hakon.

Hakon nodded back to acknowledge the flattery. "Were I not here, who would you follow?"

"Anyone who would grant me space in their ship," said Ragnvald. "I am poor."

"And honest," said Hakon.

"Flattery works best on vain men," said Ragnvald.

Hakon threw back his head and laughed. "That was well calculated. You flatter me by telling me you flatter me not. Listen to what I tell you: many men are followers. How did you know what you told me tonight?"

Ragnvald cleared his throat. "I guessed."

"You guessed better than men who have been my councilors for twenty years. Ingimarr is father to the woman my son wants to marry. He does not want the marriage to happen, even though he is my friend and ally. Can you guess why?"

"Are you certain you wish me to say?"

"I am," said Hakon gravely.

"Your son Heming is hotheaded and . . ." Ragnvald hesitated. These words would sound calculated, as if Ragnvald wanted Heming's place.

He did want Heming's place, but that did not make them less true. "I wonder if he is not too proud to be well liked. Something I know aught of." Hakon smiled slightly at Ragnvald's assessment, and did not contradict him. "He killed a jarl you valued, out of jealousy. Ingimarr fears the same for himself if he refuses, but he fears it too if he agrees. Like Runolf, he will be in a position where he cannot win."

"What should I do? I value both of them."

Ragnvald knew this was a test, as with every other word he had exchanged with Hakon this night. "Send Heming away," he said. "You hold lands in the Faeroe Islands, do you not?" Ragnvald had learned this from the tale told tonight. "He should make sure those lands still feel the allegiance they owe."

"You do not wish to go to war by his side," said Hakon.

That was not what Ragnvald had meant. He was sure Heming was brave, and he said so.

"Brave and foolish," said Hakon. "I know he tries to gather support for an unsanctioned raid."

"He wants to win your admiration."

"He should just do it, then. He frets and plans like the old woman who starved to death because she could not decide which honey cake to eat first. Still, he is my son. I would not send him away."

"You have other sons," said Ragnvald carefully.

"He is the only son of my beloved wife Asa, may her barrow be warm and her rest peaceful," he said. "I wished . . . I will think on what you said. I fear Heming is a sword at my back as long as he is here." Ragnvald almost corrected this too: his reading of Heming Hakonsson said that while he might kill anyone who took his father's attention, he would die himself before doing his father harm. But if Hakon sent him away, it would be far better for Ragnvald's safety, so he kept his lips shut over the words.

"You honor me by listening to my counsel," he said instead.

"Tell me, where was this wisdom when you stood on the trial ground?" Hakon asked, laughing.

"Olaf angered me," said Ragnvald. "I was foolish."

"Anger is a pilot who always steers his ship onto rocks. It is a poor guide."

Perhaps so, but Olaf angered Ragnvald even now. "If he had only—if he had done what he swore. I would not have turned him out. I respected him as a father."

"He already has a son," said Hakon. "Two."

Ragnvald should have seen that, of course. It was hope that had made him think Olaf would honor his promise, hope and foolishness.

"He has a son he has cosseted and raised as less than a man. And Hallbjorn is a baby still. I did not think"—Ragnvald took a deep breath—"he did not act as though he wanted Sigurd to inherit. He was my father's friend."

"Perhaps he thought he was doing Sigurd a service by going easy on him," said Hakon. "Men are often unwise with their sons." His forehead creased, and Ragnvald's anger receded enough for him to wonder if Hakon thought of himself and his own sons, or of his father.

"Drink no more tonight, Ragnvald Eysteinsson," said Hakon. "I want you to be the first man to swear to me, and I want your words to be clear." At Ragnvald's surprised look, he smiled, lifting the ends of his long mustache. "Sit. Eat your meat. Be ready."

16

THE DAYS PASSED SLOWLY AT HROLF'S FARM. WHENEVER SVAN-
hild could, she asked for work outdoors with the sheep and goats.
Hrolf had few cows, for they could not survive well on such sparse
grass. She stayed outside all day long, her hands growing brown in the
sun, only coming inside and exposing herself to the barbs and sniping
of Hilda's sisters when she had to.

Herding the animals, she was thrown into the company of Hilda's
brother Egil. Because of his betrayal at the trial, whenever he tried to
engage her in conversation, she answered as shortly as possible without being rude.

"Why do you treat me so ill?" he asked one night when he came to
fetch her from the far field for dinner. She tucked her spindle into her
belt, took the loop of wool from her wrist, and tucked that in as well
before answering him. His tone was querulous, and he thrust his head
forward on his narrow neck like a goose.

"Need you ask? You could have testified for my brother—with the
truth, not those half-lies—and you did not."

"I told the truth," said Egil stiffly.

"And did you tell the truth when you came to Ardal before?"

He frowned. "I like you," he said. "Ragnvald told me how charming you were. He thought that we might make a match."

"I am the granddaughter of a king," said Svanhild, angry at Ragnvald as well now. He had promised her better than this coward. She

could not imagine that anyone other than Egil thought this match a good idea. Certainly Hrolf could not like it. "Why should I be yoked to you?"

"Ragnvald thought it good enough that he should be married to my sister," said Egil, hotly.

"That is because he is stubborn and would not break the promises they made as children," said Svanhild. "He is with Hakon and his sons now. He will come back and marry your sister, I am sure, and it will be a great favor to your family."

"You set yourself far too high," Egil said. "What free man cannot count a king among his ancestors? Your father lost his land and then his life."

"And my brother will gain it all back and more, while you cower in fear," said Svanhild. She had little memory of her father, except the impression of brightness and happiness that he carried with him. She laid this over stories that Ragnvald told her of him—how he won their mother Ascrida in a game of dice with Ascrida's father, and when he tried to claim his winnings, she harnessed horses to a sledge and drove up into the mountains. He found her later, waiting for him, bundled in furs. She told him he was late, but a man who would ski after a woman into the woods on the darkest night of the year could be forgiven. Svanhild could never reconcile that woman with her silent mother. Olaf had much to answer for.

Egil clenched his fists, and for a moment Svanhild thought he might strike her. In her anger she almost welcomed it. If he hit her, she would hit him back, and scratch and bite too. He would see he could not talk to her that way. He turned and walked away instead, though, back toward the hall above the fields.

Hrolf came out of the house a few minutes later and dragged her back by the arm. "You will give my son respect while you're under our roof," he said as he shoved her into the main room by the elbow.

"You never wanted me here," said Svanhild. She heard Hilda's intake of breath. His women tiptoed around his moods, but Svanhild had grown up with the much more fearsome Olaf. Hrolf did not frighten her.

"Indeed, I do not," said Hrolf. "You tempt my daughter into unseemly displays. You make her unable to forget about your idiotic brother."

"My brother is worth ten of you, or your cowardly son."

"If you were a man, I would kill you for that." Egil put his hand to his knife as though he might do it anyway. Svanhild felt the eyes of Hilda's sisters upon her.

"Father, you know that—," Hilda began.

"As it is," said Hrolf, speaking over Hilda, "your guardian will pay the insult price."

"Are you not her guardian, Father?" Hilda asked. Svanhild looked at her gratefully.

"No. Yes. I'm not sure." Hrolf stroked his beard, thoughtful now that he was engaged in a question of law. "This is an odd circumstance. Her brother is her guardian, I suppose. If he still lives."

"He lives," Svanhild said.

"If not, I suppose it's your stepfather. Or even myself." He brought his attention back to her. "Svanhild, you will not speak with Egil anymore, except as a proper guest. You are not a child. You should not behave as one. I am the closest to a guardian you have in this district, unless you'd rather go back to your stepfather. And since your stepfather began the task of finding you a husband, I will continue it."

✢   ✢   ✢

SVANHILD LAY IN the bed she shared with Hilda and Ingifrid, listening to their breathing and trying to decide what to do next. She did not trust Hrolf to find her the right husband, a man of her station who she would not hate, who would not mistreat her—if possible, a man who could help Ragnvald, an ally, not a vassal. She thought immediately of Solvi—everyone at the *ting* had thought that he was trifling with her, showing his contempt for Ragnvald, and later Olaf. Svanhild did not think that was his reason, though, or at least not all of it. He, a king's son, had offered marriage in the end. True, she would be a second wife, and she was the granddaughter of a king, but she had been raised as the stepdaughter of a yeoman farmer, no better than any of their neighbors. She had no great dowry to tempt Solvi, so it must be for herself. He was handsome as well, though too short for a warrior, and under his trousers, his legs would be badly scarred. Perhaps women refused him because of that. She recalled, with a rush of heat to her cheeks, riding with him before she knew who he was. He had not felt less than a man, pressed up against her.

She shied away from the direction her thoughts were taking. Solvi was a man without honor, a man who made enemies more easily than allies, and everyone at the *ting* said he would be on the losing side of the wars that threatened. It was no great shame to sell his sword in lawful battle, but in treacherous murder—no, she could not think of him for a husband. Solvi had blithely admitted to trying to kill Ragnvald. As if killing Ragnvald were a joke to him. Now he played with her the same way. He would not think of her, except as a prize that had slipped through his fingers, no more important than a silver arm ring.

She turned over, in a huff. Hilda muttered in her sleep, pulling back blankets that Svanhild had tugged with her. Let Hrolf find her a husband, then. He could probably only manage a betrothal without Ragnvald's consent and dowry. By law, she might refuse a marriage, although if a man carried her off and raped her, and gave her guardian a proper bride price, she would still be married. Could Hrolf intend that—did he believe in Ragnvald's return so little?

Certainly, Hrolf would not be willing to dower her. He might choose one of the farmers he knew to the south, with land close to Ardal, far from Hrolf's own farm. Perhaps her husband would be overseas frequently. Perhaps he would die and leave her an independent widow. Then she might take lovers, if she wished, as long as she took care not to get pregnant. It was a wonder more women did not murder their husbands. Perhaps they were scared of being alone.

She must not tell Hilda of this—Hilda who feared even to think of the things that were a woman's proper pleasures. She wondered that Hilda had found the courage to make her claim on Ragnvald so publicly. The Hilda she knew now, at Hrolf's farm, was not so bold. She rolled over gingerly, trying not to disturb Hilda or Ingifrid, and willed morning to come soon. For a moment she missed Vigdis. Vigdis knew the tricks of being a woman in a man's world, of gaining power and anything else she wanted. What she wanted was different than what

Svanhild did, but at least she was not as passive as the other women Svanhild knew.

✢ ✢ ✢

"SVANHILD, YOUR STEPMOTHER makes a notable seedcake. Do you know how to make it?" Bergdis asked one morning. Threshing time began today, as the gods Frey and Freya had decreed, and so the household was hosting a feast.

Svanhild said yes, and showed her how it was done. She had exchanged few words with either Hrolf or his wife since the day she insulted Egil.

After the cooking was done, Bergdis sent Svanhild to take a bath as guests started arriving, saying that it was a gift on her feast day. Thralls had heated the water, and it was very pleasant. Usually she had to wait until all the sisters had taken their baths before being allowed to take hers. She brushed her hair by the bath's fire, watching the sparks that flew every time a droplet of water hit the burning wood.

As Svanhild returned to the hall, guests approached from the west. She recognized many of them from the *ting* assembly, or from nearby farms. She was about to go back into the kitchen and see what else needed to be done when she saw a familiar figure dismount from a horse. For a moment, she feared it was Olaf, and her comb slipped out of her sweaty hand, but when she drew closer, she saw Thorkell, like Olaf, tall and with coloring like yellowed wood, wearing a deep red cloak. So this was why Bergdis had given her first bath.

Hrolf would not give her back to Olaf, but he would do the next best thing. She ran into the kitchen.

"Thorkell is here," she said to Bergdis and Hilda, who was also arranging meat on platters. "Do you think Olaf sent him?"

"No," said Bergdis, tucking Svanhild's hair behind her ears. "My husband invited him. He thought you would be glad to see him."

Svanhild drew back from Bergdis's touch. "He would not think that. Olaf wanted me to marry Thorkell."

This did not have the impact on Bergdis that Svanhild was hoping. "And you did not wish it?" Bergdis asked.

"No," said Svanhild angrily.

"I don't see why not," said Bergdis. "I would think that you would want to make peace between your brother and your stepfather. That is a woman's truest work."

Svanhild supposed that some tales spoke of peacemaking women, but she far preferred the women who urged on their reluctant men to make war and revenge. "Ragnvald would not want this. Why would Hrolf?" she asked in a small voice.

"Do you truly fear him so much, Svanhild?"

Svanhild shook her head. It was not him she feared so much as her helplessness.

"Then remember, you are our guest and he is our guest," said Bergdis with finality. "You will both be courteous to each other."

"Tell *him* that," said Svanhild. It would be discourteous if he carried her off.

☩   ☩   ☩

HROLF'S HALL HAD more than enough women to serve during the feast, and Bergdis sent Svanhild to sit at Thorkell's side, sharing his cup, as she had at Ardal. She sat woodenly next to him, trying to keep her body from touching his, but she could not avoid it when he pressed up against her.

"Who is it that I pay a bride price to now?" Thorkell asked, trying to jest with her. "You have so many guardians."

"And too few," Svanhild muttered, half to herself.

"I hope to remedy that."

"You pay a bride price to no one," she said woodenly. "Without my brother's agreement, it is my right to refuse this match, and I will."

His smile faded, and she grew fearful again. "Hrolf sent a messenger saying that you would be pleased to leave here," he said.

"I would," she said, "but not with you. My stepfather means neither me nor my brother any good. Marry one of Hrolf's daughters, not me."

"I do not want one of Hrolf's daughters. You are comelier than any of them."

Svanhild supposed that was meant to please her. Thorkell was more gallant than she had any right to expect from a man a generation older than her, but that only made her feel more trapped.

"You want me because you think you can control my brother through me," said Svanhild. "I will be your hostage against him, when he comes for Olaf."

"You have a suspicious mind," said Thorkell. "You will be old before your time." He laughed, though it sounded hollow. "Squinting as you count chickens, accusing the thralls of stealing them."

"Not in your hall," said Svanhild, shaking her head. Some tears escaped her eyes, and she rubbed them away. "Please do not ask this of me. Do not embarrass my host and yourself."

He tightened his hand on her arm. "I was promised you, Svanhild Eysteinsdatter, and I mean to have you, one way or another. Who here will stop me, if that's what I want?"

Svanhild choked and looked around the feast, to see who was witnessing this. Hilda's sister Malma looked at the two of them, considering, but around them conversations continued, and men made wagers on dice, drank deeply of another man's wine, or flirted with Hrolf's women. Svanhild was alone in this throng. Thorkell gripped her still.

"No one will stop you," she said, bowing her head. No one would. Ragnvald would not come in time. Hilda might cry for her, but she would not stop it. A woman must get married, Hilda would think, one way or another.

"Understand that well," said Thorkell. "I will not be such a bad husband as that. You only need firm managing."

"Yes," said Svanhild, still with her head down. He must think that she submitted. "I understand."

✣   ✣   ✣

SVANHILD EXCUSED HERSELF as early as she could from the feast to do the night's outdoor tasks, fetching water and bringing uneaten food to the pigs. Once she agreed that Thorkell could do what he wished with her, he had become friendly again. He should marry Hilda, Svanhild thought. At least she was big enough to bear his monstrous children. Thinking of lying in bed with him, of him touching her any more than he had tonight, sparked the same panic she had felt when Olaf and Vigdis tied her up. She did not want to be at anyone's mercy.

The pigs were in a stone pen next to the kitchen. Svanhild threw them sodden trenchers and watched the ensuing fight. At Ardal, they let the pigs wander free. Here they had to fear the wolves that came out of the forest. If Svanhild must be fearful everywhere, if even here she was not protected, then she should go to Ragnvald, who at least would not try to sell her to a man she did not want.

From the kitchen door, Bergdis called her name. Svanhild set her jaw and walked across the grass. She must not betray her decision, and she must leave tonight, before Thorkell suspected anything and carried out his threat.

"You were a good girl tonight," said Bergdis, giving Svanhild a quick hug and a kiss on the temple. It was only because she had not made too much trouble that Bergdis praised her, yet tears sprang to Svanhild's eyes. She could be loved and understood by these women, if only she followed the path they had laid out for her. Bergdis wanted her in the same bondage she had pledged her life to, wanted Svanhild's threat removed, her care turned into someone else's responsibility. Svanhild ducked her head, not having to pretend shyness. Let Bergdis think her modest about her upcoming wedding.

Hilda wanted to talk that night, to persuade herself that Svanhild did not blame her or her father for Thorkell's coming. Svanhild answered shortly and said she was tired, and soon enough she heard Hilda's snoring and knew she slept. She waited until the whole household and all of the visiting farmers had fallen into the drink-sodden sleep that followed feasts. She sat up and heard muffled sounds of pleasure coming from somewhere in the hall. A farmer and his wife, or perhaps two of the thralls were doing what they could not when their masters were awake.

Svanhild got carefully out of bed and tiptoed past the curtain that hid her chamber from the rest of the hall. She made her away around the servants who slept in the kitchen, into a storeroom off to one side. Moving as quietly as she could, she took a pile of hard rye loaves off a shelf and put them into a sack.

She eased the door to the storeroom open and stepped out into the night. The gold of a false dawn shone on the horizon. Overhead stars winked. She shivered, pulled on her traveling coat, and over it, tied her dagger around her waist. She left her hair tucked into the collar and pulled her hat low over her head. She hoped no one would look at her too closely. Few women traveled alone for more than a day's walk. Near Hrolf's farm she would be known, and that might protect her, but not from being sent back.

She must make her way toward the *ting* grounds, and then hope that a path remained from there to Lustra Fjord. If she could not find a fishing boat to take her to Ragnvald at Yrjar, perhaps she could travel overland to the nearby market town of Kaupanger. There she could certainly find a boat, or news, something. She could sell her jewelry for silver coins to more easily buy passage.

The fields of Hrolf's farm looked different at night. She had tried to remember landmarks on the way here from the *ting* grounds at Jostedal, as Ragnvald had trained her, even turning to see how they looked coming the other way. Features she remembered in daylight's detail were now silhouettes, though, or lost in dark entirely.

She followed the marked path downhill away from Hrolf's farm before turning at a lopsided cairn to track across an open field. No one would know she had gone until morning. Hilda would not raise the alarm, Svanhild thought, not until she could keep it a secret no longer. And then, Svanhild did not know if Thorkell would pursue her.

She saw a cairn, but it was the wrong one, too many piled stones, traced over with orange lichen. Walking unfamiliar ground felt longer, she reminded herself. Behind her the gray of Hrolf's hall was lost against the black silhouette of the mountains. The stone fences that separated Hrolf's fields from his neighbors' looked like crouching black creatures. Anything could hide in their shadows.

She should have come to the cairn by now, but she would not backtrack. She splashed through a creek she did not remember on her journey here. Had there been enough rain in the past week for water to flow where it had not before? Through her growing worry, she could not remember. A smattering of rain began to fall.

The path went through a dark grove, and Svanhild decided to wait there for morning. Panic was waiting for her, whatever direction she continued, the reasonless panic that would waste her energy, drive her in whatever direction she feared most. Panic killed, Ragnvald had told her; it used up energy and drove men into their enemy's snares, or over cliffs in the dark. She sat down to rest.

Then a bolt of lightning struck, not twenty feet in front of her. She screamed and stumbled back, the image of an oak tree burned into her vision. Another strike sounded behind her. She started running, heedless of the branches that caught her feet and tore at her dress. She got caught in a thornbush once and wrenched herself free, tearing a long scratch along her arm. Her bundle of bread and clothes grew heavier.

She was cold, tired, and on the verge of tears. She needed to stop, or she would injure herself. It was Loki, men said, who addled their brains in the woods, turned them around so they could no longer tell north from south, even with the sun high in the sky.

She crawled under the shelter of a fallen log, tucking her sack into the driest ground and covering it with leaves. For a pillow she bundled her clothing under her head. She could rest here until the storm passed, and then continue to Kaupanger.

17

AS THE MEN FINISHED THEIR MEAL, HAKON STOOD AND BEGAN to speak. It seemed like sorcery, the way his presence quieted all talking. Even Harald stopped his flirting with—no, that was not Asa Hakonsdatter any longer, but a brown-haired thrall with buoyant breasts that showed even through the rough homespun of her shift.

Hakon's voice drew Ragnvald's attention back. It was the blood of kings that gave him that power. Ragnvald wondered if that ability flowed in his own veins. It seemed that lately he only gained attention when he was getting himself into trouble, foolishly talking himself into attacking a *draugr*, or humiliating himself at the trials.

"Welcome to our new sword hands, our new raven-feeders," said Hakon. "You must drink deeply tonight, that your swords will drink deeply of our enemies' blood." He went on in this vein, welcoming the men generally and then calling out a favored few, sons of wealthy farmers and jarls from South Maer. Ragnvald watched as the men stood to be acknowledged and toasted, trying to fix names to faces in his mind.

"And we are especially pleased that Ragnvald Eysteinsson has joined with us," said Hakon finally. "Ragnvald, come and swear, and then you will all swear."

Ragnvald stood.

"Give me your sword," said Hakon when Ragnvald approached him. Ragnvald felt the crowd's eyes on him, heating the side of his face. He drew his sword half out of its sheath and extended the hilt toward Hakon, who drew it the rest of the way.

"I make my ancestry known," said Ragnvald, then listed father, grandfather, great-grandfather, condensing generations, naming only famous forebears, until he came to Fornjot the giant, almost fifty generations back, and before that, Odin himself.

"I endured . . ." Ragnvald's lips curved sardonically. In this part of the oath he should list his heroic accomplishments, the things that would induce Hakon to want to take him on as a carl, a sworn man in his war band. "I endured Solvi and my stepfather's attempt to murder me." And his own foolish behavior at the trial. He kept his eyes fixed on the hilt of the sword held in his and Hakon's hands. "I hope I will win greater battles than that in your service."

Hakon let go of the sword. "Ragnvald is overmodest," he said to the crowd, and then, in an aside to Ragnvald, "It does him no credit."

Ragnvald's already heated face grew even hotter. He had not thought that by refusing to name his deeds, he insulted his host, his king, who had singled him out. Hakon continued, "All of you, bid him tell you of the *draugr* he slayed, just two days past. Or better yet, skald"—he gestured at the man who had accompanied them from the *ting* assembly—"teach your fellows Ragnvald's song. Let it be sung near and far, so all men know his name, and the name of his king." He turned back to Ragnvald. "Now take this sword." He handed it back to Ragnvald with two hands, and Ragnvald took it the same way.

"I accept this sword," Ragnvald continued, "and the lord who gives it to me. Until the end of my days or you release me from my oath, my death will stand between you and danger. If you fall, I will avenge you."

He glanced at Harald, who watched him in return, an unreadable expression on his face.

"Should some of these men not swear to us?" Harald asked his uncle, not troubling to keep his voice low. "I want Norway's heroes sworn to me." Ragnvald cast his eyes down, worried others would see how much he enjoyed hearing himself so described, though he did not think much of Harald's rudeness.

"Hush," said Guthorm. "When Hakon swears allegiance to you, then all these men will be yours as well."

"I pray that you make for Norway a king worth swearing to, but for now I am the strongest king in the north," said Hakon. Harald bristled, and Hakon continued, "Be silent. I must swear my part, so the gods do not punish me."

Hakon gave his version of the oath, listing his ancestors back also to Odin. He linked himself explicitly to Ragnvald by mentioning their common ancestor Sveidi, only five generations removed. Ragnvald knew where Sveidi's burial mound was. Hakon was claiming him as kin. "I will be your lord, until you have done me a service, and I have helped you regain your land from your stepfather, at which time you will be released from your oath."

Ragnvald looked up at him, surprised. He had expected Hakon to require, perhaps, a lifetime pledge not to raise arms against him.

Hakon shrugged. "It is not so fine a sword as to command your whole life, Ragnvald." He smiled and made a sign with his fingers against ill luck. "Only the fates do that."

Ragnvald bowed his head again and walked back to his seat, feeling dazed. Hakon called up other warriors to swear to him, a few more to swear individually, then the remaining men in a mass. Ragnvald drank the rest of his ale, which seemed to make him drunker than it usually did. Men he did not know congratulated him and brought him more to drink. A skald sang of his fight with the *draugr*, and Ragnvald slaked his thirst until he could no longer make out the words.

✣   ✣   ✣

WHEN HIS HEAD had cleared somewhat the next morning, Ragnvald walked down to the ships beached on the broad plain to see if he could help. He was eager to be fighting and proving himself. Hakon's chief pilot, Grim, was a small, taciturn man, with a face wrinkled leather-tough by a lifetime spent at sea. He did not seem to like anyone, least of all Ragnvald, who received a smack on his hands that stung smartly when he tried to help load the ship.

"Do you know where to put the casks of water so the ship won't founder in high seas?" Grim asked, and then, before Ragnvald could do more than open his mouth to start a reply, grunted. "I thought not. Leave this work to the real seamen."

There were plenty of other tasks for the waiting warriors. Ragn-vald assisted Oddi and Dagvith in rolling up a second sail for each ship, in case the first one was ripped away. A mast could be replaced, but each sail contained enough fabric to make full sets of clothing for every man on board and was dyed in a checkered pattern of blue and white—Hakon's colors. The wool was rough; it made his hands greasy and worked small, hard fibers into the soft parts of his fingers. Sail wool was unwashed, for the natural oils kept the rain from soaking in and weighing down the sheet until the spars broke.

Ragnvald remembered Svanhild's hands after a winter spent spin-ning the rough fibers. His sword calluses softened over the long win-ter indoors, while her hands only grew rougher, chapped with cold and hard work. Ragnvald whispered a prayer to Ran the sea goddess, thanking her for the sail that kept them from having to row every long mile between here and wherever Hakon planned his attack, in hopes that she would let them return again safely, not cast her net over them. He asked also, if she was watching him, that she would watch over Svanhild as well, no matter how far she was from the sea.

Ragnvald mentioned Svanhild's hands to Oddi as they went about their work. Oddi had enjoyed tales of Svanhild before, how often she got into trouble, and Ragnvald nursed hopes that Oddi might want to marry her when they returned.

"Did your household not have thralls to do that work?" Oddi asked.

"Svanhild spun so ill she was only allowed to spin sail wool," said Ragnvald, laughing, then worried. A man wanted a wife who spun, and spun well. "In truth, I think she liked spinning she could do outside."

"My mother made me learn to spin when I was small," said Oddi. In poorer families, Ragnvald knew, without enough women thralls, everyone spent the winter spinning, not just the women. Ragnvald smiled, trying to imagine his stepbrother Sigurd with a spindle. He would fight with it more than Svanhild did.

"And were you skilled at it?" Ragnvald asked.

"There have been worse," said Oddi. "But then she died and my father came to claim me. I suppose I would have sold onto a ship for Iceland if he had not, made myself a bondservant until I paid off my passage and grew into a man."

Ragnvald grunted his acknowledgment. He had not realized Oddi had come from such a meager background. When they met, Oddi was a brash boy already, spoiled by his father and holding a sword, not a spindle. Ragnvald had pictured Oddi growing up underfoot at Hakon's court, turning jaded and sardonic from all he observed there.

"I'm glad you did not," said Ragnvald finally, when Oddi seemed to want more from him.

"I am not so sure sometimes," said Oddi. "I am only a hanger-on in my father's court. He will not make me an heir when he has so many trueborn sons."

"Another man might kill his trueborn brothers and have himself acclaimed king," Ragnvald said, jokingly, though in truth he wondered—if Oddi had more initiative, perhaps he would have risen higher.

"Alas, I am not the type for brother-murder," said Oddi. "Either doing murder or suffering it." And so he had chosen to try to slip by under their notice, showing neither ambition nor favoritism.

"I hope it works," said Ragnvald. "I will take your part, if it comes to that."

"My parts?" said Oddi. He grabbed his pants, between his legs. "My parts are my own—it's not you I want taking hold of them." Ragnvald laughed with him, but resolved to keep a closer eye on Heming, and not just for himself.

✛ ✛ ✛

STILL, IT TOOK several days before ships and men were ready to depart. Hakon and Guthorm spent long hours in private conference, walking on the beach or sitting near a fire in the evening, talking in low voices, with guards protecting ten paces of privacy around them. Harald and Heming joined them from time to time, but each grew bored quickly and found more enjoyable pastimes, Harald training with the warriors, or alone with his new wife, and Heming betting on dogfights.

The meat of the disagreement was easily understood, no matter how much Hakon and Guthorm tried to keep their arguments quiet. Hakon wanted Harald's help attacking Solvi and Hunthiof in Tafjord, especially after the intelligence from Smola that the rovers of Tafjord stuck close to home with their raiding this summer. Guthorm wanted Hakon's help in subduing Hordaland to the south. Harald and Guthorm had put most of the area around Vestfold under their control, and Hordaland was the next step in their expansions. Tensions between their rules spilled out into fights between Harald's and Hakon's men.

Two were fighting on the beach one morning, and Ragnvald was woken from sleep to help settle it. As he arrived they fell over onto a small ship's boat, breaking the gunwale. Ragnvald sprang forward to pull Hakon's man away, while Harald's friend Thorbrand gathered up the other. Thorbrand was a small, bullish man, with curly, sand-colored hair. Pretty hair surrounding an unpretty face. Ragnvald thought him dull until he saw in Thorbrand's smile intelligence and an easy humor.

"What do you think we should do?" Thorbrand asked, after the two brawling warriors had retreated to their own camps.

"Get moving as soon as possible," said Ragnvald. "This waiting only breeds discontent."

"No, where should we attack first?"

"I can see both sides," said Ragnvald.

"I have heard that about you, but tell me, if you had the deciding of it, where would you order the attack?"

"I serve Hakon," said Ragnvald, "and Solvi Hunthiofsson has used me ill." He wanted to share a confidence with Thorbrand, though. "I am from Sogn, and Hakon wants to install Heming in Maer. It would only be a matter of time before he looked south again. Without one powerful king, Sogn would be easy to conquer. So I truly can see both sides."

"You are the son of Eystein, who was son of King Ivar who ruled all of Sogn," said Thorbrand. "Your grandfather was a great man."

"Yes," said Ragnvald, trying not to show his bitterness. "It does not take long for fortunes to change."

✣   ✣   ✣

RAGNVALD WANDERED THE grounds with Oddi, watching the men spar, first in pairs, then attacking in groups. When Harald grew weary of the discussions between his uncle and his father-in-law, he drilled his men. These were tactics, it appeared, for a single man fending off a gang. Ragnvald asked to borrow practice swords from Harald's arms master, and for Oddi and Dagvith to attack him. He tried to repeat what he had seen Harald's soldiers do, and ended up on his back on the dirt. Oddi took his arm to help him up, and they tried again.

The trick of this fighting technique seemed to be to use one of your opponents to distract the other. Ragnvald was growing closer to success when a tide of men started moving toward the center of the camp.

Ragnvald and Oddi followed, and found a circle forming around where Harald fought off groups of men, armed with wooden axes, staves, and wooden swords. They came at him in groups of fours and fives. At Ragnvald's side, Oddi hardly breathed, waiting for Harald to fall under that onslaught. He stood out, a golden head above darker fellows, and moved swiftly, sweeping legs, fending off attackers, sometimes throwing them off with main force.

Ragnvald had never seen a man move like Harald did, too fast to follow, yet with a grace and surety that made his movements look perfectly considered, without a single wasted breath. From the look on Oddi's face, he had never seen the like either. Harald did not hold himself like a warrior, proud and wary. His easy speed and ferocious strength needed no posturing. Finally, with sweat dripping from the ends of his unkempt hair, Harald put up his hand to call a halt. The men around him applauded. Harald waved them off and gestured for a servant to give him ale, his chest heaving like a dog's after a run.

"It takes more than one man to subdue so many districts," said Ragnvald doubtfully.

"Look around you," said Oddi. "If anyone can do it, he can."

As soon as Harald defeated his assailants, he sprang up on a stone and called out, "Listen to me, men. Tomorrow we travel to Hordaland. Now that Vestfold is under our control, they will be the first new district of my Norway, a kingdom that will stand against Denmark, England, even the Frankish Empire. A kingdom that will protect its citizens from raiders, either from our own shores or others. My kingdom will bind together, as you bind to me."

The men cheered, and Ragnvald applauded as well. For centuries,

Danish kings had been expanding their territories, and England had come together under their King Alfred, in order to repulse an army of Danish invaders. Ragnvald still doubted that Harald himself could unite the Norse kingdoms of valley and fjord with forested mountains and flat farmland, but with someone like Hakon, he might form a strong confederacy. An alliance of strong kings and a strong vision could become a company of wolves to protect a hall rather than endanger it. At least now he could see what had caused Hakon to ally with Harald.

✢ ✢ ✢

FINALLY, AFTER SOME private exchange of promises, Hakon announced that they would indeed raid in Hordaland, for it was rich, and those who desired might stay the winter in Vestfold, drinking Harald's ale and training for the next year's war. He made it sound like his first choice, but Heming's cloudy expression told everyone the truth. Harald and Guthorm had come north with empty words—threats for Hunthiof, promises for Hakon—and now proposed to leave with none of them fulfilled.

The pilot Grim became more talkative when they were under sail again. He sat at the steering oar and pointed out mountain landmarks and said their names: Giant's Bed, Thor's Hammer, Tyr's Hand. Heming spent the voyage trying to bet with Ragnvald and Oddi about anything and everything, how many leaps the dolphins running before their ships would make, whether Grim would call for oars when they beached or show off his skill by bringing the ship in entirely under sail, and a thousand other things.

Ragnvald rarely took these bets; to win would be to anger Heming, and he did not have the silver or the stomach for losing. Oddi bet, though, and his moleskin gloves changed hands a half dozen times before the ship passed by Sogn Fjord again on the way south.

Harald and Guthorm sailed on their own ship, leading a separate convoy. Ragnvald sometimes glimpsed the fine lines of the royal ship through the mists that lay off the prow. It moved like a sea serpent, cutting through waves, never wallowing, disappearing as its own wind sped it ahead.

After two days of sailing, all of the ships found space to beach on an island just north of the mouth of Hardanger Fjord, Hordaland's main artery.

"This would be a fine place for a town," said Harald to Hakon, when they settled around the evening's fire. "A protected harbor, space for farming, mountains for defense."

All the things he named stood before them across a narrow strait. Farms already divided the flatter lands. High above, a cliff thrust out over the fields, a fine lookout point. Fires set by men from the other ships winked down across the beach. The sky was a bottomless twilight blue overhead, with orange and pink at the horizon.

Hakon and Harald's favorites were all gathered around this fire, sons and friends and hangers-on. Ragnvald found himself seated next to Thorbrand again, no bad thing. Thorbrand was Harald's fast friend, but he had his own mind as well.

Guthorm called for quiet. "Tomorrow we sail up Hardanger Fjord into the heart of Hordaland," he said. "There is a meeting of this district's kings. We will take our army there and let them see our strength. Then they will swear allegiance to Harald. Tell your men to make ready, and to eat well tonight."

✢ ✢ ✢

AFTER A DAY'S sail up Hardanger Fjord, they hid the ships in the overhang of a cliff and waited for nightfall. Guthorm's intelligence said that the seven coastal Hordaland kings met now to settle border disputes and discuss how to keep raiders from their shores. They would bring guards, but no armies. Guthorm's force would have the advantage.

Guthorm sent scouts, fast-running young men, in a few directions to learn the local news and make sure the meeting was still to take place. After a morning of waiting with the ships, Ragnvald grew restless. He and Oddi asked for permission from Hakon to do some hunting and carry back any intelligence they might find. They climbed into the forest, where cliffs rose above the trees, until they came to a grove on the summit. The trees here were small and scrubby, anchored shallowly in the thin soil. With so little cover, the air was warm and dry. Flies buzzed around the sap that leaked out of the tree trunks.

They followed a deer path for a time over soft pine needles. The quiet focus, the single-minded purpose of hunting, soothed Ragnvald's restlessness. Then, like a gift from the gods, a deer crossed in front of them, a young buck, fuzz still clinging to its antlers. Ragnvald's arrow found its throat as it bent for a drink of water in a sunlit clearing. He and Oddi butchered it under the trees. They could not risk a fire, so instead they sat next to the carcass, eating the dried meat they had brought and drinking from a skin of ale that Oddi had been saving since Yrjar hall.

"You know, sometimes I'm not sure I like you very much," said Oddi with a grin. "You are too lucky, and when you are not, you draw too much attention." Ragnvald sucked in a breath. He valued Oddi for always saying what others thought, but it was sometimes uncomfortable. He took the ale skin from Oddi's hand and pressed the opening carefully to his lips, trying not to spill any. It was warm and bitter, and warmed his blood too, turning the jangling of his nerves into anticipation of the night ahead. A night for battle and bloodshed. He licked his lips.

"Or rather, I thought to bring you to my father's court as an ally, but now I'm worried I'll be standing next to you when someone throws an ax at you," said Oddi.

"Afraid I'll duck?" Ragnvald asked, amused.

"You are fast," said Oddi with a grin.

"I am your ally," said Ragnvald more seriously. "I hope that one day that means more than it does now."

"It does," said Oddi. "Be careful, though. I counted Jarl Runolf as a friend too." Jarl Runolf, whose blood had watered the dueling ground at the *ting*.

"Perhaps being your friend is dangerous," said Ragnvald. He meant it as a joke, until the words left his lips.

"I cannot stay in my father's court," said Oddi, nodding. "I see that now. He has too many sons already."

"Where will you go?"

"I have a friend, who will be a jarl in Ardal, and one day king of

Sogn. He might need a man to lead his warrior *hird*, or train up his brood of sons."

"Surely a king's son can do better than that," said Ragnvald, affection making him gruff. He and Oddi had been friends as boys, when Ragnvald's father was alive, and had friends up and down the Norse coast. Visitors always came to Ardal, or Eystein took his son along with his favorite warriors and favorite women to visit other halls on short summer trips. Ragnvald had made friends more easily then as well, when he was too young to be suspicious, when Olaf was no more to him than one of Eystein's quieter warriors.

Ragnvald passed the ale skin back toward Oddi, whose hands closed around it and then froze. Ragnvald looked up and saw what Oddi had seen: a small boy, dark hair tousled and face smudged, with eyes too large for his face. Choices warred in the boy's eyes, but boldness got the better of him.

"This is my father's land," he said.

"Who is your father, then?" Oddi asked.

"Jarl Lingorm," said the boy. "He is the king's right-hand man." Oddi glanced sharply at Ragnvald. Which king? Ragnvald wanted to ask, but did not. That would betray too much.

"Is he at home?" Ragnvald asked. "We want to meet him." He smiled slightly. "And pay him for the deer we took." Ragnvald's expression seemed to heighten the boy's suspicions; he drew back, shielding more of his body behind the tree in front of him. Clever lad.

"He's at home," the boy said, jutting his chin forward, far too defiant for his words to be truth. Ragnvald shook his head slightly, hoping Oddi would pick up the signal.

Whether Oddi did or not was of no matter, for the boy saw, sprang from his shelter behind the tree, and went darting into the forest. Ragnvald gave chase. The boy was sure of foot and smaller, and for a dozen steps, Ragnvald thought he might lose him, until the boy started to tire, and Ragnvald's fingers brushed the fabric of his tunic. Ragnvald put on another burst of speed. As he came alongside the boy, he scooped him up under one arm. The boy let out a yell. Ragnvald put his other hand over the boy's mouth and nose. Better the boy pass out than carry on making noise.

He licked Ragnvald's hand and then, when Ragnvald pinched his nostrils shut, bit it deeply enough to draw blood. Ragnvald cursed him under his breath and swung the boy's head into a tree, with enough force to stun him. He returned to where Oddi still sat with the deer carcass, and flung the boy down onto the ground.

"Scream and I'll cut your throat," he said. The boy looked back at him. Some rebelliousness still shone in his eyes, but he was cowed enough not to try to call for help again.

"I've no stomach for killing him. But I don't want him running back to warn his family," said Ragnvald in a low voice, without taking his eyes from the boy. Oddi made a noise of assent. "If things go ill, a hostage might be useful." He took some of the leather rope from the deer and used it to tie the boy's wrists. The rag he had been using to mop his sweat did well as a gag. Then he hoisted some deer meat onto his shoulder and took the boy's arm in his other hand. "March," he said.

He had to free the boy's hands to get him down the cliff, back to the ships. Between them, the boy stumbled, rebelliously, and more than once Ragnvald had to grab him to keep him from going over the edge. Might as well let him fall, an ignoble part of him whispered.

Ragnvald and Oddi brought the deer meat back to the ship to pack it in salt so it would not spoil. Ragnvald found a sturdier rope to tie the boy up. He secured him to one of the ship's ribs, and tied his hands and feet. It still did not look quite secure enough; he could well imagine the boy getting out of his bonds and wriggling over the side—Ragnvald remembered being that age well enough to remember getting into and out of all kinds of spaces adults could never go—but he had no surer way to hold him. He could not seal the boy up in a barrel, much as he might want to.

Dark came early in the shadow of the cliffs. The insects and birds quieted as the darkness drew in. As Ragnvald leaned over the edge of the ship to wash the blood from his hands in the fjord water, Oddi crouched next to him.

"Leave it," he said. Ragnvald looked at his hands. The blood had grown tacky as it dried, and now his fingers stuck together when he made a fist. "Blood spilled now, blood spilled later. You'll want them to fear you."

The deer blood smelled different from a man's blood, less metallic. He had spilled deer's blood many times, men's only a few. When they attacked the monastery in the Hebrides, Solvi's berserks had smeared blood on their faces and worked blood into their hair to make it stand out in all directions. And the monks had run.

Ragnvald looked up when Guthorm approached. "How did you end up with a prisoner?" he asked Ragnvald, who explained as quickly as he could.

"I suppose we'll have men enough to guard the boy as well as the ships," said Guthorm, eventually. "I don't like it, though. What if this boy has minders who wonder where he is?"

"Better for them to wonder than know what he saw."

"You could have killed him and left him in the wood. Made it look like an animal did it." Ragnvald recoiled; the boy was younger than the novice monks Ragnvald had helped kill with Solvi's raiders, still a child. Guthorm shook his head. "I had thought better of you, from the tales told of you," he added.

"I could bring him back there and do it," said Ragnvald.

"No, it is too late. We depart at nightfall. Perhaps he will be of use as a hostage." Guthorm turned to step from Hakon's ship back to his own. The creaking of many ships moored together, and the low voices of men who knew battle was coming, filled the still air.

"I knew your father," said Guthorm. "I hope you don't have his faults."

"I hope not as well," said Ragnvald to his retreating back. Fuming, he spoke to the pilot of one of the ships, who would remain behind to move them if they were discovered. He promised the man silver if he looked after the boy, and freed him once their forces had been gone for a full day. That should give them enough time.

18

IN THE MORNING, SVANHILD CRAWLED OUT OF HER SHELTER, and saw frost on the ground from the night before. A curl of bark had caught a splash of water that she used to wet her face. She took all the items out of her pack and rolled them more securely than she had been able to do in the dark at Hrolf's farm. Perhaps she should wait here until Thorkell became tired of searching for her.

No, that was the voice of fear speaking. He had hunting dogs, he had her scent. She must keep moving. Face strangers, who might not know her name or her family. Men who would—would men be willing to take her where she wanted to go? Would the daughter of the kings of Sogn, kings passed into memory and faded reputation, be able to command any respect, even to buy it with jewelry? It was all very well to dream about being a Brunhilda, bent on revenge for an insult to her husband, when she could not even stand up and continue walking.

She argued with herself a few minutes longer, and had almost resolved to rest another day when she heard the barking of dogs in the distance. That noise put enough fear into her breast that she must start moving, or shake apart with it. She put her bags over her back and started following the slope downhill, trying to keep an even pace, as her feet kept moved faster and faster, through brambles that scratched her skin and tore her clothes, making her a mess all over again.

She reached Kaupanger after another night spent outside. The only town on the western coast, it was choked with buildings, more than

Svanhild had ever seen together before. She had heard stories of cities in faraway lands, where tens of thousands of people lived together. Such things could only exist where the land was flat and fertile. The richest Norse farms might support no more than a hundred, including thralls and children. More would starve.

Before leaving her campsite, Svanhild had brushed her hair out and put on her festival dress. She fastened it with pewter brooches and a slim, unadorned pewter chain between, leaving the smaller, richer silver brooches in her pack. These were treasures from her mother, only on loan for the *ting*. Svanhild hoped her mother would not begrudge the expense. She tied her hair back neatly under a green wimple that Vigdis had said made her eyes look bright.

A stream separated her from the ship-filled beach. She stepped over a mossy rock, and lost her balance when a slop of vegetable mess came hurling out an open door. A few seconds later two huge pigs rushed over to slurp it up. Svanhild put out her hands and caught herself in the filthy water that flowed through muddy ground.

The crowd of buildings and people had looked orderly from above, where she could not hear it, where she did not have to step over the messes made by animals, by the press of humanity. If she walked close to the shore, she had to step over rotting masses of seaweed, surrounded by clouds of stinging flies, and dodge merchants' crews tossing their wares to and fro. But when she walked on the street inland, she lost her bearings.

At least she was not the only woman walking around without a male escort. Some of the women she saw were waiting at storefronts, or driving a few cows through the streets. Some people nodded to one another when they passed, and no more greeting than that. It seemed terribly rude. Svanhild had never seen a stranger come to Ardal without a greeting or an offer of food, and here she was a stranger. Yet she remembered her father telling her that these people did not live in concert as on a farm, but in small, separate households, weaving between one another, like all the types of insects that live on a single tree.

She followed a finely dressed lady to a slightly cleaner part of the town. Ditches had been dug here to carry sewage away. Men walking through would toe animal droppings into the ditch as they passed by, while women picked their skirts up high to step over them.

Svanhild lost sight of the finely dressed woman, and hurried instead to catch up with a woman who looked more like a wealthy farm wife, dressed for warmth and practicality. She carried two heavy baskets of vegetables, one over each arm, and was leading a cow.

"Excuse me," said Svanhild. "Do you know where I could sell gold or silver?" The woman scowled at her and did not answer. Svanhild wilted. "Or do you know who I could ask?"

"I'm busy," she said. "They're not far." She pointed in a direction that could be anywhere in the south end of the town, and continued on her way. Svanhild walked a few paces in that direction. All the houses looked the same, with leather shutters tied down tight.

An older man approached her, stooped, and hardly taller than Svanhild herself. "What are you looking for, maid?" he asked. "I can help you."

He looked kindly enough, with bright blue eyes creased at the corners. He walked with the aid of a stick, but quick enough he could keep up with her. "I'm looking for someone to sell some silver to," she said. "Can you help me?"

"Oh, there are a few shops, all along the back of the town," he said, pointing toward where the houses started to rise and grow sparser as the ground rose toward the cliffs above the fjord. At Svanhild's quizzical look, he added, "Farther from the smell of the shore. You'll see. I'll show you."

He spun around her and stepped in front of her, as fast as if he did not have a cane to maneuver. He used it instead as a flourish to end his footwork, and pointed the way up the sloping streets, out of the mud. She followed him up, between weathered buildings. He told her as they walked that he had been born on the spot of land that would become this strange place, Kaupanger, the only town on the western coast, and he knew it better than anyone. When she glanced behind her to try to mark her way, he drew her attention back with a joke, or another flourish with his cane.

The houses here looked like little halls, shortened so they were no longer than they were wide. Small decorations were the only way of differentiating one from the other. At least the man kept leading her uphill. She could find her way by going back down again.

Then he turned a corner and disappeared. As she called out for him, something hit her in the back, and she stumbled forward. She tried to yell and another shove buried her face in the dirt. She pushed herself up and felt a hand scrabbling at the pack slung over her shoulder. She heard a dagger leaving its sheath and passing close to her ear, before the wight on her back began sawing with it at the pack strings.

"What do you want from me?" Svanhild cried.

"Your silver, of course," said the man who had led her. Now that she was pinned down, he moved less swiftly. "Come on, give us the pack, or that dagger can be used for sawing more than just fabric."

"I need it," she said. "Please, I have to get away. It's all I have."

"You can work for it back, can't you?" said the person on her back with the knife. "She'll be a strong worker, I think." He had a boy's voice, and dug a boy's bony knees into her ribs.

"Na," said the man. "There's a ship in port. Tie her up and get done with it. They've enough men, but they're paying double for women."

A jolt of anger went through her like a thunderclap. A free Norse man would never allow himself to be taken alive and enslaved. He would rather die, and so would she. Her fear gave her strength beyond this boy's. She rolled over, heedless of his dagger, and threw him off her, onto the ground. She had begun to stand when he grabbed at her leg and pulled her down on top of him. She aimed her knee into his stomach. He slashed at her with his dagger, and she flinched away, covering her face. His slashes cut her forearms, driving her back so she no longer pinned him down.

"Stop this," came a woman's authoritative voice, "or I'll have the guards on you."

The boy stopped attacking her, and Svanhild used her advantage to kick him hard in the stomach. He choked and curled into a ball, like a grub exposed to sunlight. She wanted to kick him again. His master had disappeared.

"You, what were you doing following these scoundrels?" she asked Svanhild. It was the woman from the market whose vague directions had led her into this mess.

"You wouldn't help me," said Svanhild. "Who was I supposed to ask? No wonder all the kings want to put you under their control."

"I'm sorry," said the woman gruffly. "I should have helped you. Then I wouldn't have had to leave my cow behind and climb up here. She's probably made some mischief by now. Come with me, and I'll bandage your cuts."

"What about him?" Svanhild asked, turning to look at where the boy had lain. He was gone. She should have kicked him harder.

"You're not a Kaupanger," said the woman.

"What does that mean?"

"It means you don't pay the guard to protect you. Who is your protector?" It was a question with too long an answer, and the woman saw it in her eyes. "Come with me."

Svanhild followed her down the hill gratefully, to where a basket of vegetables was perched on a windowsill. "You can carry those." A cow nosed through some rotting produce on the ground. The woman tugged on the cow's head. It ignored her. The woman sighed and waited until it was done before continuing to walk.

They walked through the town, around back of one of the storefronts. It was not open yet, the entrance covered with wooden shutters, bound by leather thongs in intricate knots. She tied up the cow in the small, poor lot behind the house. No wonder she did not mind the cow eating rotten vegetables. Svanhild could not imagine what the cow's milk would taste like.

"Don't go shouting about your wealth in the street, girl. Are you simple?" the woman, whose name was Gerta, asked when they were out of the main thoroughfare. She led Svanhild inside, sat her down in the kitchen, and gave her a cup of ale and a cloth to wipe her face.

"I'm sorry," said Svanhild, tears immediately threatening to spill over her cheeks. "I've never been here before. I have a pair of brooches I want to sell so I can buy passage on a boat to take me to my brother. I have to get to him. I don't have anywhere else to go."

"Where are your parents?" asked Gerta, sounding interested against her will. Svanhild related the whole story as far as she could, but there was too much to tell, and she started crying in the middle of it.

"I don't know what was the right thing—maybe I should have married Thorkell, even if his big stupid sons killed all his other wives coming out. Hrolf wasn't supposed to be allowed to marry me to anyone, and I know he didn't want me there. I don't want to be where I'm not wanted, but now I'm not wanted anywhere."

"I don't pretend I understand that story of yours—but you know your mind," said Gerta. "You'll do well to go to your brother. He was supposed to have the keeping of you."

Svanhild remembered how relieved he had been to get rid of her, and did not reply.

"I can give you some advice about how to go from here," Gerta continued. "We saw Hakon's ships go by here six weeks or so ago, after the midsummer—the *ting*, I guess—and we haven't seen them come back this way, not that that means anything. I suppose he's at Yrjar still."

"Why do the people at Kaupanger not go to the *ting*?" Svanhild asked.

Gerta pulled her braid over one shoulder. By the gray in her hair, she was older than Svanhild had originally thought, at least a decade older than Svanhild's mother. She carried it well. The fine lines around her eyes made her look wise. She was tall, deep-breasted, and broad-shouldered, built like a strong man. She moved like one too.

"Most of us don't stay here that long, and those that do, we turn our eyes toward the sea, not the farmland. This year we decided to have our own assembly to decide local governance questions. Sometimes King Hakon or King Hunthiof or one of the other petty little kings comes through and extracts some taxes from us, tries to tell us our business, but not since we hired on some boats to patrol the harbor and some warriors to make them think twice. We take care of ourselves here."

Seeing that Svanhild looked confused, she smiled slightly. "But that's not why you're here."

Svanhild nodded. She was embarrassed to have broken down crying. How could she brave the seas and go to find Ragnvald if she could not even walk through a town without fear? The cuts on her arms smarted.

"You're putting yourself in danger," said Gerta, "and that's what."

"What should I do, then? I can't go back. I have to sell my brooches and find my brother."

"I came from a farm like yours," said Gerta. "Too many daughters." She paused, as though she might say more. "I'll tell you what I can. In a couple of hours a man I know will be ready to buy jewelry, and I'll go with you while you try to sell your brooches. Give me a pinch, and I'll make sure you get a good deal."

Svanhild did not know what a pinch was, but she suspected it was some fraction of the price she fetched. Hopefully not a big fraction. It made her feel better to learn Gerta was not just helping her out of kindness. Kindness meant obligation, or a motive Svanhild could not fathom. When she sat under Gerta's roof, Gerta owed her food and protection, by the laws of hospitality, but that meant nothing once they passed through Gerta's door again. "Do you even keep laws of hospitality here?" she asked with sudden concern.

"Yes," said Gerta. "Some of us do, and think of the town before themselves. We don't want blood feud with your family. But hospitality doesn't mean I'm not going to get my cut of your silver."

"Do you have a husband or"—Svanhild paused, unsure of how to put it—"a man?" Or anyone else who might object to finding Svanhild here.

"Used to," said Gerta. "Not sure they're worth the bother, but I might marry again, if I find a man with a good head on his shoulders. Marriage is not so bad when you're my age and you know what you want. A little girl like you, though, you shouldn't have to make decisions like that on your own. Now help me cut these vegetables to pass the time."

Svanhild took her dagger out of its sheath from around her waist and pared and sliced the huge heads of cabbage, while Gerta grunted over her work and put them in the soapstone pot hanging over the fire.

"Not bad," said Gerta. "What else can you do?"

"I can herd cows and sheep and make cheese and things."

"Can you spin or do tablet weaving?"

Svanhild shook her head. "No, I'm terrible at spinning." She laughed and then tried to swallow the noise when she realized it sounded more like a sob. "I don't know why Thorkell wanted to marry me."

"Now, none of that," said Gerta sternly. "Men get more foolish as they get older, I find, and women get wiser. Though it sounds like this brother of yours isn't starting out too wise. Well, few of them do. We'll get you to Yrjar if you want. If you had any handy skills, I might consider apprenticing you, but if you can't spin, you're not much use to me. Better you be a farmer's wife, the right farmer this time. Someone your brother picks."

"My grandfather was a king," said Svanhild softly, but sitting up straighter.

"So was mine, or so I hear," said Gerta. "Can't throw a stone without hitting a king or would-be king around these parts."

Svanhild could not argue with that, so she continued slicing vegetables. Gerta said that none of the shops would want to do business until after they ate their morning meal, which was closer to noon than what Svanhild thought of as morning. When they were done chopping vegetables, Gerta put Svanhild to work making a stew with the vegetables and a few shreds of cold, stringy beef.

"We don't get much meat around here," said Gerta, "unless it's festival or the like. Milk neither. I don't like to buy when I can do for myself. My cow gives me just enough."

Svanhild did not have an answer for that. She could think of nothing to say to Gerta, who lived only a few days' journey from Ardal, but had a life so different Svanhild could hardly imagine it.

"I might go up to Yrjar," said Gerta. "Lots of bored men, I'd wager, waiting for fighting. Though they won't have done their raiding yet, so they probably won't have much silver to spend. Still, they'll have sweethearts they want to impress." Gerta tied the warp of her tablet weaving onto her belt. She turned the tablets and threw the shuttle so fast Svanhild could not follow her movements. Gerta looked down every few moments, but seemed to do the work enough by feel that she could watch Svanhild and frown at her. "Mind you don't let that soup boil over. I don't want to be missing any of it."

After the vegetables had softened, Gerta said, "Show me what you have for sale." Svanhild hesitated for a moment. Gerta had been kind, in her brusque, bossy way, but Svanhild knew nothing about her. "If I don't see them, I won't know the fair price," Gerta added. Svanhild opened her pack and unknotted the sock that she had secreted the brooches in. They were of silver, with fine knotwork surrounding matched amber jewels, each larger than an acorn.

"Not bad," said Gerta. "They want polishing." She produced a rag from somewhere on her person. "Give them a good rub." While Svanhild worked, Gerta banked the fire so it would not go out while they went on their business. She looked Svanhild up and down, critically.

"We need you to look richer, so you'll get a better deal. The dress isn't half bad." Svanhild had changed into her other finer dress, which, wrapped in muslin in her pack, had stayed unsoiled despite her fall. "But your wimple won't do." She picked up a pile of cloth and pulled out a snowy white one with a blue ribbon along the edge, picked out in rust-colored thread. "This will suit you better," she said. Svanhild tied the wimple on her head, under her hair, so it spread out in a long wave over her back. "That's good," said Gerta. "Now you stand up straight, and act like you do this all the time. Mind you pick up your skirts in the street. You don't want what's flowing there on them."

Svanhild followed Gerta out into the street, between the houses. Now that the sun had risen above the fjord cliffs, the town stank even worse than it had in the morning, a mixture of meat and vegetable offal, of human waste, of seaweed and sweat. Svanhild nearly gagged with it. Gerta was a few steps ahead of her, with longer strides, and she hurried to keep up.

Crowds pressed in upon them at the center of the town. Gerta slowed her step and walked next to Svanhild. Men with bundles parted on either side of them. Men and women called out greetings to Gerta, which she acknowledged with a nod of her head. Svanhild tried to keep her head up as well, but she had to look at where she placed her feet to avoid stepping in dung.

"How do you know so many?" she asked.

Gerta nodded to another shopkeeper. "Since my husband's death, I have been allowed to speak at our local assembly. Here we are." She stopped in front of a wooden door that looked like all the rest.

"Is it—will they see us?"

"He will see me," said Gerta. She rapped loudly on the door.

A short man with a squint opened it. "Eh, Gerta, it's early."

"Yes," said Gerta, walking in, with Svanhild behind her. "Fasti, my niece Thorfrida is visiting me, and she has tired of her brooches. She would like to sell them to you." Svanhild tried not to gape at Gerta's lies. Gerta knew what she was doing here.

"Yes?" said Fasti. "My wife, may she rest peacefully, was called Thorfrida. It's a lucky name. She was a beauty too. Didn't give me children, but she was a good wife. Ah, have a seat."

Svanhild wondered how lucky the name Thorfrida could be, if she was barren and dead, but she only thanked him for the compliment. Inside the room was neat and snug. Oil burned in sconces on the walls, giving the room an orange glow.

"Haven't opened up yet," he said. The shop had a hole cut in the wall, like a little door, with shutters, and these he pushed open, letting more light into the room. "A niece of Gerta must be lucky indeed," he said. His squint deepened. "And wealthy."

Svanhild had seen little evidence of Gerta's wealth. Perhaps there was more to her than met the eye—or maybe she was only a good manager, who ate simply and kept her wealth for other things.

"Why don't you see what we have for sale?" said Fasti. He brought over a tray of brooches, some worked in gold, others in silver, all of the metal so beautiful and well cared for that it seemed to invite her touch. She looked at Gerta. She was not here to buy.

"She might consider your trinkets," said Gerta dismissively, "after she sees what you can give her for her brooches." She nodded at Svanhild, who brought them out. They seemed plain next to the gold Fasti had shown her.

Fasti took them and turned them over in his hands. "Amber," he said flatly.

"See how beautiful the pieces are," said Gerta. "They are almost perfectly matched, and clear."

Fasti held the brooches up to the light coming in from the window.

"They're from Dublin," said Svanhild, "the king's court."

"They are known for their silver workers," said Gerta.

"Put out your hand," said Fasti. He took out a small pouch of silver coins and counted them into Svanhild's hand.

She realized that she had no idea what might be reasonable, what she might need to take her to Tafjord and beyond. Transactions at Ardal and even at the *ting* were as often in trade as coin. She had heard the law recited recently enough to know the price of a free man's life, but not of her jewelry. She folded her palm around the coins. "My brooches weigh more than this," she said hesitantly.

"Is that so?" Gerta asked. "Fasti, come now, you know I'm no fool. Did you think my niece would be as well?" Svanhild opened her hand and put it out. Quickly, Fasti doubled the amount of coin Svanhild held.

"That's better," said Svanhild. She glanced at Gerta. Gerta would not scruple to speak, so Svanhild must be doing well enough. "Still, I don't know," she said to Gerta. "Didn't you say there was another jeweler we could try?"

Fasti spat on the floor. "Haki? You would trust him over me?"

Svanhild looked to Gerta, who tilted her head, as if considering. "I'm sure you are doing the best you can for us," Gerta said. "These are hard times." She caught Svanhild's eye again, and Svanhild thought she saw the corner of Gerta's mouth quirk.

"Put this silver aside for us," said Svanhild. "We will return after talking with Haki."

"Five more coins if you take it now," said Fasti. "And come back to look at my wares again." Svanhild looked at Gerta, and pretended to think it over. It seemed like a game, one Svanhild liked, and thought she was playing well.

"Yes, of course," said Svanhild. "You are a very fair trader." Gerta produced a small satchel for Svanhild to pour the coin into, and secured it to her own belt. "Perhaps I had better . . . ," said Svanhild, not liking to see it there.

Gerta gave her a stern look. "Thank you, Fasti, of course we will return."

"Yes," said Svanhild. She gave him a curtsy. "Your wares are enchanting."

She followed Gerta out onto the street, sticking close to her as a burr. If Gerta meant to take the coin from her, there was little Svanhild could do about it. Gerta was taller and stronger than her, and more than that, Gerta had the respect of the whole town, while Svanhild was a stranger.

They returned to Gerta's house the same way they had come; Svanhild noticed that the houses, which had all seemed the same before now, had subtle variations, banners of different colors hanging from them, open doors and windows.

As soon as they returned to Gerta's house, she untied the coin purse and gave it to Svanhild. "You're a sour little thing," she said. "Did you think I would cheat you?"

"Well," said Svanhild, feeling a bit ashamed now, "you did lie to Fasti."

"I help you, you help me," she said. "Not everything is swords and oaths like that tale you told me of your brother. Here, we trade instead. And anyway, I've brought Fasti nieces before—he knows it's a game we play."

"Are all your nieces named Thorfrida?" Svanhild asked, her hands on her hips.

Gerta smiled at that. "No, I've not tried that before. It will only work once, so count yourself lucky. Now, you're a fair hand with a bargain, but you never would have made that deal on your own, so I want my fair measure."

Svanhild felt badly about having mistrusted Gerta, and pulled out a few more coins than she had originally intended to give Gerta. From the way Gerta smiled as she closed her hand around them, Svanhild thought maybe that was the point of this whole little charade—Gerta had pushed Svanhild into mistrusting her and then feeling guilty for it. Svanhild poured out the rest of the coins into the sock she had been using for her brooches, and knotted it tight. She handed the coin purse back to Gerta.

"Does everyone here play these games?" she asked, gesturing at Gerta's hand, which still clasped the coins Svanhild had given her.

"Yes," said Gerta, "and you've a skill with them I didn't guess. Though you can't let yourself be swayed by a little indignance from your target."

"Thank you for the lesson," Svanhild said crisply, but without much rancor. She still needed Gerta to help her find a ship.

"Are you sure you couldn't learn to weave on the tablets?" Gerta asked. "It is not much different from regular weaving. I need a girl here, to learn my craft. If you stay, you won't have to ask your brother for his protection."

As much as Gerta had irritated her, Svanhild wished she could say yes. Gerta had as much freedom as she could buy or bargain for. She was respected in Kaupanger and did not seem to worry about the wider world, except in how it brought coin to her hand. But Svanhild had no skill at anything that could be sold here; she was born and made to run a household, to sew up a warrior's wounds, to face down summer raiders, not for this petty handling of material, here on the fringes of society.

She shook her head. "I'm hopeless."

Gerta nodded, not seeming too worried. "I thought as much. And you've family and blood," she said, meditatively.

"Will you still help me find a ship to go to Yrjar?"

"Yes," said Gerta. "Remember me when you're fine and married to a king. Now, can you at least help me sort some flax? Or is her ladyship hopeless at that too?"

"I can do that," said Svanhild, stung by the sarcasm.

She sat with Gerta the rest of the day, picking through the fine fibers, separating short stricks from long tow. During the afternoon, men and women came to talk with Gerta about various issues affecting the town, and Gerta gave her opinion. In the evening, they ate the stew Svanhild had made. Gerta drank ale—at first Svanhild tried to join her, but Gerta drank glass after glass, and fell asleep with her head on her kitchen table. Svanhild covered her with a blanket and found a straw mattress to curl up on.

Outside, the sounds of voices in the town, of animals carrying loads, continued into the night. Gerta snored. Svanhild tried to imagine what the next day would bring, until she too fell asleep.

19

BEFORE TWILIGHT, GUTHORM'S SCOUTS RETURNED WITH NEWS
that the meeting of kings would be held at King Gudbrand's hall. The
kings had been together for a few days, and next day was the great
feast. They should be sleeping off their drunkenness when Guthorm's
forces arrived. All depended on secrecy and speed, or the seven kings
would scatter, return to their halls, and muster men to fight. Guthorm
had even brought Harald's mother, Ronhild, along with them to chant
her spells and ensure that they remained hidden. Ragnvald had only
seen a glimpse of her so far on this journey, sitting cross-legged at the
foot of the flagship's mast, her long fair hair in a plait down her back.

Ragnvald was last to the ship. He pushed it off the sandy bottom
and swung himself up into the bow, keeping his mouth shut over any
grunt of effort that might escape. He made his way toward the front of
the ship through the press of tense and silent bodies.

Harald's ship *Dragon Tongue* sailed up the river, with Oddi's *Bear
Biter* behind her. They kept the dragon figureheads stowed, and did
not hang their shields from the sides of the ship.

This land seemed strange to Ragnvald. They had passed between
high cliffs while navigating the main body of the fjord, but the walls of
the tributary fell away quickly and had low, sloped banks, which widened the farther inland they sailed. On one bank, a boy waved a switch
at the backside of a fat ewe. His mouth hung slack as he watched the
ships go by.

Ragnvald flexed his hands. He had left the blood from the day before to dry on the backs, and now it prickled. He examined the base of his thumb, where the boy had bitten him. His teeth had drawn blood. Ragnvald would have to treat the wound carefully. He had seen bites go putrid within days. One of Solvi's men, who had suffered a bite from a struggling woman, had his hand hacked off by the healers, and even that had not saved him from death by fever. Ragnvald wrapped a cloth around the wound, and tied the ends.

Farther on, a pretty girl stood up from her hoeing to watch them pass. The sun behind her lit up her long, unbound hair, making her appear crowned in a golden flame. Next to him, Oddi took a deep breath. Longing stirred in Ragnvald's chest. He wondered what golden-haired Vigdis did at this moment, if she tormented his mother. How did Svanhild fare with Hilda and all her sisters? He raised his hand to wave at the girl. She waved back and then lifted her hand to shade her eyes as the ship slid by.

They sailed past other farms, then through a thick forest, buzzing with insects. Trees overhung the river, making dappled shadows on the water. The ships slowed to a halt. Ragnvald jumped out into the waist-deep water and, with Heming and Oddi, hauled on the ropes until the ship was close enough to the shore for her shallow keel to brush the sandy bottom. They would wait in the forest until twilight, then attack farther upriver. Ronhild had looked at the clouds before advising Hakon, and thrown the rune sticks, and determined that this night, the wind would blow them downriver rather than thwart their escape.

Finally Hakon spoke: "It's time."

Hakon had placed Oddi and Ragnvald in a ship of their own for the attack, giving Oddi command. Those who were not waiting in the ships crept toward them from the river's banks and climbed in. Ragnvald checked himself once, twice, and again for his weapons: sword at his right hip, lying in its scabbard along his thigh, dagger on his left hip, ax hanging from his back.

No wind stirred. Sweat from Ragnvald's scalp dripped down the back of his neck, wetting the tunic he wore under his leather armor. He felt a hand on his arm and turned to see Heming standing next to him. Ragnvald raised his eyebrows questioningly. Heming smiled slightly and shrugged, tipping his head toward Hakon's boat, as if to say, perhaps, his father had placed him here.

The most experienced oarsmen rowed tonight, dipping their oars soundlessly into the smooth river and raising them again with little to mark their passing but a smooth ripple flowing back from the bow. They rowed for a hundred breaths, and then a hundred more. The shore slipped by, trees black against the purple sky.

Then they reached Gudbrand's hall and surrounding fields. Its outbuildings were hardly visible against the dark hill behind them, save for a circle of light. The bow of the ship crunched against the bank. It sounded terribly loud to Ragnvald, as he strained his ears in the silence. Heming leapt out front. Ragnvald followed him, landing softly in the grass, Oddi by his side. Ragnvald held his sword in front of him, tip up, but low so his arm would not give out before he had a chance to drive it into flesh. All around him he could sense the watchful tension of the other men. Heming breathed low and even, as if he did this every day. On the other side of him, Oddi was taut as a new-strung bow. Ragnvald forced himself to loosen his grip. His hand tingled as blood returned to it.

Somewhere in front of him was Harald, leading the raiding party. Ragnvald kept his eyes fixed on Oddi's leather belt, which had been polished recently enough that it was a spot of gray in the darkness. He did not want to creep up too close behind him.

Hakon and his younger sons went with the main force, over the open slope that led up to Gudbrand's hall. Ragnvald and Hakon's older sons would come around through the grove, and attack from the other side. If they could, they meant to barricade the meeting kings inside the hall, and threaten to burn it unless the kings swore allegiance to Harald.

Ragnvald's party had the longer journey, picking through the darkness at the water's edge. He heard the shouts of battle, sword upon sword, the crash of shields, and then shouts of victory. Harald's voice carried above all the others, calling out the numbers of his slain.

In front of him, Oddi's shoulders slumped with relief. Ragnvald was not sure later what made him turn. Perhaps a branch snapped, and attracted his attention. Ragnvald touched Oddi's back. When Oddi turned, Ragnvald jerked his head toward where he had heard the noise and laid a finger on his lips. He took a step toward the dark shape of a grove of trees. This would be the sacrificial grove for the hall, rich and well watered with the blood of animals and men. An auspicious place for defenders to wait, so they could deliver more deaths to the gods.

Ragnvald touched the charm at his neck, praying for bravery. If the gods favored him, then they would help him when he fought on their ground.

"Men," he whispered to his companions, "in the trees."

Heming nodded, a movement Ragnvald felt more than saw. They could not risk more speech. Their footsteps took them into the shadow of a hollow in the hill, and Ragnvald jerked his head to the right, and followed the darkness of the low ground, hoping that Oddi and Heming stayed close behind him.

A silhouette detached itself from the grove of trees, moving stealthily along its margin. Ragnvald wondered if their plan was to allow Harald's men freedom of their farm and then kill them during the celebrating. It was what Ragnvald might do, though it would put their property at risk. The grove was small—perhaps they only had a few men. Those that remained hid here, to defend the hall as best they could. Ragnvald circled around behind the enemy. A cloud passed over the moon, plunging the field into darkness. Ragnvald drew his dagger with his other hand. He could kill left-handed if he had to.

Oddi and Heming were still a few steps behind. The bulk of Hakon and Harald's forces cleared the crest of the hill, their thick-armored forms making dark shapes against the sky. Ragnvald could hear them still: sounds of excitement, of carelessness. They believed they had won.

The twang of loosed arrows filled the night. Men screamed. The sound chilled Ragnvald's blood. Hakon's force had brought no bows. Were all of them now caught in a trap? Ragnvald lost the shape of the man he tracked for a moment, until his silhouette blocked the slimmer trees. Ragnvald continued walking forward as if he had not seen the figure that paced him.

The man came closer, slightly behind Ragnvald, so close that Ragnvald could smell the meat of his dinner. He waited until he heard the hitch of breath that preceded the man's attack, then turned and thrust his dagger up into the man's throat. He died without a sound, choking on steel. Ragnvald eased him to the ground. He wiped the blood from his hands on the man's tunic.

Ragnvald glanced up at the hall, through the trees. The clouds had cleared, and now moonlight showed him figures with bows clinging to its thatched roof. How long had they been waiting there? Did Ragnvald's boy captive have a friend, one who had escaped and told of their coming?

Whatever other men remained in the grove had not yet emerged. Ragnvald guessed they would not until the barrage of arrows stopped. Ragnvald motioned for Oddi and Heming to follow him. A gap between two boulders served as the gateway to the grove—a perfect choke point. Ragnvald pantomimed climbing, and Oddi took his meaning, scrambling up one of the rocks. The sound of fingers prying at dirt seemed loud, even against the yells of men pierced with arrows, but no attack came.

In the grove, a half circle of figures, hardly moving more than stumps of wood, crouched facing the two boulders. Now, hidden in the shadow of the rocks, the advantage of darkness was with Ragnvald's party. Nearby a bird flapped, surprised from its nest, and made a low call. One of the heads of the waiting men came up, but a harsh hiss told him to stay seated.

A signal. They were waiting for a signal. Ragnvald sheathed dagger and cupped his hand around his mouth, making the sound of an owl. His heart thudded in his chest. He drew his blade again slowly.

"That's it," he heard a voice say.

"Floki was supposed to make a raven's call," spoke a voice, young and uncertain.

"Floki's an idiot." An older man, this one.

"Do you think they got them all?" whispered the young one as they crept toward the shadow where Ragnvald hid.

"No," said Ragnvald, pitching his voice low and gruff as the older warrior's had been. The older warrior whirled to face him. Ragnvald saw the glint of bared steel a moment before the sword crashed into the rock where he had stood.

Then all was chaos. Ragnvald could not tell if he struck friend or foe—he lashed out with sword and dagger, finding trees as often as he found flesh. He heard a crash and a howl and hoped that was Heming ambushing one of the men from above. That was not Oddi's yell, nor Heming's, so some worthy damage had been done. He tried to keep himself behind the men leaving the grove, so his blade would only harm enemy flesh, but he found himself pulling his swings, hoping he was not wounding kin or friends.

He fought in close with one strong man who got a few shallow cuts in on him before Ragnvald stabbed him through the stomach. He fell moaning, and when his noises stopped, all was quiet. It was the sort of silence Ragnvald had heard before in battle, a moment when all the earth seemed to pause. Ragnvald peered into the darkness. No one stirred except his friends.

"How many did you get, brother?" Heming said to Oddi.

"I'm not sure," Oddi answered. He sounded winded. "I feared I'd cut one of you."

"Me too," said Ragnvald, glad Oddi had said it first.

A few more groans came from the ground around them. The noise of battle resumed up the hill. The sounds of arrows had stopped, and now there was screaming. Oddi took off up the hill, and Ragnvald had started to join him when Heming's hand on his arm held him back.

"We leave tonight for Tafjord," said Heming. "That is the land I want—not this. My father spreads himself too thin, in pursuit of this dream of King Harald's. Maer will be my kingdom. All of my father's jarls will respect me then." It took Ragnvald a moment to realize what Heming was saying: that he was planning some different assault even while fighting these men. Ragnvald would not have been able to split his attention so.

"You mean your father will," Ragnvald said. More yelling sounded from up the hill. He needed to be there, with Hakon, where he was sworn. "Let me go."

"Only if you come with us," said Heming. "Otherwise you die here. My sword is always hungry for more blood. You should be my sworn man, not my father's."

Ragnvald stayed silent. He could not make his mind move from the battle at hand to think of this, except to know that his dreams had been dealt a blow here. Between Hakon and his son was where Jarl Runolf had died.

Pressing what he must have thought was his advantage, Heming continued, "My father thinks to make himself young by surrounding himself with young men." He spoke quickly and angrily, words well rehearsed. "You can be one of my jarls when Maer is mine."

"Must we leave this very moment?" Ragnvald asked. The sounds of fighting from the hall tore at him. His place was there, by Hakon. He had sworn it.

Heming did not seem to hear the sarcasm. "No. Only do not drink overmuch when we celebrate tonight. We leave when all are sleeping."

"We must help them," Ragnvald said, pulling out of Heming's grasp, hoping Heming would not realize that Ragnvald had not agreed.

His legs felt weak as he sprinted up the hill, until he heard Heming's footsteps behind him, and fear lent him a burst of strength. Heming would not kill him in the open, not when he thought he had Ragnvald's agreement, but Ragnvald still reached the hall a half dozen paces ahead of him.

Torches lit the area now. Some of the men had dragged women into the shadows and raped them. One still screamed. The others only whimpered. A girl clutching a kitchen knife, her skirt streaked with blood, sat against a tree. She snarled at Ragnvald when he passed by, making Ragnvald think of Svanhild at her fiercest. He walked past her, trying not to see her. He would not hurt her worse.

He breathed a sigh of relief when he saw that the sounds he heard had only been those of pillage, not of the slaughter of Hakon and Harald's men. Some men had attacked with bows from the roof, but their arrows ran out before Hakon and Harald's forces did. After their men fell, women fought back when they could—some had armed themselves with daggers and kitchen knives—but they were no match for Hakon's men.

"Where were you?" Hakon asked when he saw Ragnvald approach. "I thought you were right behind me."

"There were men in the woods," said Ragnvald. He smiled, cheeks tight from the deer's blood earlier and now the drying blood of men. "There aren't anymore."

"The men on the roof, the men in the woods. They meant to trap us in between," said Guthorm. "Did they know of our coming? Did someone betray us?"

Ragnvald shrugged. "Perhaps they had watchers we did not see who glimpsed Guthorm's scouts." He hoped it had been that, and not a companion of the boy he had captured. Heming, at least, had not betrayed Guthorm in this, but he was planning a betrayal tonight.

Guthorm clapped Ragnvald on the shoulder. "You are right. I start at shadows in these fractious times."

"We have taken but few losses," said Hakon. "Perhaps they hoped to ambush us from the grove and the hall, but we brought too many men for them. It was wise of you and Harald to ally with me. Where is Heming?"

"Heming?" Ragnvald asked. "My lord, I must speak with you about—"

"Later," said Guthorm. "We have work to do."

Guthorm's men had surrounded the hall with great bales of tinder, ready to be put to the torch. Archers on the roof, with now-empty quivers, tried to climb down, only to be prodded back up onto the turf by the warriors who surrounded the hall. Guthorm's men banged on their shields.

"Kings of Hordaland," called out Harald, once the noise subsided, "we will burn you in your hall, along with your crows on the roof, if you do not come out and swear to me."

The great doors to the hall opened a crack.

"I am King Harald of Vestfold," Harald proclaimed in a mighty voice, low-pitched enough to avoid the boy's breaking that troubled him in more casual conversation. "I am the conqueror of King Gandalf of Akershus, the prophesied king of all Norway." He presented himself with authority, at least. Guthorm had chosen his figurehead well. "If you swear allegiance to me, I will make you more powerful than you could ever dream. Your enemies will shake before you, and your sons will inherit great wealth. If you do not, your lives will be forfeit."

The doors of the hall opened slowly. Two kings walked out, surrounded by a cadre of guards: Hogne and Frode Karusson, the brother kings of two adjoining Hordaland kingdoms. They were short, stout men, the kind of stoutness that gave strength. Both men looked as though they could wrestle a bear and win.

"But . . . you're just a boy," said King Hogne. Ragnvald had not heard much of the Karusson kings, except that Hogne was all bluster, and his brother Frode was all rage.

"I am what I am," said Harald. "I will grow older, and Norway will be mine. You will not grow older than you are now if you do not swear to me."

They did not swear, for who had heard of such a thing? Ragnvald could hear their thinking as though they shouted it. Harald, or Guthorm who drove him, was a madman or a visionary. Norse kings killed one another, or made alliances of equals. Men raided and sometimes set-tled, but this talk of conquering was a new language, from another land. They rushed forward, their guard band against Harald's hundreds.

Harald gave the signal for his men to burn the hall. Hordaland men ran forward to die on the swords of Harald's army. Ragnvald killed a few, for he was standing near Harald, where the fighting was thickest, but they would have died no matter who held the swords, trapped between fire and blade. The hall burned as the king's men fell. Skalds later sung that Harald killed seven kings that day.

When this spasm of fighting was over, the hall still blazed. Ragn-vald staggered off to find some watered ale to slake his thirst. Oddi stopped him, telling him Hakon wanted to speak with him.

"We've taken these prisoners," said Hakon, gesturing to men bound and gagged, lying on the ground. One curled around a bloody stomach, moaning. "Some of them may know where the other Horda-land kings have gone. I have heard tell that Gudbrand is not here. He must have been here, for this is his own hall."

Ragnvald's legs felt tired and shaky, the aftermath of battle. It left some men giddy, ready for drink and a woman. Ragnvald found it more tiring—he wanted sleep, forgetfulness now.

"We did well," said Hakon to Ragnvald and Oddi. "These kings have seen rich plunder." Hakon gestured for Oddi to step aside. He reached down and picked up a small casket with metal hinges instead of the usual leather and held it toward Ragnvald. "Open it."

Ragnvald did, and found it full of hacksilver, and many coins stamped with a slim, bearded profile Ragnvald knew to be the English king Alfred.

"This is part of the Danegeld," said Ragnvald.

"The great English ransom," Oddi echoed. "Cowards," he added, but without much heat. If the English were willing to pay a Danish army to stay away from their shores, it meant more English treasure could come east. And become Hakon's treasure.

"Are these kings allied with the Danes?" Ragnvald asked.

"Perhaps," said Hakon, without much interest. He was secure in his power. "I would give you a ring for your service in the woods this night," he said to Ragnvald. "But since we found this—I will give you a double handful of silver as well." He smiled at Ragnvald's frown of concern. "Use one handful to buy your bride. And another to buy thralls to farm your land."

Ragnvald looked down at the silver, greedy for his handfuls. He took his share, filling the satchel at his belt. Not all the coins bore Alfred's face. Some of the coins were lettered with the hard angles of Greek; some others had the graceful curls of Arabic writing. They had come, and seen blood, long before this night.

"My men have kept aside a few unspoiled women," Hakon added. "Take one, get yourself properly drunk. Time enough for speeches and gifts tomorrow."

"Some men should guard the treasure," said Ragnvald, feeling uninterested in women or celebration. He did not know if that was because of the girl who had reminded him of Svanhild, or because of Heming's threats. Well, one of those had a solution. "If you allow me, I will see to it. But first, I must speak with you." He lowered his voice. Hakon would not want Harald and Guthorm to know of Heming's plot. "There is treachery near you."

Ragnvald looked around for Heming, but wherever he was, it was not here. Perhaps he was enjoying one of those unspoiled women now—all the more reason for Ragnvald to stay clear.

Hakon waved off a few men who stood near. "Tell me," he said.

"Heming means to leave tonight when all the men are drunk, and sail back to Tafjord to attack Hunthiof and Solvi."

"How do you know this?"

"He told—he asked me to come with him," said Ragnvald. It seemed petulant to bring up Heming's threats, and Hakon might believe him less.

"And you do not wish to?"

"Solvi will keep," said Ragnvald. In truth, he did not want revenge on Solvi, not the way he did upon Olaf. "I am here now."

"Thank you for telling me this," said Hakon, his eyes shadowed. "Come with me. If it is true, Heming will answer for it."

They found Heming standing under the eaves of one of the outbuildings, together with the captains who must have decided to throw in with him. He looked so guilty when Hakon and Ragnvald approached that Ragnvald did not fear being disbelieved.

"Is what I would give you not enough?" Hakon roared, on seeing him. The captains glanced at each other and, by unspoken accord, slunk off in various directions. Hakon narrowed his eyes at their leaving, but did not stop them. "I would have made you king of Maer, had you only waited a season. Ragnvald here would have been your adviser and companion."

Ragnvald made his face as impassive as possible, trying not to show how ill that would have suited him.

"Explain yourself," said Hakon.

"I am a man's age now, have been five years gone," said Heming, his hand on his sword. Ragnvald put his own there. He was sworn to defend Hakon. "Yet you treat me like a boy."

"Because you act like a boy."

"King Hunthiof is your sworn enemy. I want to kill him for you. You defied your father and conquered Halogaland," said Heming, his angry tone turning aggrieved.

"Because I was a younger son, and my father did not mean to give me anything I could not take with my own hands. I conquered Halogaland before my older brother could."

"That is not what the songs say," said Heming.

"You call me a liar?" Hakon roared. "The songs say what I will them to say."

"I'm sure your puppet Ragnvald said what you wanted him to say too."

Ragnvald tightened his grip on his sword, in case Heming should draw on him now.

"Ragnvald is sworn to me, not you. He did what a man ought," Hakon said.

Ragnvald wanted to be far away from here. If he left, would they stop talking about him? He continued to back away, slowly, in case Hakon bid him stay, but he did not. Ragnvald had volunteered to set guards for Hakon's treasure, and that would serve to keep him busy and out of Heming's way until morning.

✛   ✛   ✛

ODDI CAME TO sit by him later in the night. Ragnvald paced back and forth in the dark, around the pile of treasure that Hakon had looted. The hall smoldered and smoked. He greeted Oddi, who sat on a rock, looking down toward the river, toward the grove where they had done their killing.

"My father has spent half the night scolding Heming and the other half torturing the captives. He is angry." Oddi spread his hands. They were still red with blood, flecked with darker specks of something thicker—from battle, or else he had been called on to help with the torture. When Ragnvald sailed with him, Solvi had said that some men had the stomach for torture, and some did not. Solvi himself did not, he said, and so he kept Ulfarr to do the work for him. He had said it was not unmanly, for true men had deep feelings. Ragnvald had wondered then, what Ulfarr thought of that, but Ulfarr seemed proud to do this bloody work, to set himself apart from the ranks of other men. Ragnvald would not have thought Oddi had the stomach for it either, at least not to seek it out.

"Did you do it? The . . . questioning?" Ragnvald asked.

"No," said Oddi. "It is bad enough to see. He cut the guts out of the first man while his fellows watched. I think he wanted to frighten Guthorm and Harald." He shook his head as if to dispel the vision. "At least I did not vomit. All we learned is that King Gudbrand is on the move with his warriors. He has heard of our coming or of Harald's. We will not catch him, not without more information, or more men."

Ragnvald was surprised at that. They had near on four hundred men, and Harald at least that many, surely more than a petty Hordaland king could likely muster, at least on short notice. He said as much to Oddi.

"Gudbrand has raised men against Harald already," said Oddi.

"Then he should be easy to find. That many men cannot pass unnoticed. Will we put more halls to the torch?" Ragnvald asked, feeling stupid from lack of sleep.

"I know not," said Oddi, looking at him curiously. "You sound worried. Do you not like killing?" he asked, more bitterly. He held his hands oddly, apart from one another, not relaxed.

"I like it well enough," said Ragnvald. "Until the middle of the night when it is done." He gave Oddi a smile that felt strange. He was in one of those odd moods that overtook him after battle, now that Solvi had wounded his face. Every battle since then had ended wrongly for him: Solvi's dagger, a false *draugr*, and now Heming's betrayal. "What will this King Harald have us do? What does he bid?"

"You can guess as well as I," said Oddi.

"Yes," said Ragnvald. "We will find King Gudbrand, and put him to the sword. We will put all the other men to the sword who opposed us. We will open more bellies. We will sell his slaves away from his lands, and ransom his women from their kinsmen, just as we are doing now. We would torture some, if we felt like it."

"You are tired and drunk," said Oddi. "Go, find a woman, and sleep some. I will guard here." Oddi looked down at his bloody hands again and then wiped them off on the grass.

"No, I took this task," said Ragnvald. "I am guarding this gold. How much gold do kings need?"

"What do you want, Ragnvald?" Oddi asked. "If you would know the shape of fates and of countries, go talk to a skald or a priest, or talk to Ronhild the sorceress. If you're not going to sleep, I will, and I don't want you sending me evil dreams."

He stood up and walked away. Ragnvald immediately regretted speaking as he had, voicing questions no man could answer: why some

men were kings, and others soldiers; why a man like Olaf would raise
Ragnvald up to be his son and then betray him. Why Hakon would set
his sons against each other; why gold flowed to his hands, while Ragnvald had to be grateful for a handful of silver. He would need more
than that to make Ardal into the farm it should be, rich as he remembered it as a boy, with cows that ended the winter fat as they began it.
And then a hundred times that to become a fine enough lord that the
men of Sogn would be willing to acclaim him king. And he should be
grateful to Hakon, but the obligation only made him feel small.

20

GERTA WOKE EARLY THE NEXT MORNING, SEEMING NONE THE worse for her drinking. She must drink that deeply every night. Svanhild followed behind her, with her bags over her shoulder, as Gerta led her toward the beach. Svanhild's head ached a bit from the two glasses of ale she had consumed.

Gerta carried herself ramrod straight. She took no provisions, though she had pressed a few rounds of bread and hunks of cheese on Svanhild. Svanhild took that to mean that Gerta would not be traveling with her. She thought of Gerta's desire to go to Yrjar, and also of her offering Svanhild a place with her. Gerta had carved out a life of independence and respect here in Kaupanger, but it looked lonely.

They walked among the ships pulled up on the beach. Gerta lifted her skirts as she stepped over slimy piles of seaweed. She gave each of the vessels a careful look, and then walked on to the next one. Svanhild could see little difference between the ships—most were wide and deep, without oar ports—knarrs, for merchants. They could not outrun an enemy, or leave a harbor quickly, but they could carry far more cargo than a dragon ship, from what Svanhild could see. Ragnvald had said they also required less skill and fewer men to sail than a narrow warship.

At length, Gerta stopped in front of a well-maintained merchant's vessel. On the deck, a stoutly built man near Gerta's age directed two younger men loading heavy chests. He had white hair, kept short and neatly brushed, a short beard, and small, dark eyes, but he looked youthful for all that, with a restless energy to all of his movements. Gerta waved the older man over, and they had a low conversation. Then she motioned Svanhild to come closer.

"This is my friend Solmund," said Gerta.

Svanhild made her greeting with a curtsy, and introduced herself, glancing at Gerta before giving her real name.

"How does the fancywork business?" Solmund asked. "My wife treasures the counterpane you gave her."

Gerta nodded at the compliment. "Well enough," she said. "When next you go to Birka, perhaps I will accompany you."

Solmund smiled. "You always say that, Gerta."

Gerta nodded again. It seemed she would not smile this morning—the only evidence of her night spent drinking. "I wish you a speedy journey," she said to Svanhild.

"Thank you for your help," said Svanhild. "The gods smile on your hospitality." Svanhild would have liked to hug Gerta, but Gerta's straight back seemed to forbid it. She watched Gerta leave, feeling bereft. Here she was, handed off yet again.

Svanhild bowed to Solmund again when Gerta receded from view. "Can I help with anything?" she asked.

"You can see if my wife needs anything," said Solmund absently, waving in the direction of the ship. Svanhild was happy to learn that there would be another woman on board, although she had resolved not to doubt Gerta's trust of Solmund. As she descended the stairs into the ship's hold, she made a prayer to Freya in thanks for her good luck. The gods must smile on this path.

Solmund's wife, from what Svanhild could see in the gloom inside the ship, was possessed of a friendlier face than Gerta's. Had she more flesh on her bones, she might have been pretty. Her shoulders and hips were narrowly framed, and her life at sea had stripped any excess from her, leaving her eyes and cheeks deeply shadowed in their hollows.

"I like company," she said, when Svanhild greeted her and told of her destination. "Though I am glad I had sons, not daughters. A daughter might keep me at home. Not a daughter such as you, it seems." Svanhild felt that was an invitation to tell her story, and so she did, as far as fleeing Hrolf's farm.

"That is a bold story," said Solmund's wife. "Are you sure this is safe for you?"

"Is any sea travel safe?" Svanhild asked. "This is safer to me than staying behind."

Solmund's ship carried gold and Frankish swords for King Hakon, as well as bolts of cloth from Constantinople. Svanhild and the wife—who gave her name as Haldora—unwound the rich fabric to make sure that it was aired and would not spoil during the journey, then rewound it back on its dowels. In this way they passed the time until high tide, when Solmund made a prayer to the sea gods Njord and Ran, bowing and gesturing over the bow of the ship, and then cast them off. Svanhild sat with Haldora near the small tent on the deck where the whole family slept if they had to spend a night on board.

Haldora gave Svanhild a length of wool roving and an empty spindle. "It's hard to spin shipboard," she said, "but you'll soon get the trick of it." Svanhild had been too busy watching Solmund cast them off to explain that she was a poor spinner at the best of times.

Solmund's sons were well made, taller than their father, loose-limbed, with the promise of attaining their father's bulk one day. They climbed over masts and gunwales like mountain goats on a steep slope. None among them looked as formidable as Ragnvald, though.

Svanhild had been too scared and busy over the past few days to think of her brother much. Soon she would pass over the same sea roads he had sailed on his way to Yrjar. She would see the things that he had seen and described to her: the diving of ocean birds, the sea fog, the seals that rested on rocks and called to each other like playful children. The wind blowing off the fjord smelled new-washed.

After they maneuvered out into the middle of the fjord, Svanhild picked up the spindle and the bolt of fine wool roving. "Do you have anything rougher?" she asked. "I'm better suited to sail wool."

Haldora plucked the spinning from her lap. "You need not spin at all, my dear, I only thought you might be happier with your hands occupied."

Svanhild smiled at that. "I can as easily comb wool for you, or something simpler."

Haldora gave her an odd look, but like most women, she detested the tedious task of picking sticks and dirt out of wool, and then the endless combing between iron spikes until all the fibers ran the same way. At least Svanhild could always make friends by offering to do that work.

✣   ✣   ✣

THEY STOPPED THAT night on a narrow beach beneath the fjord's high cliff. Solmund's sons pitched a tent on the sand while Svanhild and Haldora prepared the evening meal. Svanhild added some of Gerta's bread to the repast. She and Haldora waited on the men until Haldora sat down next to her husband on a piece of driftwood to eat her meal, salt fish boiled with some leeks, and so Svanhild sat down as well, rather than waiting until the men were done.

"How do you come to be out here alone?" asked Solmund.

Svanhild tried to tell a short version of leaving Hrolf's farm, glancing at Haldora, who smiled at her—she did not mind hearing the same story twice. So Svanhild added as much as she could of Ragnvald's story, before she meant to, telling of Solvi, how he tried to kill her brother, at Olaf's leading.

"It is like something out of an old song," said one of Solmund's sons eagerly, tripping over the words.

"And Solvi asked for me," said Svanhild, laughing and blushing. "It is too foolish to be a heroic tale, and I would rather not figure in a comic one."

"This Thorkell does not seem so bad," said Haldora gently.

Did all women think the same? Svanhild looked to Solmund. "Do you trade with Solvi Hunthiofsson?" she asked. "Or his father?"

Solmund looked taken aback, perhaps to be questioned so boldly by a woman. Svanhild bit her lip—she should have followed Haldora's lead more. Haldora was competent and brave, it seemed, to lead this life, but gentle too.

Solmund finished chewing his bread before he spoke. "I used to. Before I married, when this Solvi was still a boy. Tafjord was a rough place, always too many warriors without enough to do. When I brought servants to help me, Hunthiof's men would have sport of them, forcing them to fight one another so they could bet, that sort of thing." Warriors played cruel games, and servants and thralls were usually the butt of them. Svanhild knew this. A good king would keep his men from doing too much damage, but they must be allowed to pass the time somehow.

"That was before Hunthiof's wife died. I came there once after that. By Thor, I was glad I had left Haldora and my sons at home. It had become haunted. The boy ran wild. Men had been killed in duels—or nothing as formal as a duel—and their bodies lay unburied around the hall. It had snowed early that year at least, so the stench was not so bad until I came into the hall. I should have fled then and there.

"'I would bid you welcome,' King Hunthiof said when I came with my usual wares. 'But we are the dead here, and there is no welcome from the dead, for the dead.' His words chilled me. I could see that he had taken leave of his senses, and that his men, those that remained, had followed him into madness. His son, Solvi, had recovered from his injuries enough to walk, but he did not speak. He only wandered among the fallen men—and none could tell those fallen from drink from those fallen in death. He ate and drank whatever had been left to spoil on the table. I saw him vomiting in a corner before I left, with no woman to care for him, to wipe his face. I do not know what happened to the women who once served the hall, but sometimes I have dreams about it. If the child had not been maimed, if his father was not a king, I think I might have stolen him away. Certainly I wish I had."

He shuddered. Svanhild thought he had not meant to say this much, but now that he had begun, he was far away, back in that world. He gripped his wife's hand hard, making her tanned skin white.

"He took all my goods as spoils—for Hel, they said—for none can bring goods away from the country of the dead. And then he took my servants—one of them, Sverri, had been with me for years. He had been my companion since I inherited my first ship from my father, may he lie quiet in his barrow. He said that if I would leave the land of the dead, I must pay for the privilege. Of course I protested, and asked for him to take me instead, but he said no, that Sverri would do, that taking the life of a free man would put them in debt—I do not know what they meant. Their rituals were none I had heard of before. Whether they were from some terrible god, or only Hunthiof's madness, I do not know. I will not tell you how they killed Sverri, though they made me watch, and once they had smeared me with his blood, they put me back on my ship and sent me with my hold empty, back out into the stormy fjord."

Solmund let go of his wife's hand and shook himself. "I borrowed heavily from all my friends so I could continue to trade, for all the wealth I had left was my ship. I have heard that Hunthiof's madness is not so strong as it was, and he is a canny ruler again. Some traders still go to his hall, but I shall never go again. And I have heard I am not the only trader he served thus. Is it any wonder that his son should have grown up cruel and capricious? I am glad you are going to your brother. He will want to keep you out of Solvi's grasp."

Svanhild felt guilty for making Solmund relive those memories, and her heart went out to small Solvi, wandering through that hellish hall, with none to tell him what was wrong.

✛   ✛   ✛

HALDORA BADE SVANHILD join her in her fur-lined sleeping skin when they camped for the night, so they could share warmth. The winds blew strong here, with the high fjord walls funneling the ocean gales and flapping the tent's sides. They left in the morning, a few hours after the sun rose. Haldora spent much of her time in the forecastle tent, fashioning clothes for her family, but Svanhild did not want to hide from the sights. Soon she would be within walls again, with women. Or maybe not—maybe Ragnvald would take her in his ships as well. If so, she would need to learn how to live in one.

She passed the time in the bow, where she was out of the way of the sail as Solmund's sons swung it to and fro to catch the changing winds. When she looked at the path ahead, their progress seemed stately, yet waterfalls slipped by, and the fjord grew ever wider. From overhead, gulls dove for fish, and ravens fought with them. She longed to sail one day in a sleek dragon ship, a warship, one that would eat up the waves under its keel.

Near the mouth of the fjord, a strange calm kept them pinned to an exposed beach for two days. Solmund's sons caught minnows in the shallows for bait; Svanhild and Haldora stewed dried meat and

salted the boys' catch. Svanhild worried that Solmund would blame
her for ill luck, but he only told stories of how he had sometimes been
trapped like this for a week or more. The winds and tides were always
uncertain at places like this, he said, because of the spirits who dwelt at
the borders of places, neither fjord nor open ocean, the beach neither
land nor sea.

The next day dawned gray, with choppy seas, and they resumed
sailing north. Fog hid both shore and border island, except in rare
glimpses that showed the ship had not strayed out of this world and
into another.

Svanhild was peering intently into the mist, looking for land, when
she saw the wavering ghost of a dragon ship plying across the waves
toward them. It appeared so suddenly it seemed a product of her
imagination, and disappeared just as suddenly, behind the bulk of a
fog-shrouded island. The fog thickened, and turned to rain. The ship
reappeared on the other side of the island.

The wind was fitful, squalls shoving the knarr along, before sub-
siding and leaving the sail slack. The dragon ship moved sleekly, oar
driven. For a moment, Svanhild did not think of the danger, only mar-
veled at its speed and beauty, until it drew quite close and she saw the
shields arrayed along the gunwales. They only did that, Ragnvald had
told her, when they were primed for attack.

Too late Solmund's sons scrambled for their swords. "Get inside,"
said Solmund frantically, when he saw her standing in front of the tent.

She drew back inside and let the flap fall closed. All she could hear
was the hiss of rain on the oiled leather, and her own heartbeat, thud-
ding loudly. Haldora put a hand on Svanhild's shoulder. Svanhild
jumped.

"What—was it?" Haldora asked.

"It was a dragon ship," Svanhild whispered. Svanhild let Haldora
hold her close. The ship had been moving so fast; surely they were
already alongside. Should she be able to hear something? Perhaps they
had not thought the knarr had much to steal, or were not in the mood
to harass merchants today. But no, they would not turn without at
least greeting Solmund. And their shields had been out.

After an eternity of waiting in the tent, while Svanhild tried to hear something, anything, above the flapping of the sail, the wind shifted, shuddering the tent walls and sending drops of condensation onto her face. Finally Svanhild heard shouts, and the banging of the ships' gunwales knocking together. Someone from the dragon ship would fling a rope across, lashing them together so the knarr could not escape. The captain would come aboard, and search everywhere. He might kill the men, and take Svanhild and Haldora for slaves. There were markets in Frisia where rovers could sell their slaves to merchants from the south. They ended up in Baghdad or Constantinople, bereft of language or family, buried or burned far from their gods. Few had ever returned to tell their tales.

"Greetings," called out a man's cheery voice. One of the raiders then. She knew that voice, Solvi's voice. Her *wyrd*, come to find her.

"Greetings," replied Solmund, more warily.

"These waters belong to me," said Solvi. "And there is a tax for traveling through them."

"These waters are free," said Solmund. "And I see you are an honorable man, a warrior with a deeply nicked blade. You are not a man to steal from those unarmed."

"Your sons have swords."

"My sons fear for my safety," said Solmund.

Svanhild tried to crawl toward the entrance, but Haldora held her back, digging her fingers into Svanhild's wrist.

Some words passed between the men outside, which Svanhild could not make out, and then Solvi, with his bright voice ringing like a smith's blows on a sword, said, "Show us then, so we can choose our tax. You should have said you were selling to my father, not King Hakon. I might have spared you then."

"Why are you not raiding richer lands, my lord?" asked Solmund.

"There is something I seek closer to home," said Solvi. "Now stop delaying. My men will take their spoils, peacefully or otherwise."

"It is me he wants," Svanhild whispered to Haldora, wishing she could take away the woman's fear. "Perhaps if he gets me, he will leave you safe."

She pushed the flap open and stood in front of the mast. The rain had stopped, and the wind whipped strands of hair out of her braid.

"Solvi Hunthiofsson," she said, standing as tall as she could. "Am I what you seek?"

None spoke. Her words seemed to have quieted even the flapping of the sails. Svanhild looked around the deck. Solmund's sons had already been disarmed. One of Solvi's men held the eldest with his arm at an angle that looked close to dislocating his shoulder. Solvi gaped and then covered it quickly with a grin.

"My lady Svanhild," he said. "What brings you here?"

She stepped down off the forecastle platform. Her heart hammered in her ears. She walked toward Solvi, putting one foot slowly in front of the other, so she would not stumble as the ship pitched in the choppy water.

In the sagas the women got their way by being bolder than the men who surrounded them. What they could not do with steel, they did with will. There must be a way to spare Solmund and his family, who had been so kind to her. She squared her shoulders.

"Is my lord a thief?" she asked, pitching her voice low so it would not quaver and show her fear. "You would not ride onto a neighboring farmstead and take a man's sheep, so why would you take my friend Solmund's stores? They are his as much as the farmer his flock." If that was true, it was only because Solvi preferred to do his raiding by sea. But men liked to hear well of themselves. So Vigdis had said.

Solvi licked his lips. She waited for him to speak. He made no reply. Svanhild felt the attention of all these men on her, the weight of their eyes. Perhaps they were not used to seeing Solvi lacking for words. She crossed the few steps between them and put her hand on Solvi's arm. His sleeve had not been sewn this morning, and it gaped at his wrist. She wondered, nonsensically, if his wife did that for him when they were at home. Svanhild's thumb found flesh. His skin was hot against her chilled hand, and she hastily moved it so fabric separated them.

"I thought my betrothed an honorable man," she added desperately.

Solvi burst out laughing. "Your betrothed? My lady, you are bold. But you are right, I do seek you, so it is you who put these people in danger."

She took a shallow breath. She had hoped and feared that it was true, and having it confirmed only made her fear the greater.

"It was you who put them in danger, my lord," said Svanhild. She had dared greatly already, and she had as much as consented to marrying Solvi now. "And as this shows no honor, you must not be my betrothed. For I am sure my family would not betroth me to a dishonorable man." She risked a glance at Solvi's men. A few of his older sailors were openly grinning at Svanhild's logic, while the younger ones watched, eyes round and wondering.

"What does a woman know of honor?" asked Solvi, his smile sharpening unpleasantly. Svanhild quailed—had she gone too far? She took her hand from Solvi's arm and turned away, the picture of a woman's scorn. It was a calculated gesture, and Solvi would know it, but she played to more than just him now.

"A woman may know honor," she said. Her favorite stories had served her well so far; she prayed they would continue. "A woman like the Swedish Gudrun, who killed her own sons since they were the sons of the man who betrayed her? A woman like Unna, who spurred her sluggard husband to vengeance? I think a woman can know honor better than a man." She looked around at Solvi's other men. Even the older ones now wore thoughtful expressions, as though they truly listened to her words. She had never been heeded by so many at once. It was intoxicating, a heady draught of fear and power.

She turned to Solmund. "My friend," she said. "Will you please gift my betrothed with something suitable to celebrate our union?" Solmund glanced at Solvi, who shrugged and nodded. Solmund directed his sons to pull up the deck boards that protected his wares.

Svanhild put her hand back on Solvi's arm and smiled blandly at him.

"What are you playing at, Svanhild?" he asked under his breath.

"Let these people go, and I will come with you willingly," she said in the same undertone.

"You'll be coming with me whether you like it or not."

"Your men will be fishing me out of the sea if you do not do as I ask. Well kicked and bitten for their troubles," she said. She had never felt so clearheaded. She could walk across these waves if she had a mind to.

Solmund emerged from under the decking with a beautiful necklace and arm ring, which he presented to Svanhild and Solvi.

"May we leave now?" Solvi asked, voice loud enough for all to hear. "Finding you is worth any treasure we may have forgone."

Svanhild smiled at his sarcastic tone. He might mock her, but he still played her game. "Solmund and his family rescued your bride and brought her to you," she said. "Do they not deserve a reward?"

Solvi leaned forward to whisper in her ear as though they were lovers. "How far do you mean to push this, Svanhild? Your games are charming, but my patience is not infinite."

Svanhild flushed with anger, but still smiled, as though it was his teasing words that made her cheeks flame. A few of Solvi's men now seemed to be growing bored, for the game was ending. They rested their hands on their swords, knees moving with the rhythm of the ocean, keeping their balance as naturally as breathing. The younger ones still looked to Solvi hopefully, though. They watched a scene out of a tale, their shining eyes said, and they wanted it to come out right, the honorable rewarded, the guilty punished. Svanhild tipped her face up to Solvi's.

"Your men love a generous lord, do they not? Do they not boast to their friends of the fine rings you have given them?"

"English coin," said Solvi, loud enough for all aboard to hear. "Your wares and your services will be paid for." He jerked his chin at one of his men, who went to fetch it.

"May I say my good-byes, my lord?" Svanhild asked, now in an ordinary tone. The performance was over. She had won, but what? Freedom for Solmund's family, and captivity for herself. Her limbs felt leaden. The rain still fell, plastering her hair to the sides of her face. None would see a heroine now in a short, drenched girl.

"What trick is this?" he asked.

"None," she said sharply. "I am yours."

He grabbed her arm hard. "Are you, Svanhild?"

She pulled it out of his grasp, frightened by his harshness. "As much as I ever will be." The wind blew strongly behind her, and carried her words to him alone. "If you mistreat me, my brother will avenge me. You failed to kill him once. Think well on that." She turned away from him.

She hugged Solmund and Haldora good-bye. Solmund had no

words for her. Svanhild thought she saw Hunthiof's old hall in his eyes, the hall of the dead. She told herself that Hunthiof must have changed since then, or Solvi would not have survived to adulthood. Haldora leaned close when they embraced and whispered a shaky thanks in Svanhild's ear that made tears spring to her eyes. She blinked them back before she let Haldora go, and walked with her head held high to Solvi, who took her arm and helped her over the gunwale into his ship.

21

THE MEN ROSE SLOWLY THE NEXT DAY, AFTER THE BATTLE.
Ragnvald watched a few start fires, through eyes gritty with sleep un-
slept.

"You are not good company after a battle, Ragnvald Eysteinsson,"
said Oddi, pulling Ragnvald up out of his thoughts. He touched Ragnvald on the shoulder, a friendly gesture, and Ragnvald smiled slightly.

"I'm probably better company than your brother was last night,"
said Ragnvald. "But forgive me—it matters not whether I drink, even.
I am sorry if I gave you nightmares."

"No," said Oddi. His hands were clean this morning. Ragnvald
wondered if he would speak of it more—what his father had made
him watch. But Ragnvald did not want to ask. "No," said Oddi again,
"I found a skin of ale and a girl who wanted to share it with me."

Ragnvald lifted one eyebrow. "Did she?"

"Well, she wanted a warm place to spend the night, and I warmed
her well." He sighed and shrugged. "My brother is wroth today."

"Do you know what your father means to do?" Ragnvald asked.

"He has set down Heming's captains and raised others to command
their men," said Oddi. He gave Ragnvald a mocking look. "My brother
swears vengeance on his betrayer."

Ragnvald glared at him. "My oath was to his father, not him. Your
father. I do not like a man who would threaten me to bring me to his
cause."

"Heming will kill you," said Oddi. He said it with such a lack of affect that it chilled Ragnvald's blood. Oddi had been friends with Jarl Runolf too.

"He can try," said Ragnvald, trying to sound unworried. He should not dwell on it; since Solvi, he had known he was not safe. "What would you have me do?"

"I don't know," said Oddi. His shoulders slumped. "But I hoped you would have some better idea than I do."

"It's not my fault your brother's behaving like a lackwit," Ragnvald said. "I didn't ask to be in the middle of all this."

"You did." Oddi gave Ragnvald a rueful smile. "I know it's not your fault Heming's an idiot, but you did ask to be here."

"That's true."

"I won't kill my brother for you, but I'll shout a warning, if I see a dagger coming for you."

"I'll try not to duck and let it hit you."

"My father would speak with you," said Oddi.

Hakon breakfasted on a small knoll, surrounded by his men. In the lee of one of the barns, a collection of slaves sat, hands bound, surrounded by men guarding them. When Hakon saw Ragnvald, he stood and walked with Ragnvald out of earshot of the assembled crowd.

"You did well bringing Heming's plans to me," said Hakon. "Though he will not think it. I do not know how to make him see reason. I suppose all I can do is mind him more carefully."

"No." Ragnvald looked at Hakon's mouth—which wore a worried frown—rather than his eyes. "He chafes under your bridle. Send him among Harald's captains."

"He might think himself rewarded. But you have only been wrong once since I've known you. And that was at your trial. I think"— Hakon gave Ragnvald a piercing look—"I think that your judgment is sound, except in your own cause. I hope that I am right. I will send you, Oddi, and Heming among Harald's captains, to remind Harald that he owes me loyalty. If our armies separate as we search for other kings to slay, you will stay with them." He gave Ragnvald a speculative look. "I hope that my son does not kill you."

Ragnvald stumbled. "I hope not as well. If you fear for that, keep me here with you."

"No," said Hakon. "He might not like you, but he could learn from your wisdom, out of my shadow. He may prove himself to Harald, with you by his side. But if he does attack you, take care not to kill him, for then I will have to kill you." He laughed. Some of Ragnvald's panic must have shown, for he added, "I will put some fear into him too, and all will be well."

"My judgment is certainly not sound in my own cause," said Ragnvald angrily. "I should have remained silent. Can you not separate us?"

"You will do well." It was a command. "I want you to guide Heming, and to bring him to Harald's notice. Do this, and I will reward you—one of my sons will surely rule in Sogn, and you will be the first of his jarls, with a fine feasting hall."

Ragnvald knew that becoming king in Sogn was a distant hope, but hearing Hakon blithely plan to hand the land off to one of his sons, who never even visited except for the *ting* assembly, rankled him. "I thank you," he said tightly.

"I set you difficult tasks because I know you can master them," said Hakon. "Make peace with my son, and make him Harald's friend."

✢   ✢   ✢

HAKON AND GUTHORM divided up the slaves evenly, and sent them south to be sold at Dorestad. The raped girl who had clutched her knife and reminded Ragnvald of Svanhild was among them, and it still made him uneasy to see her mistreated, so he did not watch as their ship set off.

Ragnvald, Oddi, and Heming took their place among Harald's captains as they formed up ranks to march into the uplands, following the path King Gudbrand was said to have taken. Ragnvald was alert for any difference between their force and Hakon's, but it was much the same, composed of fresh-faced farm boys and grizzled old trappers among the seasoned warriors.

Ragnvald did not know how to behave with Heming—he would rather have avoided him if he could—but if he kept close, perhaps he would not need to fear a sword in the dark. Heming was an honorable man; Ragnvald did not think he would stoop to outright murder.

"My brother tells me I have you to thank for this." Heming gestured to where Harald sat, within view but out of earshot, laughing with his friend Thorbrand and one of the captive women. Oddi was busy overseeing the men Guthorm had assigned him.

"Yes," said Ragnvald shortly.

Heming turned to face him. He had the look of a warrior from a saga, handsome and strong, in a way that made Ragnvald too aware of the way Solvi's knife had twisted his own face, of how narrow and slight he was, compared to Heming's muscled frame. Now Heming did not look so haughty, though, but a little bit lost.

"I thought that what is between you and your father might be better for some distance," said Ragnvald diffidently. "Was I wrong?"

"I don't know." Heming shook his head. "I want him to think me a man, not a child."

Ragnvald drew back, startled at this sudden confidence, and then worried that Heming only shared this because he planned on killing Ragnvald, so it did not matter what he told him. "He wants you to—"

"I know," Heming cut him off. "He wants me to make a friend of Harald. What good can that do? My father is the most powerful king in the west. All friendship rests on that. What is there for me to do?"

"Well," said Ragnvald, "there will be opportunity to fight bravely at Harald's side, and skalds will sing of it." He looked out over the river, and added, "Is that not why you wanted to sail against Hunthiof at Tafjord?"

"I should kill you for that betrayal," said Heming, voice suddenly poisonous. Ragnvald stood and put his hand at his sword. He had hoped speaking of their conflict might take away its power, but he had chosen wrong—Heming would rather it not be spoken. Heming faced him, also fingering the grip of his sword. Fire-lit faces turned toward them.

"My father is Hunthiof's ancient enemy and would—he should—thank me for planning Hunthiof's death," Heming added.

Some tension went out of Ragnvald—it seemed Heming still meant to talk, not attack. "Or he might mourn," he said, "like the man in the tale who killed his enemy and then took to bed for a month because he would never more have a challenge like that. Perhaps your father is wise enough not to court such despair." Ragnvald said the last sardonically, searching Heming's face for some sign that he might be letting go of his anger.

"What do you know of it? You have not killed your enemy, this Olaf. If a man kills his enemy, he should not mourn, he should go out and find a new one."

Ragnvald felt the anger Heming had been trying to stoke. He wanted to ask if he had done Heming a service in becoming his enemy, but he did not want to remind Heming of that, not when they both stood ready to fight.

"I am not your enemy unless you wish it," he said instead. Heming made him feel the battle weariness that nerves had been keeping at bay. He had slept little over the past few days.

"No, you are my nursemaid and my father's spy," said Heming bitterly.

Ragnvald inclined his head. "As you say. I would sleep now."

Heming did not answer, only glowered as Ragnvald turned to find the tent that he had set up to share with Oddi. Ragnvald woke when Oddi came in later in the night and could not fall asleep again, spending the night instead turning over the words he had spoken to Heming. He had grown proud of his ability to sway Hakon with advice and clever observations, but he had nothing of the same to offer Heming. If only Heming would see that doing well in Harald's war would earn a measure of his father's trust and admiration, he might hate Ragnvald a little less.

✛   ✛   ✛

THE NEXT MORNING the combined armies pressed on. Guthorm's goal was the great fort of King Eirik in the Hordaland uplands, but as they marched overland, up into the hills, the scouts heard news of Gudbrand.

For a few days the army chased rumors across the fields and forest. They marched south, then heard that King Gudbrand's army was moving inland. The vast company could not find enough food. Deer and other game feared such a large group of humans and fled far before them. The men had emptied the first few farms, to much wailing of women and complaining from the farms' owners, until Guthorm put a stop to the raiding. Now they went hungry save what the men could trap overnight.

Hakon and Guthorm met, and Hakon determined to take his force back to the fjordlands, to protect the land that they had already conquered. Ragnvald could see that this did not please Guthorm, but Hakon had reason and a hungry army on his side this time.

Finally Guthorm decided that it was not a good use of their resources to continue this pursuit, and they tracked east to King Eirik's fort. Ragnvald had heard this fort sung of—the story went that before the gods drove the frost giants into the mountains, the giants had built it, their mighty hands, as hard as stone, carving out the earthwork ramps and ditches. It dominated a broad upland plain near the foothills of the Keel. Seeing the high-piled earth, the deep trenches reinforced with spikes, Ragnvald could well believe that giants had a hand in it. If those within were well provisioned and had enough men to guard the walls, it could withstand a long siege.

He was glad Guthorm had decided on some object, no matter what it was, for it meant a few days without marching. The bite wound the boy had given Ragnvald's hand was not healing well. He examined it each morning and found the edges hot and suppurating, refusing to heal together. He washed it and covered the wound with cobwebs before wrapping a clean cloth around it, as he had been taught, yet it only hurt more and more each day.

Harald's army camped in a grove out of bowshot of the fort, while Harald took Thorbrand, Ragnvald, Heming, and Oddi, as well as a few other captains, to scout around the fort and look for weaknesses. Their arrival had not escaped notice. Great wooden doors barred each of the four entrances. Guards patrolled the tops of the earthwork ridges.

"My uncle tells me it is double-walled, so that if an army makes it through the first wall, they can be slaughtered in the gulf between," said Harald. The idea chilled Ragnvald's blood, to be trapped there with death on all sides. "I must ask him how he means for us to take it."

On the way back to the camp, Ragnvald fell behind with Oddi, out of earshot of Harald.

"It would be faster for his uncle simply to lead these men," Ragnvald said. "It is foolish to pretend this boy can do more than stand up and make pretty speeches." He was weary from the marching, from the pain in his hand, and from the haste with which the army moved.

"He is young," said Oddi. "But I feel he will grow into a great king. His mother is a great sorceress, and she prophesied it. Would you prefer it if he made foolish decisions himself, rather than following his uncle's counsel?"

"I would prefer it if I thought he was more than a particularly well trained dancing bear," said Ragnvald. He did not know why Harald irritated him so much, except that he shone so bright, and had every advantage of strength and birth, yet these advantages seemed hollow. True, his skill with weapons, even at such a young age, had never been matched. He might make a worthy hero, but a hero needed different skills than a king. Some of Ragnvald's dislike must come from envy—he knew himself enough to admit that. Harald had lost his father and now had an uncle who acted as a father to him—more than a father. Hakon was pleased to play father to his sons and men like Ragnvald, only as long as they could help him and did not outshine him. Harald had no brothers to compete with, and no sisters to worry over either.

"Bear, do you think?" Oddi asked, pulling Ragnvald out of his thoughts. "He puts me more in mind of a well-fed wolf. Be careful, Ragnvald."

Ragnvald hurried to catch up with Harald's long, loping strides. As soon as they returned to Guthorm's tent, Harald said to his uncle, "It is indeed a mighty fort. How will we take it?"

"We hear they are not well provisioned," said Guthorm. "We will lay siege for a few days, and ask for terms. If that does not work, we will fill in a section of the ditch, at night, so there will be less risk of arrow shot. Then rush the wall at that place. Some will die going over it, but most will not, and Eirik will not be able to keep us out."

"I will go over," said Thorbrand. "What of the inner wall?" Ragnvald was glad Thorbrand had asked, so he need not.

"We must bring planks to bridge the inner ditch," said Guthorm. "And make sure not to block our retreat. Perhaps some swifter attacks at first, to confirm how things lie. We do not know enough about how they set their guards."

It seemed the beginnings of a good plan, though Ragnvald did not know how Guthorm could be certain they were not well provisioned. He would like to try to lure one of the guards away from his post and question the man, but he did not think his suggestion would be welcome, not after Guthorm's anger at him over the matter of the boy—the boy who punished him even now.

Ragnvald sat that night with Heming at dinner. Heming was never happy without an audience, so he had made friends with some of Harald's finer warriors, the sons of rich raiders, men who knew enough to appreciate Heming's graces but could not outshine them.

"How are you getting on with King Harald?" Ragnvald asked him. They dined on deer that Dagvith, one of Ragnvald's tablemates from Yrjar, had taken in the afternoon.

"He is, as you say, a boy," said Heming. Ragnvald immediately wanted to defend Harald, though he agreed with Heming. Heming did not bring out the best in Ragnvald, either. He must master the annoyance that festered from his hand into his heart, or he would become unwelcome at every hearth.

"And?" said Ragnvald. "Your father wishes you to be his companion." He hoped Hakon would rejoin them soon.

"He is stocked full with companions. Perhaps if this Thorbrand does not survive the next battle . . ." Heming gave Ragnvald a speculative look. "My father did want you to help me."

"Not with murder," said Ragnvald firmly. He had not spent much time with Thorbrand, but thought he liked him, this small blustery man. The path to turn Heming into Harald's companion would lie with Thorbrand, not over him. "Why don't you volunteer to help build the ramp onto the wall instead?" he offered. "Harald will admire you for that."

"It will be dangerous," said Heming doubtfully.

Ragnvald sighed. "I will do it too," said Ragnvald. There, now Heming's competitiveness might help him.

✢ ✢ ✢

AFTER HE HAD spent two nights building the ramp, Ragnvald's hand could hardly hold the haft of a shovel. When his digging shift was done, and the other men crawled off to sleep, Ragnvald walked a little way into the forest. He sat down with his back against a tree, cradling his hand, trying to hold off despair at what must come next.

Dawn came on gray and rainy. He should wait for full daylight to tend the wound, when he would be able to see it best, but he feared to examine it too closely, and that someone else might watch him. He unwrapped the wound. Just a small double arc of teeth marks, yet it was red and hotter than it had been the day before. Running his finger over the flesh sent a thrill of pain up his arm and into his elbow.

Now that it had gone this far, he must cut open the wound to drain out the poison. Best to burn the wound with a hot poker, but Ragnvald did not think he could do that for himself, and he did not want anyone else to learn of his injury. A healer, seeing what Ragnvald saw now, the sickly shine of it, would probably want to cut his hand off.

Better he die than live without a sword hand. Oddi would help him to die gripping a sword if it came to that, so he could go as a warrior to the lands beyond death. Ragnvald found he could just bear to think of these things if he thought of them as happening to someone else. His hand too—he would cut the poison out of a friend's hand, so now he could do it for himself.

He drew his dagger and tested the edge by rasping his thumb against it. It had been sharp enough to cut the meat at dinner, and what was he but meat?

He wiped the blade on his shirt. It would be better if he could wash it clean with sand, but they were far from a sand beach. He must not delay. He looked around to see if he was likely to be disturbed while he did this thing.

All slept at this hour; no one would stop him. He found a flat rock that he could use to steady himself, and pressed the back of his hand against it. The rock was cool—even the back of his hand was hot now from the infection. Cut it and let the blood and fluids run free, he told himself.

He pressed his blade to the edges of the wound, opening them where they had tried—and failed—to come together. The pain was like a punch in his stomach, far worse than Olaf's sword in his thigh, or Solvi's dagger to his cheek. Blackness gathered on the edges of his vision. He waited for it to fade, and swallowed down the bile in his throat. He must do this. He pressed harder now.

His hand bled freely, red blood that looked black in the gray dawn, mingling with the cloudy fluid of infection. He let it bleed for a dozen breaths. It did bring some relief, some lessening of the pressure, more than just the relief of no longer pressing a knife into his own flesh. He took another deep breath and cut the other half of the wound. That one was easier. The pain came in regular waves, and after each one crested, the trough felt almost pleasant. His hand now seemed as though it belonged to someone else in truth. A burning sensation suffused it, as though he had plunged it into ice water.

His stomach heaved. He looked away from the blood, from his mangled hand, at the quiet camp, the gray humps of leather tents, then back at the wound. Blood and pus, white, not clear. That was not good. Still, it did not smell putrefied yet, only like blood always smelled, of metal and ocean.

It seemed impossible that he could have done this without anyone noticing, for he had groaned with pain as he did it. He took up a small skin of ale with his left hand and splattered it over the wound, hardly feeling it. Then he took a clean strip of cloth that he had stolen for this purpose and wrapped it around his hand, binding tight, and biting off the knot with his teeth. He stood. The tents of Harald's men wavered in his vision, as though he were looking at it through the mist. He emptied the ale skin into his throat.

By midafternoon, Ragnvald knew that his surgery had not worked. It seemed that he floated above the camp, watching Harald move between tents, shining like a torch, warming where he passed, turning all heads. This sensation came from fever, Ragnvald knew, a fever that detached him from his body and his cares. It touched him lightly for now, though he could feel its black shadow on the horizon.

Near afternoon, one of the scouts came running into the camp, breathless with exertion. He had to lie on the ground for a few minutes before he could speak well enough to be understood. Ragnvald had spent most of the day sitting near the leaders' tents, at the foot of a tree, listening with half an ear to the conversation, while his fever ebbed and flowed. He knew he would feel better if he lay down in his tent, but feared that if he did, he might never stand up again.

"Gudbrand's army assembles in the foothills to the south," said the scout, finally. He gave counts of men and tents he had seen, drawing the shape of the land in the ash of the dead campfire.

"We should go to meet him there," said Guthorm.

"They are well positioned at the top of a hill," said Ragnvald, half to himself. "But if we draw them out, we may be crushed between them and Eirik's fort."

"We have more than twice their numbers," said Guthorm. Ragnvald had not realized his voice had carried to Guthorm, but he supposed Guthorm might be alert for anyone arguing with his plan. "We can attack from below, and brace each other if necessary."

Ragnvald frowned. His fever had robbed him of any self-control, it seemed. Harald looked at him inquisitively, and that was enough invitation for Ragnvald to stand, uncertainly, and join him at the fire. Strangely, the warmth from the flames made him feel colder, and he had to clamp his jaw to keep from shivering.

"What would you do, Ragnvald?" Harald asked.

"If you attack uphill, form a curve in the line, here. A dip." He moved forward and sketched a line in the dirt with his left hand, keeping his right pinned to his thigh to keep it from being jarred into worse pain. The line bowed inward at the center of the slope. "They will think they are pushing you back. Then, let the middle of the line fail, and their men rush downhill, through the line. You must turn quickly after that, to meet them as they try to fight back up. But then you will have the advantage."

"'You'?" said Guthorm. "And where, in this fantasy, will you be?"

Dead, Ragnvald thought. "I will be in the middle, ready to fail and turn," he said. "That is where the bravest will be." He looked evenly at Guthorm when he said it, hoping he could not see Ragnvald's pain and his desire to lie down, lie down and float away.

"If you came up with this plan, how do you know Gudbrand won't see through it?" Guthorm asked.

"My father trusts Ragnvald," said Heming.

Ragnvald did not even have the energy to give Heming a grateful look. He rested his head in his hand. "What can he do, even if he knows this? He could have more men hiding in the trees—that's what I would do—and attack from above once we face downhill. We can guard against that—our force should be large enough to send a party into the forest to roust out anyone hiding. Let the outer edges of the shield wall take that task, after we turn."

Guthorm and the captains fell to arguing about the plan, and Ragnvald drew back to the edge of the circle. He gathered his cloak around his shoulders. He did not care if they liked his plan or not. Perhaps someday, after it ceased to matter to him, they would see that it had been a good one. He listened with half an ear and started to doze. Oddi roused him some time later, with a hand on his arm.

"I think they will do it," said Oddi. His mouth quirked. "Ragnvald the Wise."

"I only spoke first," said Ragnvald, shrugging. "If it is such a good plan, someone else would have come up with it."

"You take the virtue of modesty too far sometimes." Oddi sighed. "Clever boasting is a virtue too."

"I cannot be clever, nor can I stop my mouth tonight. That is not so wise." He did stop speaking then, though, for fear he would reveal to Oddi the reason.

"Then I had best let you sleep," said Oddi.

22

SOLVI'S SHIP WAS NARROWER AND SLEEKER THAN SOLMUND'S knarr, with perfectly lapped boards, all of pine that still smelled of sap from the forests. The sail was twice as large as the knarr's, and when it was unfurled, Svanhild worried a strong wind might tear the mast off.

She should not have, though, for Solvi and his pilot knew these winds and waters too well to ever make such a misstep, and Svanhild could not make herself hope for catastrophe, not while she was on board. She had wanted this, she reminded herself. She had known that Solvi was a threat to Ragnvald—that he might even treat her ill—but this was her choice.

"Where do I stay, my lord?" she asked.

"You can drop the 'my lord,'" said Solvi. "You've played your part."

"What shall I call you?"

"As soon as we have some privacy, you can call me husband." He gave her a questioning look, and seemed about to say something else, but only added, "Until then, don't speak unless you're spoken to."

Svanhild had hitched her pack onto her shoulder and started to make her way toward the stern, where there seemed to be more space, when Solvi said, "Is that all you brought? I had hoped you'd come to me with more of a dowry." His mouth quirked, as though he wished to start some game with her.

"Did you?" She felt very tired. She looked at Solvi, and said, "And I had hoped to get a better bride price than my brother's blood. I will master my disappointment, if you do yours." His smile lost its mirth, and he turned away.

They stayed that night on a rocky beach. One of Solvi's men gave her a hide blanket to keep her warm in the wind that swept across the treeless island. She could not fall asleep for worrying that Solvi would come over and claim her as his wife this night. She dreaded being so close to him, although she had touched him willingly enough earlier, riding over the assembly grounds with him. Solvi was all fire and energy. Imagining having that focused fully on her, without his men around to distract him—the intensity of it made her squirm, and not with the pleasurable self-consciousness he had made her feel at the *ting*.

She did not sleep, aware of every rock that dug into her back, and of the men who slumbered close, snoring. The sea rocked the ship where it was pulled up on the beach, crunching it against the sand. She listened to the slaps of wave against decking, hoping it would lull her to sleep, but every noise startled her.

The next day Solvi's ship had to fight its way back to his hall at Tafjord. Rain fell in sullen sheets. Svanhild wrapped her blanket around her and sat in the stern again. Solvi called out orders and kept watch in the bow. He had not said two words to her all day. She must look a fright—no bath since before leaving Hrolf's farm, and now five days spent rough, without even combing her hair.

The rain had followed them inland, a drizzle that collected on her chin and dripped down her neck and under her clothes, making her feel even more wretched.

One of the warriors helped her from the ship when they docked, steadying her on the slippery rocks. "Solvi bids you make yourself presentable to meet his father," he said. This one was young, with a shock of red hair and the washed-out, fishlike features that usually went with that coloring. The leanness of his face, the calluses on his hands where they grasped her arm, told that he was at least fierce, if not yet an experienced warrior. He looked at her curiously. They had all watched her match wits with Solvi and win. Now Svanhild felt miles away from that girl, whoever she had been.

Tafjord looked like any other collection of halls and barns, no sign that it was still Hel's domain, as Solmund had described. The buildings were gray and muddy with rain, the grass trampled by many feet. Tafjord had two halls: the high-roofed drinking hall with its cross-beams decorated with the heads of hounds, biting at the sky, and the living hall, low and twice as long. A few thralls ducked in and out of storehouses and barns for animals.

A woman stooped low in the doorway of the next building, a turf hovel, her arms full of cheeses. Svanhild picked up her skirts, although it hardly mattered—they were already streaked with mud to the knee—and went to help her. "Are you Solvi's wife?" she asked.

"I am Geirny Nokkvesdatter," said the woman. She looked Svanhild up and down. She was taller than Svanhild, likely taller than Solvi too, with eyes the color of choppy fjord water. Her hair was bound back severely under her wimple, not a strand escaping. Something in her expression reminded Svanhild of her mother, as though something essential was missing from her. "I am Solvi's wife," said Geirny. "You are not a new thrall. Who are you?"

"Svanhild Eysteinsdatter." Svanhild's voice wobbled, and she set her jaw against it.

Geirny's eyes filled with tears; apparently she recognized the name. Svanhild wanted to apologize for this, for being here. The cheeses started to slip out of Geirny's hands. Svanhild rushed forward and caught two before they fell into the mud.

"Come," said Svanhild, as she was accustomed to speaking to Hilda's littlest sister Ingifrid: firmly, but gently. "Let us take these to the kitchen." She started back down toward the hall, and Geirny followed after her. Svanhild shoved the kitchen door open with her hip, holding it open for Geirny, and then took the remaining cheeses out of Geirny's arms and set them down on the table.

She looked down at where her hands rested on the cloth-wrapped cheese. They were chapped red from her travels, and dirty too. She tucked them into her pockets and said, "Solvi has asked that I make myself ready to meet his father. Is there a basin for washing?"

Geirny set her jaw. "It's not washing day," she said, the tears threatening to spill over again. Svanhild wondered if Geirny wanted her looking slatternly to meet her new father-in-law, but the tears made her think Geirny was too upset to plot that.

"I'm sorry," she said. "I did not think—"

Geirny interrupted her by bursting out sobbing. She sat down on a stool and buried her head in her hands. Her wimple slid forward, exposing her hair, an ashy blond, braided tight against her scalp. Svanhild sat down next to her and patted her back until the sobs subsided.

"Are you . . . ill?" Svanhild asked, feeling foolish.

Geirny stopped sobbing and sat, shaking. "You don't know what it's like," she said, the words hardly intelligible as she gulped down tears. "There are only a few old women thralls, and I have to prepare the feasts at a moment's notice, and he hasn't given me a son, he has only exposed my girl children in hopes that I will give him a son more quickly, and I—I am sorry that you are here against your will, but . . ." Geirny's eyes were red as she turned them to Svanhild again.

Svanhild hugged her close. "Shh, I'll help. It will get better, I promise." Geirny's words chilled her blood. Solvi would not leave her daughters to die as soon as they were born; she would have that promise from him before they wed.

She made Geirny look at her again. "I do need to wash myself and prepare to meet King Hunthiof," she said. "Can you help me?"

Geirny told her where the bathhouse was and loaned Svanhild a comb. The bathhouse was next to a stream that led up into the hills. The room was cold, not surprisingly, and stocked with wood to start a fire. Perhaps Geirny's management of the household was not as bad as Svanhild feared. She brought a coal in a small dish from the kitchen fire to start it, and within an hour, she had coaxed the fire into a good blaze.

Svanhild changed into a thin shift and warmed herself thoroughly before braving the icy stream waters. The cold water made her gasp. The stream ran swiftly here. She dug her numb feet more firmly into the rocks. Here was no place to give in to weeping. She had to meet King Hunthiof, who would probably pronounce them married on the spot. Svanhild should have attendants, be veiled, and be presented by her father to her groom, but all the legal formula required was that she share a cup of ale with her husband, and that a man recite the blessing of Frigga, the goddess of the hearth, over them. Hunthiof could do that quick as look at her.

As soon as she had gotten herself wet and scrubbed the mud off her feet, she pulled herself out of the water and bent over to wash her hair. She could take her time combing out the tangles in the warm bathhouse. She stood, swinging the sodden mass of her hair over her shoulder, and turned toward the shore. Not ten feet from her, under the eaves of one of the barns, stood Solvi, the same three warriors he had brought to the *ting* flanking him.

The water had made Svanhild's shift transparent and molded it to her body. Terribly aware of her nipples tightening in the cold air, she tried to cover herself. Solvi's warriors turned away, two quickly and one more slowly, but Solvi continued watching, not grinning now, just looking at Svanhild's body with a concentration that made her hot with anger.

"Did no one tell you that I come here to bathe after a voyage?" he asked.

Svanhild shook her head. She had been told to clean herself up— did Solvi not remember that? He cleared his throat. "Come back later," he said to his men. He held out his hand to Svanhild. She refused to take it, for to stretch out her hand would expose her breasts under their sheer covering, and she could not stand Solvi looking at her like that. He shrugged.

"Give me your cloak," said Svanhild.

"No, my lady." Some humor had crept back into his voice. "I would see you. We shall talk in the bathhouse."

She would have preferred to follow him, but he gestured for her to go ahead, and so she had to walk before him, her shift clinging to her backside, feeling his eyes on her where she could not defend against them. As soon as they entered the bathhouse again, Svanhild's shift began to steam. Solvi put off his cloak.

Svanhild pulled her dirty dress over her body to shield herself from Solvi's gaze, which heated her more. Solvi looked at her for a long moment and then dropped his eyes. He took a deep breath and set his lips in a thin line. He was built on a smaller scale than most men, only an inch or two taller than her. Could his burns have caused that? He was handsome, too handsome by half, with a lean, symmetrical face and bright blue-green eyes. He kept his beard cropped so close to his chin that it was little more than a dusting of hair. Most likely out of vanity, Svanhild thought, the better to expose his elegant jaw and strong chin.

"I had thought to work harder at wooing you," he said. "You said no, more than once."

Svanhild went cold all over. "You said—you wanted me," she said. Then, more angrily, "I thought you would take everything from the merchant Solmund if I did not—what else did you mean to do, if not that?"

Solvi shrugged. He looked amused. She could not have been at more of a disadvantage here, wet and by turns hot and cold, half dressed and bedraggled, while Solvi was fully dressed and grinning. "I would have taken a tax, to be sure. Perhaps required them to come along to Tafjord."

"Where your father might torture them to death."

"You've been listening to old stories," said Solvi.

Svanhild sniffed and tried to sit up straighter, still holding her grubby dress to her chest. "That is what I heard."

"Well, I've let my men have their amusements, but not here, and not from a merchant who could sail by another year and give me another tax. Ruining him or killing him would not be useful. You should know that rumors mean little. People are saying your brother killed a *draugr*."

"Are they?" said Svanhild eagerly. "Perhaps he did."

"*Draugrs* are a fable for children."

Svanhild crossed her arms more firmly. She would believe the good that people said of Ragnvald.

"So you are only here to save your merchant friends from my terrible tortures," said Solvi. "You do not mean to marry me? You will not keep your word?"

"What will you do with me if I say no?"

His face changed in some way she could not identify, but he said, just as lightly, "You will never be in danger from me."

"What about my brother? Will you help him, if I"—Svanhild swallowed—"marry with you?"

"I will not seek to harm him. But I will not promise against a fate I do not know, for a man who hates me still."

"You're awfully honest," said Svanhild. "Why? Why not lie?"

Solvi looked surprised. "I don't know. But you're right, it is not a lie." He looked down at her in a way that made her fear and half long for what he might do next, then stood abruptly and went to the door. "Tell me when you decide."

"Wait," she said. She meant to do this. "What about Ragnvald? Why did you try to kill him?" When he turned back, she grew flustered again and added, "While you are being so honest."

"My father and your stepfather cooked that plan up, and they are useless in the kitchen." He barked out a laugh at his joke and shrugged. "My father wanted allies in Sogn against the coming of Harald. I meant to lose Ragnvald early in the voyage, but he kept being—useful."

"Ah," said Svanhild.

"I would not have chosen it. It was a foolish promise for my father to make."

"And you were willing to be his murderer?"

"My father—" Solvi began. His shoulders rose as he took a deep breath. "My father thought it would be best."

"You substituted your father's judgment for your own?"

"I did. I regret it." He looked down again and slid around to sit next to her on the bench. "Can you forgive me that? I have paid. The matter is settled."

"It is all I know of you," she said, her voice rising in a wail. The tears that had threatened all afternoon burned in her eyes, spilling a few drops over.

He took her hand. "That can change." She jerked it away. Solvi's mouth grew hard. He stood. "If that is your answer, then, ask Geirny to find you a place to sleep. You need not meet my father." She had wounded him, and a part of her hurt with it, while another enjoyed his discomfort, her power.

"I am true to my word," she said, before she could lose her nerve. Solvi was a king's son, and he had been generous with her. When she said it, a painful tightness in her throat eased.

He nodded gravely. "My father will marry us this evening."

✣   ✣   ✣

"YOU SAID SHE was beautiful," said Hunthiof. He sat in a chair carved out of the hall's main beam, which was formed of a lightning-struck oak, blessed by Odin. Svanhild did not like the look of him, this man who had tried to compass the death of her brother, who had killed Solmund's friend and servant. His beard was grown in long, for he was no longer a warrior. His brow was strong, his eyes small and deep. One, she realized as she came closer to him, was riven with a scar, and a milky, blind white. The other shone bright like a raptor's eye.

Svanhild jerked her chin up. "I had no one to attend me, my lord." She had combed her hair as best she could and plaited it into two braids, but it was still wet, and her part must surely be crooked. She turned to Solvi. "You must bring me women thralls when next you go viking."

"Oho." Hunthiof cracked a smile, and Solvi smirked. "I think this will be a better wife to you than Geirny. Fire rather than tears. You will share a cup tonight, and be married." Hunthiof fixed her with a fearsome glare. "I trust there will be no wailing and carrying on."

"Not from me," said Svanhild, standing up straight. "I cannot speak for your men." Hunthiof furrowed his brows, while Solvi laughed.

Solvi took her arm and led her into the food-serving area again, to wait until Hunthiof had assembled cups and witnesses.

"I do not have a veil," she said, shy of him again now that they were alone. She would not cry, though Solvi gave her a kind look, and she feared it might crack her resolve to be brave. His crew and Hunthiof's men waited out in the hall to watch this humiliation. When Ragnvald saw her again, she would be Solvi's wife. His second wife. How much better would that be, in his eyes, than being his concubine?

"Was my brother's blood my bride price, truly?" Svanhild asked, trying to keep either tears or anger from her voice.

"No," said Solvi. "I have chosen a parcel of land. It will be yours, to be inherited by your daughters, if you have any."

"You would not make me expose them as you did Geirny's? Do I have your promise on that?"

Solvi looked at her steadily again. "I swear to you. I want nothing to do with the killing of children." His eyes flickered away. "Even should you have a child that was not mine."

Svanhild shook her head. She could not think of that now, what it might mean, what it said of Solvi. "Then who killed Geirny's?"

Solvi looked as though he would rather not say, but finally he pressed Svanhild's hand. "She said it must be done. She wants a son to rule from Tafjord."

"And you did not stop her?"

"I was away. She told me she would conceive a son more quickly if—and then the next time, she said the child was sickly. I was away, and she is not strong. Perhaps it was." The memory seemed to pain him: these children, dead before he could greet them.

"I still do not have a veil," said Svanhild, still softly, and this time with some gentleness.

Solvi stood and opened one of the cupboards. He pulled out a linen cloth woven so finely that Svanhild could hardly see the threads. It was thickly embroidered on the edges in blue, with threads of gold picking out crosses.

"These are odd hammers of Thor," said Svanhild.

"They are the crosses of the English sacrificed god. This was the altar cloth of a church. The threads are real gold."

"An altar cloth?" asked Svanhild. She looked at the fine white cloth. How could it have borne the blood of sacrifices and still be so unblemished?

"They do not make sacrifices, and so their god is weak and cannot protect them." Solvi grinned wolfishly. "Cannot protect them from me."

Svanhild smoothed her hair. "Will you . . . ?"

His lips curved slightly. He did not look as though he felt shamed to do this woman's task for her. Folding the cloth, he put it over her head so she could pull it down to cover her face during the ceremony. She fingered the fabric, which was thick and strong. "I will not be able to see through this," she said.

Solvi touched her elbow. "I will not let you fall."

✠   ✠   ✠

SVANHILD DID NOT remember much of the wedding after. The thick white veil hid most of the proceedings from her. When Hunthiof sacrificed the goat, she flinched at its panicked bleating and the gurgle of blood that followed. It ran out over the table and spilled near her feet, a stream of red that approached her shoes before running into a crack in the floor. Hunthiof called down the blessing of Frigga upon them, of children and a happy home.

Then Solvi lifted the veil. The lamplight, shining on the golden wood, made her blink. Svanhild's head swam from a few sips of the honey wine. Solvi seated her next to him. For this feast, and this feast alone, she did not have to wait on anyone. Slaves, mostly male, brought indifferently boiled mutton, without enough juice to make palatable the stale trenchers it was served on. The men dug in as if this meal was something to be enjoyed. Svanhild picked at her food. She would have been ashamed to serve this at Ardal, and it had been two generations since anyone in her family had called himself a king.

A skald chanted a story to the accompaniment of his harp. It told of Hunthiof's great grandfather, a mighty hunter, and the great beast, half bear and half man, that he had slain and then brought back to the hall, slung over his shoulders. A legendary feat: few men were so strong in these days, when heroes lived only in stories. When it ended, Hunthiof's—or Solvi's—men took up the traditional wedding songs. There should have been the voices of women, the sweet songs of children, of love, mixed in among all these baritones. Warriors made toasts, and spoke ribald jests about what would come tonight. She was a field that Solvi would plow. She was the sheath for his sword. She was the tree his ax would split.

She drank her wine and tried to disappear. If she stared enough at her food, at the jeweled goblet before her, she would not need to see or hear. She should have given herself more time to think, to see how Solvi behaved. He kept changing, a trickster like Loki, one moment terrifying, the next kind.

She had done this for Solmund, to keep his family safe. She had done this for Ragnvald; he did not need an enemy like Solvi. She had done this for herself, so she need not be her brother's unwanted burden again. She had chosen this path. Ragnvald would hardly be pleased. He had taken up service with Hakon, sometime enemy of Hunthiof. She would not be the one to buy peace between kings.

By her side, Solvi kept her from retreating entirely into her worries, giving her better pieces of meat, inquiring what sweets she liked, acting gallant and confusing her. She could bear his solicitude even less than the joking.

Near Solvi sat his closest companions. Ulfarr had pulled a young thrall into his lap. His hand lay over her wrist, pinning it to the table. Every time she tried to get up to serve ale, he pulled her back. Her eyes looked like those of a trapped animal. He was handsome, with a dark beard that contrasted with his bright hair, but his eyes unsettled her, ever roving over the feast, never satisfied, even with the little cruelties he visited upon the serving woman.

He saw her looking and held her gaze while he fondled the thrall in his lap. Svanhild's meat turned to ash in her mouth. Solvi would touch her like that tonight—at least her birth, or some honor in him, kept him from making a show of it here, in front of his men. Tonight, and any other night he wished, he would touch her. She had been prideful when she accepted, proud of the worth of her word, of her boldness. It was done now; she was a married woman. No matter what happened, no matter if she found reason for divorce, she would have to get through this night in his bed.

Against her will, Svanhild's eyelids began to droop. If only she could stay awake and steel herself. She was unaccustomed to sitting still and drinking for so long. It was Ulfarr who saw that she drowsed and raised his glass to toast the wedding again. Svanhild's cup had not been allowed to grow empty, and she had drained it with a will. Drunken women might bring shame to their husbands—but she cared less of that than of numbing herself.

His toast was good-natured enough: "To Solvi's new bride, may she grow yet more lovely with the passing years." Svanhild gave him a wan smile and took a sip from her glass. The wine tasted sour now that she had drunk so much of it.

"My bride is tired," said Solvi, standing. Bawdy jokes followed about how tired she would be the next morning.

Solvi picked her up out of her chair, to the shouted cheers of his men, and carried her out of the hall. Once they were outside, he set her feet down on the ground again. He glanced at her. Svanhild kept her eyes facing forward. Her thin shoes slid on the spring muck. Solvi kept her from falling with a firm grasp on her elbow. Behind him the guests from the wedding trooped after them. All those men. There would be no mother, or Vigdis, to lay Svanhild in the bed, to spread her hair out to be alluring to her husband, to whisper last-minute advice, to tell her that hundreds of women had endured wedding nights, and would in the future, and that it would get better, that it would only take a moment. Hundreds of women had not thrown themselves into marriage with the man who tried to kill their brother. That was Svanhild's to bear alone.

Behind them, the procession men struck up another bawdy drinking song, of the sharp keel of a ship, which split the slippery ocean. Svanhild wondered what Solvi made of all this, for she had not heard him laugh or seen him turn his head since they left the hall. Vigdis had told her how it went between man and maid, and she had seen animals at it often enough. The cows and ewes suffered no ill effects from it. Vigdis had, though; purple bruises ringed her wrists after some of her nights with Olaf. Svanhild had seen women enjoy the love-teasing that went on at feasts, as men grew drunker and their fingers grew bolder. Svanhild had once thought she might as well. Now she cringed at the thought of Solvi touching her more intimately than his hand on her elbow.

The procession carried them into the bedroom. Ulfarr went to unpin Svanhild's overdress—in some traditions the wedding party might undress the bride, continuing the jokes and drinking, until her new husband chased them away. She shrank away from him, his cruel hands. Solvi gripped Ulfarr's wrist to stop him. He pushed Ulfarr roughly, though with a grin, and bent to whisper in Svanhild's ear.

"Can you manage your dress without help?" he asked.

She nodded, glancing quickly at him before lowering her eyes. Her fingers shook on the clasps. Must she now undress herself in front of his men? That was worse than having them rip her clothing from her. She placed the pins on the shelf. Her overdress fell to the floor. Solvi lifted the veil from her forehead and folded it while Svanhild took out her braids.

"To bed, to bed," said Ulfarr. He was too close, his touch unclean. Svanhild shrank away again.

"Leave my wife and me our privacy," said Solvi.

"We must see you safe to bed." Ulfarr put his arm around both of them. He smelled of mead and blood. "We must witness."

"You've witnessed enough," said Solvi. "Now go."

Ulfarr plucked at her dress once more. Solvi gave him a warning glance, and Ulfarr pulled his hands back. He was the last to go, following the other men out and shutting the door behind him.

Svanhild took a deep breath. They were alone. Solvi had never tried to harm her. She crossed her arms over her chest. Her flesh wanted to shiver, though the room was warm. Solvi put his hand on her shoulder, hot through the thin flax of her shift. She still stiffened and stared forward at his chin rather than tilting her head the scant degree needed to look up at him. His shortness was oddly comforting—she had always been surrounded by men and women taller than her, who engulfed her when they tried to embrace her. Solvi was her size.

"Do you think you will grow to hate me less?" Solvi asked, that hard, dangerous grin on his face. It chilled Svanhild's blood.

"I don't—"

"Don't lie to me," he said, the grin disappearing, leaving him even more fearsome. Then he sighed. "This day has been hard for you. We can wait until tomorrow."

Svanhild frowned. She did not want kindness from him, nor did she want his confusing changeability. She felt numb.

"If you do not tonight, I will dread it all day tomorrow," she said dully. She turned her eyes away from the pinch of pain on his face. Tomorrow she might be more aware, less drunk from the feast. Perhaps more calm as well, though. Perhaps her hands would not shake then. She combed her fingers through her hair. It was still wet from the river and must now be hanging in unattractive strings. Its touch chilled her skin, and she could not hide her shivering now.

"You are cold," said Solvi. "Come to bed."

Svanhild turned away from him, stepped out of her overdress where it pooled around her feet, and hung it on one of the pegs. "What side of the bed do you prefer?" she asked. "It is your bed."

"It is yours too."

"What of Geirny?"

"I do not wish to speak of her tonight. Now get under the blankets and stop your shivering."

It was the most luxurious bed that Svanhild had ever lain in. The mattress was of eiderdown, thick and soft, like sinking into a cloud. She closed her eyes to enjoy it more fully, but opened them again when she felt Solvi's eyes on her.

"What?" she asked.

Solvi did not answer. He took off his belt and jewelry, the arm and neck bands that marked him a king's son, the finger rings won viking. He did not remove his hose or tunic, but climbed under the covers with her and put his arms around her.

He touched his fingers to her cheek. She gritted her teeth. He ran his hand along the side of her face and tipped it up so she had to look into his eyes. "Svanhild," he said. "I have loved you since the *ting*."

She looked away. If Solvi had been all brute, that she could have borne, but this tenderness made her feel ashamed. He tilted his head down to kiss her, though he did not have far to go. She kept still under his kiss. It was not unpleasant, only strange. She did not belong to her body now; it was someone else's Solvi was touching.

"Ah, you do not hate me," said Solvi when he pulled away, mistaking her immobility for acceptance.

Svanhild had promised herself she would find privacy first, but her tears would not wait. Her drunkenness gave her no relief now, only a lack of control. "I should have had a wedding, with my mother to dress me and my people to toast me, not this . . . perversion."

"We can visit them," said Solvi. He let go of her arm and looked so downcast that for a moment Svanhild wanted to relent. "You do hate me. I had thought . . ."

"No," said Svanhild. She was frightened of him, angry at him, and she clung to that anger. "I do not hate you."

She lay, still as a doll, as he pushed her gown up her legs. "I would see you," he said, "but perhaps you will find this easier with no light." He snuffed the lamp with his fingers, scenting the room with smoke.

Faint illumination from outside shone in through faults in the hall's chinking, making Solvi into a bulky silhouette above her. He ran a hand over her breast and then fumbled beneath her underdress until he pressed a hand between her thighs. She stifled a noise of surprise.

Tears pricked her eyes when he pushed a finger into her, and when he tried to find room for two, she cried out, "No. You're hurting me."

To her surprise, his hand withdrew. "I am told it hurts the first time," he said.

"Not like that," Svanhild insisted, with a sob, although she truly did not know; she only knew that if Solvi continued to touch her she did not know how she would bear it. If he touched her, she would lose her mind and become a helpless, screaming, crying thing.

Now his hands held her shoulders, gentle and firm. If he were not who he was, she might even find the touch comforting. His legs, still in their hose, rested against hers. She pulled away. "I do not want you to touch me," she said, her voice rising to a shriek. "Not now, and not ever."

He pulled away from her. "As you wish, my lady," he said. He breathed steadily next to her, in a way that sounded full of effort. "A divorce is easy enough to acquire. And I suppose this saves face for me better than if you had declined to marry me at all." His voice was so bitter that Svanhild wanted to comfort him. "It will take some time. If you stay until the next *ting*, we can declare it there."

Svanhild turned away from him and continued to cry until her throat hurt and her eyes were swollen.

23

HARALD HAD STAYED UP ALL NIGHT, AND NOW STOOD, AR-mored, waiting for his men to assemble. All moved softly, any loud voices quieted by gestures from commanders. Ragnvald had eventually slept even through his fear, pressed down by the weight of fever. His hand hurt less this morning, but his head felt worse, hot and strangely untethered to his body, as though it could float up, above the battlefield. He wrapped his hand tightly. He put on his leather armor and a helmet Hakon had given him after they took the hall. He must remain able to hold a sword, at least until Harald's army had the upper hand. He wanted to look no further into the future than that.

He stuck close by Harald as they arranged the men in lines at the base of the hill, only an hour's march from Eirik's fort. It was as the scout described, bare on the lower half of its flank, below a scrub of trees that grew into a dense forest on its peak. The men with experience fighting in a shield wall took the fore. Ragnvald hoisted his shield in his left hand, and thought of bracing himself on the men next to him. Perhaps they would hold him up if he fell. His ax was on his back, his sword at one hip, and his dagger at the other.

Harald pulled Ragnvald close to him. "We're following your plan," he said. "It is a good one." Ragnvald thought he might like Harald better now, if only because he saw Ragnvald's value. Or because it no longer mattered. Here was where Ragnvald would die, when his hand gave out, or when he gave way with Harald, and the battle turned.

"Then can I be in the center?" Ragnvald asked.

Harald looked at him strangely. "You are not well. I want you coming back from this. You don't need to prove your bravery today. You
have fought a *draugr*."

"I want to make sure my plan works," said Ragnvald, although in
a way Harald was right. He had only to prove himself to Odin now.

Ragnvald formed up in the shield wall, with only Thorbrand between him and Harald. As they pressed up the hill, the army of Gudbrand coalesced into a wall above them, shields overlapping as though
they made a warship out of men.

Around Ragnvald, Harald's men tightened and advanced, until they
were pressing against the shield wall in front of them. Thorbrand's
shoulder dug into Ragnvald's on the right, and another man, whose
name Ragnvald could not remember, wedged against him on the left.
Behind him, one man pressed on his back to keep him in place as his
feet tried to slip down the slope. In front of him one of the Hordaland
warriors snarled, his face mostly hidden by his shield and helmet.

Ragnvald had only heard songs of shield-wall battles before. Usually, men in the Norse lands preferred to attack by stealth, to raid and
then slip away, and rarely mustered large enough armies to fill a shield
wall. He had heard tales of Ragnar Lothbrok and his shield-wall battles in England, but he had retreated before the English in those battles
as often as he was successful.

Ragnvald had time to think of all this, since the shield wall was a
place of pushing and burning muscles, but not much movement. It
was hot, except where a morning breeze found his face, and the air
around him stank of fear-sweat and wet leather. Occasionally the man
he faced across the line, a warrior with a braided red beard, tried to
send his sword over the top of the shields, or below the bottom of
them, but mostly nothing happened except pushing. Ragnvald's feet
slipped, and the man behind him pushed him up. He looked to his left
and right, and saw that, as he had suggested, the inside of the line had
slipped down, and the men at the edges advanced higher.

He probably should have come up with some sort of signal, but
this was Harald's battle. Ragnvald was only here to bleed and die. At
least the strain in his legs from pushing up against the man in front

of him distracted Ragnvald from the pain in his hand. He glanced at Harald, who seemed determined to shove through the man in front of him. He probably could—he was that strong—but Ragnvald shook his head slightly. It would do them no good if the shield wall broke upward. Harald would lose more men that way than if they followed Ragnvald's plan.

Harald gave him a questioning look, and Ragnvald nodded. Harald smiled, just slightly, and then toppled forward, landing on the man in front of him and knocking his sword out of the way. The tide of Hordaland men crashed through the break in the wall, taking several steps down the hill before realizing that the only thing that lay in front of them was a long slope, and that the enemy had gained the ground behind them. The gap in Harald's line widened farther, letting more Hordaland men through.

Ragnvald let out a yell—"Turn, turn, turn!"—and Harald took up the call. Ragnvald caught a glimpse of Oddi and Heming, in the center of the bands of Harald's men they had been given to lead, turning to face the enemy downhill.

Harald heaved himself off the ground with a mighty push and whirled to take the foolish men who ran at him. Now that the shield wall was broken, it would not form up again. Men fought hand to hand. From everywhere came the thuds of swords hitting shield and armor, and the screams when blades found flesh. A small ax sailed overhead, thrown by one side or the other.

Ragnvald gripped his sword as tightly as he could. Once he let go, he would not be able to grip it again. He clashed against a huge man with no armor at all, and no shield either, who attacked fiercely and died quickly, choking on blood when Ragnvald stabbed up into his throat. His bravery could not protect him from Ragnvald's Odin-given certainty.

The next man Ragnvald faced was better armored, and smaller. He gave Ragnvald a good fight for a few minutes, but Ragnvald had nothing to lose, not today, not now. He hardly felt it when the man slashed at his left shoulder. It was not a deep wound, and it hurt far less than his hand, which screamed every minute for him to stop. If he would not stop for that, he would not stop for a lesser pain.

The Hordaland army started to retreat, at least from one side of the field, melting back down toward the lake. Some of Harald's men gave chase. It seemed wrong to Ragnvald, splitting their forces like this. Something was amiss. Why would one side of Gudbrand's forces retreat, and not the other?

Ragnvald dispatched the man he was fighting with a two-handed stroke that severed the man's head from his body, a blow that sent a shock up through Ragnvald's arm and tore his sword from his grasp. He tried to work it out of the man's shoulder bone. It would not come free. His grip had failed, and his hand would not close around the hilt. He tugged for a moment with his left hand, but he could not waste time here. It was a pot-metal sword. He would not need it where he went. He could as easily die with an ax in his hand and gain Odin's favor.

Ragnvald pulled his ax from where it was strapped on his back. He could hold it with two hands, let his left do more of the work. He looked around for Harald, who stood in a circle of fallen men, his skin and hair streaked with blood. A terrifying smile lit his face. He looked like a berserk, but he clearly still had all his faculties, because he called out to Ragnvald.

"That was a good plan you had." Harald tossed his hair back. "This is my favorite battle yet. You're not tired, are you?"

"We've won," Ragnvald called out as he drew closer. He wondered if Odin would still take him if his ax did not taste blood. "Shouldn't we fall back?"

"I want a full surrender," said Harald. "Where is the false king Gudbrand?" A man sat up out of the ranks of dead and wounded. He yelled a war cry and threw himself at Harald, and Harald killed him as quick as blinking.

Harald roared out, "Gudbrand, king of Hordaland! Come to me, and I will spare your life. If I have to look for you, you die."

Ragnvald's neck prickled. Something was wrong that Gudbrand was not here. He peered up into the woods that blanketed the top of the slope.

Ragnvald saw the volley of arrows coming toward them in time to crouch behind a fallen shield and protect himself, but Harald caught one through the shoulder, right at the gap in his armor. It went through the joint, a spot to paralyze his sword arm. A band of men bore down on them from the woods. No one, Ragnvald thought distantly, had followed his plan to clear out the woods after the battle turned.

Ragnvald tried to grip his ax two-handed, but his right would not obey him. The leading man was certainly Gudbrand, his hair bound around his forehead with a golden band, his beard long and gray. He led a band of fiercer warriors than any Ragnvald had seen in the shield walls. They were bigger, their shields bitten more deeply by sword cuts, the swords themselves slim and bright-polished, Frankish steel. Ragnvald stared at them for an agonizing moment longer. They moved so quickly, and his feet were rooted to the ground.

They were going for Harald. Ragnvald commanded his legs to move, his hand to grasp. He had to hold his ax up, to protect Harald. This was why the gods had put him here, given him the dream, kept him from dying in the fjord. Solvi's knife, Olaf's betrayal, all had led him here, and yet his body would not obey him.

One thing left, he told himself, then rest. He picked up his ax and ran for Harald, who was still pinned to the ground by the arrow. Harald started to sit up as he saw the men coming for him, but his arm dangled useless at his side. He looked shocked and insensible, the fire from before gone from him.

"Get behind me," said Ragnvald. "Stand up when you can. You still have one working arm."

Ragnvald was cold where the blood from his own left arm had soaked through his shirt. His right hand no longer felt hot, but boneless, dead already. He gripped the ax with his left and chopped into the first comer, then the second. He did not care if he killed them, only that he cleared them away from Harald. Dimly he noticed that others had joined them, that Harald stood next to him again, holding his sword awkwardly in his left hand.

Then something hit him wetly in the head, and he fell to earth.

✛ ✛ ✛

CROWS WHEELED ABOVE Ragnvald, as they did in the land of the dead, except he could not imagine that in any of Hel's misty realms he would be this thirsty, or hurt this much. A woman stood over him: this was Urd, with her dark hair and a raven on her shoulder. She was not a Valkyrie, but one of the fates, come to tell him what might come next for him, or here to cut off his life.

"Yes," he whispered. "Come to kill me."

She did not seem to see him from above. Her hair flew behind her like a banner. She stooped down to one of the men and gave him water. Water, Ragnvald needed water more than he needed anything else. He tried to raise his right arm, but it would not move. He shifted and wrenched at whatever weighed him down until the left one did.

"Water," he croaked. "Water."

She walked as if she would pass him by. All around smelled of blood and death, of bowels opened by swords. And of dirt. He lay in the dirt, the mud churned up from a dozen feet.

"Water," he said again. "Water," he said. He would chant it until he died. She turned and brushed her hair away from where the wind had blown it in her face, her eyes scanning the ground.

"I might have a live one here," she called out. "Noble enough. He's got a helm."

"Ours or theirs?" someone else called back. A man's voice.

"I don't know," she said.

"There'll be a reward if it's the cousin of that boy-lord, Heming—Ragnvald—that's who they're looking for. They want to give him a proper burial." That was nice, they wanted to give him a proper burial. Ragnvald would like that, to lie in a clean, sheltered barrow, to rest.

"I'm Ragnvald," he said as the woman stooped down by him, her hand on her dagger. A strand of her hair swept over his cheek. She looked like Alfrith, the island witch. "You can bury me," he whispered to her.

"He says he's Ragnvald," said the woman. She smelled like clean water.

"Water," he said. He wanted that, and a barrow—a barrow with water, or ale. Nothing more. He told her this.

"You are Ragnvald?" she asked, suddenly dubious.

"Yes," he said. "Help me."

Hands came and touched him, lifted him. He could not move parts of his body; some were numb, while others sang with pain. Did he still have all his parts? Did he have a raw wound like the *draugr*'s, splitting his head?

They took him to a tent full of the dead and dying and laid him there. Then someone touched his hand, and he started crying and begging. Someone else put a hand over his mouth.

"Honor yourself," said the voice, a woman's. Svanhild, perhaps. She always told him the right thing to do. He went quiet.

Someone touched his hand again, and this time it was too much pain for him to remain conscious. The goddess Ran and her dark waters were waiting for him, the depths of forgetfulness, her hall of drowned sailors. Where he belonged.

✣ ✣ ✣

WHEN HE WOKE again, it was dark in the tent. He turned his head and looked toward the door, where torchlight approached, outlining the figure of a man in its glow. It was Harald; no other warrior was so tall. The light made the edges of his hair shine gold, and cast his face entirely in darkness. A golden wolf. In Ragnvald's fever, he had chosen this golden boy, this would-be king.

"What has happened to me?" Ragnvald asked.

Harald started, as though he had not expected Ragnvald to speak. He said some low words to his guards, and they turned and left, taking the light with them. "You are injured," he said.

"How?" Ragnvald tried to sit up, and his head swam. Harald's face wavered. "Did you let them take my hand?"

"No," said Harald. "They wanted to, while you were gone from us, but I wanted to ask you first. A man should be allowed to choose." He edged back from Ragnvald as though he could be infected by Ragnvald's injuries. Still, he did not turn to leave. That meant something.

"No, if I am dying, let me die of it. I do not want to live without my sword hand." Ragnvald let his head fall back onto the pillow. The beams of the ceiling overhead spun and continued spinning even after he closed his eyes.

"I would say the same," said Harald. "A man who cannot wield a sword cannot be king." He grew quiet.

"What happened? How long . . . ?" Ragnvald asked.

"You last fought a week ago. You saved my life, and my mother saved yours."

"If I do die, let me take up my sword."

"It was left on the field," said Harald. "Someone will find it and bring it to you. If not, you may hold my sword, until I can give you one for yourself. I promise."

"Do you believe I will go to Valhalla?" Ragnvald asked. He did not think so. He was Ragnvald Half-Drowned; he needed to find the half he had left behind. Maybe it was out in the water, the cooling water. He was thirsty again. Harald held a cup to his lips with such gentleness that tears pricked in Ragnvald's eyes. He could not bear kindness right now, but he wanted Harald to stay. A warrior should stand vigil for a warrior's death.

"You will be king," said Ragnvald. "You are mighty."

"I almost fell," said Harald. He sounded uncertain.

"Luck was with you."

"You were with me."

"Luck." Ragnvald opened his eyes again. He felt he was back on a ship, but a ship he could not figure out how to steer, a ship's deck with no edges. Nowhere he could fall from. "Does your shoulder pain you?" Ragnvald asked. Harald held his arm to his body and shifted uncomfortably at the question. The young god had never been wounded before.

"Some," said Harald. "It will be a few weeks until I can move it again. I will learn to fight better with my left hand in the meantime."

"You will be king," said Ragnvald. "You have luck and skill and strength. You will be injured again, as all warriors are, but it will not stop you."

Harald looked at him oddly, as though Ragnvald spoke prophecy.

"What will stop you?" Ragnvald asked, in growing bitterness. Harald would live. "You have men and luck and gold, and you cannot be defeated. What stops you at the edges of your conquering? What stops you from being the man you would stop, the man who kills his neighbor and takes his land?"

"Honor," said Harald. "A king is his land and his people. You know that about your own land, your Ardal, your Sogn. The people who farm the land, who bury their bones in it, a king feels that, in his bones. He defends the land and farms the land and makes the land bring forth beautiful things. I do not conquer for myself."

"You do," said Ragnvald. "But I'm glad it is not only for yourself."

"When I am king, I will gather all of our best artists to a new town, and they will make the ugly hacksilver we take into ornaments for beautiful women. I will bring Frankish sword makers, and they will teach our smiths their craft. There will be no more blood feud, only my justice, my law."

"And that is why you would be king?"

"Yes," said Harald. The light behind him made his hair look like a crown, as it should.

"Then I'm glad I saved you. Make sure I die with a sword in my hand. Don't let them cut it off." Ragnvald yawned.

"I won't," said Harald. "Rest, my friend. We will stand together many times in battle again, I promise you." He shook Ragnvald, so Ragnvald had to open his eyes again. "Promise me. I want you as one of my warriors, my sworn companions. To fight by my side."

"I have my land to regain," Ragnvald said. Sogn. He would rest there if he could, not this strange, southern land.

Harald hardly blinked. "You will be one of my captains, my jarls, then. I will give you a land—and you will hold it for me."

"I would fight for you," said Ragnvald. "If I live."

In Valhalla his sword hand would not burn like this. In Valhalla he would be a better companion to Harald. As he fell asleep, he felt something cold rest against the bandages on his palm. A sword.

24

WHEN SVANHILD WOKE, THE BED NEXT TO HER WAS STILL warm from Solvi's body, but he had risen and left. She was wrung out from her crying, drained in a way that almost felt pleasant until she remembered how she had behaved the night before, drunken and protesting when she should have been welcoming. She had given her word to Solvi and married him. If she wanted to flee, she should have done it before.

She pinned on her overdress with bone pins that had been among her bridal trinkets. Solvi had worn fine gold jewelry last night, worked in whorls of animals devouring each other's tails. If she had been a better wife to him last night, she might expect her own jewelry from him. Not now, though. He surely had enough of weeping women, being married to Geirny.

She had no wimple, so she put the veil Solvi had given her last night over her hair. In the kitchen she found Solvi sitting and eating a bowl of gruel. The pot hung over the fire, and smelled burned when Svanhild stirred it.

"I trust you slept well, my lady," he said, inclining his head with exaggerated courtesy.

Svanhild raised her chin. "I did, thank you." She wanted to say something, to bridge the gap between them, but she did not know him at all. She hoped that he would reach out to her again, but perhaps she had lost the last chance he would give her.

"Who is the housekeeper here?" she asked. Solvi shrugged. "Your father has no living wife," she said. "Perhaps one of his concubines?"

"I don't know how the women do their work," he said shortly. "Ask Geirny, if you must know."

"Is there anything you would have me do?" At home, Olaf had mostly kept out of Vigdis's way indoors, but sometimes he had instructions for her.

"No." He stood and walked outside. She felt deflated when he left. Thralls had come in and out of the kitchen while they talked and would gossip no matter what, all the more because she had asked something of him and he had refused it.

She added more water to the barley cereal and scraped the pot until the burned bits started to come off. A few of Solvi's men wandered in for breakfast. Svanhild served them, and made small talk with those who seemed inclined to speak. She learned that Solvi would sail out for a few days, probably to harry more merchants. She hoped that he would not run into Ragnvald.

Geirny came in, yawning, after all the men had eaten their fill. She had not put on an overdress. Her shift hung loose on her thin frame.

"I hope my husband did not use you too hard," she said snappishly as she served herself a bowl of cereal.

"Would you like some?" Svanhild pulled out a pot of honey she had spied and handed it to Geirny. "Who is the housekeeper?"

Geirny yawned. "I have the key to the storeroom," she said. Which was the honor given to the housekeeper. But if so, she should have been up before the dawn.

"What shall I do today, then?" Svanhild picked up the pile of dirty bowls and started to wipe them clean.

Geirny looked Svanhild up and down and frowned at her. "Make a new dress?"

Svanhild glanced at her clothes. Walking from the hall last night had stained the hem with mud. The dress was made from a fawn-colored homespun, the finest that the farm at Ardal had produced, and a color that suited Svanhild and made her eyes look deep and lively, or so Vigdis had told her. Geirny had worn red silk the day before, a color too bright for her fairness, but which would have looked well on Svanhild.

When she went to the storage building that Geirny had mentioned, it was locked. She would not go ask Geirny for the keys. She could hardly bear this place, and it had been little more than a day. She could not wait nearly another year until the Sogn *ting*. Let Solvi bring her to Ragnvald at Yrjar, if he did not want her anymore, or as close as he could manage. She had found passage to bring her here; she could throw herself on the fates again.

Or perhaps she could change his decision over a few days at sea. She had made up her mind to be his wife, and given her word, and then revoked it when it became hard to keep. And the moment she chose had been the moment that would hurt him most. If he left her here until next spring, she would have to pass those long months, dwelling with her mistakes, and no way to rectify them.

If he wanted to divorce her, and she could do nothing to change that, she would rather pass the year with strangers at Yrjar than here.

She found Solvi in his ship, supervising the refitting of the oarlocks.

"Husband," she called out to him, her voice going high. He turned, wearing an annoyed expression, and she took an involuntary step back. Without his affection to protect her, he frightened her.

"Yes?" he said impatiently.

"May I speak with you?" she asked. He walked toward her. He was ungainly on land, but he walked beautifully on board the ship, as if the slight pitching in the lapping of the water at the fjord's end made his steps into a dance.

"Yes," he said, now close enough that no one else could hear their words. She looked up at his face, hoping he would look friendly and hopeful, perhaps even teasing as he had yesterday in the bathhouse, but he gave her nothing.

"Take me to my brother at Yrjar. You do not want me here, and I do not want to be here."

"And you will come to the Sogn *ting* for a divorce?"

"Why can we not do it sooner?" Svanhild asked. Solvi's jaw tightened.

"Some time will make the rumors sting less," he said. "For both of us." Even that gave Svanhild some hope—they were still in this together, in a small way she might spin into more.

"Then take me to Yrjar. Time will pass easier there."

"For you, dear Svanhild. My time is my own. And your word is suspect now."

Svanhild drew her chin up, ready with a sharp retort about what kind of husband he had been to her, what kind of wooing he had done, but that would lead where they had already been.

"I have given you enough," said Solvi. "You will wait until spring and then we will have our divorce, and in the meanwhile, I will be away at sea, and we will not have to see each other. That is what you get from me."

Svanhild burst into tears, not caring who saw. She wondered, as her sobs subsided, if this would move Solvi, or if she had truly killed any goodwill he had toward her. She had hurt him, and seeing that hurt made her angry with herself.

"If I begged you to forgive me," she began, the words thick in her throat. She hid her face when her voice failed her entirely. She must look ugly and twisted with tears. "If I begged, would you? What do you want from me? Should I go down on my knees here? Before all your men?"

He took her arm and marched her off the ship. "I don't think my men need to know how it stands with us."

"How things stand with us is that you are my husband, and I want you to be my husband."

"Until you change your mind again. I have had enough of that." Solvi looked at her sadly. "I have been honest with you, Svanhild. You have been dishonest with me."

"I have tried, my lord," she said. She wanted to throw his dishonesty about Ragnvald in his face, but it would not serve her well now.

"No. You have been changeable, and you have lied. You swore in front of the gods. Go to them for forgiveness."

"Please," said Svanhild. She had gone this far; if she was truly his wife for a time and it did not work between them, then there could be a divorce. To divorce now was to give up, to compound her every wrong step since the *ting*.

"I will not lie to you anymore. I wanted you when we first met," she said. "Then I knew who you were and hated myself for it. My brother will hate that I have married you, and he is my only family now, and—" Here she choked on her words. She could not bear Ragnvald being ashamed of her. "Can you not see this is difficult?"

Expressions she could not read flickered across his face. "I think"— he shook his head—"you are too much, Svanhild. I had thought—but no. As you will. I will send you away now, not wait for spring."

"Yes," she said. "Take me on your ship with you. I have not yet had enough of sailing."

He grabbed her shoulder. "It is not for your pleasure, wife. Pack your things. Be ready before noon. I will happily leave without you."

✣   ✣   ✣

THEY SET OUT on the afternoon's tide. Svanhild could not guess what Solvi had told his father, or Geirny. He seemed to come and go with the wind.

He gave Svanhild back her place on the ship's small, raised deck, above the rowers' seats, in a tent, alone, and commanded her to stay there. She kept her body inside on the first day, but poked her head out and watched the beauty of Geiranger Fjord as they sailed down its length. There was no end to its marvels. She had been blind to them on the way here, and in any case they had been hidden by sheets of rain. Now the sun played hide-and-seek with the clouds, making rock the color of weathered wood shine like gold where it touched. At every turn, more waterfalls tumbled over the cliffs.

They moored up on a small landing the first night. Half of Solvi's men slept on board his ship, and those on the other two ships, captained by Snorri and Tryggulf, found other places to sleep. Snorri, Tryggulf, and Ulfarr were Solvi's closest friends, and Svanhild tried to see what bound them together, now that she had resolved to stay with Solvi.

Tryggulf had a thin hard look, pale skin, pale eyes, and pale hair. He looked like some icy wight, but he was a gifted storyteller, whose otherworldly face turned animated and friendly when he spun out a tale. His stories revealed he was many years older than Solvi, having fought in battles that occurred before Solvi's birth.

Snorri was even more troubling to look upon. His face had been caved in by an ax many years earlier, ruining his mouth and nose. His speech was indistinct now, for his jaw had never healed right, and to eat he had to cut up his meat into small pieces that he could swallow whole. When he did speak, everyone stopped to listen.

Ulfarr she had noted at the wedding feast. He was handsome and cruel, and she saw far too much of him on board the ship, for he was Solvi's forecastle man, his bravest, his first to leap into battle. She withdrew into her shelter when he looked upon her.

That night Solvi set up a tent for her on the hard stone, and she slept there, listening to the water lap at the dock. The next day, she did not retreat inside when they sailed, but found a place at the bow, as she had in Solmund's ship. At midday they passed by a deep gorge in the cliff's face. Most of the waterfalls skimmed over the cliff's surfaces, and changed daily depending on how much rain had fallen. This one was cut so deeply that the water was only visible in glimpses. The sailors made signs of benediction, touching talismans sacred to the gods.

"What is that place?" she asked the sailors around her when they passed. They looked at her, at one another, and then at Solvi. "Will no one answer me?"

Solvi came over to her. "I have ordered them not to talk to you," he said in a low voice. "And I ordered you to your tent. Why can I command my men but not you?"

She looked up at him. "What is that place? It looks like a crack that goes all the way to Hel."

"I have heard that said," said Solvi. "I have also heard that it delves into Svartheim, where the dwarves hammer out their magical weapons."

"It is too beautiful to go into Hel," said Svanhild. Their ship's path had come closer, by luck, or some god's hand. "Can we not go closer still?"

"This is not a pleasure cruise," said Solvi, irritated.

"No," said Svanhild. "It is my last freedom, for a time at least. Unless you do not go to Yrjar, and instead take me with you on your raiding."

Solvi shook his head. "That cannot be."

"Will you take me into that gorge? If you would shame me by getting rid of me, I will never pass by here again." She sighed and peered into the depths of the ravine. No, of course, she could not expect this of him. She was only glad that he had not beaten her and forced her to remain in the tent. She would have to do more than simply ask him for favors, if she wanted him to truly be her husband.

He looked at her a moment longer before giving the command to turn the ship. It steered straight for the gorge. As they drew closer, it seemed the rent in the cliff might swallow them up. The gorge was wider at the base than she had thought, deep and dark. It would admit a ship at least partway in.

"This would be a rare place for an ambush," she said to Solvi, who was by her side again.

He did not speak, but made hand gestures that his men obeyed. One of them leapt out onto the shore and tied a rope around a tree that grew almost horizontally out from the cliff.

A narrow landing of rock led into the gorge's depths. Svanhild did not know what she would do inside it. Perhaps she had been guided here by the hand of a god or spirit. Solvi followed her in. She turned and looked at him over her shoulder.

"I could leave you in here," he said, "and claim the dwarves got you. You would make one of them a good wife."

Svanhild only smiled up at him, keeping her thoughts about his own short stature to herself. She walked slowly, allowing her eyes to adjust to the dark. The base of the falls here was lost in darkness, and only a narrow strip of light showed at the entrance they had come through. She stopped and let Solvi bump into her, his chest against her back. She had felt him like this when she had ridden with him at the *ting*, when his body and his warmth had called an answering warmth in her. The dark freed her, somehow, of her last constraints.

"Have me," she said. "Be my husband, once at least."

"Why this change?" he asked. The waterfall, hidden in darkness, was not far away. It made her face wet and cool, and only made him feel all the warmer against her. "Why did you punish me so much, Svanhild?"

She had a sharp retort at the ready. She had not punished him that much—he had tried to kill Ragnvald, after all, and he might be a king's son, but he was no prize in more than a few ways. She turned to face him and pulled his face to hers. She kept silent until her lips were almost touching his.

"We punished each other, I think," she said. Her hands shook. She put them against his waist, pulling up the edge of his tunic. He did not stop her. When her cold hands found the warm skin of his stomach, he flinched, but still did not pull away.

"Show me, please," she said, her voice shaking. She did not know what to do, how to touch him. As when she had negotiated for Solvi to leave the merchant Solmund his goods, if she stopped for even a moment, she would falter. Here, her performance was for Solvi alone, and he was a far harsher judge than his men had been.

"Careful," he said. "We will end up in the water." He pressed her back until she was against the cold stone wall. "You would rather this than a bed?" he asked, sounding both amused and resigned.

"This is the bed we have now," she said.

He kissed her for real now, opening her mouth with his tongue. She tried not to think, only to feel, to yield.

"Help me," she said. He must take the lead at some point, he must.

"You're doing well enough," he murmured against her neck.

"Now you are punishing me," she said teasingly. Her hands found his waist again. She pressed where he was hardening for her. He still wanted her, at least.

He took pity on her hesitancy then, and pulled up her dress. He pressed her up against the cliff wall where she could half support herself on an outcropping. When he pushed his fingers into her, it hurt again as it had at the wedding, but she bit her lip against any outcry. He did not seem to care this time whether she liked it or not. She thought she could detect some undercurrent of anger in his movements when he went into her, or perhaps that was what it was usually like, sharp and brutal.

There was some pleasure in it, though, after he pressed into her, and she felt his breath on her cheek, the beat of his heart in his chest, the pleasure as frightening as her own boldness. She wanted to push him away again, and off her, away from this closeness, but she had been down that road before, and there was no freedom there either, only another kind of lonely bondage.

He did not hold her afterward, only whispered into her hair, "Well, Svanhild, you have gotten what you said you wanted. How do you like it?"

"No," she said. She wanted to say something coquettish, like, I have only gotten it once. Or something true like, I heard it would get better, and I hope it does. But here was another truth: "I am only learning what I want," she said, after a moment. "Do you still want to send me back?"

"You have not changed my mind," he said. "It takes more than a willing cunt for that."

The words fell like a slap. Svanhild nodded in the dark, tears in her eyes, her voice failing her. She wiped her face. He would not see those tears. She had triumphed, in this way, as thin as the victory was. She could do this again, and perhaps Vigdis was right, it would get better. She had taken pleasure in parts of his touch. There might be more she could find.

25

"DEATH DOES NOT WANT YOU, RAGNVALD HALF-DROWNED," said a woman. She pressed a hand to his forehead. Ronhild, Harald's mother, her voice as cool as her fingers.

It took Ragnvald a moment to realize that his hand no longer burned, and his chest clutched with fear. Someone had taken it; Ronhild had taken his hand with her magic. He would live out his days a useless cripple.

Then he wiggled his fingers and found that it was still whole, and pained him when he moved it. He drew it out from under the covers. It was bandaged.

"I should change that," said Ronhild. She unwrapped the wound, releasing whiffs of body scents, the tang of blood and heat of healing, but no smell of putrefaction. She set his hand gently on his belly, palm up. Ragnvald wriggled onto his elbows so he could look at it without moving it too much and saw a shiny ridge of brown and blistered skin crossing the flesh. Someone had burned it closed and driven the evil from it. He leaned back on his pillow and sighed.

It hurt distantly when Ronhild rebandaged the hand. Ragnvald recognized the fuzzy feeling in his head now, no longer fever but strong drugs to dull pain.

"My thread," said Ragnvald. He barely had a voice. Ronhild put a cup of water to his lips, and Ragnvald remembered her son doing that, Harald, gentle and kind for a moment. Then a moment of uncertainty, when Ragnvald had voiced his questions, the darkness of his thoughts. "My thread must have been measured longer. I have been saved for your son."

"I think you have," she said.

"Have you seen anything? Can you prophecy my fate?"

"I have seen your hand, torn, bloody, and full of evil," she said, "and none had known you were injured before battle. I do not have to prophecy to see that you will drive yourself to your death, because you trust yourself too much and your friends too little."

That sounded like something Hakon had said to him. Ragnvald shook his head. "But you are a sorceress," he insisted. "Can you prophecy for me? Did the gods save me to protect your son?"

"If you believe it so, you do not need prophecy, only follow your will. Most men are better off not knowing, for if they knew their *wyrd*, they would be frightened of it."

"I am not frightened."

"Then I will tell you: you will give up everything for my son, and when you have nothing left to give, you will give up your life as well." She tucked in the end of his bandage, placed his hand back under the blankets, and took a deep breath, seeming human for the first time. "That is what I see for you," she added.

"I have already tried to do that once. It does not surprise me that I will again."

"I know. You do not need to seek death, for it will come to you."

"There are things I need to do first," said Ragnvald. This conversation seemed half like a dream, his words as fated as everything that had come before.

"Yes," said Ronhild. "Your land. Your revenge. Your wife." She looked sad when she named those things, and Ragnvald thought he knew why, with the clarity that the lack of fever had brought: those might be among the things he would lose to Harald, before he lost his life.

"Drink this, and sleep." She pressed a cup to his lips. Her potion floated him away, this time on a calm and buoyant sea, a pleasant, warm sea that had never existed in the Norse lands.

✢   ✢   ✢

WHEN RAGNVALD WOKE again, he was hungry, and as soon as he ate, his strength began to return. He walked slowly around the camp with

Oddi, who told him what had happened in the week he had missed. Harald, or Guthorm, had won the battle, but Gudbrand had escaped with a fair number of his men.

King Eirik, locked within his fort, continued to refuse parley, so Harald's men finished building the ramp over the wall. Eirik's guards never attacked in force. After the ramp was completed, Thorbrand led an attack over the wall. The inner protections were just as fearsome as the outer, he said, with an even deeper ditch before the inner wall, lined with spikes and patrolled by guards as well. They fired arrows into Thorbrand's massed men. The outer wall guards retreated rather than attacking, which Ragnvald thought wise—the bowmen could do their work for them. Thorbrand quickly called for a retreat back over the outer defenses.

"They have provisions to outlast us, but they don't have enough men," Ragnvald mused. "They did not even emerge to take the advantage when we faced Gudbrand's men."

"You should tell Guthorm," said Oddi.

"He must know," said Ragnvald.

"Perhaps," Oddi allowed. "But another voice, one that has been right before, would be welcome."

Ragnvald let Oddi accompany him over to where Guthorm sat with Harald, while they watched the life of the camp, men sharpening daggers, poking at steaming messes that hung over campfires. After they exchanged greetings and good wishes for Ragnvald's health, Ragnvald told Guthorm what he suspected.

"That seems right," said Guthorm, once Ragnvald explained his reasoning. "What do you suggest we do?" It was strange to see respect in Guthorm's eyes now, when only yesterday, in Ragnvald's time at least, he had been so dismissive.

"Show him we are not afraid to spend our own lives to end his warriors' lives. Show no mercy. Pursue and kill."

Guthorm played with one of the gold rings in his beard. He narrowed his eyes. "Yes," he said, "though we should not risk our lives needlessly. Yet King Eirik must see us show no caution." His stern face transformed entirely when he gave Ragnvald a slow, pleased smile. "He must think we would not hesitate to spend our whole army, to take this fort."

"It is true enough," said Harald. "I cannot be seen to retreat from a fight, especially at this early stage. If I ever hope to make kings swear to me without a fight, they must think me invincible."

✜   ✜   ✜

IN THE NEXT skirmish, Thorbrand poured men over the first wall. Harald was still too injured to fight, but he promised a gold arm ring to any man who brought back the head of one of Eirik's men, and so a number of fights broke out between his own warriors, once the fighting was done and twenty of Eirik's men lay dead. Harald's best warriors had made this sally, and only a few fell.

The following morning, King Eirik emerged from the fort under the flag of truce, with ten guards. He brought a woman with him, of such rich dress and haughty bearing that she could only be his daughter, the famed Princess Gyda. They met with Harald's party on the open plain, within a bow strike of the walls and Harald's men. Eirik was a slight, proud man, well-formed, with pretty features that echoed those of his daughter. Her beauty was known throughout Hordaland, and beyond it in the songs of skalds. She bound back her red-gold hair under a narrow fillet, and let it flow in rippling curls down her back. Her dress, dyed a deep blue, made her slanted, elfin eyes look like pools with no ending.

"I will consider swearing to you," said King Eirik. "You have defeated many Hordaland kings, you say, and since they have not come here to help me, even after I lit the signal fires, I think you must be telling the truth."

"We killed the men at your signal stations," said Harald, "but yes, I am. I never lie."

"What can you offer me, for my allegiance, and the allegiance of the greatest fort in all Hordaland?" King Eirik asked. He wore the richest clothing Ragnvald had ever seen, brightly dyed in stripes of orange and purest white, with gold at his shoulders and wrists. He meant to impress Harald. This display told Ragnvald he had been correct: Eirik had riches but no men.

"What can you offer us," Guthorm asked, "besides a fort built far away from the coasts it must protect, which needs many men to defend it, men you do not have?"

"We offer vassalage to the king of all Norway," said Harald. "It is what I offer to all kings, and they come to see the value of it." He spoke as though he had already conquered many lands.

"This is a wonderful idea." Princess Gyda had a clear voice, like the striking of a bell. "That one man should claim rulership of all Norway. I should like to see it happen."

Harald grinned. "Would you like to be the queen of Norway?"

She looked at him steadily. Other men might quail under such a direct, frank gaze, or seek to punish the woman. Harald looked entranced.

"I would," she said.

"Excellent," said Guthorm. "The two of them shall be married this night, and then you will be Harald's sworn king, collect his land tax, enforce his laws, and win the benefits of his friendship."

"I said I should like to be queen of Norway," said Gyda. "But I cannot do that without a king of Norway to marry." She turned to her father. "Won't you find me a true king, Father?"

Eirik smiled, smug. "You have your answer, my lords. She will only marry the king of Norway, and I see nothing but an injured, ambitious boy before me."

"You would follow the foolish words of a girl?" Guthorm asked. "When we can kill every man, woman, and child in your fort as easily as we walk across this field. It shames this fort to be held by such a man."

"I obey wise counsel," said King Eirik, "whether it comes from a girl or from the rushing wind. Come back when you are king of Norway." He and his daughter turned and walked with stately leisure to their fort, never turning to look back.

"What impudence," said Guthorm, as soon as they were out of earshot.

"She is right," said Harald. "I am not yet king of Norway." Ragnvald glanced at him. His eyes danced with delight, as though he thought this a game. Ragnvald's shoulders slumped. He had walked too far today, still weakened by his fever.

"We should take the land by force, and make the girl into your concubine," said Guthorm. "This land, this king, is nothing to us, only high fields and farmers, no strategic value, a great fort that guards nothing."

"Farmers are not nothing," said Ragnvald.

"Close enough," said Guthorm.

Ragnvald flushed angrily. "An army marches on food," he said, try-ing to find a justification for his words besides his own ill temper at his weakness. "Hordaland is not far from Vestfold, and has more arable land. If you control these fields, with a willing king, your army will never go hungry."

Harald looked at Ragnvald and then at his uncle. Guthorm nodded slowly. "This is true," he said after a moment. "So we must defeat this Eirik."

"Or make him and his daughter so happy that he will deny us noth-ing," said Ragnvald. He remembered what Guthorm had said earlier about Eirik's fort. "This fort was the seat of power in Hordaland in the early days, was it not? All Hordaland kings owe duty to Eirik by ances-tral right, or would, if he chose to enforce it."

"That was centuries past," said Guthorm. "Now all is splintered and confused, as you can see, and needs a king to unite it. Harald."

"Make this Eirik king of all Hordaland," said Ragnvald. "If the other kings don't like it, they can die. They swore unwillingly anyway. Eirik will owe much to you, and he will do much for you."

"What of his proud daughter?" said Thorbrand.

"She will not mind being married to my nephew then." Guthorm smiled at Harald.

"No," said Harald. "She wished to be married to the king of Nor-way, and him alone, and so she shall. I will swear before her not to cut my hair or shave my beard until I am king of all Norway, and she consents to be my bride."

"She is too proud," said Guthorm. "You must humble her."

"No," said Harald. "My wives must be she-wolves to be the mothers of wolves. Like my mother and this Gyda. She should not be humbled; she should be praised. My skalds will make songs of her beauty, and my oath."

It was a youth's idea, Ragnvald thought, feeling decades older than Harald. He might have liked the idea himself, before too many betray-als had made the old songs seem foolish.

"So it shall be," said Guthorm. "We will send an envoy to King

Eirik in the morning. My boy, between Ragnvald's cunning and your showmanship, you will not need me for long."

✢   ✢   ✢

THE NEXT DAY Harald and Guthorm went to parlay with King Eirik again. He agreed to their offer with haste. Unless he enjoyed betrayal for its own sake, Ragnvald predicted he would remain Harald's ally. Guthorm and Harald had set him high for no other reason than a bold daughter, a fine fort, and the fact that Harald had given every other king in Hordaland even more reason to dislike him.

King Eirik invited all of Harald's men into the fort for the betrothal feast, which made Ragnvald trust him the more. He meant to show off his wealth now, not attempt murder. Indeed, he had so few men that he could not murder a company even a quarter the size of Harald's, not without sorcery to put them to sleep.

While ale was poured around all the tables, Eirik spoke the words of betrothal, and formed oaths for Harald and Gyda to take. When Harald made his oath, he swore that he would not cut his hair, nor return to claim Gyda as his bride, until he had put all Norway under his rule. She smiled at that, looking as pleased as a cat loose in a dairy house. Skalds would sing songs of her beauty beyond the borders of Norway now. She and Harald exchanged only a few words as they sat displaying themselves together on the dais. She would not bed Harald tonight, or any man. Ragnvald wondered if she was one of those women who feared the marriage bed, and had found a clever way to keep herself from it, perhaps forever.

Gyda's younger sister made eyes at Harald from under her lashes. She had darker hair and was plumper, warm where Gyda's beauty was cool, with a pouting lower lip that any man might like to kiss. If she had not trained all her wiles on Harald, Ragnvald might have tried to flirt with her himself. Something about her reminded him of Vigdis, though this girl seemed far more eager to please a man, not merely torment him.

They passed a few more days at Eirik's fort in the Hordaland uplands. Eirik promised to send some of his men to Harald's side as a show of good faith. He did not have any sons, only his two daughters, but some nephews would act as both hostage and aid to Harald. Harald tasked Eirik with bringing Gudbrand and his few remaining forces to heel, either swearing to him or dying. Ragnvald did not think Eirik would stir much from his fort to attempt that, but at least it meant that Harald and his men could return to Vestfold.

Ragnvald watched Harald carefully in those few days. He had bedded the other daughter, to be sure, with no ill effects on their alliance or on his intended marriage with Gyda. He had walked the battlements with Gyda, Ragnvald, and a few others following a few paces behind as guards. Gyda pointed out the defensive aspects of the fort that they had not had to face during their attack. The ground between the two walls was riddled with traps, covered with matting to disguise them. Harald's men had been lucky not to stumble into any of those—another sign of his favor with the gods.

Gyda was a cool woman, with an eye for battle tactics, at least when it came to her fort. Later, when she and Harald played tafl to while away an afternoon, she beat him, even when she took the defending side, the far harder position from which to win.

Harald's army left Eirik's fort on a clear morning. The air held a touch of autumn. Harald and Ragnvald walked ahead, as behind them stretched a ribbon of his men, well fed and rested now.

As they walked, Harald said to Ragnvald, "You know, I think I shall follow my uncle's advice and keep her in Hordaland even after I marry her. She should stay to defend these lands for us."

Ragnvald nervously hoped Harald would bring up having Ragnvald swear to him, as he had done before, when Ragnvald lay fevered. It might have only been some sort of salve to a dying man. "You think so?" he asked.

"Do you not? My uncle does not think she desires marriage as much as she desires power. She would be a tyrant over my other wives. Let her be a tyrant over men instead, and do me some good."

Ragnvald was surprised anew by this bit of insight. Guthorm had taught his nephew well, but he was not a mere magpie, repeating what he had been told. He brought his own wisdom as well. When the gods made someone so perfect, a man could either seethe with jealousy or follow that perfection.

"What troubles your Heming and my Thorbrand?" Harald asked Ragnvald next.

Not so perfect after all. Harald should recognize Heming's desire to stir trouble, his jealousy. Perhaps, being blessed as he was, Harald had never felt jealous, and so could not imagine it in other men.

"Heming would—" He would please his father and be Harald's friend. Ragnvald paused. He did not know if he should tell Harald that. "Heming longs to prove himself. He is the son of the greatest king in the west, and he hopes that in your service he may make the skalds of Halogaland sing of him as much as of his father." Ragnvald looked around for Heming, who walked with his newfound friends. Thorbrand guarded Harald and Ragnvald, walking behind them, just out of hearing.

"All men in my service want to be saga heroes." Harald looked at Ragnvald shrewdly. "Do you not hope for such glory yourself?"

"I hope for wealth and men enough to take back my land, make it into what it could be, and regain my family's name."

"That is all?" Harald said. "Is it not a modest dream?"

Ragnvald wanted to speak to him of the golden wolf, of the dream he had, the leader worth following, who would make Ragnvald shine, and shine in his turn. That was Ragnvald's true dream, and if anyone could understand it, it might be Harald. Yet if Harald laughed at him, Ragnvald could not stand it. As long as the dream was his alone, none could mock it.

"I will dream larger when my land is mine again, and Olaf is dead," he said instead.

"I will give you men today, if you wish," said Harald. "If you swear to me."

"Remember, I am King Hakon's sworn man, for a season at least." The words of the oath had said that Ragnvald must serve Hakon until he had done Hakon a service, and until Hakon had given Ragnvald men to attack Ardal and kill Olaf. Hakon could withhold that indefinitely, but he would be known a poor and ungenerous king if he did. "Until I have done him a service—like bringing his son Heming some fame—and he has helped me kill my stepfather."

"I do not accept oaths from men who are sworn elsewhere," said

Harald. "No man who is an oath-breaker may come into my service. But if Hakon releases you, I still wish you to swear to me. Be one of my captains, my advisers, and one day be one of my kings. A district will be yours, Ragnvald Eysteinsson, if you swear loyalty to me. This I will promise to you."

Visions of a great hall in Sogn, overlooking a commanding view of Sogn Fjord, rose in Ragnvald's mind. He saw Hilda, crowned in gold, wearing rich colors, with a bundle of keys at her belt. He saw an army of sons clinging to her skirts, sturdy young boys.

"I will ask him," he said. "I wish this too."

26

SOLVI CAME TO SVANHILD IN HER TENT THAT NIGHT AND TOOK her again, with few preliminaries. She was so sore from the previous joining that she could only endure it, listen to the sounds of the water again, and hope that he finished quickly. She had invited him, pushed him away, and invited him again. She would not push him away now, though it felt as if she had lost the strange war they fought with one another. She had given up something—her maidenhead, her pride— and he had given up nothing. Maybe she should have let him bring her to Ragnvald.

As days went by, she became accustomed to life at sea, and after a time it did not hurt when Solvi came to her at night. She still did not enjoy it, nor did he seem to mean for her to, but when she woke up in the dark and he was sleeping next to her, she liked his warmth.

When the fjord gave way to open ocean, Solvi turned the ships south, away from Yrjar. So at least he wanted her warming his bed for this journey. He talked to her no more than he had before, and she tried not to show that she wanted him to.

His men did, when she asked them questions. Tryggulf, he of the chilly boiled-fish appearance, was gentler, at least to her, than she would have expected from his looks. He captained a different ship during the day, and when they beached at night, he made sure she had the best food from all three ships' provisions. He pointed out shore-birds to her, and the crawling creatures that came out of the sand, as

Ragnvald had done with the creatures of the Sogn woods. Tryggulf had made a study of how the birds walked in the shallows, what they liked to eat, the tricks they used to catch their meals. Some of this helped him stalk and trap them for food, but he also had a real love for the little dramas of their lives.

None of Solvi's men, except perhaps his captains, seemed to know his plans at any time, nor did that bother them. The trust his men gave him told her something admirable about him, although she could not quite decide what. Some feared him, some loved him. Some only seemed tolerant of him, yet obeyed him anyway.

At least during the day she had the joy of life here, on the ocean. Boys as young as ten sailed with them. They used small hatchets as axes, and climbed like squirrels to the tops of the masts. The men found them entertaining, trained them or teased them, and pitted them against each other in mock fights. The boys were useful ship-board, these little wind-sprites who could climb the slickest mast in any weather. They loved Svanhild. They told her stories of battle and triumph, even sometimes, in the evening, their small fears.

"You will coddle them and make them weak," said Ulfarr one night, after the boy Vigulf had cried on her. He had broken his wrist and was frightened that the other boys would grow stronger than him while it healed.

"They are brave boys," said Svanhild. She still did not like Ulfarr, though he had behaved well enough to her since the ribald teasing of her wedding night. When he noticed her at all, it was almost as Solvi did, at least during the day—impersonal.

"Who is braver, the boy who says he has no fear, or the boy who has a fear and masters it?" Svanhild asked Ulfarr. She looked at him until he turned away.

"I have no fears," he muttered.

Svanhild wondered if that was true. The gods frowned on liars, and she did not think the gods would have made a man with no fear. Ul-farr, she decided, feared things he could not control, and so he stayed far away from her after that.

Though the ships tracked south, the days grew shorter with the waning year. Svanhild clung to Solvi at night to share warmth. More than once he spoke in his sleep, words of fear and muffled cries of pain. He seemed sometimes, in sleep, to be that child who had fallen into a fire, the child who had lingered near death for days. Tryggulf had told her about that too, how he had refused to die, and then refused to be a cripple.

Every time he came to her in the night, she thought to use Vigdis's coquettish arts to win him to her, but when he rolled off her, she could not make herself flirt and banter, not when he might reject it. He did not try to kiss her, not after that first time. Whenever she caught him looking at her, he looked away. She kept up her friendship with Tryggulf, in hopes that it might make him jealous, and then he might treat her better, or at least say a few words to her, but he did not.

Ten days into their journey, Solvi stopped a trading ship, the first they had passed. Svanhild sat in her tent with her head poking out while the ships maneuvered in the breeze to surround the vessel. Solvi's three ships were like a small wolf pack, herding, playing, and skimming over the waves, making tight turns to cut the merchant ship off.

The trading ship reminded her of Solmund's, though the men on board were not a family but a company of dark-skinned merchants, too different of face to be brothers. When they drew alongside, Ulfarr threw a grappling hook across and lashed Solvi's ship to theirs, then leapt lightly across. The wind carried their voices away from her, but she could see what was happening, and imagine Solvi's side of the conversation. His men returned shipboard with a bag of oatcakes and several bolts of cloth.

"My lady," Solvi said to Svanhild, in high spirits. "Which of this cloth would you like for a dress?"

Svanhild looked down at her own dress, which was stained from days at sea. She had not had time after her wedding to make herself a new one, and must look a slattern. The cloth was all fine, and her fingers cried out to touch it.

"The red," she said. "And I will need a needle and some thread, if they have it."

He nodded and stepped across, back to the other ship. When he returned with supplies, silk thread, and a small needle of iron, rather than bone, the like of which Svanhild had never seen before, he placed it at her feet with a triumphant bow.

"Thank you, my lord," said Svanhild. "This fabric is very beautiful. Too beautiful for shipboard. I would also make myself trousers and a leather coat like your sailors wear, so I could be more comfortable. I fear my dress will trip me."

She was sitting at his feet, and he stood over her. She looked up at him—she was not trying to look particularly beseeching, but she realized that it must look like that, as though she played one of Vigdis's tricks, and she dropped her eyes.

"As you see fit," she said when he did not answer. After so many days of silent fighting, of nightly surrender, she did not want to wheedle him.

"You shall have what you need," he said. "We will see what we can find along the way. In the meantime, Vigulf's mother has overprovisioned him with clothes that are too large for him. My men would have stolen them long ago, but they are not that large." He laughed, and Svanhild smiled hesitantly along with him. "Though I suppose they might fit me. I will get you the garments you require."

Vigulf did not seem to mind parting with them. Indeed, he gave Svanhild little looks of pride, glad to do something for her. When next they camped on a beach, Svanhild washed her soiled dress in boiling seawater and let it lay out, spread over the sea grass that grew on the island. It dried with whorls of sea salt in it, and she spent the next day scraping these out with a rock, while the ships continued southward.

✣ ✣ ✣

"WE CROSS TO Frisia tomorrow," Solvi told her the next evening, while they rested at a rocky campsite, eating salt cod stewed with leeks and drinking fresh water from a rain pool Svanhild had found on the island.

"Frisia," said Svanhild. She had heard of it from Ragnvald and travelers who came to Ardal. "How long will that take?"

"A day or two," said Solvi. "We may have to sleep on the open ocean," he added, a thread of tension in his voice. Even the best sailors did not like to pass too much time out of view of land. "With a good wind, the crossing is quick, and we will see the delta of the Rhine River. But if we are calmed, or there is a storm . . ."

Svanhild whispered a charm to gain the goddess Ran's favor and then asked, "What is in Frisia?"

Solvi smiled, darting a glance at her. "The land north of the Germans. Our friend Rorik rules in Dorestad. We need friends now."

"Because of Harald," said Svanhild evenly.

"My father does not believe in his threat," he said. He traced patterns in the sand with the tip of his dagger, little furrows that seemed to paint a picture until too many passes made them all chaos again. "He thinks that nothing will change, that our land will always be a place of warring, petty kings and raiders. But you do not, do you? You think he will do it, this Harald?"

"I only know what I hear," said Svanhild. It seemed like a task for a god, to form one land out of the Norse peninsula and all of its warring districts. A king must be close by to keep raiders like Solvi from her family's farm, as the Kaupangers bound together to keep raiders off them. That was what a king was supposed to do, and Sogn had had none for two generations. "You think so?"

"I think he is a threat to Tafjord and my father. I think that he will make too many rules and leave no place for a man to be free."

"Are you so free now?" Svanhild asked, half to herself.

"We will trade in Dorestad for swords of Frankish steel," said Solvi.

"You have not yet given me a sword," said Svanhild, trying to put a note of hope into her voice, so she would not sound resentful. She had forgotten until now—that was supposed to be a part of the wedding ceremony, the sword that her husband laid in her lap, which she would give to her firstborn son, a symbol that the line of family honor passed through her as well as him.

"Give me a son and I will give you a sword," said Solvi abruptly. He stood up and walked away. Still, at least he was speaking to her now.

✛   ✛   ✛

THEY REACHED DORESTAD after a few days on the Rhine. The air grew warmer as they traveled inland, as though they had outrun the coming autumn. The town itself, when they reached it, made

Kaupanger seem like little more than a big farm. Dorestad's muddy streets stank worse, and the river stank here as well, flowing sluggish and brown over waterwheels, past women who washed in it anyway. An old stone building dominated the town, the home of the Christian viking Rorik. Solvi had told Svanhild that Rorik had an agreement with the Frankish king to keep the Frisian coast free from raiders. He had become a Christian when he made his alliance with the Frankish emperor—and served him well—but he maintained his friendship with raiders like Solvi, who brought him news and trade goods.

The ring of sharpened stakes that formed the outer boundary of the fort enclosed a network of buildings within. Straggles of bark hung from the wall; it was newly made and smelled sharp and fresh against the stench of the town. Svanhild found it strange to walk among the townsfolk and find that she was indeed no shorter than most of the women, taller even than the shortest men. Solvi should feel at home here, but he walked warily among the land-dwelling men. He took Svanhild's hand once to pull her out of the way of a cart as they passed through the gate to the fort.

Rorik waited to greet them at the entrance of his hall. He was a great bear of a man, tall and dressed in the Norse style, setting him apart from the Frisians who guarded him.

"Solvi Klofe," he cried, crossing the muddy ground swiftly, to pull Solvi up into a bear hug that half lifted him off his feet.

"This is my wife Svanhild," said Solvi. Svanhild curtsied deep. She was not sure whether to like Rorik yet—there was something in his manner that put her off, an aggression in his bluster, and she could not tell what Solvi thought of him. Solvi kept his opinions close. No wonder he had been able to cross an ocean and back with Ragnvald, and stab him in the end.

"Nokkve's daughter?" Rorik asked. "She is not as I had heard her described."

"No," said Solvi. "This is Eystein of Sogn's daughter. I like her better than Nokkve's daughter, although I think my father likes this alliance less."

"I met Eystein," said Rorik, surprising Svanhild by speaking directly to her. "I liked him. He talked too much, but such men are better company than those who talk too little. It was a pity that he had none to avenge him against his betrayer."

Svanhild liked Rorik better now. She stood taller. "There is someone to avenge him—my brother Ragnvald."

"I have heard something of that—he is making war on the side of King Harald now, with Hakon's sons," said Rorik.

"Really?" Svanhild asked, greedy to hear more.

Solvi made a noise, and Rorik stepped back. "Welcome to Dorestad, Solvi Hunthiofsson and young Eysteinsdatter." He spread his arms to encompass Solvi's company as well, arrayed behind him. "You and your crew have my hospitality as long as you need it." He smiled broadly.

"We accept your hospitality," said Solvi. "We have much to discuss."

Svanhild glanced at him. He sounded more tense than a trade for swords with an old friend should warrant.

"We can talk business tomorrow," said Rorik. "For now, my hospitality includes a bath." He made a show of sniffing at Solvi. "I'm sure your wife would appreciate it if you smelled better."

"I'd appreciate it if I bathed," said Svanhild gratefully. "My husband can do as he pleases."

One of Rorik's women helped Svanhild to a bathhouse that stood over a clear-running tributary of the Rhine River. Thralls had already heated iron cauldrons of water. When Svanhild finished soaking and steaming, she felt clean and warm for the first time since before embarking on this voyage. She brushed her hair out and let it dry free, into the soft waves it would take, given the chance, and talked with Rorik's women, who came to steam with her after she had finished washing.

"Did you really come on a ship with all those men?" Lena asked. Svanhild gathered that she was Rorik's favorite right now. She had a pretty, petulant face, and a breathy voice that made her sound half simple. The other women rolled their eyes.

"Yes," said Svanhild, who thought Lena might be putting on some of her foolishness. "I—I didn't mind it. Solvi was going to send me back to my brother, but—" She realized that perhaps she ought not be telling these tales. This was between her and Solvi. Yet these women here were kind to her, and she thought she discerned something lonely about them. From their conversation, it seemed that Rorik grew tired of his women quickly, and their lives were not so comfortable when he did. Svanhild had to speak carefully with some of the women, whose command of the Norse language was not perfect and spattered with Frisian words that she did not recognize.

"Wasn't he worried for your safety?" Lena asked.

"No," said Svanhild, slowly. "He did not—I was not a very good bride, at first. I am still not sure I am a very good bride."

Truly, she had been a fool and a child on their wedding night. Instead of reliving that humiliation, she told Rorik's women of how he had tried to kill her brother but then paid him off, and finally captured her. The women expressed shock and astonishment just when Svanhild wished them to. They were right—it did sound like a song. Lena sat forward expectantly.

"Is Solvi—whole?" Lena asked. One of the other women scolded her, but Svanhild smiled wickedly.

"Oh yes." Svanhild knew how to play this role, even if she did not understand why Lena should care so much about it. If he was not whole, in the way they meant, she could not imagine what it might take to be whole. He had felt right in her hand, when compared with other men she had seen.

"Is it true his legs are twisted and scarred from . . . from what happened to him?" asked Kolla, an older woman with a disdainful air. Svanhild liked her anyway—she must be clever to have lost her beauty and kept her place here.

"He does not let me see them."

"And you think he does not love you as he should?" asked Lena. "I think he does—I saw him looking at you as you came here, as though he would murder anyone who hurt you, and wanted to take you right then. And you looking like a boy, with your hair all tangled."

"Lena," said Kolla sharply.

Svanhild laughed. "I don't mind. She's right, I wasn't dressed very well. Maybe he likes that."

"He likes you," said Lena. "You have to make him show it. Make him give you jewelry."

"Don't listen to her," said Kolla. "He's scared he repulses you—that's why you've never seen his legs. If you see his scars and show him you love him anyway, then he will be yours forever."

Svanhild did not want to think about that. She had not had much luck when she was forward with Solvi. They had just begun to dance closer to one another—this might push him away again. And his scars, whatever they might be, did repulse her. At least Snorri wore his worst deformity on his face, for all the world to see. These were hidden. Though it could not be that bad, surely. Solvi could walk, and even fight.

"I will think on it," she told them.

That night, Rorik feasted all of them. Svanhild wore the dress she had made from the new fabric, which seemed tighter over her breasts than she had expected, measuring it from the soiled dress she had worn shipboard. It felt luxurious, slippery silk over the clean shift that Lena had given her. Lena said they had many, of a kind of smooth, imported flax that was near transparent. Rorik and Solvi talked of movements of armies and men, and Svanhild tried to listen for news of Ragnvald, who traveled now with Harald, it seemed.

"Harald hasn't come here for an alliance, even though we've cousins in common only three generations back," said Rorik.

"I think he's too occupied with the lands nearest him now," said Solvi. "He needs a strong base if he intends to leave it while he pursues other conquests. But he'll come here for swords." Solvi looked pensive. "He has declared against my father."

"Hunthiof never had a knack for making friends," said Rorik. "He thinks if he sits in his hall and does nothing, nothing will happen to him."

Solvi bristled. Rorik raised a placating hand. "He used to be a fierce warrior," Rorik said, "but he did not recover from the death of your mother, and you know it. Let us not talk of it now, though. This is your welcome feast."

Solvi looked frustrated. Yes, this was to do with more than swords. He wanted to make Rorik an ally. Svanhild edged closer to him, pressing herself against his side until he relaxed somewhat against her. Eventually the feast turned to drunken insult contests and a few fights, and Rorik's woman Kolla pulled Svanhild from her seat.

"Come, you are half asleep," she said. Svanhild followed Kolla from the hall. Rorik's servants had prepared for her and Solvi a chamber with a bed with a down mattress, more comfortable than anything she had lain in since leaving Tafjord. She listened to the noises of men in the hall talking and joking. When the rhythm of the voices turned to that of toasts—a speech followed by cheers, followed by quiet—Svanhild fell asleep. Solvi would be too drunk to join her, so she need not worry about putting Kolla's suggestions into practice, not tonight.

27

VESTFOLD LOOKED TO RAGNVALD LIKE A LAND AT WAR. THE weather turned cold on the journey from Hordaland around the southern edge of Norway, bringing driving rains and winds that blew them off course as often as it pushed them toward their destination. As Harald's ships sailed between the low islands of Oslo Fjord, farmers stopped in their labors to watch them pass. They stared, and Ragnvald looked back. Ragnvald gave one of the farmers a wave in greeting. The man did not respond except by keeping pace with the ship until it reached the margin of his fields. He waited there until he passed out of Ragnvald's view, around a bend. Farther up the fjord, burned fields and the blackened ruins of halls and smaller buildings bore witness to the war that had passed over them. Communities that had stood with Harald or against him—they had been punished by one side or the other.

Bare fields gave way to pine forests as the fjord grew narrower. Around a last bend, the land opened up again, broad fields rising from the water. This eastern side of the Norse peninsula seemed flat compared to the high mountains and deep fjords of Sogn. The pines here grew taller than any on the steep slopes in Ardal. Cows that would have to be tethered together to keep from slipping off a steep fjordland pasture back home wandered here on gentle slopes. Strange, that a fighter as strong as Harald had come from such an easy land.

At dusk they reached the fabled fort of Harald's father, Old Halfdan. Heming ordered the sails stowed, and they rowed into the natural harbor at the fjord's end. The stone docks that provided spaces for warships were already taken, so Harald's ships had to be lashed to the ships that had arrived earlier. Ragnvald grew nervous when he saw Hakon's flagship. In Harald's company he had been able to put this meeting out of his mind, but now it must come; he must ask Hakon to release him.

At the feast that night, the table sagged under the weight of food on it, spitted boar, stewed beef, the side of a whole stag. Ronhild directed her women to serve Frankish wine, and provided a girl to share the cup of every warrior present. Ragnvald believed even more in Ronhild's magic. A land as impoverished by war as the land they had sailed through should not be able to offer such bounty.

Hakon told what he had done since splitting from Harald's forces, harrying Hordaland jarls over the countryside, chasing them among the islands, until those who would not swear fled out into open ocean.

"They will need to find another land," said Hakon. "Norway is not for men who will not bend to their king."

"That is a great victory," said Guthorm. "We too have conquered since we last spoke. Your sons all do you credit: Ragnvald, Oddbjorn, and Heming." He and Harald exchanged a look. "Well, I know that Ragnvald is not your son, but his bravery still does you credit."

One of the skalds at Harald's hall gave his rendition of their attack on Hordaland, making much of how mighty King Eirik's fort was, how beautiful and haughty his daughter, how gallant Harald's oath. Ragnvald earned his own mention, for nearly dying to save his king, the skald said. Ragnvald grew nervous as he heard the words that made Harald his king, and he tried not to make eye contact with anyone from Hakon's party, which he sat among. Not long ago, being grouped with them would have filled his heart with pride and happiness; now it made him feel guilty.

"I had always thought Vestfold women the most beautiful in the land, but I have learned that Hordaland boasts their equals," said Harald when the song was done. He raised his glass.

The warriors took up the toast, and the hall grew quiet while men drained their cups of ale. When the clatter of pewter on wood told that the toast was drunk, Heming said to Thorbrand, who was sitting across from him, "This Harald has married with my sister as well. He should not say that Vestfold women are most beautiful. Or Hordaland. My sister is from Halogaland, and she is fairer than any of these slatterns."

"My wife is from Vestfold," said Thorbrand, mildly. "So I agree with Harald. Men doubtless love the women of their own regions best."

"Your own bride is fairer than Gyda?" Ragnvald asked, for he knew Thorbrand loved to speak of his wife.

"Erindis is fairer to me, for she is mine," said Thorbrand. He waved her over. "I have been speaking well of you." She blushed. She was a tiny thing, short enough she could have walked under Ragnvald's outstretched arm. Gyda outshone any woman Ragnvald had ever seen, except perhaps Vigdis. If Ragnvald killed Olaf, Vigdis would be a widow, free to give herself to any man she desired. Ragnvald shifted in his seat and bent his mind instead to Hilda, with her serious face and her unswerving loyalty. She who he had promised himself to when they were children, who stayed loyal to him even when he had nothing to offer her. He thought her better than these women who made bargains for power, who would be one wife among many if they could tie themselves to a king.

His mind wandered, and so he did not hear what caused Heming to leap to his feet, sending the bench he sat on clattering to the floor. Thorbrand had his teeth bared like an angry bear. Men around them cheered, for all enjoyed a fight. Men who had been brewing fights of their own stopped their squabbling to watch. But Ragnvald had seen Heming fight at a feast before, and he did not want this one to end as that had.

"My lord Heming," Ragnvald said, "you are drunk, and looking for reasons to fight." He stared at Heming until Heming looked down.

"Yes," said Heming. "I must clear my head outside." He stood and stumbled out.

Ragnvald went to speak to Harald. "Perhaps some games," he suggested. "Tensions are high where I am sitting."

"A fine idea," said Harald. He looked to Guthorm, who stood and announced a series of contests, and ordered another barrel of ale to be opened. He divided some of the men into a living game of tafl, which he played against Hakon. They could not play it to completion, for the men were too drunk to stay in the places where they had been set, but Guthorm declared it a triumph of entertainment anyway, perhaps more than if it had finished.

"What next?" Harald asked, his face bright with drink.

"Arm wrestling," called out Heming. "Let us see who is the strongest, between my father and Harald's warriors."

That sort of suggestion always met with approval at a feast. A line of men formed to challenge one another. Heming quickly organized the tournament, separating the men into two groups, who would take turns against one another. Ragnvald wondered how drunk Heming truly was. Drunkenness would be a good excuse for starting the sort of brawl he seemed to want with Thorbrand, and a clear head would be a good way to win it.

"Will you judge, Lord Guthorm, as our host?" Heming asked. "Or will you join the competition?" Guthorm agreed to judge, as long as Harald did not compete. Ragnvald also chose not to take part, since his hand still pained him.

Men sat across from one another at the head of the table to take their turn in the challenge, common soldiers mingling with captains, though the common men were smaller and not as strong as the sons of nobles who had been well fed their whole lives. The sides were whittled down as men retreated, with aching arms, until only a few were left. Ragnvald cheered for Thorbrand, Oddi, and Heming when they took their turns. Every time Ragnvald drained his cup, a charming young thrall with a short cap of dark hair refilled it, letting her fingers linger on his. He would have her tonight, when this contest was over.

Heming defeated all of his challengers handily—he had both long arms and great strength. He attacked quickly, before his opponents could take his measure.

Finally, in the third round, when only ten or so men remained, Heming faced Thorbrand. One of Harald's men looped the leather thong around their hands and tied it—not too tightly. Heming bent Thorbrand's wrist and drove his arm back. Thorbrand winced, for the first time since the contest began. Heming must be gripping tight.

Thorbrand fought him to a standstill in the middle. Then Heming grinned and tightened his grip until his fingers went white. The muscles in Thorbrand's jaw stood out as he fought Heming. His arm began to shake, first at the wrist then all the way up into his shoulder. Sweat poured off his face, while Heming's smile shone even brighter than his golden beard, a fierce, predatory grin.

Thorbrand fought the full distance, his face growing red, tears of effort leaking out of the corners of his eyes, but eventually Heming pressed his hand down to the tabletop, and Thorbrand raised his other hand to show that he yielded. Harald's man came back and unlaced the thong that held them together.

"Let me see that," said Thorbrand. The man glanced at Heming, who nodded.

"Yes, show it to him," Heming said haughtily. "Let him see I beat him fair and square."

Thorbrand ran his fingers over the thong and looked at his hands. Ragnvald came closer and tried to see what he was looking at. There was a red mark in the middle of his palm that looked as though something sharp on the leather had come close to drawing blood.

"Well?" said Heming. "Can you not admit that I won?"

Thorbrand threw the leather down and grabbed Heming by the collar of his silk tunic. "You did something to the leather," he said in a low voice. "I would swear to it. It felt like a knife was cutting into my palm."

"You would swear to your own weakness?" Heming asked, refusing to let Thorbrand pull him any closer. "I can take a little pain without complaining. Can you not?"

"You cheated," said Thorbrand. "I don't know how, but you did."

"Do you challenge me?" Heming asked. "I have fought seven duels, and always killed my man. I would be happy to make it eight."

Thorbrand clenched his hands by his sides, his jaw working, his face still red from the contest. "No," he said finally. "Your father is an important ally for Harald, and I am more loyal to him than that." He lunged forward and grabbed Heming again, forcing Heming's face down to his. "But know this—cross me again, and your father can try to find you a kingdom who will accept a maimed king. I do not lose duels either, but you are too good for killing. I would rather mar that pretty face, so women run screaming from you."

Ragnvald looked around for Hakon. He had been deep in conversation with Guthorm, near a quiet fireplace, away from the contest. He stood up and strode across the hall.

"I could challenge you now," said Heming. "You have threatened and insulted me. It would be a legal duel."

"Do it," said Thorbrand.

"Son," said Hakon. "Do not do this."

Heming broke free of Thorbrand's grip, shaking his head, and called out in a clear voice. "Thorbrand Magnusson has insulted me, threatened to maim me, and called me a cheater. I demand a duel to defend my honor."

Harald looked up. "Perhaps you have not heard, Heming Hakonsson, that I plan to outlaw dueling when I am king. It is wasteful and leads to blood feuds, which drain whole districts of their best warriors. No, if you and Thorbrand quarrel, tell me the meat of it, and I will pronounce a sentence."

"Yes," said Thorbrand. "Let us have a trial. Heming cheated at arm wrestling. I call your man there to testify"—he gestured at the warrior who had the job of looping the thong around their wrists—"before the gods, his *gothi*, and his king that he did nothing to the leather to give me more pain in the grip so I would lose."

"Let Heming decide if he wants to pursue this," Harald said. "He did not know how I governed my court until now."

Heming looked wildly at Ragnvald, Hakon, and then Thorbrand. Ragnvald shook his head. "I withdraw my challenge," Heming said finally.

"That is well," said Thorbrand. Heming lunged at him, his dagger in his hand, then pulled himself up short, laughing, as Thorbrand flinched.

"Yes, hide behind your king," said Heming, too quietly for Harald to hear, but loud enough that Ragnvald and the other men standing around could. "Only a coward refuses a duel. We will find a time and place for this, I promise."

"As do I," said Thorbrand.

Hakon pulled Heming down to sit next to him on the bench and waved his hand for more ale. If he drank until he passed out, that would be an end to this tonight, at least.

"More tales," said Harald. "Who here has not heard the tale of Ragn-vald Half-Drowned, who slew the *draugr* of Smola?"

A cheer went up, and Ragnvald cringed. Well, Hakon and Har-ald's men would need something to distract them, to heal the rift that Heming had opened.

"I have heard you called Ragnvald Draugr-Slayer," said Thorbrand. "Tell us the tale."

Ragnvald glanced at Heming, whose head now rested heavily on his hand. "Heming should have been the one to slay it, but his father would rather risk me than his son. If it were a saga, I should have died and let Heming live a hero."

Heming smiled drunkenly. "Ragnvald rarely does what is expected of him, especially not dying when others wish it." Everyone laughed, and Ragnvald felt easier.

"I have not faced a *draugr*," said Harald. "I did not even know if they were real."

Oddi gave Ragnvald a warning look that he could read well enough. He could tell Harald in private the truth of the *draugr*, as he suspected it, if it even mattered. Perhaps Oddi was right, and the story was more important than the truth. "I still do not know if they are real," said Ragnvald. "All I know is that he was a strong man"—in life, Ragnvald wanted to add, but stopped himself—"and in death too. He could feel no pain."

He told the story as well as he could, making much of the power of the sorceress, the beauty of her daughter, but as he came to his own battle with it, he could not find the words to make it heroic. He had been fearful, he had stumbled, he had been too weak afterward to cut the thing's head from his body. Oddi rolled his eyes.

"He does not tell it well," said Oddi. "A warrior should have a bold tongue as well as a bold sword."

"And is yours?" Harald asked. Oddi took the invitation to launch into a tall tale, which he seemed to invent on the spot, of a giantess he had wooed. Ragnvald recognized bits of the story from tales told at Yule-tide feasts, though Oddi put his own stamp on it, and Ragnvald found himself laughing at the faces Oddi made when he spoke of plowing the insatiable giantess. Harald roared with laughter when he was done.

"But a boaster outwears his welcome," said Heming. "Ragnvald does well not to brag." Ragnvald was surprised to have support come from that quarter until Heming added, "His father was known as Eystein the Noisy—Ragnvald checks his own faults well."

"Yes, he does," said Harald. "His family has many virtues. I shall tell a story now, one that I just heard, and do the children of Eystein the justice they deserve." Ragnvald and the rest of Hakon's men leaned in to hear.

"You know this Solvi Hunthiofsson, better than I, so you know that he is lame. He was married to King Nokkve's daughter, but she found him disgusting, and in his pride, he put her aside, to take up with another girl instead.

"She enchanted him, they say," Harald continued. "He was roving and took the ship in which she sailed. She stood up in the prow of the ship and offered herself to him rather than see him harm the merchant who carried her. He was so moved by her bravery, he made her his wife, and put aside his other wife. They say that she so bewitched him that he would not be parted from her. She made him sail away from his father, and now they go roving together, he and she pirates."

"You sound as though you admire him," said Heming. "I thought Solvi was your enemy."

"So he is," said Harald. "I would meet this girl for myself, I think, and take her from Solvi. I would not be enchanted by a mere woman, but I would know the woman who did this to him." He smiled at Ragnvald. "I will have many promised wives to win allies, but she I would marry for herself."

"Who is she?" asked Ragnvald, feeling cold. "What has this to do with my father?"

"I thought you would know best," said Harald, frowning.

"Who is she?" Ragnvald asked.

"Svanhild Eysteinsdatter." Harald met Ragnvald's eyes. "Your sister. I thought you knew, and that was why Solvi was your enemy."

"Solvi is my enemy because he dealt me this," said Ragnvald, gesturing at the scar that tugged on the corner of his mouth with every expression he made.

"That was not over your sister?"

"No," said Ragnvald.

Harald laughed, though his eyes were uncertain. "She is well named: Svanhild, Swan Battle, for she has won her own battle on the swan's sea road. I shall have my skald make a song of it."

"And add to her shame?" Ragnvald asked. His anger was so deep, it felt like a perfect, fragile calm. "Pray, do not." He stood and stumbled out of the hall, without asking for leave to go.

✛ ✛ ✛

OUT INTO THE twilight, Ragnvald threw up the rich feasting meat onto the patchy grass. He retched until he had nothing left in his stomach, and still it heaved when he looked at the mess he had made. No one paid him any mind, though it was early in a feast for a man to become too drunk to keep food in his stomach.

He walked weakly toward the rear of the hall, putting out his hand to rest against the tall posts from time to time. He could hear laughing and singing from within. It sounded as if they laughed at him, and already sang a song at Svanhild's expense.

The moon had risen above the horizon, a pale ghost in the dark blue sky. Oddi fell into step next to him.

"How can the skald be sure? How could he know?" Ragnvald asked, though his stomach already knew it was truth. "We have been gone from Sogn a few months. She was safe with Hilda's family, far from Solvi's sea roads."

Oddi kicked at a stone by his feet. It skittered off into the shadows. "You know how swiftly word travels, with so many ships crossing and recrossing." He squinted at Ragnvald. "I asked, though. For you, I did not want to believe it."

"And?"

"The skald told me how the news had come. A fisherman on an island where Solvi camped had it from one of Solvi's men, a young man, who liked the tale. The fisherman passed on his tale to the next passing merchant. Harald meant to compliment you, I think. He did not think he was telling you something new."

"Yes," said Ragnvald tightly.

"I will go with you to avenge her," said Oddi. "Heming would too, though for his own reasons."

"I should have gone with Heming to Tafjord, and attacked," said Ragnvald. "Your father might have forgiven us, if we won, and Solvi might be dead, and my—Svanhild spared this."

"Or you might not have found him there, and you would have angered my father for nothing," said Oddi. "Come now, you would never have done that."

"Because I am not bold enough, you mean." Ragnvald kicked a small rock on the path as Oddi had done and sent it careening into a nearby tent. The owner of the tent yelled and put his head out. Ragnvald ducked and hurried his steps.

"No," said Oddi, "because you are not foolish."

"I have been foolish," said Ragnvald. "Many times."

"Be foolish again, then. Ask Harald for men to chase down Solvi. Ask my brother to go with you now." It was tempting, but Ragnvald knew Solvi, better than any of the men here who swore him an enemy. Solvi's ships sailed so swiftly they might be carried by magic. He claimed welcome at hearths from Iceland to Brittany, had friends among the Baltic viking states, and might hide anywhere a ship could reach.

"If she is on the move with Solvi, they might be anywhere," he told Oddi. "And your father would not thank me for doing exactly what he tried to keep Heming from doing."

"I see you have already given it much thought," said Oddi. "If it were my sister, I would take the nearest ship and do what I must."

"What you must? Sail the North Sea until you drown? Tell me about the sisters that you would ride off to rescue. Would you do that for Hakon's daughters, truly? You have never mentioned them before."

"Fine," said Oddi. "I have no true sisters. I am trying to give you sympathy. You speak of Svanhild as most men speak of their best beloved, or the friend of their heart. I am telling you, badly I fear, that I understand you would do anything for her." He paused. "And I would help you."

"Thank you," said Ragnvald. "Truly. I would do anything, but I can do nothing, not at this moment. And now I am half sworn to that foolish boy, and sworn to your father, and Svanhild is lost to me."

"You are right to call me a fool," said Harald from behind him. "I have come to apologize. As I said, Solvi and his father are our enemies, so you may be sure that your sister will be avenged. And I spoke true: I would take her for one of my wives or concubines."

"My sister is not meant for a lesser wife." Ragnvald did not want Harald's sympathy; he wanted Harald to take back his terrible story, to put Svanhild back where Ragnvald had left her, safe with his betrothed. Oddi put his hand on Ragnvald's shoulder to try to calm him.

Harald pulled himself up straight. He towered over Ragnvald, this young giant. "None of my wives will be lesser," he said. "Have a care. I will be the first man in Norway, and my wives its first women."

"Will be, will be," Ragnvald repeated back to him, mocking.

Harald put his hand on his sword. "You will accept my apology. It was done in error. I did not mean an insult, but if you challenge me, I will kill you." Ragnvald took a step back. "No man may challenge me and live."

"Yes," Ragnvald said, grudgingly. "I accept your apology and"—he gritted his teeth—"I thank you for giving me this news. I hope we are still friends. I spoke in haste. Now I ask your leave not to return to your hearth tonight."

"Of course," said Harald, the frightening warrior hidden again beneath the face of the friendly boy. "This is a harsh blow. My hospitality is yours as long as you need it. When you are calmed, we must speak of how to get your sister from Solvi the Short. He does not deserve her."

Ragnvald thanked him again, and Harald returned to the hall. Ragnvald walked to his ship to retrieve his skin sleeping bag and the tent that he and Oddi had shared while on shipboard. It was a fine night, a late summer night. Above, curtains of northern lights shimmered. A mild breeze came off the flat water of the fjord.

"I will stay with you," said Oddi. "It will be no hardship to sleep out of doors tonight. The hall will reek with so much feasting and drinking."

His words made Ragnvald gag again, and Oddi laughed, before turning it into a cough.

Ragnvald smiled sourly at him. "No more words of food, I ask you." He began setting up the tent. "At least Solvi has made her a wife."

"And a heroine," said Oddi. "I wish I had paid her more mind at the *ting*, this Svanhild, the beloved of kings. You should let Harald make his song."

"Svanhild would like that," said Ragnvald. He sat down on the ground and put his head in his hands. He felt shaky. As he took a deep breath and sat up, his own odor came to his nose. He was covered with sour sweat from being ill, not to mention the dirt of a week at sea. "Let us find the bathhouse," he said. "No one will be using it during a feast."

28

SVANHILD DOZED, IN AND OUT OF SLEEP, THE NEXT MORNING until Solvi put his arms around her. His movements were slow and sleepy, so she did not know if he had yet woken.

Eventually she got out of bed and looked down at him. A stab of sunlight from a gap near the roof lit his hair and close-cropped beard gold. In sleep, his mouth wore the ghost of a smile. He was handsome—she had thought that when she first saw him—and he had strong shoulders. Perhaps she should think of him as a sea creature, a merman, man above the waist and strange below.

He opened his eyes, and the smile faded from his face. "Why do you look at me like that?" he asked.

"I am thinking of our meeting." She lowered her gaze.

"You liked me then," said Solvi.

Svanhild smiled and nodded, fearing that if she said anything, she would have to lie to keep him happy. She would like him now, if he let her.

He pushed himself up on his elbows and grimaced. "Rorik had firewater from Ireland," he said. He let his head fall back, and frowned again. "Ugh, no better. Send for some ale and a bucket."

Svanhild did so, and though Solvi looked green for the first hour after sitting up, he did not need the bucket. He bade Svanhild sit next to him in their bed. Svanhild felt suddenly shy. They did not talk much when they were alone together. In private, Solvi had use of her body.

In public, she strove to be his adventuress wife, and enjoyed playing the part.

"I know you are half my enemy still," he said, playing the ends of her hair through his fingers. Sitting this way, they touched, and Svanhild did not have to look at him. She made a noise of denial. "I don't know what game you are playing," he continued. "I'm not sure you do either. But Rorik likes you, and you must stand with me here."

Svanhild worried her lower lip with her teeth. Stand with him—he did not mean like this, in private; he had some political aim. Ragnvald was with Harald, and Solvi opposed Harald. Perhaps the rumors they heard were nothing, and Ragnvald only followed Harald because Hakon did. Ragnvald would return to Ardal, and with Hunthiof—and one day Solvi—his neighboring king, he might one day value Solvi as an ally.

"I will," she said. "If you tell me more, perhaps I can even help you."

His fingers tightened in her hair, pulling it somewhat. "No, you will fight me."

"I won't," she protested. She had held her tongue so many times over these weeks of travel when she wished to say something harsh to him. She wondered if he knew how hard she worked.

"You will, or you will want to. I have no stomach for fighting you now. Continue pretending you are my faithful wife. I am enjoying that."

Svanhild took his hand and unwrapped the strands of her hair from it. "I will continue what I have been doing," she said. "Now drink your ale."

☩   ☩   ☩

RORIK TALKED OF Harald again that night, and with great admiration. Svanhild watched Solvi to see how he reacted as Rorik told of how Harald's mother had visions of his putting all of Norway under his power.

"And now we hear tell that he has promised not to cut his hair or shave until he has done so," Rorik added.

"He must look a fright," said Svanhild. "At least you comb your beard." She laughed and caught Solvi's eye. He nodded at her, so he must not mind this flirting.

"That I do, for I know maidens like a neat appearance." Rorik leered at her. "But they say Harald looks like a god nonetheless, and it doesn't matter if he combs his hair or not. He is taller than me, and any woman would swoon to be in his arms."

"I am sure I would not," said Svanhild haughtily. "I don't like tall men." This she directed at Solvi, who smirked at the compliment, but when Rorik made an expression of mock affront, she touched his shoulder and said, "Except you."

"If he admires Harald so much," said Solvi in bed later that night, as they lay warm together in the dark, "I wonder that he hasn't declared for him."

"Must he declare for anyone? He is free here in Dorestad. Why would anyone follow a king if he could be one himself?" All of the kings who followed Harald must disagree with her though. Ragnvald had sworn to Hakon and now, it seemed, was following Harald, tying himself into a hierarchy of obedience from which Solvi and Rorik stood apart.

"Why indeed," said Solvi. "I would not, will not."

"But Harald is coming to take your land, you told me. And Hakon—he means to follow Harald as well."

"Hakon will only follow himself," said Solvi with some disdain. He traced Svanhild's shoulder. "Do you think Rorik would support me—perhaps loan me some ships to defend Tafjord?"

Svanhild could feel the tension in Solvi's body. So this was what he had meant when he wanted Svanhild to stand with him. "Do you think Harald will return to Tafjord, or was it empty boasting?" she asked. "He has only conquered Vestfold and Ringerike, to hear Rorik tell it."

"He said he would," said Solvi. "But I don't think he would, except that bounder Hakon has gone to him. Hakon will tell him that Tafjord is ripe to fall."

Svanhild did not answer, for she had heard the same at the *ting*. She could offer no comfort. Perhaps there was hope, though. Many men flocked to Solvi's banners when he went raiding. Hunthiof seemed as wealthy as Hakon, though he disdained to show it in any other way than heaps of treasure. Hakon had flaunted his fortune at the *ting* by living higher than anyone else, making his whole presence into a demonstration of wealth and elegance. That was not the style of the sea kings who hailed from Tafjord, who valued gold and a small, loyal band of raiders over a large court.

"My father was once a great king," said Solvi. "I heard the stories, always. From Tryggulf, and from his skalds. But he has not done much to keep happy the farmers of Maer. If Harald comes to Maer, I do not know who will rally to my father and who to Harald." He moved his hands, rough and scarred from the years at sea, over Svanhild's skin. She shivered.

"What would you—if you did not need to please your father, if you did not need to please anyone except yourself, what would you do?" she asked, in a low voice.

"I would take three ships," he said. "I would plunder and raid, and spend my coin all winter, and then raid again the next year. I would die in a sea battle, and let fish eat my bones. I am no farmer, to own land and be buried in it. I am only—" He cut himself off abruptly. Svanhild did not need to ask what he would say next. He was a king at sea, while at home he was only his father's disappointing son. On land, he walked crooked and crabbed. On land, he could not climb a mast to be taller than everyone else. On land he could not flee.

"I cannot, though," he said, his voice rough. "Harald and his uncle came to insult my father, to tell him that he might as well leave without a fight. That cannot go unanswered."

"So it is a matter of honor." Svanhild could understand that, even if it set him against Ragnvald.

"I owe duty to my father and his father and his father's father, to hold Tafjord." Unspoken, though Svanhild could hear it: a wish for a son to rule Tafjord and Maer after him, to carry that duty forward. Svanhild touched her belly, taut and hard from the hardships of the last month. She had missed her courses once—too early to tell anything. Would she be the one to give Solvi what he wanted too much even to name?

⁜   ⁜   ⁜

A STORM BLEW in the next day, keeping the men indoors. Some dozed and drank, others gambled, still others made free with Rorik's female thralls. Solvi diced with Rorik that night and lost a few throws, using what Svanhild knew were weighted dice.

"I have heard that Harald means to keep Norway's shores free from raiders, and tax any trade that leaves the country," he said to Rorik, with little preamble. Svanhild tensed. Rorik must know that Solvi was leading him somewhere.

"How do you know this?" Rorik asked.

"It is what he and his uncle said when they came to threaten us."

"They cannot succeed," said Rorik, uneasily.

"Not if the kings they would conquer stand together against them. Your trade would suffer. Send men with me, or come yourself. My captains know the western shore better than anyone. We will sail to meet Harald wherever he strikes." Solvi paced in front of Rorik's chair. Svanhild would have smiled, had she not been worried. Her husband had a knack for showmanship.

"What then? I hear five thousand men march with him," said Rorik.

"Ten thousand men will be against him, if someone only leads them."

"And you are that man? You brought me how many—a hundred? What do you know about the battles such as Harald fights, thousands of men on solid ground, a shield wall that stretches past the horizon?"

"Fighting him will not need that. It will need fleet raiders, men who can hide on bare islands and sail well. Meeting Harald's armies on open ground is foolish."

"And men from the mountains," said Svanhild. "Trappers and hunters. They will not want Harald's rule either. They can do on land what raiders do on coasts."

Solvi and Rorik both turned to look at her. "My wife is right," Solvi said. "With your support, other kings will listen to me. You can lead us. I would follow you."

"You are my friend, Solvi," said Rorik with an uncomfortable laugh, "but no."

"Men, swords, whatever you can spare then." Solvi jumped to his feet.

"I cannot take sides."

"What if I gain other allies? If Harald rises, kings everywhere will tighten their grip. If he outlaws raiding in Norway, how many more raiders will come to the shores you are meant to protect?"

"As long as I don't anger the emperor of the Franks too badly, he lets me do what I want. I pay him some taxes, and I loan him men and ships to protect himself when he wishes to look fearsome. Harald will not turn his eye to me, unless it is to buy Ulfberht swords from me."

"What will you stake on that?" Solvi asked. "Now is the time to strike Harald, before he gains too many more allies."

"I will give you swords."

"Swords that will end in Harald's hands, if I do not have men to wield them."

Rorik held up a placating hand. "You are right, Solvi. A splintered Norway will be better for me. If you can raise more allies, I will give you men as well."

"Will you come?" Solvi asked.

"My warring days are over. But I have a fine sword for you, and one for your wife's first son."

"Let us drink on that," said Solvi. "If I gain another ally, you will have men for me."

"A strong ally," said Rorik. "Another king." They drank and toasted, and were heard by Solvi's men and Rorik's.

✛ ✛ ✛

"HE COULD CALL up a thousand men from the Frisian coast," said Solvi that night when they made ready for bed. "Harald will look here, or the Danish jarls will look here, if Harald ousts them from their Norse holdings."

"And they are yours if you gain another ally," said Svanhild.

"What if the next king I ask says that, each waiting for someone else to make the bold move?" Solvi sat down on the bed, and then stood up again.

"And your father can call up no allies?" Svanhild had heard of Hunthiof's friendship with King Nokkve, repaired by Solvi's marriage to Geirny. Though how strong it remained, with Svanhild in Solvi's bed, she did not want to know.

"My father does not—he would prefer I stay in Tafjord with my men to defend him there. He rages about Harald's insult, but he will do nothing."

So let him do nothing, Svanhild wanted to say, but she would not encourage Solvi to abandon what honor he had. "The kings of Hordaland, every other Norse king—would they not be on your side?"

"They might," said Solvi. "If they could put aside their own quarrels. But I fear that uncle of Harald's will set them against each other."

"You can always ask."

"And abase myself again?" said Solvi.

Svanhild felt ashamed—he could be speaking of their relations, not his political ones. He did not look like he wanted an answer, so she put her hand out to him. "Come to bed," she said.

He looked at her for a moment, then stopped his pacing. He turned to put out the rushlight, and Svanhild got up on her knees and caught his wrist. "No, let me see you."

Solvi clenched his jaw and curled his hands into fists at his sides. Perhaps he would hit her. A part of her hoped for that—then she would not have to go through with this.

"You are beautiful," he said, but accusing this time, not wonderingly, as he had said it on their wedding night. As if her beauty was an affront to him.

"You are strong," said Svanhild. "Brave, and a leader of men. Honorable." He was, in his way, putting kin and land above all, as Ragnvald had done, and perhaps he understood the world better than Ragnvald did. "I want to see the man I couple with." She spoke the words to evoke the law against a man tricking a woman into sex by pretending to be someone else. "It is my right."

Solvi looked lost. Whatever she had expected of him—to scold her, take her and punish her—he did not look like he would do it now. Svanhild came forward on her knees and tugged at Solvi's shirt. She took her scissors off the bedside table and cut the threads that she had sewn around his wrists this morning, sewing him into his shirt to keep out the cold. She slipped her hands under the edge of the tunic, skimming over his waist and lifting it up over his shoulders. She touched his uncovered skin—this part was easy enough. Like this, he was beautiful to her.

She took a deep breath and undid the strings of his trews and pushed them down, keeping her eyes on his face. He cast his eyes down, on his hands where they caressed her breasts. She kissed his chest and sat back on her heels, in front of him, now looking down to see what she had feared. His legs were badly scarred, and foreshortened. Shiny white scars crisscrossed the healthy skin of his thighs. His right calf had half the muscle of the left, and was all scar tissue. That foot, too, lacked toes, while the other had only three. No wonder he walked with difficulty on land, even wearing his high, hard boots.

Her stomach turned, the way it always did when she looked on an injury. She wanted to touch her own legs, seized by some strange instinct to make sure they were still whole. Tears prickled in her eyes. How hard it must have been for him, learning to walk again, to fight, always too short, always crippled. What kind of man could have done it? None she had ever known, except maybe Ragnvald, but even he was too hemmed about by what should be to strive against the fates as Solvi had.

Solvi's legs were shorter from the scarring, and he was proportioned smaller than most men, as though the burn had stunted all of his growth. He was her size, her Loki, her trickster husband, born from fire. She ran her hand over the scars of his thighs, feeling the strong muscle underneath, and glanced up at him. He looked stricken.

"What are you trying to do, Svanhild?" he whispered.

"To know you," she said. "To show you that you should not doubt me."

"You want to weaken me."

She pulled her hand away. She would start crying in earnest if he continued to hate her, when she had seen all of him. Kolla had been wrong, or she had done it wrong.

"There would be no better match for me than you," she said, "if only you did not stand opposite my brother." She blinked, and tears did flow over her cheeks. She wiped them away angrily. "You have given me—the sea, freedom, adventure—you let me sail with you. He shut me away. I do not want you to fight my brother, but I am yours."

She bowed her head. He put out the light, and pushed her back. He touched her slowly, without saying anything, gentler this time than ever before, until she pulled him into her with her legs around his back.

He held her and kissed her neck afterward, pressing the length of his body against hers, sweat sticking them together.

"Next time, will you let me leave the light burning?"

"Wanton," said Solvi. "That is for me to ask."

"Yet I do ask it," she said, turning to face him. He kissed her again and pulled her to him so she had to put a leg over his waist again.

"What if I cannot give you a son?" he asked, his voice low and muffled, for his face was buried in her hair.

"Then a daughter," said Svanhild. "With both of our looks, she would be comely, would she not? If not over-tall." She could only see a son, though. Her son would have Solvi's handsome face. Her son would inherit Tafjord, and perhaps be the king that Maer had lacked since Hunthiof stopped doing his duty.

"Svanhild—" He sounded broken. She knew he feared his seed was no good for sons, or anything else.

"Do not speak of ill omens this night," she said. "This is a night for good magic."

Solvi was quiet for such a long time that she thought he had fallen asleep. Finally he kissed her again and said, "Yes, it is," before wrapping his arms around her and throwing a naked leg over hers. It felt whole in the dark, skin against skin.

She fell asleep thinking of her son, how he would be a sea king like his father and a farmer like his uncle, the best of all that Maer and Sogn had to offer. She dreamed of him too, but instead of dreaming of a golden boy running over the hills of Tafjord, it seemed instead that she sought him on a treeless plain, wreathed in mist. In the distance a mountain belched fire, and under her feet lay ice. She woke troubled, and Solvi's drowsy touch could not soothe her back to sleep.

✣ ✣ ✣

"YOU ARE DANGEROUS to me, Svanhild." Solvi traced the outline of her breast through the shift she had pulled on in the middle of the night. She thought she should cover up, but part of her enjoyed the brazenness of this, the luxury of it, lying long abed in the morning. Kolla had been right after all, about how to bring Solvi to her, but she had not said that the spell would work both ways. Svanhild wanted him to touch her again.

"Am I now?" she asked, leaning up on one elbow. Her hair cascaded over her face. She laughed and draped it over him as well, drawing it back so it slipped over his skin. He enjoyed that, she could tell by the way his eyes half closed.

"Yes," he said. She ran her hand over her stomach, still flat. If she gave Solvi a son, he would deny her nothing. He would deny Ragnvald nothing.

"You are always thinking of something else," she said. "I watch you, and I see that."

"I watch you too," he said. "And when I watch you, I can see nothing else."

She rolled over onto her back again. "Then I am dangerous," she said, not teasing this time. She was pleased, but also saddened—would he blame her for her attractions? "Shouldn't you put me away, then?"

"I could leave you home, where you would be safer," he said. "Would you stay at Tafjord and raise our children while I raid abroad?"

She could not tell from his tone of voice what he wanted. She had loved the past few weeks, even with Solvi's early cruelty and indifference, more than she had loved any time before in her life. She did not mind the constant moving, sleeping every night on a different shore. She knew what Vigdis would say, that her hair and skin would become rough, that no man would love her anymore, but she could not bring herself to care about that, not when every day brought a new horizon, new adventures.

"Would you leave your father to die in his hall, leave Harald to his conquering, and sail off across the seas with me?" Svanhild asked. "Let my brother follow his kings and his fate without your interference?"

"Svanhild," said Solvi, a note of pleading in his voice, "you know I cannot."

"I would not stay in an unhappy hall and wait for an unhappy fate. Even if you commanded me." She looked at him directly in the eyes, as she had not since their lovemaking, since he had given her pleasure that made her feel like an animal lying out in the sun, complete and unashamed. "If war comes to Tafjord, I will be no safer there."

"And war is coming to Tafjord." He looked at his fingers on her breast again, rather than her face. "Nowhere is safe now. I would rather have you by my side."

Svanhild did not answer. She had done what she wanted to, if she could keep this, Solvi's love for her, like a bird grasped gently in her hand. It was powerful, but fragile right now. She did not want to damage it, this newfound trust.

29

RAGNVALD SLEPT DEEPLY AND WOKE HAPPY, CLEAN AND WELL rested, until he remembered what he had learned—that Svanhild was with Solvi, and all men knew it. The story had not made clear how she had gone from Hrolf's farm to Solvi's bed. It chilled him to try to guess what had come to Hrolf's farm to make her flee. If Svanhild had not been safe there, was Hilda? She was his intended; it would be a double shame to him if something had happened to her.

He felt helpless thinking of it. This was Solvi's revenge upon him for not dying, and he wondered if Svanhild might be pleased to be Solvi's mistress or wife, at least in a small part. Ragnvald could not give her the excitement she craved.

While he ate dinner that night in a corner of the hall with Thorbrand and Thorbrand's wife Erindis, Oddi came to him and told him that Hakon wanted to talk with him on the next day.

"He thinks you have been avoiding him," said Oddi. The stewed meat in Ragnvald's mouth tasted suddenly foul, though the kitchens of Harald's hall produced nothing but rich, well-flavored dishes.

"Of course I have not," he said, after he chewed and swallowed. "I will be glad to hear what he would say." He said his good-night to Thorbrand and his wife, and followed Oddi outside.

It was a chilly night. A breeze shivered the surface of the fjord and set the ships that were not beached rocking against one another.

"You fear to tell my father that Harald wants you," said Oddi. "It is a terrible problem you have. Too many kings wish you for their sworn man. Every man in that hall wishes he had the same worries."

"You don't," said Ragnvald.

"I'm a bastard with no ambition, except to please my father," said Oddi. "Makes life easier."

"I want to please my father too," said Ragnvald.

"Do the dead talk to you, Ragnvald Half-Drowned?"

Ragnvald shook his head. Leaving Hakon's service meant leaving Oddi too, perhaps, and he would miss this. Oddi knew just how to distract Ragnvald from his moods.

"What do you think your father will say?" Ragnvald asked.

"It will not be pleasant," said Oddi. "He is jealous. Of Harald's power, of the greatness that accrues to his name, of many things. My brother Heming comes by his faults honestly."

Ragnvald had seen those faults, even while he looked for Hakon's virtues. "Knowing that will not help me sleep," he said with a short laugh.

"I know," said Oddi. "But try, anyway. For my sake, at least."

✢   ✢   ✢

RAGNVALD HAD HIS chance to speak with Hakon the next morning. Harald's hall and the landscape around it seemed crowded to him, hemmed about by fields that he did not know, and by responsibilities that kept him from exploring them. He could see that Hakon felt the same. At Yrjar he had a long shore to walk, where he could see his fort and all his ships beached, like dogs sleeping next to one another in front of a warm fire. Here the ships were crowded into the small harbor, stacked deep.

"Harald will need a new capital, I think," said Ragnvald, "if he would be king. He could be easily trapped in here."

"If he would be king," said Hakon. "Do you still see as clearly as when I sent you off with my son? Can you tell me what I must know of Harald?"

Ragnvald hesitated, though he was sworn to Hakon now, and Harald would want him to fulfill his first oath. Those words of Harald's had troubled him—the idealism was all very fine, but a young king, still growing into his power, could not afford to be so picky about his allies. He might need the services of an oath-breaker one day.

"He is young," said Ragnvald carefully. "I must tell you—he has asked me to swear to him, to be his captain for life."

"And he flatters you with songs," said Hakon. "You who said he hated flattery."

"The skalds sing the truth of that battle, no more," said Ragnvald diffidently. He did not hate flattery. No, he craved it so much he distrusted that craving. He walked a half step behind Hakon as they trod the beach.

"So I should fear your advice?" Hakon asked.

"No," said Ragnvald. "I would not lie to you, nor even bend the truth. I see certain things: you wish the districts of Norway for your sons. Harald wishes the districts of Norway for his allies, and him over them all. There is not necessarily a conflict."

"Yes, I know this," said Hakon impatiently. Ragnvald's face heated with anger and embarrassment. He only wanted Hakon to know that he saw it too. "Have you already decided—or do you wish me to buy your favor back?"

"He has other allies, though, beyond your sons," said Ragnvald, trying to steer the conversation back to his oath.

"Yet he wants you. You bring nothing to him, though, except—" Hakon pressed his lips together. Ragnvald could read what he would not say: he had liked Ragnvald well when he was raising him up, but now that Ragnvald surpassed his sons, Hakon liked him less. "Well, what would you tell me of Harald?"

"He is young, and inexperienced. He is too idealistic for his own good," said Ragnvald. Hakon nodded. "Yet he is blessed by the gods. He can fight. The tales do not lie about that. That alone would make him a formidable leader. Guthorm drives his strategy, but Harald is more than a figurehead. He has vision and wisdom of his own. He stirs men's imagination, and has wealth enough to keep them by his side. He is god-blessed and lucky."

"I expected better of you," said Hakon crossly. "You are young, but not credulous. Where is your clear sight? I had hoped you would tell me that he was only a puppet in Guthorm's hands."

"I see what I see."

Hakon peered at Ragnvald as though he could look directly into his mind. "You truly think he can do it? Put all of Norway under his rule?"

"I do." Ragnvald let out a long breath. "It will be harder without you by his side. It may even be impossible. If you stood against him, you would destroy each other. With him, you would be great allies." But Harald would be Hakon's king, and Hakon's sons must be Harald's subjects. Hakon might not be able to swallow that.

Hakon picked up his pace along the rocky margin of the water. Dead reeds made the ground marshy. "What of my sons?" he asked. "How do I put them in his way?"

"I have done what I can for Heming." Ragnvald fingered the edge of his tunic, running his thumb along the hem, which was shiny with wear. Adviser to kings, wearing threadbare homespun. He should spend some of the silver he had won in battle on a new tunic, so he looked the part he wished to play.

"Had you not taken me in, I would have . . ." Ragnvald had tried not to think of it. Would he have gone to Hrolf's farm with Svanhild? Would he travel with Solvi now, and raid again on the open ocean, always having to look behind him, in case Solvi thought it good to try murdering him again? He would not have met Harald. "I would not be here. I would be a poorer man. I owe you duty for the rest of my life, and you can always count me an ally."

Hakon waved him off. "Speak plainly, Ragnvald. This flattery becomes you ill."

"It is gratitude."

"Yes, with your ambition and pride, you wear gratitude like a too-small tunic." He glanced at Ragnvald's clothes, and Ragnvald colored. "You are Harald's man now, in your heart."

Ragnvald nodded.

"But your Harald does not like oath-breakers."

"I have broken no oaths. I am your man. I did what you asked."

"And now you want to be freed." Hakon's eyes gave no clue of what he wanted Ragnvald's answer to be. There was no freedom where kings took an interest, only power and favors.

"I want too many things," said Ragnvald. "Solvi Hunthiofsson is your enemy and mine. And Harald's too. Now that you have helped Harald in Hordaland, will you give me and Heming leave to go after him, and take Svanhild back?"

"What of your father's land, Ragnvald Eysteinsson? Would you not see that restored?"

"I would," said Ragnvald. "But my sister's honor must come first."

"Had you asked me for a force to sail against your stepfather, I would have given it. That was the oath you swore to me. No, I'm sorry that Solvi has taken your sister, but I cannot have my son and my ships chasing him all over the North Sea, with winter coming upon us."

"Then here is your answer," said Ragnvald, angered. "I believe I can convince Harald to make Heming one of his captains, his companions, if you free me from my oath and let me swear to him."

"Is that how you would sell yourself?" Hakon asked. "Since I will not send men out to die on the sea for your sister? Why should Harald count you so much higher than my son? I come to him with ships and wealth beyond counting, and you come to him penniless and poor, dour company. What do you have besides your knack for always being right? Kings do not like men who are always right."

"How well I know that," said Ragnvald hotly. "It is one of my curses. But Harald values it. As you did once. As for your sons—" He cut himself off. He had spoken to Hakon of his sons before, but always carefully, never in anger.

"What of my sons?" Hakon's voice was dangerous.

"I only know Heming. He is a brave man, but jealous and foolish. He wishes for your good opinion above all, and you hold him too close to let him earn it. He wants to think of himself as a man. You tie him to you so tightly he can hardly breathe. Harald can see that Heming has no use besides what you give him, for he has earned nothing for himself."

Hakon's face went red with anger. He stepped forward and slapped Ragnvald across the face, as though Ragnvald were a mere boy. "I have killed men for talking to me this way."

And Ragnvald had grounds for a duel with that slap. He was glad no one was here to see it, so he need not confront a king. "Kill a man who speaks the truth, and you will only be surrounded by liars. I am your sworn man, until you release me. I am no oath-breaker. Do what you will." He turned and left.

+   +   +

"I HAVE HEARD that you want this Ragnvald for your own?" Hakon said to Harald at dinner that night, while waiting for thralls to bring out trenchers. "Is not my daughter enough for you?"

Ragnvald flushed angrily as men laughed. It was a joke that cut very close to insult.

"Yes," said Harald.

Hakon paused, waiting for an explanation or defense. When none came, he smiled. "My warriors are yours. This Ragnvald is of an old ruling family, an equal with mine or yours." Ragnvald sat up, surprised. He had not thought to win praise from Hakon now. "He is not mine to hand over. His vow to me will be at its end when I send him with men to kill his usurper stepfather."

"That is well," said Harald. "Then Ragnvald can swear to me before we go warring in the spring."

"Tell me, though, will you help him regain his sister?" Hakon grinned unpleasantly. "I refused him, so he wishes to find another master. I told him he should not sell himself so cheaply." Ragnvald stood, ready to fight. It was no more than he should do for Svanhild, yet Hakon painted him as a whore for it.

"Is that so?" Harald asked.

Ragnvald glanced from Hakon to Harald. Hakon looked amused, waiting to see how the drama he set in motion would play out. Harald appeared ready to be offended.

"Solvi has many enemies," said Ragnvald, still standing. If Hakon wanted to see a drama enacted, he would have it. He smiled slightly. "And many of them are here tonight. I know that all of you will help bring my sister back to me, soon or late."

"Yes," said Harald. "Solvi will winter over somewhere, and we will hear of it. Then we will send ships and men there to fight him. But I am not trading your sister's honor for your loyalty. I ask for oaths for life. A new nation cannot be built on less."

Ragnvald nodded; Harald had used those words before when telling Ragnvald of his plans, his vision. "That is not why I wish to swear to you," he said. Men had turned from all over the hall to watch him where he stood. He looked down the long fire, at the faces of the warriors. An anticipatory murmur wended through the crowd. There was precedent for this: a man standing to praise his lord, to give an example all men would follow.

"You all see this scar on my cheek?" Ragnvald asked. Harald nodded. "Solvi Hunthiofsson gave me this, and he gave me something else as well." He looked at Oddi. "No, not a nephew, Oddi. Stop grinning at me." Though it pained him to make a joke at Svanhild's expense, Harald and Hakon's men laughed appreciatively. Hakon looked bemused. He must not have expected Ragnvald to make a speech, to craft his story into a weapon. It was not one of the skills Ragnvald had honed, but he had heard skalds speak, and he had been saving this one tale until it could do him the most good.

"When Solvi threw me in the water, I began to sink. The cold arms of Ran's handmaidens were pulling me down, and as I sank, I had a vision." He described it then, the hall hung with gold that shone green under the water, the fire that gave off no warmth. "And into that hall came a wolf, with fur of gold that shone in parts and was matted in parts. Some of the men who touched him burned, like King Gandalf, King Frode, King Hogne. Some grew brighter, like King Eirik." Ragnvald swallowed. "King Hakon Grjotgardsson."

Ragnvald paced the floor once more, drawing out the tale. "Then I touched his fur. I could not stop myself, whether I burned or no." He paused again. "Where I touched, the matted fur burnished, the dirt became bright. And I did not burn. Since that dream, I have been looking for that golden wolf. I thought . . ." He faltered; he could not say that Hakon or his sons had failed him—"I thought it might be the search of a lifetime, but it has come to me swiftly. King Harald is the golden wolf that I saw. With him, the men of Norway will shine, or they will burn, but they will not be able to resist him. I will swear to King Harald, as should every man of this peninsula. He is my king."

"I am well pleased," said Harald. "Ragnvald is a sorcerer as well as a warrior." He spoke quietly, but in the hush, his voice still carried to the farthest reaches of the hall. "You have even predicted that I would not cut or comb my hair. I will grow matted indeed!"

Ragnvald let out a breath. Men started to speak in low voices, until Harald held up his hand. Into the silence, his mother spoke—Ronhild the sorceress, wise in prophecy.

"Ragnvald dreams true," she said. "I had a dream at Harald's birth, which you all know, and I have dreamed of a brother to stand by his side."

"I have many brothers," said Harald. "The gods bring them to me."

"And all of them will make you shine, my son," she said. "Because you choose them well."

Harald stood and drew Ragnvald into a hearty embrace. "Ragnvald will be the first of my sworn captains in the spring. Now we spend our winter making ourselves strong for war."

Ragnvald sat down, dazed. Then the cheers began, chants of Harald's name, and a few of Ragnvald's, while other men called for their own captains, men already sworn to Harald. All raised their glasses to toast, all except Hakon and his trueborn sons.

☩   ☩   ☩

THE FIRST WINTER storms blew with them snow, ice, and ships bearing the rest of Hakon's household from Yrjar. His wives, his daughter Asa, who was married to Harald, and his younger sons Geirbjorn and Herlaug were among those carried south. Ragnvald was surprised that Hakon would impose himself on Harald's generosity all winter. Harald might not mind, though. Winters grew long and dull for men trapped inside with the same faces.

Harald had many plans to keep his men busy as the daylight hours grew shorter. On clear days, Ragnvald drilled with Harald and his captains. He worked hard to make sure his hand did not stiffen up. The scar was a thick ridge across his palm and still, even healed, looked like a bite mark. He worked tallow into it every morning and night, and stretched the scar tissue until it ached. In idle moments he thought of finding the boy who had given it to him, bringing the lad into Harald's service. It would make a fine story.

He thought of Svanhild, and hoped that at least she was safe this winter, even if it was in Solvi's bed. Tales reached them of Solvi travel-ing and gaining allies to stand against Harald. Guthorm thought that Solvi was not the type to unite anyone, but Ragnvald wondered. Solvi did as he pleased, and had men following him wherever he went. If he turned his talents toward gathering more than the warriors it took to make a raiding party, he might form a true rebellion against Harald. He might only be the messenger, putting his daring against the harsh winter winds to good use.

The day before Yule was gray and blustery. The wind blew the snow around in spindrifts, forcing it through chinks in the hall's planking. Harald's allies who could make the journey to his Vestfold hall in less than a day thronged the halls. They brought wives and daughters who filled the halls with the sounds of women's chatter that had earlier been scarce. It made Ragnvald miss his home and Svanhild all the more. He promised himself that he would host a great Yule feast with Hilda, as soon as they married.

Guthorm and Harald had arranged a number of contests, the usual tests of speed and aim: a ski race, a snowshoe race, arrow and ax tar-gets. Men fought out a huge mock battle with wooden practice blades over a pig's-bladder prize. Harald's side, which included all of his cap-tains, won handily against Hakon's captains and his younger sons. Ragnvald wished it had been a more evenly matched battle, but per-haps such an outcome would put to rest any question of who would win a true fight.

Guthorm said the last game was an old Vestfold tradition, which had claimed lives each time it was contested. Dark had fallen by the time the other games were done, though the midday meal was only a few hours past. Men were already tired from the days' exertions, and many were drunk, having slaked their thirst all day with Ronhild's strong fruit ale.

"The last event is a race," said Harald, standing on one of the stone docks. A few men grumbled. A race did not seem exciting enough. "The ice in the harbor needs to be broken up before it grows too thick. And not with axes this time. We will race across it. Men have asked me how I became so agile, and this is how—racing across breaking ice all winter, for sport and speed. And you will do the same."

"What are the rules?" someone called out.

"No rules except this: no weapons but what you find on your way." Harald grinned as men started talking with one another, excited.

Guthorm spoke up. "We will have boats standing by to pull men out of the water, or rescue you if you become marooned."

"A boat will fish me out," said Oddi, who had made his way to stand next to Ragnvald. "But what will become of my poor frozen balls?"

Ragnvald laughed, though anticipating the race made him shiver. This water would be far colder than the waters of Geiranger Fjord that had nearly drowned him this spring. No visions waited there this time, only death.

"The prize is a Frankish sword for all who beat me," said Harald. "And this, for the first man to reach the opposite shore." Guthorm handed him a sword in its scabbard, and Harald drew it forth. It shone in the torchlight. Runes adorned the length of the blade, and ruby cabochons shone on the pommel, yet it was its shape and simplicity that drew the eye, not its decoration. Frankish swordsmiths knew secrets, and made light, unbreakable swords. This sword might dower a princess or buy Svanhild back from a king's son.

Men massed at the shore. Ragnvald pushed himself up to stand next to Harald.

"If you win, you must promise to boast of your victory all winter," said Harald to him, with a grin.

Ragnvald smiled ruefully. "That is cruel. Now I do not want to win."

The fjord was a mass of twisted ice, which looked immobile now, but would break as soon as men's weight touched it. Ragnvald was not faster than any of the fastest men, but he was still a bit lighter than the full-grown warriors. He had won Solvi's arm ring racing on the oars, and this would require the same surety, the same quick leaping.

The race began at the sound of the horn, the most important men first, followed by waves of warriors. Ragnvald leapt lightly over the upthrust, snow-covered crusts of ice. Within a few seconds, he and Harald had gained the lead. Harald bared his teeth in a fierce grin. His hair stood out in a halo around his head.

Ragnvald redoubled his effort. He could not beat Harald in any other contest, but he might here, with luck. The ice began to shudder from the men behind them, and cracks opened up in front of Ragnvald. Luck favored Harald here again, for the cracks came more quickly in the lane that Ragnvald had chosen, a few arm spans farther from shore. Or had it been Harald's canny choice to take the inside path? Ragnvald had moved outside to escape the spill of torchlight that would expose him to the missiles of men behind him.

He missed one step, and his foot plunged into a crack in front of him, instantly widening it. He still had enough purchase to recover from that step, and the water did not reach his foot immediately through the leather. When it did, the cold stabbed like knives.

Ragnvald's breath rasped in his throat. Of course Harald liked this contest: a man could not simply throw himself into the physical effort of it and forget thought. He must always be thinking, deciding. On the other side of the fjord stood Guthorm and Hakon. They had appointed themselves judges of this, the most important race.

Ragnvald was a body width ahead of Harald when he made his final leap, then slipped on the bank and plunged in water up to his thighs. Harald's leap found solid earth, before Ragnvald managed to scramble up onto the bank, cursing at the cold that gripped his legs.

Over the chattering of his teeth, he heard Guthorm and Hakon arguing over whether he or Harald had won.

"Ragnvald did reach the shore first," said Guthorm.

Ragnvald's breath still heaved in and out of his lungs. He beat at his thighs and feet weakly, trying to force cold from them.

"I think the rule was that I must be standing on the bank," said Ragnvald ruefully, "not flailing at it."

"A gracious loser," said Harald.

Ragnvald made a face. "I was faster," he said, "but you have the gods' own luck."

"It is better to be lucky than skilled," said Harald evenly. He would never doubt the gods' gifts.

"And better still to be both," Ragnvald answered.

The growing cracks had slowed down the other runners. Thorbrand and Heming were in the lead. They moved slower than Harald and Ragnvald had, as much because they kept jostling each other as because of their lesser skill.

Thorbrand was not built for this, too blocky and easy to overbalance. Heming looked as though this contest should favor him, but he was more cautious. This might be the first time he had ever shown caution.

Heming began to pull ahead, finding a path of ice rafts that led him toward the shore. He reached a larger sheet, crossed with a network of black cracks and seams. Thorbrand made a wild leap to where Heming stood. His shove sent Heming sliding into the water. The force of his exertion made Thorbrand flail his arms and tip backward on his ice floe. The front end came up, spilling water from its front like a waterfall. Thorbrand threw himself forward onto it, and nearly sent it tumbling over the other way before its rocking ceased and he was able to regain his footing. Ragnvald peered into the dark water for Heming's bright head, feeling sympathetic stabs of cold in his own limbs.

"Get up," Hakon muttered from behind where Ragnvald stood. Heming waved his arms in the air, his head disappearing behind the drifting ice. A boat came by to offer help. By the time it reached Heming, he had found the strength to pull himself up onto a stable ice floe as big as Harald's feasting table. He waved off the boat, his cold lips black in the moonlight.

"Thorbrand, you coward," he called across the ice. Thorbrand made the last few steps to the shore and bent over with his hands on his knees, panting. Heming began to walk again, but moved jerkily, like a poorly managed puppet. The cold was taking its toll on him.

Thorbrand, meanwhile, made the shore, and received a hearty congratulations from Harald. "Which of you won?" Thorbrand asked. "I could not see."

"Harald," said Ragnvald absently. Like Hakon, he still watched to see what Heming would do.

"Coward," Heming called out again. He was coming closer, his face a mask of ice and frozen beard. He did not look a hero now.

"It was allowed," said Thorbrand. "You should have had better balance if you did not want a ducking."

Heming, nearly at the shore now, roared with wordless rage as he launched himself at Thorbrand and pulled him down into the water. Thorbrand shrieked as the water hit his privates, a womanish noise that made Ragnvald choke down a laugh.

"Come, both of you," said Harald. "You'll freeze to death, and I need you." Ragnvald helped Heming out of the water, while Harald did the same with Thorbrand. The ice was too broken to allow any of the other racers to continue. Those that remained on the harbor picked their way back, single file, along the margins of ice farther out, while boats rescued the most stranded.

"He's a coward," Heming muttered as Ragnvald helped him along the path back to the hall.

"Don't be foolish," said Ragnvald. "It was within the rules. You would have done the same to him."

Once they were inside the hall, their clothes began to steam. Heming went to his chamber, and returned wearing a set of thick wool trews and a heavy silk tunic.

As soon as Thorbrand returned, also wearing dry clothes, Heming straightened up and marched over to him. "You are a coward," he said. "I challenge you to a duel this night."

"It was part of the contest," said Harald. "And I have outlawed duels."

"We need some way to settle this," said Thorbrand. Ragnvald was surprised. Thorbrand seemed too loyal to Harald and his ambitions for a more peaceful Norway, but he must have reached his breaking point with Heming.

"No duels," said Harald. "I need both of you as my captains." He said it by rote, as if Guthorm had coached him.

"It was within the rules," said Thorbrand. "But if you like, you may consider it payback for what you dealt me in the arm-wrestling competition."

Heming fumed. "No," he said to Harald. "I will be satisfied. My father is your most important ally, and this jumped-up farmer is not near me in birth. I will not be captain with this coward by my side."

Harald rolled his eyes. "Very well. Do not be my captain. Run back to your father."

"You should value him more," said Heming. Ragnvald took a step forward. Heming seemed angry enough tonight to challenge anyone, even Harald, and then he would certainly die.

"If I valued him less," said Harald, "it would be far worse for you."

"Come, Heming," said Ragnvald. "I'm sure some lady here wants to make sure you are well-warmed tonight." He drew Heming away from Harald and Thorbrand, and found them both warm drinks to take away the fjord's chill. Heming would not do violence tonight, at least.

30

IT WAS TIME TO LEAVE DORESTAD. SOLVI WOULD GET NO MORE from Rorik. Yet more days had slipped by, while he found excuses not to set his men to preparing the ships.

"You have found out how to please her, it sounds like," said Tryggulf. He had joined Solvi where he sat, foolish, watching Svanhild hold court with Rorik's ladies. She had charisma and command Solvi would be happy to see in any son of his.

Solvi smiled and looked down at the rushes on the floor. He had never been one for boasting of his conquests, and Tryggulf did not either—that was Ulfarr's task. Svanhild did seem to enjoy it now, and was not quiet; in a hall with curtains for walls between chambers, all must know.

"The weather turns cold," said Tryggulf.

"Yes," said Solvi. He must move them on, settle things before the winter, and find a place to spend the winter where Svanhild might be safe. Travel meant nights spent on the open ocean, without even the privacy of curtains, on uncertain water, where things had been sour between them. Travel also meant visiting at the halls of all the kings he must court and make into allies if he wanted to sail against Harald. If Rorik had given him warriors, or been willing to stir from Dorestad himself, Solvi could visit the halls of other kings and laugh if they refused him. He could not follow the tale he had spun for Svanhild of a life of pure freedom, but if he remained here too long, it would be all that was left to him.

True, he would not have to gather an equal force. Solvi and the kings he had in mind had followers who lived half their life on ships, and in a sea battle should overwhelm Harald easily. All the songs spoke of pitched battles on high fields, men in shield walls, and the noise of a melee on a bloody field. They would not fight so well when every misstep meant a fall into the water. Still, the gods smiled on Harald, while Solvi had had to wrest his life from the fates at an early age. Sea battles turned even more on luck than those on land.

Solvi bid his men prepare the ships for sailing back up the river from Dorestad, but still dallied a few days after the work was done, lying long abed with Svanhild in the morning and seeking her bed early in the evening, before his men were done drinking up Rorik's ale.

"Do you think Rorik is tired of your men brawling in his hall?" Svanhild asked when they lay together in the night. Her hair flowed over his skin like a dark stream.

"Tryggulf is also telling me we should leave before the weather turns too much against us."

"Is he right?"

"Yes, he is right. I think you enjoy having a roof and a bath too much for me to want to take that away."

Svanhild did not respond. Her silences did not seem to come easily to her. They gave voice to the constraint that still lay between them— she was quiet when she could not speak pleasantly without falseness.

"What are you thinking, Svanhild?" Solvi asked.

She turned so her head no longer lay on his arm. Only her hair touched him now. "I cannot advise you, when you would fight Harald, for that is where my brother is," she said slowly.

He brushed her hair off him and sat up. "I did not ask for your advice," he said, a lie. She was not worldly, but she was clever. Her counsel would be wise even if it were not correct.

She sat up as well and wound her arms around his shoulders. "I am loyal to you. I would never betray you. I would swear on the lives of"—she swallowed—"any children we may have. Which I will value far more than Geirny did hers."

He grew still, thinking of the children that he had never named. It should have been his choice, whether to acknowledge her daughters or leave them to die. Instead she—and probably his father—had made that decision for him. No more. He and Svanhild had not spoken of sons or children since that magical night. Solvi could not think of it without a sick sort of longing that he tried to keep at arm's length. He did not fear to cross the open sea between Frisia and Norway, even in the fall, at least not for himself, but now he must fear it for Svanhild, and what child she would bear for him.

"Please, I am sorry for it," said Svanhild, misinterpreting his tension. "I only fear that when I speak, my fears for him may be more—if I speak something that harms you or him, I will not forgive myself for it. I will tell you what I can, but now I want to say that we should leave Norway and never return. When we are there, I will always be divided."

"Tafjord and Maer will fall to Harald, then," said Solvi. Now he understood her silence, and pulled her close to him. "Whatever else he has done . . . it's my father there, in Tafjord. He let me live when he should have left me to die."

"I have heard . . ."

"I do not remember those times," said Solvi quickly. He had heard the stories too, of his father's dark hall, of the rites to Hel, of tortures. He had been too young, as he was too young to remember the fire, except in dreams. He remembered only when his father spoke to him again, and gave him his companions. Enough spoke of his father's madness that it must be true; he would defend the father who had let him live, made a maimed boy his heir. "I will defend him, and that does not mean sitting in Tafjord waiting to die. I will keep the fight from his door." And prove that his father had not been wrong in his decision.

"And I will be with you," said Svanhild. "I swear."

✝   ✝   ✝

THE NEXT MORNING Solvi concluded his business with Rorik, adding a few more bolts of cloth and other treasures to his hold, presents, perhaps, for kings.

"Three magic swords," said Rorik, during their leavetaking. "My gift to you and your lovely bride." He gave Svanhild a wink. "Perhaps you will have two sons."

Solvi felt Svanhild at his side take a quick breath. He kept himself from looking at her. He thanked Rorik, and unwrapped the first of the swords.

"It is an Ulfberht sword," said Rorik, "made of star-metal from the far east, and forged by our best smiths." Solvi's own sword was brother to the one Rorik held, but a man could never own too many. Alliance with a king and all his men might be bought with such a sword.

"Other swords will break upon them," Rorik continued. "They are swords fit for kings, and kings' sons. Never forget that I am your friend. If Harald should take Tafjord, you would be welcome here."

"He will not," said Solvi. He wrapped the sword again.

"If you gain other allies, send word here," Rorik said, "and I will dispatch men to join you. May Odin's crows pluck out my eyes if I lie."

✢ ✢ ✢

THE WEATHER WAS stormy when Solvi's ships reached the mouth of the Rhine, sheets of rain slipping one after another over a muddy sea. They spent a cold night on the riverbank, Svanhild shivering against him, then set out for the Norse coast.

Mist and squalls moved over the water, pacing the ships. Solvi kept them close together. When they reached Hardanger Fjord in Horda-land, they learned from the fisher folk that Harald had come and made various kings swear to him, then left again. Solvi laughed when he heard this.

"He comes and asks for words, and then leaves again," he said to Tryggulf and his men. "It is as if he never came at all."

During a lull in the sailing, when the sound of the wind kept their voices from other ears, Svanhild asked him, "You think these kings will not keep their word? I wonder that your men follow you, when you believe so little in oaths." She looked a bit surprised at her own bluntness.

"I miss your silences," said Solvi sardonically. "My men follow me because I lead them to treasure, in and out of danger. They follow me because they trust my judgment. It is the only reason any man should follow another. This Harald is young and stupid if he thinks the oath of a king with a sword to his neck means anything." He gave Svanhild a

piercing look. All she knew of the world beyond her farm, and the journey she had taken that put her in Solvi's hands, was what she had learned
from songs. Her mixture of innocence and ruthlessness was charming,
and he could never decide whether he wanted her to keep her pretty
pictures of the world, or learn his own cruel lessons. "What would you
do, Svanhild, I wonder, to save your life? To save the life of your child?"

Another woman might have bent then, acknowledged that he knew of
things she could not. Svanhild lifted her chin and said, "I don't think you
know what mothers must do, have done, to save their children's lives. My
mother"—she shook her head—"my mother sacrificed her spirit, I think
sometimes, so that Ragnvald's land could be protected until he grew up. I
wonder if it was worth the cost, her marriage with Olaf."

"It was her fate." Solvi did not want her to think of marriages and
their costs. He touched her on the cheek before returning to his work.

✣   ✣   ✣

SOLVI TOOK HIS ships around the outer islands, into the sheltered
embrace of Hardanger Fjord. He stopped and talked to whichever
shore folk they found, listening to the stories of raiders. Those who
carried knowledge traded it like coin, and so he gathered a picture of
what had passed during the fall.

"We make for Gudbrand's hall in the morning," Solvi announced
to his men. "He is the strongest remaining king, and he hates this
upstart Harald." Harald had killed seven kings, or so went the tale,
and Gudbrand had not been among them. Indeed, Harald had fought
Gudbrand twice, and never killed him. This might be the king to defeat Harald.

Solvi's men were loyal to him, but they still talked over the other
story, of the upland King Eirik, his mighty fort, his haughty daughter.
Svanhild told him what she had learned about Harald's oath for Gyda
as they settled in to sleep. The wind rippled the walls of the tent.

"Harald will marry every woman in the Norse lands, if it helps him
rule," said Solvi.

"It is the story, not the betrothal," said Svanhild. "It will win men
to him. Don't forget how you won me."

"Yes," said Solvi. "My men did like you for that."

"You did too," she said, snuggling up to him. He kissed the top of her head in answer, and told her more about King Gudbrand. They had met a time or two. Gudbrand had sent his sons raiding with Solvi in years past, and those sons had settled in Iceland, where they would have more land.

"He may call them back now," Solvi added. "He has more land to give them, with so many kings dead."

"So Harald has done him a favor," said Svanhild.

"And humiliated him. I hope he feels that more keenly."

"Is that how you will win him to your side?"

"Yes," he said. "And offer him the wealth of Vestfold. He trusts me to know more of the world than he does. I can tell him that Harald is young and not truly tested, and Vestfold will fall easily if we gather enough allies."

"Is that true?" Svanhild asked. Solvi shrugged. Svanhild pulled the blanket over them. She pressed her legs gently against his, warming the scars that made them grow easily cold.

"It is believable enough," he said. "His victories are not as notable as the tales make them seem. Harald has always had far more men on his side than his adversaries could muster in time, and the advantage of surprise. If we sail against him, in force, too early in the spring for him to gather men who will have gone home during the winter, then we can defeat him where he lives."

"Force against force," said Svanhild. "I suppose it is more honorable than a sneak attack."

"It has nothing to do with honor," said Solvi. "It is a trick that will only work once, now, before he gains too much power. If we lose, then raiding will be all we have left." He yawned. "When we win, I will take you to Dublin and drape you in Irish jewels."

"I don't care as much for jewels, and I would rather not see you fight." Because then he would fight Ragnvald, Solvi supposed. As long as she thought of Ragnvald first, she would never truly be his.

✢   ✢   ✢

ONCE INSIDE THE embrace of Hardanger Fjord, the wind grew less and the temperature plummeted. Solvi sailed up a river to Gudbrand's hall. When they finally found it, night was falling. The hall had been razed; only charred posts remained, sticking up out of a thin dusting of too-early snow. Early snow, easy winter, was the proverb, but no winter was truly easy.

"A hall burning," said Solvi. He walked around the charred foundations. "But they did not burn it with people inside, see."

Svanhild followed behind him without saying anything. He wished he had left her in Dorestad. She should not have to see this. She followed him to the sacred grove, which stood on a slope that was slippery with ice and fallen leaves. Runes were carved into the bark of the trees. Something crunched under Solvi's foot, something that did not feel like wood. Solvi bent down and pull out a pale shard of bone. He wiped his hands on his trousers. Unburied bodies brought bad luck.

"If Harald's force has already been here, does Gudbrand still live?" Solvi asked, more to himself than to his men, who followed behind.

They found a small camp at another clearing. Some tents had blown over in the wind, and no one had set them up again. Under the leather shrouds of the rotten tents lay the bodies of old women and children, only those too old or young to be useful as slaves. They had eaten small animals, to judge by the untanned skins and tiny bones discarded here, and then, horribly, begun to eat each other. These people had been waiting for rescue, for men who never came.

"This place is evil," said Svanhild. Solvi was glad she spoke. As a woman, she could voice fears so his men need not. "We must leave."

"Yes," said Snorri through his ruined mouth. "These dead will walk."

Solvi ordered his men to build a huge bonfire to consume the dead, with wood from the grove that had been poisoned by their terrible final days. When the fire burned out, close to dawn, he led his men back to the ships. Harald's promise of safety should not have allowed him to leave families to starve, even if they were his enemies.

Farther inland, they found a few more abandoned farms. Near the end of the fjord a larger group had banded together, forming a collection of lean-tos and temporary buildings around the nucleus of a hall. The community was disorganized, composed of refugees, mostly women and children, and a few men too old and lame to fight.

Solvi did find one man of a warrior's age who told them what had happened. "It was King Hakon's men," he said. "They come and raid. They ask for us to swear to Hakon as king, and if we say yes, they only take everything. If we say no, they kill and burn."

"Not Harald?" Solvi asked.

"He said he conquered for Harald."

"What did you say?" Svanhild asked. "When he asked you to swear?"

"I said no," the man said, proudly.

"Yet you live," she said. "This hall still stands."

The man looked sullen. "He left us the hall to see us through the winter. Vekel, jarl who ruled here—he took his men and ships and went to his cousin in Rogaland. He said there was no fighting there yet."

Solvi glared at the man. "If you said no, how did you live?"

He looked at his feet. "Vekel had me outlawed. Hakon said I could be jarl for him here. I didn't want to die. We had a meeting. These people elected me. I will stand against Hakon if he comes again." He put his hand on his sword.

Solvi shook his head. These people looked like they would elect anyone strong enough to lift a sword, even if he could not wield it. "There's no help here," he said in a low voice to Snorri.

He spoke with the new jarl, treating him as though he deserved that title, as though he would live through the winter to enjoy it, and heard from him a rumor that Gudbrand had gone to his island in Hardanger Fjord. Its location made it nearly impenetrable, protected by high rock walls and views in every direction. It was a good place to spend the winter. Staying there, Gudbrand would not need to see his starving people either, or count up what Hakon and Harald had cost him.

They slept in tents arranged in a ring around a fire that Solvi set one of his men to feeding all night. Even so, the cold from the ground stole into Solvi's more injured leg. Even on the coldest night at sea, it never felt like this, stiff as though lifeless already.

"I do not like this," Solvi whispered to Svanhild in the dark of the night. She might not even be awake to hear him—the best kind of confession.

"Like what?" she murmured.

"Alliances and kings. Vekel had many men, and now his halls are in ruins."

"Hakon must have had more."

"He will have as many districts as he can get," said Solvi bitterly. "There is no limit to his ambition. Between him in the north, and Harald in the south . . ." Before Svanhild, he might have voiced these fears to Tryggulf or Snorri, though he could not forget he commanded them, and they must trust his decisions. "Let us sail out of Hardanger Fjord to the open ocean, and continue sailing like you wanted." He wrapped his arms around her.

"You wish me to remind you of honor, I think." She nestled closer against him. "Is that what you would have me be, Solvi Hunthiofsson? The keeper of your honor?"

"Perhaps," he said.

"I cannot. I see what war has brought to Hordaland. If you wish escape more than you wish to spare your father . . ."

He sat up and pushed the blankets off him. "I would rather you scold me than say it like that."

She sat up as well. He expected her to reach out to him. He had grown used to her caresses in the last month, as though their early fights had never been. She hung her head down. In the darkness, all he could see was the curtain of her hair, blurring the outline of her shoulders.

"If you want us to sail away, I would," he said. "At least I would consider it. I do not want this, and neither do you. It is only my father . . ." Could he face his father in the lands beyond death, having left Tafjord open to attack?

She remained silent.

"Where is your certainty now?" he whispered to her. "Now, when I need it?"

"I have no certainty for you, and none for myself. I have only this." She hugged herself, in a gesture that seemed strangely familiar, though he had never seen her make it. Women in his father's hall—his wife Geirny—had made the same gesture, though.

"Svanhild," he said, reaching out toward her.

"I am with child," she said. "I am sure now, though it is still early.

So no, I do not scold you. I want this child safe. I do not want him born into war. I do not want his father to bring war to anyone else." She shook her head. "At this moment, I wish you were a farmer that no one would think to bother, not a king's son."

He pulled her to him, but she remained stiff in his arms. "Svanhild. You think it is a son?"

"Yes. I do not want to tempt the gods by guessing, but yes. I had a dream about him."

"But you have not been ill," he said. This was too much blessing to accept.

"No," she said. "And that worried me, but now I am sure. It must have caught early."

He felt a twinge of disappointment that this child would have taken root from one of their first, rough couplings, rather than these recent days of honey. Still, that was only a small sour note.

"Our son will inherit Tafjord," he said. "If I flee—no. My father may not value my help, but he"—he put his hand over her belly—"he needs it. I will give our son a kingdom to rule." Her body stayed tense. "Svanhild, you would have me abandon my father, avoid this war?"

"I don't know."

"I do," he said. "The Norse kings will hate Harald and Hakon for taking their land and calling their theft lawful. They will join to-gether."

"You are very certain now." She shook her head, her hair flowing over his arms where he clasped her.

"You have given me certainty," he said. How fragile Svanhild felt against him, her narrow shoulders, her fine, soft skin. She must shelter their child, and he must shelter her.

✧   ✧   ✧

A COLD FOG gathered around Solvi's ships as they reached Gudbrand's hall on an island in the middle of Hardanger Fjord. They had sailed by it before, never knowing men lived here, for the hall was hidden in a grove high above the water. One of Solvi's pilots knew where to dock to find the narrow path that led up the cliffs.

They passed by ships hidden among the trees while climbing a

track that left them exposed to any attack from above. Solvi bade his
men put space between them so no one sally could kill many of them.
The rocks were slippery with ice, cracked gray and black, too steep
for any life. If Gudbrand was truly here, and not rumor, he had dug in
deep for the winter.

When Solvi reached the crest of the cliff, he saw faint lights through
the trees, and what he thought was a plume of smoke that quickly became part of the low clouds. At least they could demand some sort of
welcome by traveler's right.

A sentry came out of the woods and met him, his sword bared.

"My men ask for hospitality," said Solvi. "I claim King Gudbrand as
a friend. Is he here?"

"If you are a friend, you will give me your sword."

"I am Solvi Hunthiofsson," said Solvi. "Go tell your master that,
and see if he still requires I give up my sword."

The sentry jerked his chin up. One of his fellows appeared out of
the gray, only to disappear again, lost in the shadows in the grove.

Solvi's feet grew cold from standing still. Men came over the cliff
crest one at a time. He felt Svanhild's warmth as she drew next to him.
She was dressed in her trousers, and bundled in a coat and cloak, so
this sentry would surely take her for a boy, not his wife.

At length the other guard returned. "Gudbrand bids you welcome,"
he said.

"And my men?"

"Gudbrand is a generous ring giver," said the guard. "Of course he
will welcome your men as well."

Solvi still feared a trap until he stood within the bright hall, full
of living, cheerful men, and saw King Gudbrand sitting near a fire,
dicing with one of his men. The king called for hot wine and a feast to
heat their chilled bones.

✛   ✛   ✛

"HE IS A young fool," said King Gudbrand when Solvi raised the subject of Harald at dinner. Gudbrand told of fighting Harald, the overwhelming force, and how King Eirik had remained snug and protected
in his fort while Gudbrand's men died on Harald's swords.

"Yet he beat you," said Solvi.

"He never found me," said Gudbrand, waving his hand. "And his uncle—he is not a fool. Harald had luck, and more men than I could muster in a short time." Gudbrand had an ill-proportioned figure, too long in the arm, too big in the stomach, protruding teeth, and close-cropped gray hair over a long straggly beard. His uneven teeth were white and strong, though, and he seemed the sort of man who commanded through competence, not dazzling speeches or grand gestures. Solvi liked that about him.

"Yes, at least you have outrun him," said Solvi. Gudbrand looked affronted. "No, it is better than losing a battle to him. You can live to fight again."

"Yes," said Gudbrand, banging his fist on the arm of his heavily inlaid chair. "Do you come to offer aid, Solvi Sea-King?"

"It is time," said Solvi. "We must band together, or all of our lands will fall to Harald and his allies."

"What do I care for your lands?"

"I will care for yours, if you will care for mine. And if you do not care for that, Vestfold is rich."

"You mean to attack Vestfold itself?"

"Yes," said Solvi. "We cannot help each other if we are defending our own lands, but if we take the fight to Harald—"

"Yes," said Gudbrand. "We will teach this Harald a lesson."

"Of course," said Solvi, smoothly, as though he had expected Gudbrand's quick capitulation all along.

"Do you mean to lead this force yourself?" Gudbrand asked.

"I am not power-mad as this Harald is. But if you can promise to ally with me, then Rorik of Dorestad will send men and swords as well."

"Rich old Rorik is willing to leave his cozy nest for you? I would venture that men of Rogaland will join as well." Gudbrand banged his fist on his chair again. "I went to that battle like a fool, and only left a day ahead of Harald's force. My fellow kings did not believe the stories. Then this Harald sneaks up on me, while you move like quicksilver and wring promises from men like Rorik. You know Vestfold. You should lead us."

"You do me too much honor," said Solvi, perfunctorily. He was probably more suited to leading this force than Gudbrand, whom Harald had beaten once. Men would be more confident in him. But he hesitated. He might not be able to set down this responsibility again, if he took it up. "Can we tempt your sons here from Iceland as well?" he asked. "If Vestfold falls, the bounty must be shared."

"Indeed we might." Gudbrand looked very satisfied at the prospect. He called for more ale, a warming brew of summer fruits. "You'll make a greater man than your father, if the gods are just. Let us drink and make our oaths, and then we can talk of who else will join us."

✣   ✣   ✣

SVANHILD HAD NOT believed all the tales from her mother and the farm's women, the way a woman might turn inward and think only of her child during pregnancy, but she found such tendencies in herself. She wanted Solvi by her, took more comfort than ever in his touch. And she could not try to dissuade Solvi from his course when it might mean wealth and security for their son. After concluding his business with Gudbrand, Solvi sent her with Tryggulf's ship back to Tafjord.

Svanhild had plenty of energy during the winter, once the early days of her pregnancy had passed. She put it all into remaking Tafjord into something more like what a hall should be, beginning with the meals. She inventoried all of the food stores, and made calculations and plans to keep the household and all the warriors eating well. Tafjord had enough food from harvest tributes, but poor management of it. Thralls must be fed if they would do work. The lowliest farmer who owned at least one servant knew that much. It should shame Hunthiof that he did not.

She missed the adventure of being on board Solvi's ship, but at least she knew her place here. Geirny had gone back to her father at some point during the fall, so Svanhild was spared her strangeness and any guilt she might feel at taking Geirny's place.

Solvi returned to Tafjord before Yule, with further promises from Rorik, and more—the Danish king had resolved to send ships against Harald. He did not want a strong Norse king.

A traveling skald joined the household for the winter, and from him Svanhild learned news from Vestfold, of Harald, Hakon, and his sons, and, of course, Ragnvald. She heard that Ragnvald had come near death, and risked his life to save Harald. She heard that Ragnvald had switched his allegiance to Harald.

Ragnvald was Harald's close companion now, his adviser, the skald said. He would be happy for that, Svanhild knew, as happy as he ever allowed himself to be. Ragnvald had intelligence beyond what was needed for a farmer and warrior, and that was where his ambition came from. She did not wonder that he would seek a king he could respect. She wished she could be happy for him. Instead she saw that he and Solvi were bent on collision again, like ships in a narrow passage, no room for either to escape.

"You work yourself ragged," said Solvi when he came to the kitchen for breakfast one morning. It was true. Svanhild did not even know how Solvi passed his time these days, she was so busy managing the hall. The kitchen was her favorite place, for she had remade it in the image of the best of Ardal. Another year, and she might have all the ingredients she wanted as well.

"There is much to do. The mismanagement that your father has allowed is shameful."

"Not shameful," he said, defending his father as he always did. "We are sea kings, not farmers. Gold flows to us, and through our fingers. We do not serve men, nor expect them to serve us." Of course, he could say that, but someone had to feed men and clothe them. They looked after themselves when they were at sea. Solvi took pride in provisioning his ships well, and when they ran low on stores, replenishing them.

"A hall is much like a ship," said Svanhild. "It lives by its stomach."

"Yes," said Solvi. "What do you need?" He ran his hand over her swelling belly. She half wanted to pull away from the touch, feeling a surge of protectiveness over this new life—she would protect it even from Solvi. Even from Ragnvald. She would protect her child from anyone, for he was hers. "I would not have you risk our child to feed grown men who should know better."

Svanhild smiled at his words, as he surely meant her to. "I do need help," she said. "Perhaps there are some local girls who would like to spend some time at the hall. Surely some nearby family has more daughters than they need." That thought reminded her of Hilda—Hilda who waited and dreamed of Ragnvald. Now Svanhild would help Solvi take away that dream. She sighed. "I work so I need not think of the spring," said Svanhild. She put her hand over his to still his touching. Her blood beat against his fingers, and against her womb.

"You will have the best care," said Solvi. "I promise. You will come through this childbed and live to give me many more children. You are strong." Svanhild had never doubted that. Solvi must be voicing his own fears.

"I fear for Ragnvald," she said. Solvi tried to pull his hand away, and she held it fast. One of the kitchen thralls was staring at the two of them. "Leave us," said Svanhild to her.

"You should fear for me," said Solvi when they were alone.

"You have no brothers," Svanhild answered. "If you did, you would know. If I lost him, it would be as if I lost a part of myself. And you go to fight him." It was true, but more true was that her growing care for this child, for Solvi, made her feel guilty. She should think of Ragnvald more.

"Yes," said Solvi. He pulled his hand away then. "This will always be the sword between us. Ragnvald has chosen. You have chosen."

"He does not want revenge on you."

"How can you be sure of that? I stole his sister. I cut his face." So he had been thinking of it too. What did it mean to him, that Ragnvald had risen so far since Solvi had tried to end his life? Did he fear Ragnvald? He knew a part of Ragnvald that Svanhild never would. The warrior, the leader, even.

"I know," she said. "Still, if you face him . . . do something for me, in the name of the child I bear for you." His expression was stricken. She knew she could only use the child thus once. "Do not kill him. If you can. If he is not trying to kill you. If you can capture him, if you can separate him from Harald. I have only one brother. I have no father. I have my brother, you, and this child."

"Svanhild," said Solvi. "You do not know what you ask. We are enemies. I do not wish it so, but it is both of our fates. You must see that. The fates have set us on this path as surely as they set you between us."

"Promise me," said Svanhild. "I do not ask you to put yourself in danger for it, but if there is a way to take him as a prisoner in this battle rather than killing him, please try." Solvi did not answer, and Svanhild continued, hoping that with enough words, she could make him see this way through, this thread through the needle. "Harald values him. He would make a good hostage. You do not know how the battle will go. It might be useful to have a bargaining chip."

Solvi was silent for a while, and Svanhild had no more arguments to make. Finally he met her eyes. "If I promise you this, will you let yourself rest? Will you stop your worrying?"

"A thousand things can happen in a battle," said Svanhild. "I know this. I know too that I have chosen you. It was a choice that cost me dearly, and will cost me more in the future. Do not seek to add to the price, I beg you."

"Do not beg of me, Svanhild." He took her hand and pressed it to his lips. "I do not want that of you. I promise you that if I can find a way to let Ragnvald survive this battle, I will. I will tell all my men. Punishment will fall on the man who tries to kill him, and rewards on the man who captures him. Will that serve?"

"Yes," she said. "That is all I can ask."

"Yes," said Solvi, his voice letting her know that he already thought it was too much, that this burden oppressed him deeply. "If there is even a battle, if my allies come. Who knows what the spring will bring?"

31

AS THE DAYS GREW LONGER, RAGNVALD STARTED TO FEEL LIKE a spring bear, too long kept inside—though he was hungry for vengeance, for action, not food. He was too well fed. They all were, with little else to do save eating and drinking. At least he was stronger from all the sparring with Harald, and the training that Harald's uncle had devised for him, and adapted to all of his men. They carried heavy stones, raced up steep slopes, faced down poor weather, at least until the cold became dangerous to their fingers. But Ragnvald ate and drank heavily too, spent late nights gambling. He was tired of the same faces, tired of the inside of halls, tired of the stench of too many men who did not bathe frequently enough.

Tensions had grown between Hakon's men and Harald's since Yule. Ragnvald and Oddi still traveled between the two halls, but Hakon rarely did, nor did his trueborn sons. Ragnvald did not know whether Hakon still meant to honor his promise and send Ragnvald to revenge himself on Olaf. He must be gone and discharge that task quickly to return in time for spring warring.

Rumors came with spring, along with wet, sodden snows. Solvi was dead. Solvi had fled to the protection of the Danish king. Solvi had mobilized all the kings of Norway against Harald, even Hakon and his sons. That, Ragnvald knew was false, yet it was continually repeated around the halls, carried between the two factions.

He and Harald climbed the hills above the hall on an unexpectedly clear day. Ragnvald had to scramble to keep up, pulling himself along on tree branches.

"What do I do?" Harald asked Ragnvald, frustrated. A fight had broken out the night before between one of Harald's men and Hakon's. Harald had let them wrestle it out, encouraged other men to make bets, praised the winner and the loser for their technique. "I cannot turn them all into contests."

"What does your uncle say?" Ragnvald asked as he fended off a branch that Harald let snap into his face.

Harald stopped, looking impatient for Ragnvald to catch up. "He says I should wait for the snows to stop, then go to war again. War against someone else will heal our divisions."

"Or at least disguise them for a while," said Ragnvald. "Your uncle is right. Fine weather and making war will help."

Oddi came running up to them, out of breath. Oddi had been pulled between Harald and Hakon worse than Ragnvald had, though he had a sixth sense for when some argument was about to break out, and would suddenly disappear. Ragnvald wished he had that ability himself. It must come from long years with Hakon's sons.

"What is it?" Ragnvald asked.

"Heming and Thorbrand are dueling," he said. "On the sparring ground." Harald took off running, with Oddi and Ragnvald loping behind him.

"Stop this immediately," Harald roared as soon as he drew close. Heming and Thorbrand had measured out a true dueling space. They must have planned this, in secrecy, no rumors coming to Ragnvald or anyone else. Each had staged the requisite three shields against the fence, and each had chosen a second. A rope marked the edge of the dueling ground. If either stepped over the margin, he would be counted the loser.

"I cannot, my king," said Thorbrand. He and Heming only circled each other now, their shields still whole, their breathing still easy. "It has gone too far. We must settle this." Men stood watching the duel, stone-faced, resolutely looking anywhere but at Harald.

"Your boy king cannot save you now," said Heming to Thorbrand.

"I command you to halt this at once," said Harald. "Or the winner will be outlawed. You will never set foot on any lands I rule for the rest of your life."

"What of the loser?" asked Herlaug, Hakon's youngest son, belligerently. He was short for his age and had a febrile restlessness, always looking for a fight. "They only fight to first blood."

"The loser will also be outlawed, if he survives," said Harald. "You must stop." He looked at Ragnvald desperately. Ragnvald shook his head and shrugged. There was nothing to be done here. They would not stop on Harald's say-so, and the more he commanded them to stop and they failed to, the weaker he looked.

Harald seemed to understand that as well. They needed to feel the sting of his wrath, to show that even friendship was not stronger than his law. Ragnvald almost felt relieved that this was finally happening. Heming must learn that he could not solve everything with his father's name and his fine swordsmanship. If the lesson had to come at Thorbrand's expense, there was nothing to be done. And an unworthy part of him knew that he would be even closer to Harald without Thorbrand and all their history.

Heming and Thorbrand circled around one another, making feints with their swords, but neither attacking with full force yet. To first blood, Ragnvald thought; at least they had shown some restraint there.

"Will you accuse me of cheating this time?" Heming asked Thorbrand. Thorbrand used the moment when Heming's attention was more on his insult than on his swordwork to dart a cut that parted the fine silk of his peacock-blue sleeve.

Heming backed away, laughing. "I have many tunics," he said. "You can slash them all to ribbons if you like, but you won't touch my skin."

Heming came close the next time, slashing at Thorbrand so fast his sword whistled through the air. At the last minute Thorbrand brought his shield up, and Heming's sword crashed into it, shearing off a piece of the ash wood, which clattered to the ground.

They had paced a bare circle in the center of the dueling ground, though patches of snow still lingered near the rope boundary. Thorbrand forced Heming to the margin, where his foot slipped, and he swung his shield up into Thorbrand's chin, knocking his head back with a clatter of teeth. If it had been Heming's sword, Thorbrand would be dead now.

Heming regained his footing and attacked quickly, before Thorbrand had a chance to do more than shake his head to try to clear it from the jolt that Heming had given him. Heming fought him ever closer to the border behind him, daring Thorbrand to step out of circle, losing in the most shameful way possible.

Thorbrand would not do it. He spun around, just out of Heming's reach, and then behind him. It seemed Thorbrand's sword found skin then, for Heming flinched, but no blood dripped down his arm from where Thorbrand had touched him.

Ragnvald could not tell what Heming's aim was in his next thrust. What Ragnvald saw was Heming's sword rip upward—perhaps he meant to lay open Thorbrand's cheek, take an eye, leave Thorbrand's bullish face forever marred.

The point of Heming's sword caught under Thorbrand's chin and went upward, through his throat, so easily that Heming looked shocked. He dropped the sword and backed away. The wound could not be other than mortal, but Thorbrand grasped the sword anyway, as if he could pull it out and somehow save himself. As soon as his hands touched the sword, he crumpled to the ground.

Ragnvald heard screaming from the crowd, so high and wild it sounded more like a tortured animal than anything human. Thorbrand's wife Erindis broke through the crowd and threw herself over Thorbrand's body, heedless of the sword still stuck in him.

When she tied to pull it out by the blade with her bare hands, Harald rushed over to her and drew her away. Her hands were covered with Thorbrand's blood and her own. In Harald's arms she stopped screaming and made a quiet keening noise instead, muffled by Harald's furs. Harald's eyes were wide with shock, all of his preternatural confidence gone. He was only a boy at that moment, a boy who had lost his friend and could not quite believe it yet.

Hakon had been absent for the whole of the duel. Now one of his younger sons came running back with him. Harald carried Erindis inside, and then stalked out again. Guards flanked him.

"Take him," Harald said, pointing at Heming. "Bind him, and do not let him go."

"What is this?" Hakon asked, striding up to Harald.

"Your son"—he said the words as though they tasted ill to him—
"has killed my dearest friend and my best captain in an illegal duel.
I demand his life in payment." He refused to look down at Hakon or
meet his eyes.

Ragnvald drew an astonished breath, along with the rest of the
crowd. Hakon took a step back as Harald loomed over him.

Harald's men bound Heming hand and foot. "Where should we
put him?" the lead guard asked.

"I will kill him now," said Harald.

"No!" said Ragnvald, at the same time as Hakon's men started to rush
toward Harald. "He is bound. This must not be done in haste. Heming
Hakonsson has violated your laws. You wanted him to be outlawed for
this, and so he should be." Hakon narrowed his eyes at Ragnvald. "That
is what Harald said would be the punishment for both of those who
participated in the duel," Ragnvald explained loudly, for those who had
come late.

"He killed Thorbrand," said Harald. "His wife—"

"My king," said Ragnvald. "Please think on this. You are grieving
right now. We all are. But killing cannot be undone. Some bonds cannot be reknit when they are cut." Harald looked as though he might
listen, and Ragnvald continued. "Mourn Thorbrand. Give him a funeral feast. Keep Heming in your custody, if you must. But wait until
you can render a fair verdict. A king owes that to his people."

Harald did not like these words. He looked shaken by what had
occurred, by the strength of his anger. Ragnvald glanced around for
Guthorm. He would help Harald see reason. Guthorm stood near Hakon, tensed as though he would bodily restrain their most important
ally himself, if it came to that.

"Everyone return to your halls," Ragnvald yelled. It was not his
place, but no one else seemed likely to take command now. "No one
has leave to depart. Any violence will be punished severely." He caught
Guthorm's eye. Guthorm nodded slowly. Thorbrand had been as a son
to him, but Guthorm was older and wiser than Harald. He would see
that tempers cooled before any decisions were made.

"This is our command," said Guthorm. "Do not depart. Do not

make ships ready. This will be settled peacefully. There has already been enough bloodshed today."

Harald's men followed the order and took Heming toward Harald's hall. Hakon pulled his remaining sons to him, including Oddi, and made for the lesser hall his men occupied.

Ragnvald waited until all had departed the dueling ground—common soldiers, guards, even servants. He was Hakon's man by law, and Harald's by fate and in his heart, and he knew that Harald must abide by the rule he had already set. He would never be king if he made an enemy of Hakon now. Even if Solvi had not formed the rumored alliances, he would certainly be able to take advantage of Hakon and Harald being at odds. And Ragnvald would never be able to win Svanhild back from him. Ragnvald squared his shoulders and walked toward Hakon's hall.

"You," said Hakon venomously, as soon as Ragnvald had emerged from the shadows near the door. "You are not welcome here, Harald's man."

"I want to make him see reason," said Ragnvald.

"You are a spy here."

"Do you plan something here that Harald must not know?" Ragnvald asked angrily. He stopped. Anger would not help him here. "Would you accept outlawry for Heming? Harald has always made it clear that is the punishment for unsanctioned dueling."

"I will accept nothing but my son returned to me," said Hakon. "He will pay this captain's wergild, and I will send him away from Harald's court." His eyes narrowed. "Harald needs me more than I need him."

Ragnvald was not at all sure that was true, but he would not convince Hakon tonight. "I will tell Harald that, if I have your leave to go."

"You never had my leave to be here in the first place," Hakon responded. "Do not return."

✢   ✢   ✢

GUTHORM JUDGED THAT tempers should cool over the course of a week. He and Ragnvald worked together to make Harald swear not to harm Heming in that time. Ragnvald feared that speaking with

Heming would undermine his standing in Harald's eyes, but he kept watch over him whenever possible to prevent any of Harald's men from doing him harm. From time to time he caught Heming's eye and saw a desperate and frightened look there, like no expression he had ever seen on Heming's face before.

Harald and Guthorm held a funeral for Thorbrand and buried him. Erindis haunted Harald's hall, unspeaking, deep blue shadows around her eyes. It would be better if Guthorm could get her out of the way, send her to a nearby retainer—Harald's anger might cool without always having her as a reminder—but the weather had turned cold again, a soggy spring blizzard making travel impossible.

After the week was over, Guthorm brought Hakon with a large contingent of guards, as well as his sons, into Harald's hall to speak about Heming's fate. Harald had not been willing to consider anything other than killing Heming. Ragnvald and Guthorm's patience had grown thin.

"It was a mistake," said Hakon as soon as he came in, as though the words could wait no longer. He made for the space at the head of the hall where Harald trod back and forth, waiting for him.

"That doesn't matter," said Harald, his voice pitched high. "They should not have been fighting."

"You want to make a kingdom of men without honor," said Hakon. "Not a kingdom for me or my sons."

They stood toe to toe again, and Ragnvald thought they might come to blows themselves. Guthorm interposed himself between them and pressed them both apart. "You come here today to determine Heming's fate," he said formally. "This must be settled." He turned to Harald. "Men must be able to settle their differences. Harald does not want to outlaw duels, only put requirements on them so they do not lead to blood feuds. And he did not want to see two of his dear captains injured or killed." Harald sneered at the inclusion of Heming in that description, but did not speak further.

"Now that you are both here, is there any way we can make peace?" Ragnvald asked. "We have a common enemy in Solvi Hunthiofsson and his allies."

"You," said Harald angrily. "You and my uncle have kept me from taking my revenge these seven days. Thorbrand's spirit will not rest until he has it."

Guthorm turned to Hakon, ignoring both Harald and Ragnvald. "Heming fomented this conflict. At every turn, Thorbrand would have been willing to see it end. And Heming killed a man in a duel to first blood. He could have taken blood much more easily."

"Anything can happen in a duel," said Hakon. "I will pay this captain's price. You will not like to pay my price if you hurt my son."

"You threaten me?" Harald asked, stepping in close to him again.

"Enough," Guthorm roared. "We will come to an agreement."

Hakon sneered. "With you to broker it? I can see how you will want this to come out."

"Who would you have?" Guthorm asked. "No man here stands above this fray."

That might be Hakon's purpose in raising the issue. He could refuse to abide by any agreement, if he did not like how it came about.

"Ragnvald Eysteinsson," said Hakon after a moment. Ragnvald did not even recognize that Hakon had spoken his name at first, so unlikely did this choice seem. He looked at Hakon. "Yes, Ragnvald," Hakon continued. "I have always found him fair."

"He is sworn to you," said Harald. "His judgment is suspect."

"Ragnvald is a man of honor," said Hakon. "And all know he wishes to be your captain more than mine."

"I am sworn to King Hakon," said Ragnvald. "I cannot judge."

Guthorm beckoned Harald over, and they consulted quietly for a moment. Harald turned back toward Ragnvald and Hakon, still looking stormy, but less wild.

"You must," said Harald. "Hakon could choose no other man whose word I would also abide."

Ragnvald looked to Guthorm, hoping he would speak to end this. If he could thread a path between these two giants without being crushed between them, he would need the silver tongue of Loki.

"As you judge this dispute, so may the gods judge you," said Guthorm.

Ragnvald bowed his head. "I owe both of you duty. I will do my best to broker a fair agreement."

He paced for a moment. He could think of nothing but the *ting* trial, and how the law speaker must call witnesses, how the verdict and decision must at least appear fair for all to accept it. He walked over to the fire and took up a poker of thick, twisted iron that hung nearby.

"This will be our speaking stick," he said, "if none object." None did. "I do not believe that anyone doubts the facts of what happened," Ragnvald continued, "but since Hakon was not there, let them be restated."

Again, no one objected. Ragnvald related what he had seen. He called witnesses who had seen them set up the duel, who had heard both Heming and Thorbrand threaten any man who ran to tell Harald or Hakon. All of the witnesses said that both men had been bent on the duel.

Next Ragnvald called Heming to give his own version of events. His story did not deviate much from what the witnesses reported. "Thorbrand sent his man to me to propose a duel," Heming said. "We arranged it through those men." He gave Ragnvald a beseeching look. "Do not punish them. They only did what we asked."

"That will be decided after," said Harald. Ragnvald shot him a quelling look.

"I did not mean to kill Thorbrand," Heming said finally. A duel to first blood could always go to death, with a lucky strike, but Heming said that had not been his intention. He swore it on every god he knew.

He hung his head. He looked much the worse for spending a week tied up in Harald's hall. His hair hung down lankly, and his mouth was smeared with bits of food. Ragnvald had seen that he was untied often enough not to suffer injury from it, but Harald's men had still found ways to abuse him.

"What did you mean to do?" Ragnvald asked.

"I meant to give him a terrible scar." Heming gave Ragnvald the smallest of smiles. "Like yours, but far worse." He looked around at everyone, the men gathered to judge him, at least in their minds. "If I could change this fate, I would. I do not want to die, but I will accept outlawry—"

"No," cried Hakon.

"No," Ragnvald repeated, more calmly. "We do not speak of punishment yet." He raised the poker again and said, "King Harald and King Hakon, the two most powerful men in the Norse peninsula. When a jury gives a verdict, the men of the district swear to uphold the decision. Here, none can make you abide by a decision except your own will, and the gods'. I do not plan to decide for you. I only hope for you to agree, and swear out your agreement."

Neither Harald nor Hakon said a word. "King Harald," Ragnvald continued. "Hakon's son Heming killed your captain, Thorbrand, by error. You have demanded his death. Is there any other payment or punishment that would satisfy you?"

He handed the poker to Harald. Harald looked uncertain. He glanced at Guthorm, and his shoulders slumped. "Heming must go into exile and never return to Norway," he said. "King Hakon must turn over rulership and taxes from all Norse lands other than Halogaland and Stjordal. I will install kings of my choosing to rule Hordaland and Maer, when we take it. Finally, Hakon must pay Thorbrand's wergild: his weight in gold."

Hakon had been growing angrier as Harald spoke, and when he finished, Hakon put his hand to his sword. "Never," said Hakon. "My sons must have land." He pushed Ragnvald aside and stood chest to chest with Harald. "You will never rule western Norway. You will not even leave here alive."

Harald had handed the poker off to Ragnvald, who banged it on the stone floor. "This is a negotiation," Ragnvald yelled. He continued in a calmer voice. "King Hakon must make a counteroffer." He held out the poker to Hakon.

Hakon swiped it out of Ragnvald's hand, and spoke to Harald. "You will take the common payment for a man of Thorbrand's stature, and leave my son with me, and I will forget the insult you have done me by taking him captive. If you have the strength for it, you can share rule of Norway with my sons."

Ragnvald held out his hand for the poker. "You will not offer a more generous payment to King Harald for the loss of his captain and friend?" he asked, starting to feel desperate. At least Harald no longer wanted Heming killed, but Ragnvald cared more about this alliance than about Heming's life.

"That I do not kill him where he stands for his treatment of my son is payment enough."

"King Harald, will you allow King Hakon to expand his territory if he pays you your land taxes?" Ragnvald asked.

"I thought you might try to be fair," said Hakon to Ragnvald, before Harald could answer. "You are sworn to me."

"Fair to you?" Harald said. "Heming should die for what he did."

The anger that Ragnvald had been trying to tamp down needed an outlet. "You should have guided your son better," he said to Hakon. He turned to face Harald. "And you should have been satisfied with a wergild." With everyone looking at him, Ragnvald smiled mirthlessly. "A king must think of more than his personal pain. Would you rather hurt each other than rule Norway?"

For a moment Harald looked shamed, but Hakon rushed at Ragnvald, and stood within spitting distance of him. "How dare you speak to me this way? You swore to me. You swore to *me*."

"He was never yours," said Harald. "But he shows me no loyalty either."

"I swore to uphold your interests," said Ragnvald to Hakon. Then, to Harald: "You are my king. You need Hakon, and you may have lost him forever."

"Get out of my sight," said Harald. "I swear, I will kill Heming tonight."

"Then you are a fool," said Ragnvald coolly. He dropped the poker. He had passed beyond the heat of anger into some barren place where he felt no emotion. He was grateful for it—he could be angry and sorrowful later. "Do I have your leave to go, my king?"

"Go," said Harald. "Go and do not come back."

Ragnvald left.

32

GIVEN THE CROWDED CONDITIONS OF HARALD'S HALL, RAGN-
vald had kept his belongings few and well packed, to occupy as little
space as possible. He now owned a few more sets of clothing than he
had set out with, and many handfuls of silver. Silver enough to hire
men at Dorestad or Kaupanger to help him retake Ardal, perhaps. It
would not take many men. Once he had Ardal, then he could think of
Svanhild and Solvi.

Some fishing boats still plied the waters of Oslo Fjord. They came
and sold their fish to the Vestfold halls. Merchants, too, came and sold
their wares to bored warriors and their wives. Ragnvald found a man
named Frosti who had sold all his goods and wanted to leave now, before the wars resumed. He had a small crew, and was content to ferry
Ragnvald wherever he wished. The tide even favored leaving this night.

Ragnvald was helping Frosti move some packages into the boat when
he heard footsteps behind him. He turned, and saw Oddi on the dock.

"You are leaving us?" Oddi asked. "That was ill done."

"I did what I could," said Ragnvald curtly.

"I meant my father and Harald. I've no mind to follow either of
them right now."

"I cannot help you. I leave on the next tide."

"All alone? To retake your Ardal? Why do that, when men here
would follow you?" He looked away. "When I would follow you?"

"I cannot be your escape from your father's court anymore," said Ragnvald. "I will win Ardal, and be a farmer."

"You will be more than that."

Ragnvald shivered in the damp evening air. It sounded like a curse. "What men?" he asked.

"Dagvith, of course," said Oddi. He named other men, from both Hakon and Harald's camps. Men with whom Ragnvald had sparred and bled. "They are not filled with admiration for Harald and Hakon now either. You do them a disservice to leave them behind."

The scar on Ragnvald's hand ached. Ronhild had scolded him, as he lay recovering, for not telling anyone about it, for pridefully enduring alone. He wanted to be gone, but it warmed him that Oddi and others might want to fight by his side.

"Then I shall not," said Ragnvald. "What—how should I ask them?"

Oddi laughed. "I already asked them for you. Delay for a few hours, and you shall have twenty men, in the ship my father gave me, ready to take Ardal with you."

✝   ✝   ✝

IT TOOK NEARLY a week of sailing to reach the western end of Sogn Fjord. The weather was chill and threatening, but did not impede their cautious progress. Ragnvald kept watch for squalls and other threats while replaying Heming's trial in his mind. He remembered all of his words as though they had been carved in stone, and each time he imagined saying something different, something that forged peace between Hakon and Harald. Part of him wanted to turn around, to see if he could find a way to make it right, to speak some of the better speeches he had since composed. Then he thought of Harald telling him to go, and it fed the anger that drove him north.

Oddi was the ablest pilot of the group, and he grew worn and nervous as the days passed. They beached the ship to camp each night on sheltered islands, well before nightfall.

The last night, they camped on the rocky beach that sloped up toward the lakes and hills of Ardal. Ragnvald looked around. It soothed his eyes to rest on hills whose contours he knew so well, where every path that cut over mountain and field had known his feet before. He glanced at his men, still disbelieving his fortune that they had chosen to accompany him and Oddi. Oddi was the type that made friends easily. Ragnvald was even more grateful for that now.

Some he had not known well; he had only learned more of them over the journey. They were independent-minded, all of them, and had not liked the way Harald and Hakon had dealt with Ragnvald. He remembered them for deeds of bravery in Hordaland, and many had further stories to their names that they shared on the voyage.

"Olaf has few men to defend him," said Ragnvald to the men after they had eaten. "A dozen farmers' younger sons, who have picked up a hoe far more often than they've picked up a blade." This drew some appreciative chuckles.

Ragnvald described the layout of Ardal, using rocks on the ground to indicate buildings. He did not voice his fear that Solvi might have sent reinforcements to Olaf.

"They won't be prepared to fight, and most of them like me better. The only kin he has is his son Sigurd." Ragnvald tried to picture Sigurd's face, at the other end of his sword, and could only call to memory his shock of blond hair, his slouching posture. "Sigurd is no swordsman, and I don't want him killed. Unless he insists." His last words were almost drowned out by the sound of the surf on the shore rocks. Ragnvald cleared his throat and spoke louder. "A half day's walk, fifteen minutes of fighting, and then a night of feasting. Sleep well tonight, so you are rested for the celebration."

"You want Olaf for yourself, I remember," said Dagvith, the fair, friendly giant Ragnvald had met at Yrjar. Ragnvald felt a pleasant, foolish affection for him and all of these men.

"Yes," said Ragnvald. "I have stomached the memory of his insults for long enough."

Ragnvald, of course, did not sleep that night. He tossed and turned until Oddi kicked him out of the tent they shared, and then went to sit by the shore, pacing around when he grew cold. When he saw the first gilding of orange in the southern sky, he fed the banked cooking fire back to life, and heated some dried fruit and meat for his men's breakfast. They ate quickly, and by sunup were tramping across the frozen fields in the valley that led to Ardal.

The path led up a steep slope until they drew even with the tops of the cliffs that lined Sogn Fjord. Below, an overhang hid his ship. Gray clouds scudded across the sky, threatening snow. Though it was early in the season, a few farmers were out in the fields, inspecting fences. They could not have mistaken Ragnvald's warriors for anything but what they were—men bent on killing and destruction—but none raised an alarm. They watched Ragnvald's party pass, and then turned back to their labors. Ragnvald resolved that when he ruled these lands again, his tenants would be required to light beacon fires if they saw marauders. Olaf should have known better.

Ragnvald set a harder pace than he should have, eager to meet whatever this day would bring. Sweat dripped down his neck and froze on his back, and he had left the other men far behind him. He waited until they all reached the base of the last small hill that hid them from the hall at Ardal. Then he told them to walk farther apart, so he could call a warning if he walked into a trap.

The farm at Ardal stood still and peaceful in the midmorning light. A plume of smoke issued from the forge—Einar, hard at work—and another from the kitchen. Ragnvald drew his sword.

Ragnvald had so long perfected the practice of avoiding Olaf that he imagined he could sense where Olaf was now. He should be returning from his morning ride on his prize and only stallion, Sleipnir. Ragnvald looked forward to taking the horse from him. A mud track through a snow-covered field showed the path he had followed.

Ragnvald saw no guards. He waited until his men caught up with him again, and whispered to them that they should hide themselves near the stone fence around the yard where Sleipnir's barn lay. Olaf would return there soon. Instead, they surprised young Svein, one of Olaf's guards, as he was bringing the carrots and barley Olaf would want to feed Sleipnir when he returned. Svein opened his mouth to sound a warning, but Ragnvald caught him quickly around the neck and clapped a hand over his mouth, wedging his jaw shut with his other forearm so Svein could not bite him.

"Hush, it's me," he said. "Stay quiet." Svein continued struggling. "I'll break your neck if you scream," said Ragnvald, putting a warning pressure on Svein's throat. He slowly released Svein's mouth, but kept his grip around Svein's neck.

"You were what Olaf said we should guard against," said Svein.

Ragnvald smiled slowly. "Did he?" Of course—Olaf had tried to have him killed. Now that Ragnvald was surrounded by men who would kill for him, Olaf's fear was a pleasant draught indeed.

"Beware!" Svein screamed at the top of his lungs. Suddenly the snowy practice ground was filled with gangly boys wielding pot-iron swords. Ragnvald counted fifteen at least, but none looked to be above the age of majority.

"Don't kill them if you can help it," Ragnvald yelled above the fray. These were the sons of local farmers; he would want them on his side when he ruled here.

He saw Dagvith take one of the boys by the wrists and shake him until he dropped his sword. Ragnvald fought one of the more skilled for a minute or two before getting close enough to smash him in the face with the hilt of his sword. The boy's nose exploded in blood, and he fell over on his rear. He held his hand to his nose and looked up at Ragnvald balefully.

Ragnvald glanced around to see if he might be under any other threat, but Oddi and the other men seemed to have the boys well in hand. Ragnvald hit the boy on the head, and he slouched to the ground.

"You, you, and you," said Ragnvald, pointing to three of his men at random. "Take these"—he gestured at the fallen boys with his sword—"to the barn and bind their hands. I wait for Olaf."

"Is this your stepbrother?" called out Oddi. They stood in the shadow of the barn, where Ragnvald could see only Oddi's dark shape and Sigurd's bright hair.

"Yes," said Ragnvald. "Bind him securely. I do not wish to kill him."

He had expected some show of defiance from Sigurd, but he went docilely with Oddi and seemed content to be bound hand and foot and placed in the barn with the other farm boys, trussed up like a fowl for the cooking.

Looking around for someone else to fight, Ragnvald saw that almost all of the boys had been disarmed. One held a broken arm carefully with his other hand. Another's head lolled at an odd angle—probably dead, but by accident. Ragnvald would pay the boy's father the wergild owed for him.

He rested against a wall, as the excitement of battle left him. If only Olaf had been here: then Ragnvald could have killed him while he was still fresh. Now he must wait and fret.

Ragnvald's mother emerged from the kitchen door, followed by Vigdis. His mother's hands were covered with flour; Vigdis looked fine and golden, as if she were dressed for a feast.

"Ragnvald," said his mother, running to him, her arms wide. "It is dangerous for you to be here."

"You should get inside, Mother," he said. "Olaf could return, and I mean to kill him."

She gave him one blazing look—of pride, he thought, pride he had rarely seen from her—then grabbed Vigdis's arm and wrenched her back. "My son is going to kill your husband," he heard her say to Vigdis, triumphant. "You come with me."

Ragnvald smiled at the thought of what Ascrida might do to Vigdis when she had the upper hand. She would at least keep Vigdis from warning Olaf. Perhaps she would serve Vigdis as Vigdis had Svanhild, tying her up and stopping her mouth.

The clamor drew the notice of the servants and thralls who stood watching over the wall. Oddi flung one of the unconscious boys over his shoulder like a sack of potatoes.

"Don't just stand there watching, bring me some water," Ragnvald said to one of the gaping thralls.

The sun reached its zenith. A wind began, chilling Ragnvald in his leather armor. His sword grew heavy in his hand. He cleaned it on the snow and sheathed it again. He continued scanning the horizon for the silhouette of Olaf a-horse, come to meet his doom.

It was Einar who came instead, rushing toward Ragnvald from the door of his smithy. He screamed and waved his sword overhead, sounding more frightened than threatening. Some of his men laughed at Einar's limping gait. Later, Ragnvald wondered how long Einar had sat inside the smithy, listening to the battle, listening to Ragnvald say that he would kill Olaf. He must have spent some time weighing his friendship for Ragnvald against his duty to Olaf before he gathered his courage and charged out.

Ragnvald scrambled to his feet and met Einar on the muddy ground of the practice yard where the two of them had sparred as boys. Ragnvald parried him easily. Einar had the advantage of years and smithy-built muscle, but he was lame, and he had never been on a raid, never been to war. He had never killed a man.

"Don't do this, Einar," said Ragnvald. "Olaf tried to kill me. You know this. You must have heard." Einar's wild slashes scared him more than a controlled enemy's would, for Einar's sword might touch him where a better swordsman would be more careful of his own skin. Ragnvald darted a thrust under Einar's raised arm. A line of red parted Einar's shirtsleeve. He wore no armor.

"I must defend Olaf," said Einar. "I must."

Ragnvald tried to get inside Einar's guard enough to hit him in the head as he had the boy. Perhaps when Einar had calmed, he would consent to live, and let Ragnvald live as well.

"He attacked me in the dark at the *ting*," Ragnvald said desperately. "Did you not hear?" Einar's breath wheezed. Ragnvald, though his heart hammered, still breathed easily.

"I heard," said Einar.

"Then you know he has no honor."

"You must have deserved it," Einar cried, backing away from Ragnvald. "He is my foster father, the only father I've ever known."

"He's my stepfather as well, but he is a man of no honor." Einar would put down his sword, Ragnvald thought, and they would be friends again.

But he kept the tip up and advanced at Ragnvald again. His footwork looked like what Olaf had taught them as boys. Ragnvald knew how to defend against this. He brushed Einar's sword away with his own.

"He never betrayed me. I will defend him," said Einar again.

He rushed Ragnvald headlong. Ragnvald stepped out of the way, but not before Einar made a shallow wound on his upper arm. This would not do. Ragnvald needed to be rested and unwounded if he meant to kill Olaf. That would be a harder battle, one he must fight on his own.

Einar would never forgive him this. Ragnvald jerked his chin up at Oddi and Dagvith. "Help me disarm him."

"No!" screamed Einar. He ran at Ragnvald again, his sword raised high, as though it were an ax and he meant to cleave Ragnvald in half. Ragnvald raised his sword to defend himself, and Einar ran upon it, driving the point up through his shoulder. Blood covered Ragnvald's blade and his arms. Einar collapsed to the ground.

"Tend him," Ragnvald yelled. He ran forward and pressed his hand over Einar's wound. Blood flowed between his fingers. Why did no one come? "Please, someone help!"

He heard a struggle behind him, and then Vigdis came forward.

"Let me," she said. Ragnvald stood. Vigdis pressed Einar's shoulder with her wimple. It went instantly red with blood. Ragnvald watched as her long golden hair, freed from its covering, trailed in the dirt and turned dark with Einar's blood. She looked like the goddess Freya, ministering the fallen, as she tried to stanch the blood. Einar was her nephew, Ragnvald recalled.

"I have seen men survive such wounds," said Ragnvald. Einar had rushed at him, and Ragnvald had parried. He had not meant to kill, but death seemed to come easily at his hands. The *draugr* had fallen thus.

Vigdis shook her head. "Einar will not. See how the blood pumps out." Indeed, Vigdis's wimple was not enough to stanch it. There seemed no end to his blood. Ragnvald recalled the legend that a corpse would bleed anew in the presence of its murderer. Einar should be taken away from him, or his blood would make a new lake. Einar's face was corpse-white now, his head tipped back, his eyes staring as the dead did, at something only they could see.

"I had to," said Ragnvald quietly. Einar had run on the sword, but Ragnvald moved it to meet him. Ragnvald had come here to do murder, and now he had.

Vigdis said nothing, only rose to her knees. She and Ascrida would prepare this body tonight, as they would Olaf's.

Now the courtyard stank of death. Ragnvald had done this. He paced about in the sun, trying to keep his arms warm. A thrall brought him a basin of water to wash Einar's blood from his hands.

✢ ✢ ✢

OLAF CAME AS Ragnvald's stomach started to rumble for his dinner. He was still only a shape on the horizon when his horse scented danger and reared up. From there he approached more slowly, picking over the small dips and hillocks in the fields. All Ragnvald's weariness was forgotten.

Olaf dismounted from his horse just inside the wall. He wore no armor, but he did have his sword at his belt—no man would do otherwise.

"You bring death, my son," said Olaf, looking around. "A fine king you will make."

"I am not your son," said Ragnvald. He was vaguely aware of eyes watching them, shapes of warriors and servants, men and women of the household, but he kept his fixed on Olaf.

"No. I already knew you for a serpent when I killed your father."

That should not have stung. Ragnvald had long suspected his father's death at Olaf's hand. Olaf spoke of it to anger him, and succeeded.

"You're the one who paid a man to kill me," said Ragnvald. "Come, if you would have me murdered, do it yourself."

"I will," said Olaf, and lunged. He moved slowly, as if through water. Ragnvald had all the time in the world to step out of the way.

He had not seen Olaf fight in years—perhaps he had not truly fought since the last raid on Ardal, the time Ragnvald had killed his first man. Olaf's movements were predictable and unpracticed. Ragnvald had fought many better men than him in his time with Hakon and Harald.

Olaf made another lunge and exposed his flank. Ragnvald drew a ripping cut up the back of Olaf's leg, tearing flesh on the point of his sword. Olaf stumbled forward. He tried to catch himself, and his leg collapsed, the tendon in the back of his knee cut.

After that Olaf's end came quickly. He lurched off his good leg to close the distance between them, and Ragnvald deflected him with an elbow to Olaf's nose that broke it with a wet splinter. Ragnvald cut him twice more, once along the shoulder, and once more, out of spite, across his cheek, then finally hit Olaf's hand with the hilt of his sword, causing Olaf to drop his own.

Ragnvald kicked it away and raised his sword to Olaf's neck. "Kneel," he said. Oddi pushed Olaf to his knees with a kick to his back.

Olaf knelt, his back straight and proud, though he bled from half a dozen cuts. His nose was purpled by Ragnvald's elbow, and his chest heaved with the effort of staying upright. He kept his eyes fixed on Ragnvald, who paced in front of him. Ragnvald lowered his sword. There was no chance of Olaf running now. Even had Ragnvald not lamed him, he had nowhere to run.

"Do you know why your uncle Gudrod never came to avenge himself on me?" Olaf asked. Gudrod was Ragnvald's mother's brother, a friend of his father's, or so she had always said. Now Ragnvald lifted his sword and put it under Olaf's chin. Olaf spat in the dirt, blood and saliva, barely missing Ragnvald's foot, and pressed his neck against the blade. "You think I care?" he asked. "I know you won't let me live."

"No, I will not," said Ragnvald. "But I might let you die standing, with a sword in your hand. Perhaps the gods will overlook that you dropped it before." Ragnvald owed him that much, for the training at arms Olaf had given him.

"Then do it," said Olaf. He swayed on his knees. Oddi rushed forward to prop him up again. "I can stand long enough for that."

"No, you tell me," said Ragnvald. "Why no revenge?"

"Gudrod knew that if he came against me, King Hunthiof would burn him in his hall, and leave none of Eystein's kin alive."

"And you think he will still do that for you?" Ragnvald asked. "I no more believe that King Hunthiof will come to your aid than that a frost giant will come marching down from the Keel Mountains and offer to trade his life for yours. You die now."

"Your father deserved no defense," said Olaf, sounding more desperate now. "My sons will avenge me."

Ragnvald laughed at that. "Where is Sigurd? Why is he not defending you now?"

He jerked his chin at Oddi, who came over, bearing Olaf's sword.

He put it in Olaf's hand, and before Olaf had a chance to stand, Ragn-vald swung a mighty blow and struck off his head. The neck stump spurted blood for a moment, a strange vision that made Ragnvald want to laugh, though he did not think it was funny. The body fell forward onto the ground, soaking it wet again where Einar's blood had already soaked in.

Ragnvald turned to Ascrida and Vigdis, who stood to one side. They did not touch, but their bodies were turned toward one an-other, as if they wished to shelter each other from the death Ragnvald brought. He pictured the sorceress Alfrith among them, so vividly he had to shake his head to dispel the vision. He wondered if he would see her again.

"He may have a pyre," said Ragnvald, "and a cairn to mark his pass-ing. But no mound for him. No son of Olaf Ottarsson will ever claim dominion over these lands. The runes will tell truly, 'Olaf Ottarsson, Eystein's usurper, fell here,' nothing more."

"I will make the cairn for him," said one of the older servants. Ragn-vald thought he and Olaf had raided together once, though he had not stood in Olaf's defense.

Ascrida stepped forward. "And I will wash his body," she said, her voice harsh with some emotion. In the ten years since Eystein's death, Ragnvald had rarely seen sorrow in his mother's face, but he read there now sadness and a deep anger.

"I will aid you," said Vigdis, and moved to join Ascrida. "He was my husband too."

"Are you sure you do not need to make your new master welcome?" Ascrida asked, viciously. "Rolling over for men has always been your play."

Ragnvald went over to them. "Mother," he said, "you do not need to do this."

"I do," she replied.

Ascrida walked past Ragnvald to where Olaf's head lay facedown on the ground, a stream of blood trickling from the neck, and picked it up by the hair. Its eyes regarded Ragnvald for a moment before As-crida's purposeful strides hid it from his view.

Two of the servants picked up Olaf's body from the ground and carried it after her. Olaf had been a strong man in life, but carried this way in death, his body looked like a discarded rag doll.

Vigdis took a half step toward Ragnvald, looking uncertain for the first time since Ragnvald had known her. "You are master here now."

"I am," said Ragnvald, hoping his voice came out commanding enough. "My men are hungry and thirsty. Have a feast prepared."

There was more to be done, though. He went into the barn to unbind Sigurd himself. He needed to see his stepbrother's reaction.

"I need ale too," Sigurd said gloomily. "Everyone does. You left us bound up all day."

"It will make them tougher," said Ragnvald, holding Sigurd's gaze. Sigurd could not bear up under it, and ducked his head. He raised his arm as if he expected Ragnvald to help him to his feet.

Bemused, Ragnvald did. "I'm sorry it came to this," he said, following his stepbrother back out into the courtyard. He had expected much worse from him, but he had gotten it from Einar instead. Maybe Sigurd was only biding his time. "If your father had given me my birthright, I could have made him my steward, while I went out to make us richer." As he said it, his anger at Olaf gave way to sadness. Such a waste, the blood soaking into the ground from Einar's and Olaf's fallen bodies.

"What are you going to do with me?" Sigurd glanced at Vigdis, who now held young Hallbjorn in her arms. Hallbjorn was getting big, his white legs dangling from under Vigdis's arm. "What are you going to do with us?"

Ragnvald had not decided that yet, but if he were truly done with Harald and Hakon, he would remain here, and have enough time to raise Hallbjorn up to be friends with the sons he would make.

He put his hand on Sigurd's shoulder, feeling uncomfortable with the gesture, but hoping the camaraderie would make his stepbrother feel that Ragnvald bore him no ill will. He swallowed. He could say that at least.

"I bear you no ill will," he said slowly. "Ardal is mine now. You did as a son must—you obeyed Olaf, and you tried to do as he bid at the *ting*. It is to your credit that you did that, and to your credit that you did not die for a man who had lost his honor."

Sigurd looked eager to put his life and his decisions into Ragnvald's care. So this was what it was to be ruler, and hold the lives of lesser men in one's hands. Ragnvald should be grateful for Sigurd's weakness, for it meant he would not have to kill a boy who had been his brother, but he wished Sigurd was a stronger man. Olaf should have sent him to the priests of Frey rather than force his feet into warrior's boots, though perhaps he did not have a mystical bent either.

"Tonight keep vigil with Olaf's body and Einar's, and say your prayers when we burn them," he instructed Sigurd. "Tomorrow we will discuss the future."

33

THAT NIGHT RAGNVALD AND HIS MEN FEASTED AT ARDAL, though not the sort of feast that skalds would tell tales of later. The meat had not cooked long enough, and required heroic chewing to choke it down. Ragnvald's men drank deeply, though, and behaved as warriors should at feasts, fighting and dicing, throwing bones to the dogs that circled the tables, and betting on the outcome of their squabbles. Ragnvald called out some of their achievements, as was fitting, but no one wanted to boast of defeating a gaggle of fifteen-year-old boys.

"Are you sure you should not have killed your stepbrother?" asked Oddi quietly in Ragnvald's ear. He sat near Ragnvald during the feast; indeed, he had not been far from Ragnvald's side since the fighting was done.

A shadow fell over Ragnvald's trencher, and he looked up to see Vigdis carrying a cup for him. She pressed it into his hand, and Ragnvald tasted Olaf's best wine, of which he had never had more than a sip until now. His face went hot. He hoped Vigdis had not heard Oddi's question.

"Hallbjorn is but a boy," said Ragnvald, purposefully misunderstanding. "Yes, I am sure." Vigdis gave him a small smile. She did not betray unguarded emotion very often, but she loved her son.

"I meant the overgrown boy Sigurd," said Oddi.

"Sigurd did not compass my death, and he is growing into a fine swordsman." Lies, but he could not think of more killing now. He looked at Vigdis, who had moved to the head of the table. She should be with Sigurd, standing vigil, shedding tears for her husband. She had not loved him, Ragnvald thought, but she had been his favorite for many years. Even Ragnvald's mother did her mourning tonight.

Then Vigdis looked up, meeting Ragnvald's eyes. Oddi glanced between them and smiled. When she moved down the table to serve another of his men, Oddi raised his eyebrows. "She'll be in your bed tonight, unless I miss my guess."

Ragnvald scowled at Oddi for reading his mind, and took another drink of the fine, sweet wine. "I think not. She is my stepmother."

"No longer." Oddi grinned. "If you do send her away, give her a shove in my direction. She looks like a woman who knows what she wants from a man." He gave Ragnvald a knowing look that made his face heat more. Ragnvald knew nothing of Vigdis's sort of woman. He could count the women he had been with on one hand, thralls and slaves all, women with no choice, and never more than a few times. He thought of Alfrith in Smola, the sorceress. She seemed less dangerous than Vigdis.

He hated the idea of Vigdis with anyone else, though. If Vigdis came to him, he should bid her go out to do her duty to her dead husband, so Olaf would not walk uneasy from his grave.

"Don't send her away," said Oddi. "You do ill to be alone on the night after a battle."

"You are a procurer now?" Ragnvald jested.

"No," said Oddi, "but I don't want you finding me to voice your sour thoughts again. Fuck a woman and fall asleep. That is how it is supposed to go."

Once Ragnvald had drunk enough to dull the memory of Olaf's head falling in the dust, he stood up from the table. He gave a brief speech, thanking Oddi and the rest of the warriors. Then he put Oddi in his old sleeping chamber, empty now of Einar and Sigurd: one dead, one standing vigil. Ragnvald tried to turn his heartsoreness into anger. Einar should not have attacked him. He had to know he could not survive. Ragnvald would have traded Sigurd for Einar in a moment. The wrong brother lay dead.

Olaf's chamber was along the south side of the hall, far enough from the kitchen that the heat was not overwhelming, but close enough that the smells of cooking meat penetrated here. The bed was large, larger than any Ragnvald had slept in alone. Although, he supposed, Olaf was not often alone.

In this room Olaf kept a latched chest of his treasures. Ragnvald opened it and found the expected silver, along with a few pieces of gold and some finely wrought bronze brooches, the like of which he had never seen grace the breast of either his mother or stepmother. Hilda's now, Ragnvald decided.

He was turning one of these pieces over in his hand, admiring the way the lamplight rippled over the burnished surface and lit the garnet eye of one hound, whose mouth opened to swallow the leg of its fellow, when the lamp's flame wavered and Vigdis walked into the room. Her hair was uncovered, still wet at the ends. Ragnvald saw a flash of her tending Einar, her hair dragging through his blood.

"I thought you might come to me," said Ragnvald. He had imagined this moment as soon as he was old enough to want a woman. Not quite like this—in those fantasies he had not killed Olaf, though Olaf was usually dead and far away, and Vigdis came to him, her hair down, a smile on her face, saying that she desired Ragnvald.

"All of those men knew I would come to you," said Vigdis, as though that did not shame her.

Ragnvald kept silent. He wanted her, and perhaps taking her was his right, but she had been half mother and half goddess to him for so long, and this was strange.

"So here I am." She seemed also at a loss.

"Why, Vigdis?" Her name was strange on his tongue. "I will not harm Hallbjorn. He is only a boy."

She lowered her eyes. "Do you want me to go?"

"No," he said roughly. He should send her away, but as she smiled at him, a knowing, satisfied smile, he knew he would not. He took her hand, gently for a moment, then wrenched her closer. Why should she be different than a thrall? Why should he care what she thought of him? He had power over her now. He sat and pulled her on top of him, to make her work for it, make her prove that she was here by choice, though when her weight pressed him into the down mattress, her breasts soft against his chest, her hand between his legs, he feared it would be over too quickly.

"Wait," he said, and reached up to snuff out the candle.

"Would you not like to see me?" Vigdis asked. "I am your spoils."

Ragnvald rolled her over onto her back and pressed her hands above her head, leaving the candle lit. "Are you mocking me?" he asked, though he decided he did not care if she was. She was here, and that meant more than whatever she said.

"Why should I mock the boy who has grown into more of a man than my husband was?"

"Don't flatter me."

She cocked her head to one side. "Should I not? Young men enjoy flattery." She took hold of him between his legs again, over his britches.

"I do not."

"I think this fellow does."

"He likes a firm hand," he answered. "Take off your gown."

She gave him another amused look and pulled her gown up over her head, then helped Ragnvald take off his tunic and unlace his britches. She pulled him in to enter her as soon as they were both unclothed, and remained irritatingly unmoved as Ragnvald spent himself in her.

When they lay cooling, he played with her breast and watched her nipple stiffen between his fingers, until she wriggled away.

"Was it what you imagined?" Vigdis snuggled up against his side again, as though she had not just herself pulled away.

"Like many things, it was better in the imagination than in reality," he said. "I imagined you would take more trouble to pretend you desired me."

"I thought you didn't like flattery." Her smile still held the same magic it had from before they joined, a teasing, promising smile, as though nothing had changed between them at all.

"I don't. I thought some women enjoyed it, though."

"They may," she said. "Do you want to please your wife? With more than just jewelry and servants?"

"Yes," said Ragnvald tightly, though he did not want to think of

Hilda like this, not when Vigdis's hair still stuck to his sweaty skin, and her breast lay heavy on his arm.

She hesitated, and Ragnvald worried he had given all his power away by wanting something from her. She propped herself up on her elbows. Her hair framed her face, and the candlelight made her skin gold. All of Ragnvald's muscles felt tired, but he wanted to trace her features with his thumb, to touch her and make her gasp and cry out in pleasure. To reach her in some way that was more than just his body on hers.

"You've made a good start," she said, "by not falling immediately asleep. I will show you more, if you like. But may I say not tonight?" Pain tightened her face. "Today has not been easy."

He loved her a little at that moment, more than any other. In her way, she had been brave to come to him like this, after he had killed her husband. Like a man, like his own mother, even, she did what was needful.

"Yes," he said, pleased to be able to give her something she truly wanted.

✛   ✛   ✛

HE WOKE WITH aching shoulders in Olaf's bed, next to Vigdis. She stirred as he watched her, and opened wary eyes. For a moment, he felt they looked at each other as two strange animals must when they are in the same territory, ready to fight, and then her smile went warm and liquid. A smile he could not trust.

"Why do you look at me so?" she asked. "What do you mean to do with me, now that Olaf is gone?"

Gone, dead, dead, after Ragnvald had killed him like an animal, like a slaughter. He had died with his sword in his hand, at least.

"I will decide tomorrow," he said. "After you give me that promised lesson." He raised his eyebrows at her, and she smiled archly. "This is a trade, isn't it? What do you wish? I could send you to your family across the Keel, and you could take Sigurd and Hallbjorn with you."

"Sigurd is not my son," she said. "What do I want with that weakling?"

Ragnvald shook his head. He must not pity Sigurd now. "You could go to Thorkell. He looked for a bride, I think."

"You know kings, and I think one day you will be a fine jarl. Perhaps even a king," she said. "I would rather be a king's mistress than a farmer's wife. 'A woman is lucky who is a widow.'"

She had misquoted the proverb. "A rich widow," Ragnvald corrected her. Vigdis as his mistress—Hilda would not like that, when she came, not until she had borne him a few sons at least. Vigdis could never live with another woman without striving against her.

"For now, we have not many women here with my sister gone," he said. "You should not be lying so long abed." He sat up and picked up his tunic from the floor, brushing off the dirt before pulling it over his head. It smelled of the sweat and blood of yesterday's battle. "You will defer to my mother in all housekeeping duties."

She sat up and gave him a look he could not read. "You do like to give orders, Ragnvald."

"I am ruler here," said Ragnvald, feeling she had cast him as a boy again. "You will do as I say."

"Of course," she said with a secret smile, letting her hair fall partially over her face. Of course, her voice said, you will be ruled by me. Ragnvald got out of bed and pulled on his hose and tunic. That would not be the way of things. He must bring Hilda here. He must put aside any thought of the rich rewards Hakon and Harald had offered. He must put Ardal in order, so when a king, any king, came in conquest, they would ask for his oath of obedience, not his surrender.

✣   ✣   ✣

VIGDIS WAS A fair hand at managing the farm, and though Olaf's grasp on Eystein's land had slipped over the years, the farm itself was stocked well enough to feed the men Ragnvald had brought with him until summer. As the snow cleared from the lower slopes of the mountains, Ragnvald lost himself in planning for spring. Oddi and the other men were willing enough to work, for meals and turns with the women thralls. Some began training the boys who had been Olaf's only defense.

"What will you do?" Ragnvald asked Oddi. It was a cold day. Snow threatened again. The cows nosed through a crackling of ice to reach the dry grass underneath. They would probably cut their lips and need salve. He made a note to ask his mother if she had enough prepared.

He should send for Hilda soon, but he hesitated. Once he did that, he would be truly resigned to this fate. A wealthy farmer, owner of Ardal. At one time, it had been his only aspiration, but now it felt small.

"I suppose I must return to my father eventually," said Oddi. He frowned and kicked at a tussock. "War is coming. War that will sweep over all of this land. Perhaps I can convince my father to send me to the Faeroe Islands until it passes over."

"Do you think he will?" Ragnvald asked. He had suggested Hakon send Heming there, he recalled. They lay in the farthest reaches of the North Sea, north even of the Orkneys, far away from any Norse wars.

"No," said Oddi. "That is why I remain here."

✛ ✛ ✛

THE FIRST SPRING breeze, smelling of green things, brought with it a messenger from Heming. It was a young man, hardly more than a boy, who came at midday with news from the outside world. Ragnvald recognized him, and Oddi greeted him.

"Arnfast, coming with the speed of eagles," said Oddi, making a jest on his name. "What have you come to tell us?"

The boy was slender, a born runner. He had run the hill quickly, covering the ground with a loping stride. His breath was still coming hard when he answered, "Nothing very urgent. I only wanted to run."

"You did not race at the *ting*," said Ragnvald, remembering the race he himself had won.

"King Hakon did not want anyone to know how fleet I am." Arnfast grinned. "Give me some ale, and I will tell you the news."

He told them that Hakon had taken Heming and returned to Yrjar, not long after Ragnvald left. There was an unbridgeable rift between Hakon and Harald. After a few weeks in Yrjar, Heming grew tired of his father's scolding.

"Hakon blames Heming for souring his alliance with Harald," said Arnfast.

"That surprises me," said Ragnvald sourly. "He would have broken it on some pretext sooner or later."

"Ragnvald," said Oddi warningly.

"Am I wrong?"

"Arnfast is too young for talk like this," said Oddi, so serious-faced that Ragnvald knew he spoke in jest.

Arnfast continued: "Heming gathered as many of King Hakon's men as he could convince and is planning to sail against Tafjord." To Oddi, he added, "Your father is wroth with you. You should have stayed in Vestfold to leave with them."

"I'll not be lessoned by you," said Oddi, with some heat. "You're with Heming now."

"I was bored," said Arnfast, shrugging. "I think your father did not mind Heming's plan."

"What have you heard of Solvi?" Ragnvald asked. "Did he return to Tafjord?"

"We have heard many things," said Arnfast. "Some say he spent the winter in Dorestad, or even with the Danish king. Others say he returned to Tafjord." He laughed. "I guess Heming will find out."

"Heming is as foolish as ever," said Ragnvald under his breath to Oddi.

"He sent me here to find out if you would join him," said Arnfast. He sat up and continued formally, "Oddbjorn Hunthiofsson and Ragnvald Eysteinsson, Heming Hakonsson requests your aid in defeating a sworn enemy: King Hunthiof and his son Solvi. To Oddbjorn he bids me say that brothers should stand together. To Ragnvald he says that you have been a friend when he deserved it least, and he wishes you by his side. As you help Heming grow his lands, so will he help you grow yours. Will you join him?"

Ragnvald barked a laugh, both at the message and Arnfast's formal delivery. So Heming finally had his wish: to sail against Solvi.

"I did not try to save Heming's life for friendship," he said.

Arnfast shrugged. "He is grateful still."

"You might win Svanhild back," said Oddi. "Is it not worth stomaching my brother for that?"

Of all the men who had asked for his loyalty, Heming was the one

Ragnvald wished to follow least, and yet here was his chance. Svan-hild might be at Tafjord. If Heming were successful, he would win his father's good graces, and Ragnvald might gain the gratitude of a king again—a king who would never trust him as he had before, but it would be better than his enmity.

"I would like some time to decide," Ragnvald said.

"Heming is waiting in the barrier islands outside Geiranger Fjord," said Arnfast. "He will wait another week and then proceed without you."

"A day," said Ragnvald. "You will have my answer tomorrow."

✦   ✦   ✦

"DO YOU HESITATE because of my brother?" Oddi asked when he came upon Ragnvald, lost in thought by the fire. When Ragnvald was a boy, he remembered watching the fire while adults talked over his head, trying to see the shapes in the flames. Now whenever he looked, he saw reminders of his vision of Harald.

"No," said Ragnvald.

"Because we might take back your sister—I do not see why you should hesitate at all."

He hesitated because he wanted too much. He wanted to believe that Heming could succeed, and by his success Ragnvald might rise. Then at least Harald might see him as worthy of notice. Harald had loved Thorbrand better, and thrown Ragnvald aside for his vengeance, while Ragnvald had delayed his vengeance upon Olaf for Harald, or so it seemed to him now.

"I fear for Ardal if I go," said Ragnvald. "I have killed its protector."

"Tafjord is not far from here," said Oddi. "You will be back before the raiding season begins."

"And I have Sigurd," said Ragnvald sarcastically. "He will be a great help."

"Perhaps you do him wrong," said Oddi. "I have spoken with him. He wants responsibility."

"So he can stab me in the back?"

"My father did wrong by keeping Heming down all these years," said Oddi. "You told him that when all others feared to. Do not make the same mistakes with your brother."

"Stepbrother," said Ragnvald, but Oddi was right. Hakon had told Ragnvald that he saw clearly in all but his own cause. He could do worse than take Oddi's advice in this.

"I have taken back Ardal and killed Olaf," Ragnvald said to Oddi. "Does this mean that I am free from my oath to your father?"

"I would say you are free of all oaths now," said Oddi. "You may do as you wish."

☩   ☩   ☩

AFTER EATING BREAKFAST, Ragnvald woke Sigurd up from where he dozed on one of the benches in the hall. Sigurd rubbed his eyes, and Ragnvald guided him into the kitchen for his milk and porridge.

"Does Oddi not let you share his chamber?" Ragnvald asked.

"He had Thora with him last night," said Sigurd, naming one of the thralls. He sighed. "She used to share my bed."

"He'll be gone from here soon," said Ragnvald. "Come let us walk the fields, and see if the hay needs reseeding."

The sun was shining. A cold breeze came down from the mountains. Above, white clouds looked like ships' sails. A promising day. They walked in silence for a time, until they had come to the stone fence that marked the western edge of Ardal lands. From here, on a day like this, the waters of Sogn Fjord were just visible, sparkling under the sun in the distance.

Ragnvald had thought long on how to solve the problem of his stepbrothers, Sigurd and Hallbjorn. The songs told of boys who grew to men, waiting to avenge their fathers' deaths. Ragnvald had done just such a thing himself. No one made songs of the boys who only grew up to fight in other men's raids, and let their fathers' killers die in their beds. Perhaps Oddi was right, and the way to make Sigurd into a friend was to ask him to do a favor. Wisdom might make it seem the other way around, but men resented the favors they were given, and loved themselves for the favors they granted.

He stopped and looked out toward the faraway fjord. Sigurd stopped too, looking at Ragnvald warily, at his right hand, which hung by his side, not far from the hilt of his sword. Sigurd took a step back.

"I don't want to be killed," he said, looking miserable. "It's not my fault that—"

"I need your help, Sigurd," Ragnvald cut him off, before Sigurd could shame himself further. He might have time to think of what he said, and hate Ragnvald even more for hearing it.

Sigurd made eye contact with Ragnvald briefly before looking down at his feet. "Vigdis needs you," Ragnvald continued, immediately wishing he had not. Vigdis was Sigurd's stepmother too, and she had shown what she was capable of, to get what she wanted. "My mother needs you too," he added hastily. "Ardal needs you. I must sail north to get Svanhild from Solvi, with the help of Hakon's sons. I need you to guard Ardal for me. Let Fergulf help you turn those farm boys into warriors to defend Ardal from raiders. I do not want us to be enemies. Will you help me?"

Sigurd looked at Ragnvald and gave him a sly look that Ragnvald remembered from their growing up, when he would torment Svanhild, or find some way to shirk his duty. "What will you do if I do not?" He squinted against the sunlight.

"You may go where your *wyrd* leads you, of course," said Ragnvald. Every option that had once been open to Ragnvald, to find land across the sea, now stood open to Sigurd if he wanted to take it. Ragnvald could push him that way. That might be safer.

"Why should I help you?" Sigurd asked. "You killed my father."

"Your father killed my father," said Ragnvald, exasperated. "Do you want to continue this? Do you want to fight when we return to Ardal, in the holmgang, with witnesses? What do you want, Sigurd?"

To Ragnvald's surprise, Sigurd's face crumpled. "My father is dead," he said, brokenly. "And he always liked you more." Ragnvald made a noise of denial at that which Sigurd did not seem to hear. "My mother is dead, and I don't even remember her. I don't want to kill you, and I don't want to die."

Ragnvald touched Sigurd's shoulder gingerly. He did not want this guilt: his guilt over Einar, which threatened to spill over into guilt over Olaf, or at least what Olaf's death meant to Sigurd. "You don't have to, Sigurd. Your father made many mistakes. You can be my steward at Ardal, while I go raiding, and if you do well, your sons may inherit that title. I will owe you that for protecting it."

"You think I can protect it?" Sigurd's face was streaked with tears, and Ragnvald's stomach twisted in something like disgust. "Father always said I was weak."

"It is your actions that make you weak or strong," said Ragnvald, though he did not quite believe it himself. Olaf had called him weak too. "Make a choice now, and be strong. Fergulf is a good armsman, and he can give you good advice. You should follow it when you can, and learn to use your own judgment as well."

34

RAGNVALD AND ODDI MET WITH HEMING ON THE SMALL strand of Alesund, among a warren of islands and sheltered coves. The trees that capped the peninsula's small hills had dustings of green upon them.

Heming greeted their ship of twenty warriors as warmly when they arrived as if they had brought five times as many. "Ragnvald, I am glad to see you," he said, giving Ragnvald a strong embrace and a pounding on his back. "Have you finally killed that stepfather of yours?"

"Yes," said Ragnvald.

"I owe you much for taking my part and my father's in Vestfold. He is too rigid to thank you, but I am not."

Ragnvald was surprised it had seemed that way to Heming. He nodded uncertainly. "I was only attempting to be fair."

"Cheer up," said Heming. "I lived, and so did you." He looked pleased with himself. "We're going to get your sister back, now, and kill Solvi."

"Yes," said Ragnvald. "Do you know he's there?"

"If he's not, we'll take his hall and stay there until he returns. I have heard Tafjord is easy to defend."

"Yes, and difficult to attack."

"Indeed. It was you who told me," said Heming.

Heming wanted to set off with next morning's tide, so in the blue light before dawn their ships pushed off into the network of channels around Alesund. Ragnvald sailed with Heming in the lead ship, for he knew these channels as well as any, having come this way with Solvi and his expert pilots.

The ships had to anchor for an hour or two near Alesund to wait for a complicated bit of water to run the right way to swell them through a narrow gap between two islands. Ragnvald watched a small skiff careen through over the hummock of water that two colliding currents made, a skiff that tugged at his memories.

"Let us hail this fisherman and see what he knows," said Ragnvald. "It would be well to find out if Solvi is at home."

Ragnvald waved the boat over, and threw a line to the fisherman. He was bemused though not surprised when the man tipped up the brim of his hat and showed himself to be Agi, son of Agmar, fisherman of Geiranger Fjord.

"Ragnar," he said happily when he saw Ragnvald. Heming raised his eyebrows at the name, but said nothing. "Your face has healed well. And I see you've found some friends."

"Yes," said Ragnvald. "You're farther from home than I thought to find you."

"A mess of ships came this way yesterday and took all of my catch for themselves," said Agi. "Scared the other fish away too. My wife doesn't like it when I come back empty."

"A mess of ships?" Ragnvald asked.

"King Hunthiof and his son—Solvi the Short." Agi barked out a laugh. "Took my fish himself. Had his new wife with him."

"How many ships?" Ragnvald asked, his back stiffening at the mention of Svanhild.

"A double handful at least," said Agi. More than ten, and Agi might not have seen them all.

"We have heard of this," said Ragnvald to Heming. "There were rumors he had gathered allies to fight Harald this winter." He turned back to Agi. "Which way did they sail?"

"South," said Agi. "They stayed in the channel. Usually they head out west." Out west for raiding across the sea in Ireland. South for raiding on Norse shores. Or Frisia, but Solvi was a friend to Rorik of Dorestad, and he had just been there. No, this must mean that those rumors about Solvi gathering allies were true, and that now he took a force south to make war on Vestfold. Harald's forces would be too small to defend it without Hakon's to swell them.

Ragnvald took some silver out of his pouch and counted it out into Agi's chapped palm. "Thank you, Agi Agmarsson," he said.

"Ragnvald, we must make the tide," said Heming.

"Ragnvald?" said Agi, as he threw the rope back. "I've heard of you."

"Ragnvald Eysteinsson of Sogn," said Ragnvald, ready to be proud of his name for once. "My hall and my hospitality will always be yours."

Agi gave him a half bow, then maneuvered his boat expertly over the swells and beyond an outcropping of land.

"Ragnvald, the tide," said Heming again.

"No," said Ragnvald. "Solvi sails to attack Harald." His voice sounded choked to his ears.

"What of it? Tafjord will be unguarded," said Heming. "I'm sorry your sister won't be there, but it will still be good plunder."

Plunder Tafjord, take his gold back to Ardal, live to turn that gold into more men and more land. It was the obvious choice. Dark fjord waters washed at the ship's keel. Ragnvald's skin felt chill and drowned again. Even gone from Harald, it had made him feel secure knowing that Harald was there in Vestfold, his golden future still assured. If Solvi and Hunthiof could snuff it out, then the gods truly were cruel, and Ragnvald's vision had been false. It could not have been false. Ronhild the sorceress had said it was true. Ragnvald had felt it was true.

"No," said Ragnvald, half to himself. Then, to Heming, "We must sail to Harald's aid."

Oddi had brought his ship around to lie next to Heming's while they spoke with Agi. He leapt across the gap between them as soon as they drew close enough. "Why are we waiting?" he asked.

"Ragnvald met a friend," said Heming, sarcastically. "Although he did not know your name."

"That man fished me out of the fjord when Solvi tossed me in," said Ragnvald. "At the time, I thought it prudent not to give my own name so close to Solvi's home." He told Oddi what Agi had said. "Harald needs our help."

"Why do you care?" said Oddi. "We're going to miss the tide."

"No," said Ragnvald. The ships began to rise as the change of tide approached, eddying around them. "We cannot go to Tafjord. Solvi is not there. Svanhild is not there. I will not."

Oddi looked down at the swirling water. "Harald is not our father's ally anymore."

"Yes," said Ragnvald. "Because Heming broke the alliance. Now Solvi will defeat Harald, and return stronger than ever." He turned to Heming. "If you sit in his seat in Tafjord, you will only keep it warm until he returns." The water began to back up against them, push the ships back out of the channel. Oddi and Heming's pilot exchanged a look of exasperation. Ragnvald pressed on. "It is too late. Let us beach and make a new plan." They could always make the following tide in the evening.

Heming signaled the ships that were waiting behind them. Men went to their oars. They rode the bolus of water out of the channel and into open water again. After Heming's fleet pulled up on the beach, his captains rushed to him, demanding answers.

"Ask Ragnvald," said Heming.

"I have had a vision," said Ragnvald, thinking of the golden wolf. That vision must still guide him.

"Ragnvald's visions are important," said Heming to the crowd. "I have learned this. My brother and I will speak with him privately, and then we can catch the next tide." Ragnvald glanced at Heming to see if he was being sarcastic. He looked entirely sincere.

Ragnvald held his tongue as the captains dispersed. He did not know what to make of Heming's words, but he knew must show no uncertainty if he wished to convince Heming of anything.

"What is your vision?" Heming asked.

"That you will gain the gratitude of a king if we sail to his side now."

"Why are you so certain your golden Harald will lose without us?" Oddi asked.

"Because he does not know sea battles as he does land. Because he will be unprepared. If he loses one battle—" Ragnvald closed his mouth. Harald must not lose a single battle, or he would never be king of all Norway. Harald was Ragnvald's *wyrd*, his fate, the source and object of his vision. And Harald would be the one who would unite Norway and keep it whole against the pressures of the wider world, against King Gorm of Denmark, who would make it part of a Danish empire that now included the whole north of England, thanks to Ragnar Lothbrok and his sons.

None of those reasons would impress Heming and Oddi.

"Solvi has, let us say, twenty ships," said Ragnvald. "He has more allies in Dorestad, and who knows where else. Harald only has his winter forces—not many more than a few hundred warriors. His men will gather back slowly in the spring, until he is ready to strike out again. He has never had to defend Vestfold." Heming and Oddi listened, their faces grave, so Ragnvald continued before they decided to argue.

"Heming, you broke your father's alliance with Harald, an alliance that would have enriched you both. If you do this, if we take our forces south to Harald's aid, you will repair the alliance, and break Solvi." He could see Heming wavering. "How much more will your father admire you for that than if you take an empty hall?"

Anger and shame warred on Heming's face. "My father—," he began.

"Forget about the south," Oddi cut in impatiently. "No king can rule both south and western Norway, not Harald nor anyone else. Defending Harald will not help either of you." He shook his head. "Solvi may humiliate Harald, and he is welcome to it."

"He will come back to Tafjord, though," said Ragnvald.

"Let us simply raid Tafjord, then," said Oddi. "We can sail there, and away, and leave the halls burned to the ground."

"Yes," said Heming. "My father will admire us for that. Then we can send to him, and with his aid we will hold all of Hunthiof's lands, and perhaps even take Sogn for you—that is what Harald offered you, is it not?"

Ragnvald shook his head. Hakon would not be eager for Heming to give over Sogn, but if his son ruled Maer from Tafjord and valued

Ragnvald, Hakon might change his mind. A strong king who owed Hakon service would be a wise choice for Sogn. No king had ruled there since Ragnvald's grandfather.

"Harald sent you away," said Oddi to Ragnvald. "He does not value you."

Now it was Ragnvald's turn to falter. Harald would not give him Sogn, not now. This was his chance to redeem his father's mistakes—but how? By taking Tafjord, or by bringing an army to Harald when he needed it most? If Solvi won in Vestfold, he would return with tenfold strength to Tafjord, and make foolish what Heming planned.

"He sent me away," said Ragnvald. And then the fates sent him Agi again to remind him of his vision. That is what he must remember now. "Perhaps that was the will of the gods. So I could come to you, and bring you to him."

"The gods do smile on you," said Heming, with an odd, twisted smile of his own. Ragnvald could not read what it meant; he had never heard Heming speak like this, or wear such a face.

"If this is them smiling, I would hate to see their enmity," Ragnvald muttered. Sogn, or even a part of it, was never offered to him except the moment before it was taken away. At the trial, with Harald, and now with Heming. Following that lure had always led him into danger.

"I know the gods' enmity," said Heming quietly. Ragnvald looked at Heming and saw gold and good luck, a man blessed by the gods. "Do you truly think this is their plan?"

"I think that if you restore the alliance between your father and Harald, he will bless you more than he would for raiding Tafjord," said Ragnvald. "Believe that if you do not care for my plans or visions."

"You thought my father meant to betray Harald," said Oddi.

Ragnvald was taken aback that Oddi would throw those words back at him in front of Heming. "And you said he wanted it to be in his own time," Ragnvald replied. "I do not know what your father has planned, Heming, but I do know he was angry at you for breaking the alliance. If you sail to Harald's side, Harald will give you land and men. Harald will value you for your own sake."

Heming gave Ragnvald a look of desperate hope, almost like the one he had worn in Harald's hall, when his fate lay in the balance. Hakon must have been harsh to his son since they left Vestfold.

"I have been a fool. Since my duel with Runolf at the Sogn *ting*, or even before." He sighed. "I have been wrong many times, and you have been right, and I have hated you for it."

"You were not so wrong," said Ragnvald. "How different would everything be now if we had sailed against Solvi after we went raiding in Hordaland? You were right then, and I was wrong."

"If right, then for the wrong reasons," said Heming. "I will do as you advise. If you think Tafjord would be a hollow victory, then let us follow your vision back to Vestfold." Ragnvald peered at him, looking for signs that he might be making some strange jest, but he looked sincere. If it were true, if Heming had truly changed, he might now grow into someone Ragnvald could respect. This man would be a worthy successor for Hakon, with his hard-won wisdom.

Oddi had been watching both of them, growing more and more incredulous, until finally he burst out, "You cannot be willing to give Harald aid, brother."

"Think how much more glorious the tale than sacking an empty hall," said Heming, with a hint of his old lightness. Then, more firmly, "The ships are mine to command."

Oddi shrugged. "At least we'll get to kill Solvi's men."

"We are both right now," said Ragnvald to Heming. "Your father will be pleased when he is Harald's friend again, Solvi is defeated, and all of his allies are scattered."

"If we win," said Oddi grimly.

"We will win," said Heming. "You speak to the captains, Ragnvald. This plan is yours."

✠   ✠   ✠

ODDI STILL INSISTED on sending messengers to Hakon, telling what they had done.

"I had meant to bring him Solvi and Tafjord as a finished victory," said Heming when he found out.

"Perhaps he will send aid," said Ragnvald. He doubted Hakon

would, but the chance only cost them a small ship, and the men to crew it. They still had to wait on the tide to depart. Ragnvald feared they would never catch up with Solvi, his fleet ships, his preternatural knowledge of currents and weather. Their force might arrive after the battle was over.

When the ships finally did leave, in the waning hours of the next day, Ragnvald took up a position in the craft captained by Grim, Hakon's best captain. Oddi and Heming had wanted to sail with him, but Ragnvald persuaded Oddi to take the next ship, the one whose job was to stay always in view of Ragnvald and Grim's without letting any of Solvi's ships see him.

Heming brought up the rear. Ragnvald was glad to be away from both of them, and that he had persuaded them to separate from one another. Oddi would probably continue to fret over this, and he could too easily change Heming's mind. On his own, though, he must put on a brave front for his warriors.

Grim was more pleasant to Ragnvald than he had been on the way to Hordaland last summer, though he looked the same, like the first man Odin carved from an ash tree. "This is a clever plan of yours," he said when Ragnvald came to check on him where he sat at the steering oar.

Ragnvald ran the words over in his head, looking for any sarcasm. Hearing none, he nodded. "How is our speed?"

"Good," said Grim. "The sail is cold and damp in this weather, so it will not fill as easily, and that hampers our speed, but we have a good wind."

Ragnvald thanked him and turned to walk toward the front of the ship again. There was nothing he could do to bring Solvi's ships into view except wait and trust in Grim's skill, and whatever gods would direct the winds, then trust in Grim's skill further to keep them close enough to Solvi's ships without being seen.

The first night they camped on a beach where Ragnvald had rested a few times before. He knew the sand would cache pools of rainwater for fresh drinking and stewing some dried meat into something more digestible.

"See here, my lords," said Grim, when they discussed their plans for the next day's sailing. He scraped a rough map into the coarse sand.

"Solvi will keep to the inner passage here, among the barrier islands, to protect his ships."

"Won't he want to avoid being seen?" Ragnvald asked. "Wouldn't he keep to open ocean?"

"No," said Grim with surety. "It is far too early in the year to trust the weather in the open ocean, and there are many more beaches to camp on. We will brave the open ocean and catch him here"—he pointed to a spot among his scratchings where Solvi's ships would have to emerge—"and follow him to Vestfold from there."

Ragnvald gave his approval, and Oddi and Heming seconded it. But on the next day, when the wind whipped spray around them, and none could hear them if they spoke quietly, Ragnvald questioned Grim further.

"I trust you and your knowledge of the sea," he began, "but I want to understand your thinking better."

Grim gave him a sardonic look. "You credit Solvi Hunthiofsson with supernatural powers as a pilot and a commander, but I know him and his father too. He is more cautious than you think. The reason his men trust him to lead them into danger is because he rarely does it when he's not sure of victory."

Ragnvald thought back on his time with Solvi, and it struck him as a true assessment. He gave Grim a measuring look. Hakon had a treasure here in Grim. Ragnvald wondered if he knew it. He glanced back at Oddi's ship, a gray apparition in the thin sea mist to the north. The other ships behind them could as easily be wisps of cloud, not formed of solid planks, full of armed men. Ragnvald shook his head to dispel the vision. It was nearing time to give Oddi another signal and look for a response, to make sure that they stayed within sight of one another.

"If the rumors from the winter are true, he may have gathered enough allies to him defeat Harald three times over," Ragnvald said.

"And if sea witches enchant our ships, we could fly there," said Grim, with his old sarcasm. "Hear this: if he departed Tafjord when you said, we should sail through the night once, to catch up with him. You must prepare them for night sailing."

The gods were with them, Ragnvald reminded himself. Otherwise he would never trust the weather this early in the year, in an open ship, overnight. At least the moon was bright, but it set quickly this time of year, and then there would be hours upon the ocean with only the stars and the dark, dark water for company.

"If this works, you will be richly rewarded," said Ragnvald to Grim.

"I imagine we all will be," said Grim. "Especially you, Ragnvald Half-Drowned."

Ragnvald shuddered at the ill-starred byname. He had been trying not to think of the spoils, the honors that might accrue to him, for fear of tempting the gods to punish him. "Thank you for your counsel," he said. "I value it greatly."

"I know you do, my lord." Grim peered ahead and made a slight adjustment to the steering board. They did have a good wind, filling the sail, pushing them almost straight ahead. Ragnvald went to the stern of the ship to light the signal for Oddi. After a few minutes, Oddi signaled back, and Ragnvald breathed a sigh of relief. If they lost one another out on the open ocean, they might never find each other again.

✣   ✣   ✣

HE THOUGHT THE men would rest better without the worry, so he waited until the next morning, before they set out, to give the news of the overnight sail. He let the steadiest men nap during the day, for they would be needed at night. Ragnvald could not sleep, and he knew he was keeping others from sleep, so he stationed himself at the stern until sunset.

Then, as planned, the ships drew closer, to keep view of each other during the night. A mild breeze continued, bringing in clouds overhead. They needed it not to fall off, for this to work. Ragnvald went to the bow to keep watch through the night. Men shared small portions of dried meat and fish with one another and drank cups of ale for their nighttime meal. None spoke above a whisper.

The hours passed slowly. A dim light came from all around, the shining of moon through the clouds, perhaps, though it seemed to come up from the sea itself. Ragnvald took up the task he had set himself to pass the time: working fat into the ship's seal-hide ropes, a task that was never finished, for sun and salt stole their suppleness daily. It was too easy to see outlines of his fears and fancies in the murky shapes of wave and cloud: the golden wolf, Ran's dark hall.

Ragnvald grew more and more tense as the night wore on. Over the trackless sea to the west, clouds gathered, denser. A storm. He looked at the surface of the water, to see how it shivered with the wind. The breeze that carried them along grew stronger. He remembered falling from Solvi's ship. The cold pulled at the scar on his face. Fear, his own and his men's, made him tug his cloak tighter around his shoulders.

If any sorceress had sent this storm, it was the sea goddess, trying to call Ragnvald back to her. He had almost been hers; she might not let her claim go so willingly. She wanted something, a price for seeing them through this night alive, not scattered, to bring them up on Solvi's flank without him noticing.

Ragnvald kept his favorite treasures at his belt, including the golden arm ring that he had gotten from Solvi as his insult price. He weighed the pieces of gold in his hands, one heavier than the other. One had been meant to pay for insulting Olaf, but Olaf had rendered that moot, and now he was dead, his ashes fertilizing Ardal's land better than he ever had as an indifferent farmer. Ragnvald stood up. He would rather have this be a private moment between him and the goddess who had half claimed him, half drowned him, but he knew that the men would like to see it.

He did not have to say anything to draw the men's attention. All who remained awake quivered with watchfulness, attentive to any movement. They turned to look at him. Even Grim's deep-set eyes settled on Ragnvald, stealing only occasional glances at the dark line of the horizon.

"We are in Ran's hands tonight," Ragnvald said, not above his usual speaking voice. The still-calm sea, the heavy air, would carry his words well enough. "I know her of old." His lip curled in what he wanted to be a self-deprecating smile, but he knew it was something much less comforting. "She wants a sacrifice to keep us safe, and so I offer this." He held up the two halves of the ring.

"I won this gold from you, in a way," he said to Ran. "And to you should it return. And I promise much more gold to you for a safe passage through your dark ocean." He lifted the pieces high overhead and then flung them out, into the water. They only glinted for a moment in the air before disappearing.

An hour later the storm was upon them.

THE MOST ALERT MEN TIED UP THE SAIL, AND THE SIX STRON-
gest went to their oar ports. They might lose the oars tonight, but
without the sail, they would be needed to provide power to turn the
ship into the swells.

Grim ordered everything tied down, skins lashed over anything
that could be covered. He stationed men with buckets to bail at the
center of the ship. Ragnvald put himself near Grim to help shout his
orders if needed. Then the storm struck with all its fury, lightning
crashing around them, soaking rain driving against the ship, forcing
water through oiled leather jackets, through the lapped seams of the
ship itself. Ragnvald could hardly see the other ships, which was a
mercy; they must keep far enough away to avoid crashing into one
another in the chaos. And this night, at least, they had a place to meet:
the headland that Grim had indicated.

Ragnvald bailed until his arms felt boneless, then handed off his
bucket to another man. He almost dozed, clinging to the gunwale
so he would not be washed overboard—the noise of waves and rain
combined to isolate him in a sort of silence—until someone shook his
shoulder and handed him the bucket again.

He did not know how many times he repeated that cycle before
dawn came, gray and dreary, with a lessening of wind and shrinking
of swells. He felt numb and wrung out. The men around him had blue
lips, and those who were not shivering wore a dullness in their eyes

that said they had passed through shivering to the dangerous shores beyond. This ship had survived, but Ragnvald did not know if the others had.

He would not learn that until that afternoon, when Grim sighted the headland. Sometime after the sun passed its zenith, the clouds lifted, and streams of light poured forth underneath them. Ragnvald turned to see a line of Hakon's ships, Heming's ships, his ships, stretched out behind them. He nearly cried with relief. He said another blessing to Ran. She deserved that chest of gold, animals, human lives, everything she wanted. But not his own life, not yet.

✢ ✢ ✢

THE SHIPS BEACHED in a hidden cove near Grim's headland in the afternoon. Some men napped or rested during the day. Ragnvald set those who were still wakeful that night to hide the ships as best they could, covering them with grasses or hauling them up inlets, in aimless tidal rivers between higher hills. Grim ordered the masts stepped down.

Ragnvald sent runners to the watch points to keep a lookout. He followed Arnfast over the crest of the headland, through scrubby brush and low trees, to the place where they should see Solvi's ships coming. If they came. Ragnvald had already resolved to wait no more than a full day and night. If Solvi was not spotted, they had missed him, and would be too late. He planned to push Heming onto Vestfold no matter what, if he could, but Heming might recover his good sense and push back.

Arnfast was nineteen—older, Ragnvald reminded himself, than his king Harald, and only a year younger than Ragnvald himself. He looked a teenage boy still, though, skinny and ungainly, with nothing to recommend himself except a fleet step and eagle eyes. He waited for Ragnvald to catch up with him at the best vantage point of the crest, overlooking one of the inner channels. Ice clung to the high places here, above the smooth running water. From this spot he could even see a further channel inland, in case Solvi's ships emerged from there.

Arnfast crouched on his heels for a few minutes, watching with Ragnvald, then stood up again. He was too restless to remain still. "I must see . . ."

Ragnvald did not know where he meant to go, but they might as well watch from different vantages. He nodded his permission, and sat to wait. Here on the crest of the hill, the wind blew fierce, a wet spring gale that chilled as quickly as a winter storm. He rubbed his hands together, then walked aimlessly around the flat top here, stamping his feet.

To pass the time, he began climbing down the steep slope on the inner passage. He might get a better view up the channel, and concentrating on his footing made it easier to forget how cold he was, how much was riding on the slim chance that they had overtaken Solvi's men and might continue to follow them without being observed.

Solvi's fleet was too big for stealth. Ragnvald's breath caught in his throat when they came around the bend. He had added more allies since Agi saw him leaving Tafjord. Here were more than twenty ships. Their multicolored sails shone bright against the gray of cliff and sky. Ragnvald wanted to leap up and run back to his camp, to tell them the news.

He ran for a few steps before it occurred to him that his lead ship must follow Solvi's rearmost one, and he would have to know which one that was. He had not discussed this with Grim, yet it must be so. So he sat to wait while the endless stream of ships passed single file through the channel. Was Svanhild among them, or had Solvi left her behind, somewhere safe and well guarded? He worried that Solvi might have divided his force. The last ship could be a day or more behind. Ragnvald meant to spring a trap, and might be closed in it instead.

At length, after his hands and feet had grown numb from standing still with his arms hugged tight around his ribs, a gap opened up between ships. The last ship was narrow, a dragon ship that earned the name, with a vast sail, nearly as wide as the ship was long. It was striped blue and yellow, with dyes so costly Ragnvald could hardly imagine spending them on a sail's colors. The rearguard must be an important man. He would not likely be followed by a lesser ship, with a plain-dyed sail. Solvi had gathered wealthy allies. After Ragnvald watched for a few more minutes to assure himself he was right about that, he finally retraced his steps back to the camp.

He still feared that Solvi would come around to find a place to camp and stumble into his force. He told Oddi, Grim, and Heming what he had seen, which ship he thought to be the last.

"No fires tonight," he ordered. "If men are cold, they should share sleeping bags, or stay awake." The men grumbled, but quietly.

"They will do it," said Oddi. "All have heard of how you placated Ran."

Ragnvald waved his hand. "I fear she will have me someday," he said. "But not until I am a wealthier catch."

"All the same, these men will do as you ask. That was well done," said Oddi. Ragnvald was grateful for it, if this was the right path, and grateful too that Oddi had resigned himself to this path. Ragnvald feared too much had gone right, that the gods owed him some ill luck for all this good. He was working on Harald's behalf, though. Harald was their beloved.

He passed a chilly night himself, under blankets with Oddi, sharing as they had done in Hordaland for warmth and companionship. He startled himself out of sleep every few minutes, worrying that he had overslept and Solvi's force had passed too far ahead of them.

When he consulted with Grim the next morning, though, he realized that their biggest worry would be staying far enough behind Solvi. He was bound for Vestfold, and so were they.

✛   ✛   ✛

IF THE DAYS of trying to catch Solvi had been nerve-racking, they were nothing to the constant effort to stay far enough behind him to remain unseen, without losing his force entirely. Ragnvald peered into the distance until squinting at the horizon gave him a pounding headache. Even when he closed his eyes, the world remained divided into dark and bright.

At least the wind favored them. Only a day and a half after leaving the southern headland, Ragnvald's ship entered Oslo Fjord toward Vestfold. Ragnvald ordered them to slow further. If Solvi's force turned and engaged them before making Vestfold, they would be slaughtered to no good purpose. Ragnvald sat in the stern, watching and waiting.

Without the moderating effect of the ocean, the land of Vestfold was still snow-locked. A storm had come and delivered snow to knee height since Ragnvald left. At every bend in the fjord, Ragnvald feared they would come upon Solvi's ships.

At the last turning, Ragnvald put Arnfast ashore.

"Vestfold is just over this hill, and then turn down into the valley." He took a brooch that Harald had given him from his pouch and handed it to Arnfast. "Give this to Harald or his uncle Guthorm, and say it comes from me. Tell him that Solvi and his allies are coming, and that I follow with aid." He gave the numbers of Heming's forces, far too small for Ragnvald's comfort, but help if they remained a surprise.

He made Arnfast repeat the message back to him several times before sending him off. Arnfast moved between trees like a silverfish in the water and was soon out of view in the forest.

"What should we do now?" Heming asked.

"Wait," said Ragnvald. "We must wait until Solvi's ships are lashed to Harald's and he cannot easily turn and escape, and then we attack."

Ragnvald did not know how long that might take. The fjord made another bend before it reached Vestfold, an hour's row, and even less time still to sail. He wondered if he might hear something, and then, when some time had passed, whether the silence was due to a battle already fought and lost. He should have sent Arnfast with another runner, to come back with news. Yet how many different things could happen? Solvi's men would attack Harald's, either on land or at sea. Ragnvald thought Solvi might prefer a sea battle. Harald knew his own land and defenses, and Solvi did not walk quickly.

Ragnvald heard something that might be fighting. If his messenger had gotten through, if Harald listened to him, if Harald's forces could move in time, they would be out on the water as well. Ragnvald ordered the ships to move. He could not tell what kind of battle it was, and the agony of the last few days of waiting, the weeks since he had left Harald, made it impossible to wait any longer. The ships raised their anchors, and men began rowing toward the noise, the clash of what sounded like ships' flanks against one another, the yells of battle, the thud of swords on shields. Or that was what Ragnvald imagined. It was too easy to paint any number of pictures in his mind.

When his ship made the last turn, Ragnvald saw that Solvi's ships had been able to beach, and his men streamed toward Harald's hall, milling among the buildings. The roofs of several structures smoldered, but none were yet ablaze. At once Harald's warriors burst from among the buildings to confront Solvi's, a moment of surprise. But they were far too few to defeat Solvi's forces, unless he had called his allies earlier than Ragnvald hoped.

Ragnvald saw banners from Frisia, Iceland, and Denmark, among the Norsemen: Solvi had gathered his forces from far and wide. Ragnvald could not think what to do. He had hoped for a ship-to-ship battle. Still, some of Solvi's ships had not beached yet. Ragnvald ordered Grim to bring his ship near enough to attack one of Solvi's or his allies' that held the rear, and for the others to do the same.

His ship came in close to one of Solvi's, still filled with warriors waiting for their time to advance. With the attention of the enemy ship's men turned toward the fighting on land, Grim piloted Ragnvald's ship in tight before anyone noticed their approach. His men threw grappling hooks across to lash the ships together and form a fighting platform.

Ragnvald jumped across the gap as it narrowed. The moment he landed, he faced a grizzled warrior with gray in his yellow beard and a graveyard of half-rotted teeth in his mouth. Ragnvald attacked. This warrior was a steady fighter, but slower and less skilled than Ragnvald, less suited to a shipboard battle. Ragnvald fought him to the edge of his ship and finally dispatched him with a cut across his throat. He shoved the man into the water before he could fall. His body would only clutter the deck. Let someone fish him out later, if they wanted his sword and armor. Or better yet, let Ran take him as a sacrifice.

His next opponent, a young boy with dark hair and a pockmarked chin, widened his eyes in fear when he saw Ragnvald advance. Ragnvald killed him too, as quickly as he could, without thought for his age. He needed to keep a steady pace or he would grow tired, his body realizing how his pursuit, the days of tension and terrible weather, had taxed him. The grip of his sword chilled the scar on his palm, numbing his hand. He held tighter, so it would not slip on the blood and sweat wetting it.

He had a respite before the next warrior attacked, and in the strange clarity that he sometimes gained in battle, he realized that his trap could still work. Fight through Solvi's ships that remained manned, then send men ashore to trap Solvi's men between themselves and Harald's. There was still a trap, only it would be on land.

Ragnvald and his men dispatched the remaining forces on this ship. From the strange words of their shouts, Ragnvald thought they might be Danes. These were not Solvi's sea-weathered, battle-hardened warriors. They died too easily.

Oddi's ship and Heming's engaged with other ships, and seemed to be beating them as well. Those who remained behind were the weakest. Solvi must have put them here, not intending them to fight.

Ragnvald ordered his ship's lashings cut from the now-empty enemy ship, and rowed ahead to engage with another. This one they dispatched as well, and the rising tide pushed them forward into a crush of empty ships.

Awareness of Ragnvald's attack passed through Solvi's ships more slowly than he had thought it would. Men abandoned the next ship in the face of his overwhelming force, while the one beyond still pressed toward Vestfold's shore, unaware of the threat behind them.

Ragnvald and his men followed this awareness, driving Solvi's ships before them, scattering some to the side. When Ragnvald's ship drew nearer to the shore, he caught a glimpse of Harald where the fighting was thickest, his blond head standing out above the other warriors. He wore that same wild smile he had during their race, daring himself to go farther, faster, to reach for godhood. On land, Solvi's men outnumbered Harald's by at least two to one.

"To land," Ragnvald cried. "To Harald!"

He leapt on the chaos of ships that stood between him and land. Heming's men, his men, Harald's men, now thundered behind him, rocking the ships under his feet.

On land, Solvi's forces had surrounded Harald and his men in a circle that contracted as they fought inward, while another group of

Solvi's men barricaded the hall, and had begun to move wood from the woodshed to surround the hall for a burning. There must be men, women, even children, trapped inside, but Ragnvald needed to save Harald first. It would take time to set a fire.

"To Harald," he called to the men behind him. "Attack from the shore. Protect our flanks. Do not let them come behind us." He yelled, a battle cry without words, and charged toward the men surrounding Harald, whose backs were to the water.

A warrior turned, surprised, and Ragnvald killed him before he had time to get his sword into position. The next man gave him more of a fight, until Ragnvald caught him with a blow that ripped up the back of his leg, sending him screaming to the ground. Ragnvald kicked him hard under the chin as he took a step forward to face the next foe.

Solvi's men, or whoever's men they were—Ragnvald refused to believe that Solvi commanded this disparate force himself, especially on land—turned slowly to face their new attackers. Heming's men obeyed Ragnvald well, turning outward, keeping Solvi's warriors from getting between them and the shore, which freed Harald and his warriors from the knot of men where they had been trapped.

The battle shifted. Solvi's allies had expected easy plunder, a one-sided battle to begin their season of raiding. They did not expect a real fight. Once their fellows began dying around them, some men ran back to their ships. Ragnvald saw King Hunthiof among them, calling for a retreat, before an ax caught him in the back and he fell forward into ankle-deep water at the fjord's margin.

Ragnvald fought his way to Harald's side, through men who scattered before him rather than face him. Harald was covered with blood; his teeth were red when he grinned. Ragnvald did not have the same joy of battle, but knowing it would be over soon gave him a new burst of energy.

"I knew you would return," Harald called out to Ragnvald, as their foes retreated. Ragnvald was briefly angry—of course Harald would not doubt a thing, and his mother would tell him, prophecy Ragnvald's return. Harald needed a little more uncertainty. "We must save the hall," Harald added.

Ragnvald let himself catch his breath for a few seconds, his sword tip resting on the ground. "You first," he said, gesturing for Harald to lead. Harald took off in a run. Many of the men working to build the fire saw Harald and his men screaming toward them and joined the flood back to the ships, but some remained.

Harald cupped his hands around his mouth and called out, "Solvi's men, Danish men, you have come here to attack, but you see how the gods favor me, and bring me allies in my time of need. Throw down your swords now, and you can be mine instead of these outlaw kings'. I will make you rich beyond imagining, make your wives and children safe, and give you land to farm."

It was a generous offer. Ragnvald saw a few men exchanging glances. Those who stood closest to Harald began putting down their swords.

"Do not do it," Solvi yelled. "Harald will make you into a slave." He had a carrying voice as well. He must have been on the other side of the ring of warriors around Harald. Now he stood close to the shore, ready to escape into a ship. Ragnvald watched dumbly as Solvi's men swept him along. Now that the danger was passing, the weariness of the last week's flight, the hours of battle, made Ragnvald's muscles go weak.

"Do not let him escape," Harald ordered Ragnvald. "Do it for your sister."

Ragnvald looked around at the men surrounding him: Solvi's allies, tired and sweating from the battle they knew they had lost, and lost not because they did not have the advantage but because they lacked the will. "You do not need me here?"

"Don't take too many men," said Harald. Near the shore, Solvi's men still defended themselves, though their energy had gone. No one seemed to remember why they fought.

"Oddi, Heming, Dagvith, Arnfast," Ragnvald called out, and added other names, all the names of Heming's men and his own that he could remember. Solvi fled before him. He ran poorly on land. One of his men—Ragnvald recognized him as Ulfarr—scooped Solvi up like a child and ran, carrying him. Ragnvald laughed, and began to call out an insult, but stopped himself. It would slow him down. He could make sure later that when the skalds made the song of this battle, they mentioned Solvi's flight.

Ulfarr carried Solvi out to their ship, the fast, narrow dragon ship from which Solvi had flung Ragnvald nearly a year ago. Men already sat at the oars, ready to take Solvi away. Ragnvald ordered his men to another ship, more or less at random, and bid his men put out the oars. Every moment's delay gave Solvi a further lead.

Solvi's ship rowed out of the clutch of ships in the harbor, then raised its sail, catching a breeze that did not reach Ragnvald where his ship lay. By the time Ragnvald's men had their oars out, Solvi's ship had already disappeared behind a bend. Ragnvald still ordered his men to row, and to raise the sail when they could.

Ragnvald worked the steering oar. As soon as he rounded the bend, he saw Solvi's ship, and Solvi standing in the prow, a small brown form in armor and a helm, raising a sword.

They must have lost the wind, and had few oars out, while Ragnvald's men still rowed with a will.

"Row, row," he cried. "We can catch him."

They pulled alongside the ship. It was not the dragon ship Ragnvald had thought Solvi fled to, but much shorter and stouter. Still, Solvi was in it, watching them approach. Ragnvald must have been mistaken before.

He and his men threw grappling hooks across and tugged the two ships together. Ragnvald made the first leap across, his sword drawn.

The ship was empty but for a few men with the close-cropped hair of thralls. And it was not Solvi but Svanhild standing at the prow, wearing ill-fitting armor, her face brown with dirt.

"You," Ragnvald cried, not sure whether to be angry or not. "Solvi sends you in his place?"

Svanhild looked up at him, her face serene under the dirt. "He did not send me. I was waiting to do this for him, so he could escape. He will be angry with me, but it was worth it." Her words came fast. "Now you can trade me with Solvi for an alliance with him. Hunthiof is dead. Solvi need not be Harald's enemy."

Ragnvald took her by the elbow. "If that is how you think the world works, you have been ill taught. Come with me. You shall not see Solvi again."

"Yes, I will," she said, following him. "He will win through to me, or I to him. You will see, brother."

36

SOLVI'S ALLIES HAD SCATTERED BY THE TIME RAGNVALD returned to the hall at Vestfold. Harald had not given chase. His men were too busy killing those who would not surrender, and disarming those who had.

As soon as Ragnvald was freed from these tasks, he found where Ronhild had taken Svanhild, to a quiet corner of a woman's room, full of batts of carded wool, which made the space look as though it were stuffed with clouds. Svanhild was visibly pregnant now, though Ragnvald was not sure how far along she was. It sickened him to see her swell with Solvi's child and seem pleased at it, her hands resting on her belly, an inward and contented look on her face.

"How could—I should have kept you with me." He sank down on his knees. He had thought he would be harsh with her, she who had arranged Solvi's escape, but it was Svanhild. He could not. "I should have made Hakon take you to Yrjar with us. Hrolf Nefia will pay for this, I promise. Solvi will pay for this."

"No," she said. "Solvi is my husband."

"Svanhild, it does not matter that you are"—he swallowed—"pregnant. Many fine men have offered for you."

"And my child?" Svanhild asked. There was a strange smoothness in her speech that reminded him of Vigdis. Her face showed none of what Ragnvald felt at seeing her again. This storm of anger and regret was his alone.

"Whatever you want, sister. You can raise the child. I can take him back to Ardal—we can both go back to Ardal. Olaf is dead. I am master there."

"Will your master let you do that?" Svanhild plucked at some of the wool and rubbed it between her fingers

"What master?"

"What master, indeed," Svanhild said. "For I have heard that you serve Hakon and Harald, or neither."

"It does not matter," said Ragnvald. "Why are you arguing with me? Svanhild, don't you see that we have won?"

"Almost," said Svanhild. "We will have won when you have made Harald into Solvi's ally."

"He stole you," said Ragnvald, wishing he had better words to convince her.

"Solvi is a good husband. He is my husband." She eased herself down to sit on one of the wool bundles.

Ragnvald frowned at her. "A good husband would not drag his pregnant wife into the middle of a battle."

"I would not let him leave without me," she said. "I must be by his side."

"I will not hear this," said Ragnvald. "You did not have a choice before, but you do now."

"Do not—," she began.

"They sing songs of your courage in Harald's court," said Ragnvald. "King Harald thinks you brave and would make you his wife." He looked at her until she smiled ruefully. Yes, she did like that. "You are not disgraced by this—" He gestured at her growing belly. "You can still marry well."

"No, I am not disgraced. I am proud to bear the son of Solvi Hunthiofsson, mighty sea king."

"A man with no honor," said Ragnvald. "A man who tried to kill your brother."

"He said he was sorry," said Svanhild. "He paid you." Now she sounded like a child again.

Ragnvald turned to go. She would not hear reason yet, but she would eventually, or he could keep her long enough that she would have no choice. "Svanhild, think on this. Solvi's followers are fled. He will have no home. Your child will have no home."

"We will have enough of a home for me." She crossed her arms. "You can keep me prisoner, but it will not make me less his wife. My home is with him."

✠ ✠ ✠

THE NEXT DAY Ragnvald walked with Harald and Guthorm, to take stock of who had survived the battle and who had died. Ragnvald had slept like one of those unburied dead the night before.

Svanhild would speak little more to him. She insisted that she would be sent back to Solvi, and nothing would dissuade her, except time.

"We should not have won," said Ragnvald to Harald as they surveyed the damage in the harbor. Several ships still floated free. Harald would need to send men out to row them in and beach them. His luck was so good that he now had more ships than he had begun this battle with.

Someone had found the body of King Hunthiof, washing in the water at the shore. King Gudbrand, it was said, had perished too, though his body lay at the bottom of the fjord. Women thralls washed Hunthiof's corpse and laid him out in the barn, to bury or trade for the bodies of their slain. For no one knew if Heming was among the dead or one of Solvi's hostages. The mood in Vestfold was full of exultation, and Ragnvald wanted to celebrate with his men, but Oddi could not be calmed. Hakon would come soon, and Oddi had lost his father's most precious son. He feared Hakon's anger, which would find him an easy target.

"They expected an easy fight," said Guthorm. "You made sure they could not get it. Expectations are dangerous. Remember that." It seemed good wisdom, but Ragnvald could not think of lessons now. He had Svanhild, but he had lost her. Harald had almost been defeated, and did not seem to realize how close his dreams had come to dying.

✠ ✠ ✠

HAKON ARRIVED THAT evening. He did not wait for his men to assemble a guard around him before striding across the grounds, stepping over the bodies that still lay in the mud and trampled hay.

Harald, Guthorm, Ragnvald, and Oddi all walked out to the harbor to greet him. Hakon looked as angry as Ragnvald had ever seen him, his face red with rage before he spoke a word.

"I am here to carry a message from Solvi Hunthiofsson, who let me through only on the condition that I would deliver these words," he said. "He has my son Heming, and will return him to me if his wife is returned to him. He let me see Heming. He has a wound that is festering." Hakon's voice faltered. He set his jaw. "Why was my son captured?"

Harald's guards closed in around Hakon. He was still an enemy, even if his sons had become Harald's allies. Oddi clasped his arms over his chest, as if to give himself comfort. He walked forward, his chin low, and told Hakon what had happened, of Ragnvald persuading him and Heming to abandon their planned attack on Tafjord and return to Vestfold.

"Heming wanted this?" Hakon asked. "How convenient for you, that you have an excuse."

"He did want this," said Oddi. "Ragnvald—Heming wanted his name to be remembered for this battle, against Solvi, and repair the alliance he broke."

"Ragnvald convinced him, of course," Hakon guessed. He looked at Ragnvald. "I curse the day I took you into my band of warriors. You have brought me nothing but ill luck." That was unfair, yet true enough, Ragnvald supposed, at least through Hakon's eyes. "Still, you have the girl? At least she can be useful."

"Solvi stole her," said Ragnvald. "I cannot allow her to be forced to go to him. You know where Solvi is. We must lead a force to fight him."

"Solvi has my son," said Hakon wearily. "He has blockaded Vestfold while you have been too foolish to notice. I did not come here to fight or to make peace. I came to get my sons out of trouble, and so I shall."

✠   ✠   ✠

AS THEY WALKED into the hall, Ragnvald passed by the room where he had met with Svanhild. A guard was now posted by the door.

"What happened?" Ragnvald asked. "Who put you here?"

"The lady Ronhild," said the guard. "The lady within tried to escape." Pregnant and alone, of course she would. Between her will and Hakon's needs, Ragnvald felt helpless. Harald would doubtless be persuaded to send her to Solvi, and everyone would get what they wanted, except Ragnvald, and Svanhild would grow to regret her choice. How could she do otherwise?

Harald and the party had gotten ahead of him, and Ragnvald hurried to catch up. They sat near the fire for some midday bread and cheese. A thrall brought mugs of watered ale.

"Your son did well," Guthorm was saying.

"It is true," said Harald, glancing at his uncle. "I still wish my friend Thorbrand not killed, his wife not widowed, but Heming was a true warrior and a friend to Norway in the end."

"Norway," said Hakon. "What is that? You dress your own ambition up in these false colors. There is no Norway. There are lands separated by kings and valleys, lands that will never be reconciled to one another. Your Norway will be a weak land with a weak king."

"I hear your own fears in your words," said Guthorm.

"My Norway will have many kings," said Harald. "You and your sons among them, if you will be my ally again. Must we make war on each other again? Remember, I defeated Solvi at a fraction of my usual fighting strength."

"Because you had my men," said Hakon.

"And many of those were killed, while mine were not. They are still at their farms."

"What kind of king are you, to boast that you let other men do your fighting for you? You should be ashamed even to say this to me."

"It is not a boast," said Guthorm, stepping between them, as he had at the trial for Heming's life. "It is only truth. Harald is at better strength now than you, if it comes to a fight. Furthermore, your men have fought alongside him and his captain Ragnvald, as have your sons. Are you sure they will be loyal to you?"

One of Hakon's men, who had come with him into the hall, shifted uneasily. None of the men would like to be accused of disloyalty, and Ragnvald did not really think they would follow him rather than their sworn king. Hakon looked as though his angry certainty had been shaken, though. He tugged at his beard, rubbing the ends between thumb and forefinger.

"Help me get my son," he said, sounding tired now. "He helped you; Now you must help him." He gave Ragnvald a look of disdain. "Ragnvald will not mind trading his sister to Solvi for him, if he is as loyal to you as he would claim."

"We will sail out and attack him. I mean to marry the girl," said Harald, at the same time as Ragnvald began to voice a protest.

"This is the cost of my friendship," said Hakon firmly.

"Your friendship is precious," Guthorm assured him. He looked at Harald and Ragnvald. "We must think on this."

✝ ✝ ✝

HARALD AND GUTHORM considered for a few days, while the snow melted and Hunthiof's body moldered. Harald wanted to speak to Svanhild, but until Guthorm made up his mind about what to do, he would not let Harald in to see her. Harald might be too swept away by the heroism of fighting Solvi for Svanhild, and Guthorm could not allow it. Finally, they called Ragnvald in to help decide.

Harald had a chamber he shared with whatever woman took his fancy—until Heming's duel, it had been Hakon's daughter Asa. It contained a bed as well as some chairs and a table, which was where Guthorm and Harald were sitting when the servant brought Ragnvald in. He had never been invited here before. There were circles within circles of belonging to Harald.

"King Hakon has ever been more trouble than he is worth," said Harald.

"He has few enough men with him now," said Guthorm. "But he can still muster from all of the north and much of the west."

"Ragnvald, what do you think?" Harald asked.

"Svanhild is my sister. How can I give a fair answer?"

"You always give a fair answer."

Ragnvald sighed. "Let me talk to her again."

"What will you say?" Guthorm asked. Ragnvald did not know. He was grateful when Harald spoke.

"I do not wish to send her back against her will," he said. "Perhaps we can trade King Hunthiof's body and some prisoners for Heming." If he still lived. Hakon had looked drawn and worried, and he spoke of a wound that festered. If Harald and Guthorm waited too long, they would certainly make an enemy of Hakon.

Guthorm shook his head. "Hakon swears Solvi will only trade for her. He said he does not care where his father lies." Ragnvald was troubled by the blasphemy. He did not want Hunthiof's body resting at Vestfold. "Do you think you can convince her?"

Ragnvald sighed. "I do not think it is against her will. Would that it were otherwise."

Harald gave him leave to go speak with Svanhild, and he went to the room where they had put her. She had shared a chamber with Harald's mother these past few days.

"Ragnvald, I do not wish to be here," she said as soon as he entered. "Return me to Solvi."

"You have only one song, dear sister." He sat next to her. "I have done as I promised, and found you a fine husband. If you refused to go, I might convince them to defend you."

"I refuse to stay."

"At least help me understand. What is Solvi to you now? Why do you prize him more than me?"

She drew her knees up and pulled her skirt down over them, so she sat as if within a tent. For a time she did not say anything, but then she tilted her head and looked at him. "Solvi is my freedom. Will any of your fine choices for husbands take me raiding with them? Or will it be halls and children and first wives whose word is law? Will I be left at home while my men go out and live?"

"You loved the farm at Ardal."

"Not as I love this. Not as I love him."

Ragnvald did not want to hear more of this. He stood and paced the room, this soft women's room where he did not belong.

"And what of you, brother? Are you content to be the messenger of kings, always dependent on their will? I always wondered why you did not go and carve out your own land."

A path closed to both of them now. He did not ask if Svanhild would follow him then, across the sea. She had made her choice. "The bones of our ancestors lie in Sogn's earth," he said. "We were born to keep that land safe, and with Harald as king, that will happen."

"And he is your golden wolf," said Svanhild. At Ragnvald's surprised expression, she put out her hand to him. "Ronhild and I have spoken. Now tell me what you came to say."

He took her hand in his. "This is what is happening: Harald, Guthorm, and Hakon are all agreed. Do you know what you are being sold for?"

"Hakon's son."

"Yes," Ragnvald replied. "And a renewed alliance between Hakon and Harald, an alliance that will only hurt your Solvi." He watched to see how she would react. Her face crumpled. She withdrew her fingers from his.

"No matter where I go," she said, "I hurt someone."

"How did you come to leave Hrolf's farm, truly?" he asked.

She told him, haltingly, of Thorkell's coming, of feeling trapped. Then she told him too of being at sea with Solvi, and her voice grew clear. "Solvi must already know this," she said, finally. "He must know that by allowing Hakon to come to Harald, so that I might be traded for Heming, he might cause their alliance to be restored. What can I do, rather than go to him?" She scrubbed her hands over her face to wipe away tears, and looked up at Ragnvald. "I do not want to make an alliance that hurts him. He is my husband." She put her hand on his arm. "Take me away from here, brother. Bring me to Solvi. Without this trade. Come with us. You do not want to bind your life to Harald's ambition. Follow your own ambition."

Ragnvald turned away from her. It was one path. He could break his promises, and leave Harald with Hakon his enemy again. He remembered what Ronhild had said he would sacrifice for Harald. Here was one thing, a first precious thing.

"He is my ambition," he said.

"You have not yet sworn to him. You are free."

"No one is free. I have not yet sworn, but I will."

"You said you'd care for me when our father died, and you did. You used to. What now?" The words stung less than he thought they would. They were Svanhild's last weapon. Ragnvald stood and rubbed at the scar on his face.

"You made your choice, Svanhild. If you wanted to stay here, to abandon Solvi, I would try to help you in that, but I will not help Solvi. Do you wish to stay, or go to him?"

She only hesitated for a moment. "I want to go."

+ + +

SVANHILD LOOKED PEACEFUL as Ragnvald helped her onto the ship. How could Solvi have driven this much of a wedge between them? She was his Svanhild, the best and most charming of sisters, the bravest. And now the most wrong. She could be a king's wife, and she would rather be Solvi's.

They found Solvi with a few ships, beyond the bend in the fjord. When Solvi saw Svanhild, Ragnvald almost understood. Solvi was the most accomplished liar Ragnvald knew, lying not only with words but with every movement he made, every expression. Even his eyes could glance with lying intent. But he could not mask his love for Svanhild—or at least his desire for her and the child she carried.

"Ragnvald Eysteinsson," said Solvi when he helped Svanhild step across from one ship to the other. The weather had turned warmer. Trees dripped bits of snow into the fjord. "You said no one could turn Svanhild's mind but herself. I have seen that you are right."

"She loves you," Ragnvald said, pushing her at him ungraciously. "I cannot think why." Solvi gave him a smug smile. "Svanhild, no matter what, you will always have a place with me. Your child too. You do not need to go with him now. I will find a way . . ."

"I want this, brother." Svanhild moved lightly, even weighed down by her pregnancy, with the sort of step that sailors of long experience had, the knowledge that the ground beneath her foot might give way at any time. It would, too, with Solvi.

"You want to be shackled to an outlaw, a man with no land, no country."

Svanhild raised her chin. "The sea is our country. Our land is any shore on which we rest. How much better is that than the chains you bind yourself with, to land, to king?"

Ragnvald shook his head. He did not want to envy her, her body taken over by Solvi's seed—that was her binding, and a stronger binding even than any oath Ragnvald would swear to Harald. No, he did not envy her anything except her certainty. He had believed that she would never love someone more than him; even when she was married, it would be to a man Ragnvald chose, and so bind her to him closer, not separate them.

Hakon made a rude noise. "Solvi Hunthiofsson, you promised me my son in this trade. You and your wife can pretend to be heroes of some ancient song later."

Svanhild's face went red. Solvi merely shrugged. He put two fingers in his mouth and whistled sharply. A few minutes later, men rowed a small boat over to the two ships. Within, Heming's fair hair showed above a gag. His head lolled forward, and the guard behind him pulled him back from toppling over. He was not well.

"You may keep the boat as well as the hostage," said Solvi. "My thanks for returning my wife."

"You probably stole it from some Vestfold fisherman," said Ragnvald.

Solvi grinned. "I did." Harald's men took possession of the boat. "Are we done now?"

"No," said Harald. "You are outlawed, Solvi Hunthiofsson. I call upon the gods to witness this. Your father is dead. Your lands are forfeit. Any man who sees you may kill you without penalty. Indeed, should he come to my court with your head, I will reward him."

Solvi looked white for a moment—no man could think lightly of exile and outlawry, not even Solvi Hunthiofsson—and then he grinned again. "I never wanted to be king," he said. "Come, Svanhild." She crossed the last few steps to him and stood next to him, clasping his hand, as though it did not matter to her that Harald had declared it the duty of Ragnvald and every free man to kill her husband on sight. She might never see Ragnvald again, and she did not even appear to care.

Harald's party returned to his ship. Ragnvald watched as Solvi's ships receded into the distance. Svanhild looked back. She waved good-bye, a flash of white wrist, as Solvi's men raised his sail.

Harald stood by Ragnvald's side. "We will pay and pay again for this alliance with Hakon," he said, hardly above a whisper, too quiet for Hakon to hear him where he stood at the prow. "I wonder when it will be too much. You have sacrificed greatly. Never has a man served me as well as you. I wish you to be by my side for the rest of both of our days, and I wish to reward you as you see fit."

"You sent me away," said Ragnvald. It still rankled.

"If I ever do that again, you may laugh in my face." Harald spoke louder now. "I call all men present to witness this. You will be first among my captains and advisers, saving only my uncle Guthorm. No man has ever been a truer friend than you." The men on board the ship applauded, all except Hakon himself. "You have told me that your grandfather was king of Sogn," Harald continued, "and his fathers and forefathers before him. So you must be king—my king, now. It is spring, the seas are open. We will go to Sogn, and claim a kingdom for you."

"Thank you, King Harald. You do me great honor."

"Do not thank me," Harald said. "It is no more than your due. It is I who should thank you."

Ragnvald could not speak. Harald turned to Hakon. "Then we will go on to Tafjord and win the kingdoms of Maer for your sons. I will build my northern capital there. Together we will rule this new land."

A land where his sister was not welcome; he had sacrificed her, just as the sorceress Ronhild predicted. He pressed his fingers into the scar on his palm as he walked with Harald up the beach and toward the hall. The sun lit up Harald's tangled, shining hair.

CHARACTERS AND PLACES

PLACES

Maer. A district ruled by King Hunthiof's family; sometimes divided into North and South Maer

> **Tafjord**. King Hunthiof's seat of power at the end of Geiranger Fjord

> **Geiranger Fjord**. The fjord in Maer

Sogn. A district in western Norway, south of Maer, formerly ruled by Ivar, Ragnvald's grandfather, but now without a king

> **Ardal**. A rich farm in Sogn, formerly owned by Ragnvald's father Eystein, and now owned by Ragnvald's stepfather, Olaf

Sogn Fjord. The fjord in Sogn

> **Kaupanger**. A market town on the north side of Sogn Fjord; one of the few towns in Viking Age Norway

The Keel. The mountain range that runs the length of Norway, dividing east from west

Halogaland. A district in northwestern Norway, ruled by King Hakon

Yrjar. King Hakon's seat of power in Halogaland

Smola. An island near Yrjar

Vestfold. A district in southeastern Norway, ruled by King Harald

Hordaland. A district in southwestern Norway, ruled by several kings: the brother kings Frode and Hogne; Gudbrand; and, in the uplands, Eirik

Frisia. A country on the North Sea, ruled by the viking Rorik, now part of present-day Germany and the Netherlands

 Dorestad. The trading center of Frisia

CHARACTERS

Olaf Ottarsson, Ragnvald's stepfather

 Ascrida, Olaf's wife, widow of Eystein Ivarsson

 Ragnvald Eysteinsson, Olaf's stepson

 Svanhild Eysteinsdatter, Olaf's stepdaughter

 Vigdis, Olaf's favorite wife, Ragnvald's stepmother

 Hallbjorn Olafsson, Vigdis's young son by Olaf

 Sigurd Olafsson, Olaf's son by a previous marriage and Ragnvald's stepbrother

 Einar, Olaf's foster son and Vigdis's nephew

 Fergulf, armsman at Ardal

Agi, fisherman near Tafjord

Hunthiof, king of North Maer, with his seat in Tafjord

 Solvi Hunthiofsson, Hunthiof's son

  Geirny Nokkvesdatter, Solvi's wife

  Snorri, sails with Solvi

Tryg_gulf, sails with Solvi

Tryg_gulf, sails with Solvi

Ulfarr, sails with Solvi

Barni, Hunthiof's steward

Harald Halfdansson, king of Vestfold, would-be king of Norway

Guthorm, Harald's uncle

Ronhild, Harald's mother

Thorbrand Magnusson, Harald's trusted captain

Hrolf Nefia, farmer in Maer

Bergdis, Hrolf's wife

Ragnhild Hrolfsdatter, called Hilda, Hrolf's daughter

Malma and **Ingifrid**, Hrolf's other daughters

Hakon Grjotgardsson, king of Halogaland

Heming Hakonsson, Hakon's trueborn son

Geirbjorn Hakonsson, Hakon's trueborn son

Herlaug Hakonsson, Hakon's trueborn son

Oddbjorn (Oddi) Hakonsson, Hakon's illegitimate son

Rorik of Dorestad, king of Frisia

Lena, Rorik's favorite wife

Kolla, Rorik's wife

Eirik, a king in Hordaland

Gyda, Eirik's daughter

Hogne and **Frode**, brother kings in Hordaland

Gudbrand, king in Hordaland

AUTHOR'S NOTE

HISTORY

The Half-Drowned King IS A WORK OF FICTION THAT TAKES ITS inspiration from the saga of Harald Fairhair in Snorri Sturluson's *Heimskringla*.

Norway in the late ninth century is only beginning to emerge from myth into written history. Most of the existing sources for the life of Harald and his contemporaries were written many centuries later. Ninth-century Norway did not have written language besides runes, the angular writing found on Viking markers like the Danish Jelling stones, which were raised in memory of great deeds and departed family. Runes in Viking Age Norway were used for fortune-telling, as well as marking some religious and other monuments, but not for historical record-keeping.

In the thirteenth century the Icelander Snorri Sturluson, a historian, poet, and politician, would write down the *Heimskringla*, and many other sagas—roughly the equivalent of someone today writing the story of the founding of the United States with only oral tradition on which to base his narrative. The *Heimskringla* almost certainly has gaps and inaccuracies. Furthermore, many scholars believe that Snorri Sturluson used the saga to make certain implicit arguments about Iceland's political situation at the time, leading him to highlight some stories and leave out others. The works of Saxo Grammaticus, a twelfth-century Danish historian, and *Historia Norwegiae*, a history of Norway written in the thirteenth century by an anonymous Scandinavian monk, also attest to Harald's conquest of Norway and his reign, while focusing on different aspects of the events than the *Heimskringla*.

In writing *The Half-Drowned King*, I have used the stories in the *Heimskringla* as a jumping-off point, and also asked myself what might have been the real events behind the stories that Snorri Sturluson and others passed on and recorded. My sources mention Ragnvald, Harald, Svanhild, Solvi, and many others, but I have invented aspects of these figures' relationships—such as Svanhild and Solvi's romantic involvement—and also invented some new characters, like Ragnvald's stepfather, Olaf, and stepmother, Vigdis.

Still, those wishing to avoid spoilers for subsequent novels should probably avoid Wikipedia and the *Heimskringla*.

NAMES

BECAUSE SO MANY NAMES AND NAME PARTS ARE REPEATED IN the history of Harald Fairhair, I've had to make some tough choices. For instance, Ragnvald's brother Sigurd (here I've made him a stepbrother) shares his name with many other Sigurds, including a son of Hakon Grjotgardsson. It would be terribly confusing to have two important characters named Sigurd in a novel, so Hakon's eldest son takes the name of one of his other sons, Heming.

Similarly, the prefix *Ragn-* (meaning council, wisdom, or power) is found in the names of many characters in Harald's saga. For the sake of clarity, I've used the spelling Ronhild rather than Ragnhild for Harald's mother. I also shortened the name of Ragnvald's intended, Ragnhild(a), to Hilda, again for clarity.

Old Norse—similar to modern Scandinavian languages—is an inflected language, meaning it has noun cases. Old Norse names in the nominative case, the case used when the person is the subject of a sentence, end with the suffix -r, so Ragnvald would be Ragnvaldr (sometimes transliterated Ragnvaldur). For ease of pronunciation, in most instances I have omitted the -r suffix, and used more anglicized versions of the names without diacritics, e.g., I use Solvi rather than Sölvi.

SOURCES

HERE ARE A FEW, BUT NOT NEARLY ALL, OF THE BOOKS I HAVE FOUND VALU-able in researching Viking Age Norway and Early Medieval Europe. Christie Ward's Viking Answer Lady website, www.vikinganswerlady, is also a useful resource.

Bauer, Susan Wise. *The History of the Medieval World: From the Conversion of Constantine to the First Crusade.* New York: W. W. Norton, 2010.

Davidson, Hilda Ellis. *Gods and Myths of Northern Europe.* New York: Penguin, 1990.

———. *The Roles of the Northern Goddess.* London: Routledge, 2002.

Fitzhugh, William W., and Elizabeth I. Ward, eds. *Vikings: The North Atlantic Saga,* Washington, DC: Smithsonian, 2000.

Foote, Peter G., and David M. Wilson. *The Viking Achievement: The Society and Culture of Early Medieval Scandinavia.* London: Book Club Associates, 1974.

Griffith, Paddy. *The Viking Art of War.* London: Greenhill, 1995.

Jesch, Judith. *Women in the Viking Age.* Woodbridge, England: Boydell, 1991.

Jochens, Jenny. *Women in Old Norse Society.* Ithaca, NY: Cornell University Press, 1995.

Jones, Gwyn. *A History of the Vikings.* Oxford, England: Oxford University Press, 1984.

Larrington, Carolyne, trans. *The Poetic Edda.* Oxford, England: Oxford University Press, 2014.

Lindow, John. *Norse Mythology: A Guide to Gods, Heroes, Rituals and Beliefs.* New York: Oxford University Press, 2002.

Sturluson, Snorri. *Heimskringla; or, The Lives of the Norse Kings.* Translated by Erling Monson. New York: Dover, 1990.

Wells, Peter S. *Barbarians to Angels: The Dark Ages Reconsidered.* New York: W. W. Norton, 2009.

ACKNOWLEDGMENTS

THIS BOOK HAS BEEN A LONG TIME IN THE MAKING, AND MIGHT not have come to fruition without the support of my husband, Seth Miller; my parents, Mark and Karen Hartsuyker, who instilled in me a love of myth and history; my sister, Julianna Lower, who believed in my path; and a large number of friends and cheerleaders. My first readers—Diana Spechler, Diana Fox, Caroline Burner, Beth Derochea, Elena Innes, and Margo Axsom—gave me invaluable advice and feedback, and their fingerprints are all over the finished work. Patrick Arrasmith, Milan Bozic, Fritz Metsch, Jillian Verrillo, and Miranda Ottewell did beautiful work to turn the book into its final, polished form. And lastly, thank you so much to my agent Julie Barer and her colleagues at the Book Group, as well as Clare Smith at Little, Brown, for believing in this book and bringing it out into the world.

ABOUT THE AUTHOR

LINNEA HARTSUYKER can trace her ancestry back to Harald Fairhair, the first king of Norway. She grew up in the middle of the woods outside Ithaca, New York, and studied engineering at Cornell University. After a decade of working at Internet startups and writing, she attended New York University and received an MFA in creative writing. She lives in New York City with her husband.